THE ORACLE

Eaman Murrar

THE ORACLE

Matador
9 De Montfort Mews
Leicester LE1 7FW, UK
Tel: (+44) 116 255 9311 / 9312
Email: books@troubador.co.uk
Web: www.troubador.co.uk/matador

ISBN 1 905237 39 1

Cover illustration: Maxine Chung

Typeset in 11pt Stempel Garamond by Troubador Publishing Ltd, Leicester, UK
Printed by The Cromwell Press, Trowbridge, Wilts, UK

Matador is an imprint of Troubador Publishing Ltd

In memory of the person she once was
and in honour of the person she has become.

Prologue

The night was dark and overcast. Not a star could be seen through the purple velvet clouds that obscured the black sky, and the air hung heavy as if the entire universe was holding its breath; an inauspicious night, by any standards. Faran paced about outside the house wearing away the dry earth beneath him as he crossed over and over the same spot. He couldn't bear to venture back into the house, filled with intermittent screaming and the pungent smell of dried herbs mingled with sweat, both fresh and stale. His wife had been in labour for nearly seven hours now. He knew his thoughts should be with her, but all he could think of was that there would be yet another mouth to feed. Moreover, there was this night. He was not a superstitious man, his common sense frowned upon such foolishness, but there would be idle whispers in the shadows of doorsteps among the women, and he knew even the men would be wary. There was a deep feeling of uneasiness in the pit of his stomach. No, he was not a superstitious man, but to be born on the night of a dark moon did not bode well. He only hoped it would be a boy. If it was a boy, things would go easier for everyone.

The door of his cottage opened, releasing a beam of light into the darkness. Rika, the midwife's young assistant was standing in the doorway. She peered into the shadows outside. Faran could hear loud weeping coming from the room behind her. It occurred to him that the child might have been stillborn and, to his shame, he felt a momentary sensation of relief.

"Tis done. Your babe is born and mother is fine, if a little tired," Rika called out to him.

She hesitated before adding, almost apologetically, "It's a girl."

Faran's expectant face fell. He swallowed hard as he walked

towards the house to console his wife.

Rika returned to the midwife who was cleaning the blood smeared baby in the back of the house.

"Ah, she's a jewel," the old woman commented with maternal feeling.

"Yes, but what a night to be born on. People will talk, especially her being a girl an' all," whispered Rika.

"Hush your poisonous talk and if you want to earn your keep, you'll learn to keep your mouth shut."

She carefully handed the baby over to the girl who accepted the small bundle with reluctance.

"You hold life in your hands, precious life. She is as you once were, innocent. Never forget it. Her name is Ahlia."

"Ahlia," repeated Rika. "A pretty name. Did the mother choose it?"

"No, I did."

The midwife looked sad for a moment. "It seems a boy was hoped for."

"'Tis shameful how the father hasn't even asked to see her yet, his own flesh and blood an' all," remarked Rika. "She is lovely isn't she and see how she smiles already. Oh, but look at her eyes, how dark they are. Almost black! And she already has hair too! Black as the night she's born on."

The girl made to pull open the baby's lip, but the midwife slapped her hand away.

"What did I just tell you? Anyway, save yourself the trouble, there's only gums in there."

"They'll still talk, you know," Rika said sulkily, shaking her stinging hand.

"Not if it is recorded that she was born in the morning. Only we shall know different."

The girl carefully placed the child back into the midwife's hands. "You'll not be able to hide her eyes. She has the Knowing. Even I can tell. You know what the elders think of those who have the Knowing. Each time the crops fail or an animal takes sick, she'll be blamed."

The midwife gently stroked the baby's soft cheek. Little

Ahlia looked up at her with eyes as dark as obsidian.

"One person's curse is another's gift. If this one be truly touched, then the Spirits will look after her and love her."

"Just as well," interjected Rika, "for no one else will."

The midwife shot her assistant a scathing look as she rocked the tiny gurgling bundle in her arms, but she knew in her heart that Rika was probably right.

Part
1

Chapter 1

A wizened old man sat in a large leather chair by an open fire. His long grey beard all but obscured his mouth, from which protruded a gnarled wooden pipe. His robe hung loosely over his thin body. The garment was weathered, but showed traces of having once been a rich blue, and the intricate embroidery upon the hem, though now faded, was clearly done by an expert hand.

The old man's eyes had the brightness of a person who had witnessed many wondrous things, but his face bore the gravity of one who had lived a life of responsibility. He was a man who had made many difficult decisions in his life and, in retrospect, was not altogether certain that he had always made the right ones. With the care of an artist, he took a long drag of his pipe and exhaled gently. A curl of grey blue smoke slowly escaped from his mouth and wafted upwards, snaking its way towards the ceiling. Patterns shifted and rearranged themselves in the smoky spiral as he searched them with alert eyes; eyes that did not seem to fit his tired and withered face. He nodded with satisfaction that he had understood the message.

"She does not have long left," he said quietly, more to himself than to his companion sitting beside him. His voice held a hint of sadness. Then more loudly he said, "Our time is coming to an end. Yours is just beginning, Sebastian. The challenge will soon be upon you and you must meet it. You must pluck the key of opportunity from the grasping hands of your opponents."

"What did you see, Master Viad?" asked Sebastian with uncharacteristic eagerness. He raised himself to his knees, from his crossed-legged position by his Master's feet. The stone floor was uncomfortable against his kneecaps, but his anticipation made him oblivious to the pain. Besides, this spot on the floor by his Master's favourite chair, before the roaring hearth, had been his accustomed place since he was eight years old. After years of sitting thus, the floor on this spot had become smoother, at least, if not warmer.

"Her moment is coming. She, who is the keeper of the Oracle. We shall not be responsible for her death, but when her time is come, you will be there. You will claim the Oracle and become Supreme among Sorcerers."

Sebastian nodded emphatically. He had endeavoured his whole life to master his craft in preparation for this challenge. He felt he'd been waiting for this moment for what seemed like forever. He had almost begun to fear that it would never come. At last it had.

"The Oracle is all power, Sebastian. All power... but to wield the Oracle also takes great power."

"I understand, Master."

Sebastian's blue-grey eyes were as bright and alert as his Master's, but he had not seen nearly so much through them.

Viad shook his head. "No, my young apprentice, I am not sure that you do. I am not even sure that you ever will. In fact, I think I am only now beginning to grasp a vague inkling myself. Yet, I have taught you all that my Master taught me, and more too. The rest is up to you now."

Viad retreated into the depths of his great armchair and chewed on his pipe. For a moment he simply looked like any ordinary old man. Sebastian's look turned to one of concern.

"Master?"

Viad shifted his ancient bones into a more comfortable position and took another drag of his pipe. This time he blew the smoke out more forcefully. In the hearth, the flames danced their language of life and fate for those able to read it.

"I shall not be with you much longer, not in body anyway. My time is also coming to a close."

Sebastian shook his head, "Master, I understand that you are old, but..."

Viad interrupted him. "You have no idea how old, my boy." He pointed to the flames. "See there, they tell me that the powers who loaned me this form require their materials back for another. For all my abilities, nature has beaten me. It is time for my soul to move on."

Sudden fear gripped Sebastian, but it took him just moments to resume his characteristic calm composure. He said nothing. Even in his last moments, his Master was using the experience of life and of death to teach him. He must not squander the lesson. A wave of grief welled up inside him, but he expressed nothing of it, clenching his teeth until the sensation had broken and ebbed away, all the while keeping his gaze fixed intently upon the dancing flames and opening his mind to their language.

*   *   *

She had closed the shutters to leave only the light of a single candle flickering in the near darkness. In the shadows, the sweet hypnotic smell of incense worked its magic. She summoned up her most mysterious voice.

"He is tall, and dark..." she paused for effect, "and most definitely handsome."

There was a gasp of delight.

"Tall you say?"

"Oh yes very tall."

There was another gasp.

"And dark? You are quite sure he is dark?"

"Oh yes." Hmm, she thought, better leave some leeway, "Darkish at any rate."

"Ah! Could he have dark brown hair as opposed to jet back, say?"

"It is... possible."

"And you say I know this man?" asked the excited voice.

"Oh well, what I am saying is that he most definitely knows you. Yes..." she twirled her fingers dramatically over the cards on the table in front of her.

"Yes, I see he has admired you from afar for quite some time, but of course he is far too discreet to let anyone see."

"But why hasn't he said anything?" asked the voice urgently.

"Why? Why?"

"My lady he knows he cannot have you. You are a married woman."

The client nervously began rubbing the heavy, expensive band on her ring finger with her thumb.

"Yet I sense he will pine over you, my lady, for years to come."

The lady giggled with glee.

"Oh how wonderful. Wait until I tell my friends. They'll positively die with envy. I wonder! Who is this admirer?" Her brow knotted in thought for a moment before her eyes opened wide. "Sir Afrid! It must be! He is forever hovering around me."

"Be warned, my lady, it might not be someone you expect. In fact it might be the person you least expect."

It never did to let them focus on a particular person. Spirits knew what trouble that might cause. Now was the time to take a more serious tone.

"I must warn you, my lady, of your husband's great jealousy regarding your affections."

"My Rufus, jealous? I hardly think he notices me half the time."

There was more than a hint of sadness in the woman's voice.

"A ruse, my lady! He knows how desirable you are to other men. He is terribly proud. He is not able to display emotion easily, especially emotion that runs so deep."

There was a whimper of amazement.

"I never realised. Oh, how I have neglected his feelings!"

"You must be terribly discreet to spare the feelings, not only of your husband, but also the life of your admirer. I see that your husband might kill a man to keep you and protect your honour."

"Oh!" The voice trembled with rapture.

"You must be cautious, my lady and act as if you know nothing."

The excited voice turned to an emphatic whisper. "Of course! Of course!"

"Tell me, my lady, I sense that you still love your husband."

There was a shy nod.

6

"Do you love him deeply?" she asked, "Passionately?"

A more assertive nod as the woman was swept along the current of the speaker's sensuality.

"Is there any other that compares to this man who wooed you, who chose you above all others?"

The lady was silent for a moment. She remembered how he had come to her father's house all those years ago. He had been young and slim in those days and full of fervour. How he had gazed at her with such longing. She remembered the tenderness of those first embraces on their wedding eve. The memory caused a spark to reignite within her, making her cheek flush slightly. The fortune-teller watched her client intently, reading her as closely as she might read the cards. The woman's jewellery bore all the signs of having been chosen by a man, the sort of man who found it easier to present his affection than speak it. That was not such a bad thing, thought the fortune-teller to herself. Any love was better than none.

"Talk to him, my lady. Remind him of that which you are now remembering."

There was the clatter of coins on the wooden table.

"I shall. Thank you."

The fortune-teller bowed her head graciously and saw the lady to the door, locking it behind her. She sighed heavily as she heard the tread of expensive shoes down her worn staircase. She licked her index finger and thumb and put out the candle, plunging herself into complete darkness for a moment then made her way to the window to open the shutters, a tiny chink of light that had burrowed through a crack in the wood serving as her beacon. From her window, she saw the lady tiptoeing over the dirty cobblestones and being helped into her waiting carriage. The lady looked up in the direction of the window for an instant. It was the face of a less than beautiful, rather weak-chinned merchant's wife, but at that moment the face glowed with hope and the prospect of encountering a slightly more interesting life than the one she had before coming to the fortune-teller. She had arrived here with a fat, balding, husband who she felt was more interested in chicken legs and commerce than in her, but had left with a secret admirer and a husband who was ready to fight to the death for her.

The fortune-teller looked at the coins on the table: 1 gold, 1 silver.

"Not bad Ahlia," she said to herself. "Not bad at all."

She went back to sit at the table and began absent-mindedly shuffling the cards.

"I see me paying the rent this month, with a bit to spare."

She stopped shuffling the cards and laid them out face down before her in the shape of a horseshoe.

"Now let's see what they really say."

She turned the cards over one by one. Her brow knotted as she looked at the pattern before her for a few moments, then she sighed loudly and messed up the spread.

"Gibberish. I don't know why I bother."

There was a knock at the door.

"Who is it?"

There was muffled laughter from behind the door.

"Ahlia, you're supposed to have second sight. You should know who it is!" called a jovial voice.

Ahlia grinned to herself as she went to let her friend Chara in.

"Actually I am a Fortune-Teller, Soothsayer and Seer," she paused, "at the moment... and sometimes I'm even a bit accurate."

Something hidden twisted her insides into a knot of yearning. She gave a loud long sigh and looked distant for a moment. Chara looked at her friend with concern, then groaned in dismay as she noticed Ahlia's disorderly living quarters. Half empty cups stood about on every spare surface. Ahlia's answer to making her bed had been to roughly throw the covers across, the under-sheet left untucked. There were books sitting in untidy piles everywhere and scraps of cheap parchment with notes scribbled on them in Ahlia's messy hand. Two ink bottles lay open, uncovered and slowly evaporating. It was Chara's husband's firm belief that Ahlia was more than a little strange. He blamed it on the fact that her nose was always buried in some book or other. Chara had nothing against book learning, but these were the sort of books that took Ahlia into the odd side streets and back alleys of Avor to buy, books that came from faraway places and had unpronounceable titles and expensive price tags. Chara was beginning to think her husband might be right.

"More books, Ahlia? Aren't you sombre enough already? You know that's why you haven't got a man."

Ahlia pulled a face. "Oh please!"

She pinched the root of her nose with her fingers to ward off the headache that was looming threateningly.

"What's wrong?" asked Chara.

"It's just not right, none of it. I can't help feeling like a fraud, but even when I try to tell people what I see they don't want to know, and they certainly don't pay me half as well as when I fabricate stories. They aren't interested in the truth. It's madness."

"Ahlia, my dear, it is human nature. Besides, the truth often brings misery with it. You bring a bit of mystery into people's lives, a bit of excitement. Isn't that meaningful? I've never known anyone to take such care and consideration in the stories they weave for their clients. You really think it out. It's quite an art in itself, you know. It's not easy making people happy all the time. You find them a beautiful dream to drift off into every time their life gets too awful. Isn't that something?"

"A beautiful lie, that's what I give them. I lie for a living. The Spirits will have me for that one day."

"Oh, for Spirit's sake, Can we be sure what is true and what is not? I believe my son is the most gifted and handsome child in the world. In my eyes it is the truth. Am I wrong to hold onto that?"

"No, Chara, but..." Ahlia tailed off. She knew she would not win an argument with her friend. Chara had a form of logic that always made her right, even when there was no way that she could be. Her friend continued on, relentlessly.

"Too good to be a charlatan and not good enough to be what you think you want to be. Worst of all, you can weave a dream for everyone, but yourself. You are the only one you hurt

9

because it is you alone who is disillusioned."

The comment hit a nerve.

"I just want more!" Ahlia burst out full of agitation, "I feel like I'm missing something. Something important, but I don't know what." She pulled her hand through her hair in frustration and rolled her eyes up towards the invisible Spirits that never seemed to be there when she needed them.

"Why can't I ever just be happy and content with what I've got? What's wrong with me?"

Chara, who was a good-natured person and simply got on with living the best way she knew how, did not like the tone of Ahlia's voice. She knew her friend was of a difficult temperament and given to bouts of melancholy, but Ahlia was someone you just couldn't help but feel drawn to for some reason, even if you didn't really understand half of what she was trying to tell you most of the time. It was her duty as a friend to pull Ahlia out of whatever pit of desolation she was trying to dig herself into. Chara looked at the upturned cards and shook her head.

"No good ever comes of reading your own. You know that. Anyway, you're not that accurate, remember? It's just as well you don't have more of the gift. The little bit you have makes you moody enough!" She slapped the table top.

"Come on, let's spend some of your hard earned wages. I hear Risan will be in the Three Tons drinking tonight." She dangled the line like an expert angler.

"When I said I was missing something that was not what I meant, Chara."

"Maybe not, but I'm sure he'll manage to take your mind off your worries, for tonight at least!"

Ahlia's dark eyes sparkled. "You are truly incorrigible."

"I should hope so!" chuckled her friend. "I knew that would bring a smile to your face. Maybe tonight he'll gather his courage and come over. He's been watching you for long enough. Come on, you look gorgeous as you are. Just give your hair a quick brush and maybe a dab of colour on your lips. Perhaps another dress too and..."

Ahlia gave her a look that told her well-groomed friend very clearly to say no more.

Chara gazed at Ahlia in despair as her hinting fell on deaf ears. There was no doubt in Chara's mind that her friend was beautiful, but Ahlia's long raven-black hair, roughly pulled up in a knot, had clearly not been brushed since the morning, if indeed it had been brushed at all. She wore nothing by way of jewellery and though she was lucky enough to have a fine set of full lips that bore their own natural colour well, a dab of paint would not have gone amiss, in Chara's opinion.

"Alright, alright, but at least let me help you with your hair."

Before they had time to move, there was a knock at the door.

"I didn't know you had another appointment," whispered Chara.

Ahlia shook her head, "I don't," she whispered back, walking up to the door.

"Who is it?" she called.

There was no answer. She opened the door to find an old woman standing in the hallway. She was almost doubled over in half by the great hump in her back, which made it difficult to look her in the face and gave the impression that she was almost as wide as she was tall. Like many old grandmothers, it appeared a combination of age and childbirth had made the lower half of her body expand in width. Her spindly legs seemed impossibly thin and far too unstable to support her ample bulk.

"I've come to see about having my fortune told," the woman croaked.

"Well, old mother, one of us might be able to help you there," said Ahlia good-naturedly.

"Good."

Chara and Ahlia stood aside as the old woman shuffled across the room and with some effort seated herself on a chair at the table. She peered through lank dirty grey hair at the cards.

"Ah cards, is it?"

"If that is alright by you, old mother."

The old woman jabbed Chara in the side with a bony finger, causing her to jump in surprise. "She any good, your friend?"

11

Chara looked at Ahlia with amusement.

"Why, yes she is."

"Good. It's the truth I'm after, mind. No claptrap."

Chara gave her friend a mischievous look.

"Well, you are indeed in luck, for Ahlia also has a love of the truth. I shall leave you in her capable hands," she said, patting her friend on the back on her way out and whispering in her ear, "Be careful what you wish for! Eh?"

Ahlia felt unexplainably flustered. She swallowed nervously. She had had hard clients before, the ones who were looking for proof of some kind, who gave little away. It seldom mattered. The cards were a strange tool. They spoke to people in a language of pictures. They held in them timeless symbols of human dilemmas such as love, loss and hope. Even the most sceptical could not help seeing some part of themselves and their life reflected in the images before them. People were not as unique as they thought they were. So why did she feel so edgy this time? Had she not asked for an opportunity to test her ability? She came to sit opposite the old woman. Her nose involuntarily wrinkled as she was hit by the odour of mothballs wafting from across the table. The old woman fumbled in the layers of her grey smock before producing a worn pewter coin and placing it carefully on the table.

"Is there any particular question or area you would like me to focus on for you?" Ahlia asked, after glancing at the woman's meagre offering.

"Just tell me as much as you can for that coin, please child," replied the old woman.

"May I ask, have you come far?" Ahlia asked, as she shuffled the cards.

"Yes, as it happens, a bit of a distance."

"Have you been to a fortune-teller before?"

The woman seemed to find the question amusing. Her laughter was inaudible, but her hunched shoulders shook from the force of silent peals. Finally, she said, "I can't say that I have, no."

What was so funny? She handed the cards over to the woman.

"If you could shuffle please, old mother and then cut the pack."

The woman took the cards carefully into her hands and shuffled them. She cut the pack exactly in half to make two piles. Ahlia picked up one of the piles and dealt out a spread.

On looking at the cards, she felt some relief as the images on the cards linked together in her mind. Yes, there was definitely a clear pattern. Lists of well-worn opening phrases automatically came to the tip of her tongue, but she pushed them away. The old woman had asked for the truth. Ahlia didn't know much about that, but she could say what she saw for real. She relaxed a little, glad that for once there was no show to put on.

"Well, there is an issue concerning justice in your past and I should tell you that when the cards speak of a thing in the past, it is a thing that often colours the future. I see there was a time of great struggle," she turned another card, "and loss. The card of grief, but I see that you were finally able to overcome the obstacles and see here, the card of victory." She turned over more cards.

"There is a lady. She is one who feels deeply for causes and cares for the happiness of others. I am afraid, old mother, there appears to be a bit of strife in the future. Lots of swords, see in the picture?" Ahlia held the card up for the woman to see. The woman scrutinised the card intently, but said nothing.

Ahlia continued. "The cards advise endurance and see, here this picture of a hanged man. A sacrifice of sorts presents an obstacle for you. The outcome is good however, there is hope."

Ahlia fell silent and waited for the woman to speak.

There was an awkward pause before the silence of the room was broken.

"Can you tell me more about this 'lady'?"

The old woman pointed to a card that bore a picture of a woman dressed in sea green, standing in a shallow pool of water.

Ahlia nodded, picking up all the cards except the one with the picture of a woman on it and shuffled them. She gave them once more for the old woman to shuffle and cut. Then she laid five cards out, one of which she placed over the picture of the woman.

"Well this first card is about hopes and dreams. I would say this person has a dream or high hopes for herself and look here, there is the mark of the apprentice. She is a student of some kind. Ah! Here we see something disturbing lurks about her, an enemy or perhaps a bad influence, and here there is again a card of loss. Perhaps there is poverty looming? The end is a journey, it seems. Look, this picture is of a boat." She held it up for the woman to see.

"Nothing more?" asked the old woman.

Ahlia took one last card from the pack. "The wheel, I am sorry, old mother, I can say little more. The future of this woman is in the hands of Fate, if you are a believer in Spirit, and Chance if you are not."

She bowed to indicate the reading was over. "I hope that has been of some use to you."

The woman nodded as if satisfied. "Is my coin all used up?"

The woman's coin was not enough to pay for the turning of even one card, but Ahlia was in full flow now and had forgotten all about payment.

"What else would you like to know?"

The woman considered for a few long moments. As she thought, she absent-mindedly rubbed a worn leather cord about her wrinkled neck. Ahlia found herself wondering what might be at the end of the cord. Finally the old woman spoke.

"This will suffice. Thank you child. May I ask your age?"

"I am near thirty this next equinox."

The woman's unruly eyebrow arched slightly.

"You look younger. I expected younger," she murmured.

Ahlia was used to hearing this comment.

"Oh I don't look my age I know. It's a blessing."

The woman chuckled huskily.

"Is that so, and who taught you to read the cards?"

"Oh I taught myself. I never got around to finding a teacher."

The woman muttered to herself something that sounded a lot like, "That explains it."

Ahlia pretended not to hear, but she was beginning to have suspicions that this woman was not as frail or helpless as she had assumed. She was beginning to seem just that bit straighter and

14

thinner and her voice just that bit sustained. Her hair began to seem more silver than grey, her face less contorted. The woman met her gaze.

"Been reading long?"

"Oh yes, old mother."

The old woman's brow arched.

"Before your first moon blood?"

Ahlia was surprised by the question, but she knew the elderly had a different attitude to the etiquette of personal matters.

"...er no," she answered a little bashfully. "Not that young, after that."

"Tell me. Do you like what you do? This cards thing, it fulfils you?"

A strange cold sensation rippled down Ahlia's spine as she recalled the conversation she had just had with Chara.

"Well, I like it well enough. It is a way to live," she said.

"Is that so?"

"Yes" replied Ahlia out aloud while in her head a deafening NO resounded.

The woman nodded as if something was making sense to her.

"I wonder child if I might call on you again in two days' time, but not here. The steps are a bit too much for an old woman like me. There is a tavern at the end of this street. Perhaps we could meet there?"

It was hardly worth it, but it was better than nothing. Ahlia was finding it hard to say no, although somewhere in the back of her mind, she felt she wanted to decline quite strongly.

"Very well, old mother. I can meet you there in two days' time. How does the third hour after midday suit you?"

"Thank you my child."

Suddenly, the woman looked like any frail old grandmother and all thought to the contrary was completely wiped from Ahlia's mind, as though she had never doubted it.

"Come let me help you down these death-trap stairs."

She helped the old woman out into the street and bade her farewell.

Ahlia smoothed down her dress and patted her hair straight.

15

She went to her bedside table and opened a small bottle of perfume. This was one of her prized possessions. The shop-keeper had told her it had come from the Eastern provinces. It had been expensive, but worth it. Every time she put the bottle to her nose she was transported into a beautiful rose-garden. Few roses grew in the dirty grey streets of Avor where the most pervasive scent was that of the rubbish rotting in the gutters. Carefully, she dabbed a few drops on her neck and wrist. She may not have much in her favour, she thought, but at least she would smell like a princess. She banged on Chara's door on her way down the stairs.

"Come on then!"

Chara needed no second invitation. She linked her arm in her friends as they made their way out into the cobbled street.

"My Brynan is already down there saving us a table. Let's eat too, I'm starved."

"Chara, did you not cook for your husband?"

Chara laughed at the question.

"Spirits, Ahlia, you know I'm a terrible cook. He'll be much relieved if I suggest eating at the Three Tons. You know how he loves their meat stew."

As soon as they entered the tavern, they spotted Chara's husband at a table. To Ahlia's surprise Risan was with him. She gripped Chara's arm nervously.

"You didn't say! You didn't say!"

"Yes I did. I said he'd be here."

"But not at the table!" she said in a flustered voice.

"Don't be a coward now. Don't make a mess of things."

Ahlia looked over to Risan and smiled. At least she hoped the face she was making was a smile. It must have been. He smiled back. Chara went over to her husband and kissed him.

"Well my love, I hope you ordered some food."

Brynan grinned at his wife, "Of course I did. I know you as well as I know the back of my hand. I know what you'll ask for before you even think it."

Being married herself, Chara was of the opinion that no one was ever truly happy until they resided in the land of marital

16

bliss and she loved nothing better than to match make. She smiled sweetly at her husband after taking a quick glance over at Risan who was already talking to Ahlia. "Why my love, I think you do."

Ahlia had never really spoken to Risan before, at least not what she called really speaking, but they had chatted and exchanged pleasantries. He had deep-blue eyes framed by a shock of wild brown hair and a smile that made her melt. Risan worked with Brynan as an overseer on the farmlands of Duke Efew, which, as Chara often pointed out, was a good steady living for a man who might wish to wed. As Chara had also pointed out, it was high time Ahlia found herself a husband before all the good ones were taken. Risan was definitely classed as 'a good one' by many women and Ahlia guessed him to be spoilt for choice. Yet, he was here sitting with her, listening to her attentively as she talked, and answering her questions. She thought she could not have been happier. As she laughed, ate and drank, the small, troublesome place inside of her closed itself tightly shut.

Chapter 2

Ahlia complained to herself as she trudged down Sefer Street towards The Spear Head Tavern. Why had she agreed to this? It all seemed ludicrous now. As usual, she had allowed herself to be pushed into something she really did not want to do, she thought angrily. The Spear Head was a ridiculously strange place to meet. Ahlia seldom came in here. It was often horribly busy, and unlike the Three Tons, whose clientele were more 'respectable', this place was a known haunt for the more unsavoury types of the town. The old woman could not possibly have known what manner of place this was. Ahlia should have mentioned it at the time, but somehow her tongue and mind had failed her. It was too late now. Gathering her courage, she pulled open the tavern door and was greeted by a cacophony of loud, raw sound. The room before her was large and filled with people. As the door closed behind her, daylight was left outside. The tavern windows had been blacked out to create the illusion of continual night, and candles had replaced natural light. Still, during the day it must be safe enough, she thought in an effort to convince herself. At the same time, she carefully skirted past a rowdy table of unshaven men. A man with unkempt hair flung his head back as he roared with laughter at some joke or other, almost knocking into her. She started and jumped back instinctively like a deer evading a hunter. He turned around and gave her a toothy grin, then leaned in to make a comment to his drinking comrades. The whole table burst into hearty laughter, and the man turned around again to say something to her, but Ahlia was already halfway across the room.

She had spied the old woman sitting in a quiet corner of the inn with a beaker in front of her. There seemed something a little different about her this time, something Ahlia could not put her finger on, but then everything seemed more menacing in this place. She chided herself at her own foolishness. After all, she thought, this was just a sweet elderly lady who was probably more interested in a little company than she was in the future. Nevertheless, she made a mental note never to come here, ever again.

"Hello, old mother. I fear I should have warned you about..."

"Oh this place?" interjected the old woman. "Seen much worse, believe me and I like a bit of uproar now and then. Keeps me young!" she chuckled. "And please, call me Mora. That is my name. Sit down, sit down."

Ahlia eyed the dirty bench suspiciously before carefully seating herself, while Mora watched her with some amusement.

"I was just about to call for another drink."

"Please, allow me," said Ahlia graciously.

Ahlia looked about her and tried to catch the eye of the serving maid who was busy chatting with the party of men across the room. Mora smiled to herself as she watched Ahlia's futile efforts. Ahlia huffed in agitation as the maid turned and walked even further away. She smiled apologetically at Mora.

The old woman raised a finger to call the serving maid. To Ahlia's surprise, she came over straightaway, even though she had clearly had her back to them.

"An ale for my friend."

"Oh no," Ahlia interjected, "I don't need a drink."

Both Mora and the serving maid ignored her and a few minutes later, there was a frothy beaker of potent brew in front of her.

Mora pointed to the beaker, "Drink. You'll thank me for it later."

The old woman was sounding a lot more forceful than Ahlia remembered, and seemed to be anything but fragile as she took a long swig out of her own beaker and wiped the foam from her dripping mouth with her grotty sleeve.

"Um I've brought the cards," Ahlia said with uncertainty.

"Eh? Oh the cards. Not what I meant. I've another reason for

19

calling on you this time." She motioned at the beaker with a bony fore-finger. "Take a drink. You'll need it."

"No. I'm fine," replied Ahlia firmly.

The old woman raised her hands, in mock surrender.

"If you insist, have it your way. I'm an old woman and I'll come straight to the point because there is no time to explain the whys and wherefores. Suffice it to say, I have my reasons for doing this. I don't need your cards to see things."

She pointed her gnarled finger at Ahlia, "And neither do you. You can see pretty well without them, if you'll only let yourself try."

"Mora, I fear you overestimate my ability. Perhaps a more gifted reader might…"

"Ever feel like you can see things more clearly than those around you?" Mora interrupted, ignoring Ahlia's protestations. "I mean, you know exactly what it is people want to hear from you when they come to you."

"Maybe," replied Ahlia guardedly. "But that is just being perceptive."

"Ah, being perceptive. Is insight not the ability to perceive and understand the true nature of a thing? Some might consider that to be a form of power. Some might even call it magic."

"I am sorry, I don't understand," said Ahlia.

"I'm saying 'second sight', as you people know it," she waved her hand about the room, "is at best misunderstood and at worst misused. I can teach you."

"You mean to read the cards better?"

Mora huffed contemptuously.

"Do I look like a fortune-teller to you?"

She glared at Ahlia in a way that brought to mind warnings like "danger" and "DANGER". Ahlia answered by lowering her gaze submissively.

"Not that there's anything wrong with that, mind, provided it is done as it should be," added the old woman, her eyes boring into Ahlia who cringed in shame. "But it is just not my way." There was a painful pause, as Mora seemed to muster herself up for something.

"Right, I don't know how else to tell you, except to tell you, so here is my proposal. You have heard of a Sorcerer's apprentice, have you not?"

Ahlia looked at her blankly.

"Suspend your disbelief for a moment. You understand the terminology at least?"

Ahlia nodded.

"Well I am a Sorceress, and I am offering to make you my apprentice."

Mora continued, ignoring the stunned look on Ahlia's face for the moment.

"You're a bit old, mind. Normally you'd be done by your age and a Sorceress in your own right, but that can't be helped. All things happen according to the Great Map and who am I to criticise."

She paused a moment before resuming. "I won't lie to you and tell you that you have a choice. I mean you could say no, but it would mean very little in the scheme of things. This is your destiny."

With a huge amount of effort, Ahlia finally collected her senses and found her voice. "You are a Sorceress?" she asked.

"I thought I said that. Didn't I just say that?" replied Mora sharply.

Ahlia struggled to find a suitable set of words to string together.

"What?" asked Mora.

"It's just that…"

"What?" Mora asked in a more threatening tone.

"I guess I expected…"

Mora glared at her with eyes full of derision. "I see. Judge things by their appearances do you? Exactly how many Sorceresses have you seen in your long, eventful life here in Avor? What standard are you judging me by exactly?"

Ahlia was at a loss.

"Thought so," replied Mora triumphantly.

"But how do I know you're telling the truth? I am not sure I even believe in Sorcery."

"If you are too blind to see the signs then you are just going to have to make a leap of faith," Mora said simply. "I'm not about to put on a fireworks display for you. If you don't believe in magic then why do you spend half your income on magic books?"

Ahlia looked alarmed for a moment, then realised the old woman must have seen the books in her room.

"I am interested, that is all. It doesn't mean I believe. I, for one, have never seen any sorcery or magic before and I can only believe in what I experience."

The old woman looked at her in wonder.

"Is that so! Hold on to that notion, for you shall see sorcery enough if you take my offer."

"And why are you offering to teach me?" asked Ahlia.

"Don't look a gift horse in the mouth," came the sharp reply. "Just be thankful that I am."

Thankful! Ideas were crashing about in Ahlia's head like a frenzied herd of cattle. It was becoming harder and harder to harness her brain and operate her mouth.

"And what exactly does being an apprentice entail?"

Mora sighed.

"Let's not mince words. It is power we are speaking of, though I should mention such talk is bound to generate…" she searched for an appropriate word "… 'effects'. You sure you don't want to take a drink? Marvellous for grounding is a good swig of ale. Reminds you where you are."

"No, thank you."

"Ah well. There is hardship for sure, lots of work, a great deal of solitude, and at times fathomless loneliness. Then there is the danger," she said nonchalantly. "Your life will be under constant threat, of course." Her green eyes all the while sparkled with a brilliant intensity and her voice became utterly lyrical and haunting. At some point the room had started spinning. Ahlia was not sure exactly when, but she had a physical premonition that she was going to throw up, probably quite soon. Seemingly unaware of Ahlia's digestive turmoil, Mora talked on.

"But on the other hand there is knowledge and power and experience beyond a thousand lifetimes; a chance to climb to the very heavens themselves, a chance to gain perfect completeness. A chance to hear the music of the spheres and the language of the universe and…" her voice turned into a ghostly whisper, "a chance to understand it."

She paused for a moment and took a long look at Ahlia. The girl had gone completely pale. Mora was sure she was going to faint any second. "Now child, I really do recommend you drink something."

Ahlia could think of nothing she wanted to do less. It was as though a huge weight had suddenly landed on her shoulders and yet, instead of feeling heavy, she felt horribly light. The spinning room was making her feel dizzier by the second. She mumbled incoherent words of apology and rose from the table. Everything sounded muffled as though she was under water. Her vision blurred. Her lungs felt compressed. Everything seemed too close, there wasn't enough space; no space to breathe, to think. She had to get out. She began to stumble through the crowded room.

"You saw it yourself, you know," Mora called after her. "You saw it in…" she lowered her voice again as Ahlia was already out of earshot, "…the cards."

Ahlia gasped frantically, drawing fresh air into her lungs, as she finally made it out of the oppressive tavern and into the street. She put her hand to her forehead, shielding her eyes from the bright sun. Her brow was clammy. Had the woman put something in her drink? She was desperate to get to her bed and lie down. If only the world would stop spinning, she wished, as she tried to remember where exactly she lived.

Back in the tavern, Mora finished off her ale. "I told her to drink something," she said to no one in particular, "but would she listen? Oh no. Stubborn! I've my work cut out for me, I can see. Oh! I don't have time for this." She frowned for a moment, before breaking into a smile.

"But she has the Knowing though, for sure. Buried deep it is, but there nevertheless and stronger for its hibernation."

Lost in deep thought, she drummed her coarse nails on the wooden table top.

*   *   *

Ahlia awoke sometime later to find herself in her own bed with a vague recollection of what had happened at the inn, but no idea how she had arrived back home. Chara was sitting beside her bouncing one of her children on her knee.

"Oh look Pauli, Aunty Ahlia is sobered up."

"How did I get here?"

"A tenant from two floors up found you passed out at the foot of the stairwell. Lucky for you I happened to be passing. Your hair was all over your face and he didn't recognise you. He thought you were a drunk and was about to drag you into the gutter and leave you there."

Ahlia was barely listening.

"I don't know what happened, Chara. I didn't drink anything. I just felt very dizzy."

Chara smoothed the hair away from Ahlia's wet brow. "Moon cycle?" she asked, her voice full of female empathy.

"No! One minute I was talking to that old woman. You know, the one who came over the other day and the next…"

Chara looked confused. "What old woman?"

"You know, the one who dropped by without an appointment, dressed in grey, humped back."

Chara felt like she should remember. The description definitely stirred a hazy half-memory in the back of her mind. It was strange because she normally had an excellent memory for people. She prided herself on knowing everything there was to know about everyone, but she just could not quite recall having seen any such woman at Ahlia's room. Never mind, she thought, it would come back to her. She never forgot a face for long.

"Go on," she said.

"Well, I went to meet her at the tavern, oh what's its name, The Spear Head, that's it, and…"

"That veritable pit?" her friend interjected, "How did the old hag convince you to go in there? No wonder you're in a state. I'm surprised you got out alive!" she remarked dramatically.

"Oh, it wasn't that bad Chara, I don't think…"

"Spirits! All sorts of horrid cut-throats are said to drink in that place. What manner of woman is she?"

Ahlia paused as she tried to recall the details of the conversation they had had. It just didn't seem real.

"A mad one I think. You won't believe this. I know you won't. I mean, I cannot say I believe it myself. Her name is Mora. She says she is a Sorceress and wants to make me her apprentice."

"Oh please!" said Chara dismissively, "As if Sorceresses, should they exist that is, go apprentice picking in the backstreets of Avor among struggling would-be fortune-tellers and then haul them into horrid taverns. It makes no sense at all. In any case, Sorcery is myth, a legend of the past. There haven't been Sorcerers around these parts for generations. We may get the odd witch out in the forests, but a Sorceress?"

"I'm just telling you what she said. I didn't say I believed her."

Ahlia felt angry for some reason. Somewhere in her mind a war was raging between what she thought was real and what she wanted to be real. Perhaps a part of her had wanted to believe. No, that was ridiculous.

"Actually, I can't say I even know what Sorcerers do. What do they do? I can't remember them doing anything except killing each other according to the old stories. Yes, always killing each other over something or other. Probably why there aren't any left!" remarked Chara.

Ahlia was too busy fighting to bring her mind back into focus enough to listen.

"I don't know what's wrong with my head. I just can't seem to think straight at the moment."

Each time she tried to think about what had happened the same dizzy feeling reappeared. A group of words floated about her head though she did not recall the old woman actually ever saying them to her. They kept appearing in her mind from nowhere. In fact, they were all she could focus on clearly.

"When you are ready, I will return."

*   *   *

25

On the snow-capped Islan Mountains, Sebastian practised with painstaking precision, his lunges and thrusts and parries. Magic was all very well, but one should not neglect the other skills in life. Sometimes one had to use steel to make a point. Master Viad had emphasised that. One should never put all one's eggs into one basket, no matter how powerful that basket was. So each morning, he braved the cold air that paled his already alabaster complexion, in order to perfect his sword skills.

"Sebastian."

Sebastian did not stop what he was doing or look up. He recognised the voice and the presence.

"What are you doing here, Marcus?"

"Master is speaking with Viad. Something of some importance is looming, it seems."

"I know."

Sebastian had not felt comfortable all morning. Now he knew why. Sorcerers tended to give each other a wide berth. Even apprentices did not get too close to another's territory. It aroused too much competitive feeling and more often than not resulted in bloodshed.

"May the best Sorcerer win, eh?"

Sebastian threw his sword up into the air. It continued upward, propelled by an invisible force, coming down with increasing speed to halt suddenly above the head of the young dark-haired man speaking to him. With a flick of his wrist, he returned the sword to his hand.

"Quite," he said simply.

The man had not moved an inch throughout the episode. He smiled with visible contempt.

"Still doing your cheap party tricks, I see."

Sebastian thrust his arm out. From his open palm, a ball of fire leapt out towards Marcus. Without even raising an eyebrow, Marcus deflected the shot with a wave of his hand.

"Oh grow up, Sebastian."

He made a flick of the wrist that sent Sebastian hurtling into the snow. Marcus laughed with delight.

"You're no match for me. The Oracle is as good as mine!"

Sebastian scowled at him and shook the snow out of his loose blond hair.

"Marcus!" called a short grey-bearded man who had appeared on a ridge by Viad's stone house.

"Yes, Master Carlaf."

Marcus bowed in deference to his Master. The Sorcerer beckoned him over.

"I must go, but it's been fun, Sebastian. See you on the playing field soon, I expect!"

Sebastian scowled even more and made his way back to the house without bidding the guests farewell. As soon as he had his back to Marcus, he dropped the scowl instantly and resumed his usual sedate expression.

Viad, who had been watching out of an open window, called to him.

"Yes, Master?"

"That was a curious thing."

Sebastian feigned ignorance. "Master?"

"You allowed Marcus to appear stronger than you when you could have easily beaten him. May I ask why?"

"I prefer people to underestimate me. It gives me the edge of surprise."

Viad smiled with approval. "A mighty Sorcerer you will be because you do not rely on magic as your only tool. Excellent, Sebastian, and what, if I might ask, is the 'playing field'?"

"Oh that's just his term for the world. He regards life in its entirety as one big game. For him it will be a short game," Sebastian paused before adding in a more serious tone, "I have seen his death."

"You have?" asked Viad, raising a bushy grey eyebrow in surprise. It was unusual for so young a Sorcerer to see into another Sorcerer's last moment. This was a portentous sign that Sebastian's powers were growing fast.

"Do not worry Master, it will not be by my hand."

"I am glad to hear it," replied Viad with some relief. "His Master is a great friend of mine. Of course, we were bitter rivals in our youth and tried to end each other on countless occasions,

27

but time changes all things."

"Why were they here, Master?"

"Carlaf came to consult with me regarding Mora's whereabouts. He is finding it difficult to locate her. I suspect Mora is up to her old tricks, false paths and so forth."

"False paths?"

"A Sorceress like Mora can fabricate lines of past, present and future: ghosts of the true happening, with regard to her own life, in particular. Thus, when we scry for her, she may appear to be in one place doing one thing at one time and some or all of what we see may be untrue. Carlaf, has just discovered this. I, of course, have known for some time, but for my own reasons neglected to make it public knowledge."

Sebastian wondered at his Master's cunning. Viad tapped the side of his nose and continued,

"Carlaf's great mistake is that he listens to the fire. Fire is Mora's particular friend and I have no doubt it will lie for her if she presents her case well. I have always known never to look for Mora in the flames or attempt to use fire against her."

"Did you enlighten Carlaf, Master?"

"No," Viad winked at his apprentice in a rare display of humour, "After all, we are in competition once again! Prepare yourself, however. Marcus is the least of your problems."

Sebastian nodded. He knew there would be others, many others.

"Mora usually roams about like a nomad, weaving false trails here and there, making it impossible to pinpoint her. I am quite certain however, that I am near to finding her. It appears she is much closer than she has been for many years. Closer and stiller, which means she is preparing."

"Preparing for what?"

"For the end. Mora is dying."

"And what is to stop Mora handing down the Oracle to her apprentice, Master?"

"Nothing, but it is known that Mora's apprentice died some years ago, of that I am sure. There was some speculation that the apprentice actually chose to leave Mora some time before she died, though no one knows for sure the truth of the matter."

"I don't understand. If Mora holds the Oracle and is as powerful as you say, how could she pick an apprentice that might leave her or that she surely knew would die?"

"I do not know. Of course, it is a very rare thing to foresee a person's moment of passing and even then it is not often obvious until death is nearly upon them. Death is a strange force. It can hover around a person for years before it finally swoops down. Other times it makes a sudden, flying visit. The Great Map is a wondrous thing, and make no mistake, it is a complex and dynamic thing. Hence, it can encompass both our inevitable destinies and also those moments, those very rare moments, where we are truly free and able to make choices. Mora's apprentice began as a child and, as she grew, made choices in her life, choices that were free. One of those free choices led to her death. Mora grieved loudly. We all heard it." He pointed to the flames. "It was a sound even the flames could not cover. To find another person worthy enough to train as apprentice and to hand the Oracle on to would not be easy. If there were such a person, they would stand out for all Sorcerers to see. When you were a child Sebastian, the light of your power called to me from hundreds of miles away. I brought you here before any other could claim you."

He paused for a moment, as if reliving the memory.

"I have watched for such a one as Mora might choose and I have seen none. If she has taken an apprentice, they will be inferior to you and to many others too. Mora will cling to the Oracle until the last moment. She knows what is at stake."

"This revelation makes me think this mighty Sorceress is not as flawless as you would have me believe. Perhaps she has never fully been able to master the Oracle," Sebastian ventured.

"And thus we look into a deep pool whose clarity fools us into thinking that the bottom is within our reach. Mora is a terrible force to be reckoned with. In her youth, she slew many Sorcerers who stood in her way. I cannot say why she did not better protect her apprentice for I imagine it was certainly in her power to do so. It seems that each time I think I have finally understood her, the woman, like a shape-shifter, re-creates herself. Though it appears that she has seemingly made a lapse in judgement, I would not wager even a pewter coin that it is so. She is the wielder of the Oracle. The only 'mistakes' she makes are conscious ones where she is fully aware of the outcome. Can they then be really classed as mistakes? Now there is a riddle for you to unravel, Sebastian."

"What a fool that apprentice must have been. What manner of person could give up a chance at the Oracle?" Sebastian mused aloud.

Viad said nothing for a moment, but watched his apprentice intently. He noted how brilliant and wide the young man's eyes had become at the sheer thought and mention of the power object. The very air about them seemed to crackle with the energy of desire, the desire for power. For a moment, Viad saw himself standing there, as he once did, embracing the moment of what he had deemed to be his destiny. How differently it had all turned out to what he had expected. Would his apprentice meet with more success? Here was one thing that it was not in his power to see."

"Still Master, if there is no apprentice to stand in my way…"

The Sorcerer sighed heavily.

"There are many other Sorcerers, powerful Sorcerers, ambitious apprentices. There will be many battles to fight. You say you saw Marcus' death? It is an omen perhaps."

"What does it mean?"

"Ah, it could mean many things, but for such a thing to reveal itself to you means that it is likely his death will change your future in some way."

With a wave of his hand, he gestured for Sebastian to leave him, adding as an afterthought, "Poor Marcus. It is a shameful waste. He had potential, but the moment is the moment and it cannot be avoided."

Chapter 3

Ahlia had put all thought of Mora out of her head, as much as she possibly could. For the first few days, she had half expected the old woman to appear at her doorway, but when she had not, Ahlia assumed that the entire strange episode was over. Besides, she had other more pressing concerns that required her immediate attention.

"Are you sure you counted right?" she asked the shopkeeper.

"Positive. The cabbage was four Pewters and the apples six. The carrots and potatoes come to a Silver, then you wanted the salt, the sugar, oh, and the beans..." he counted on his fingers, "Yes, definitely, three Silvers and a Pewter."

Unconvinced, Ahlia opened her purse. There was precious little left in it.

"And before you ask, I don't do credit. Perhaps, you'd like to put some of these things back," said the shopkeeper without feeling.

Ahlia shook her head. She placed the coins on the counter. There would definitely be no meat on her table this week. Hoisting the full bag over her shoulder, she left the shop, still going over the prices in her head. It was beginning to drizzle and she pulled her cloak about her to keep herself dry as she trudged home. The drizzle soon became heavy rain.

"Wonderful!" she exclaimed to the grey sky. "What next?"

A small, troublesome part of her fought hard to speak out, but she quelled it with experienced expertise. She concentrated on the cobbled stone floor in front of her as she walked. A passer-by knocked into her, but she paid no attention. Then suddenly, without warning she felt her bag being pulled away from her. Instinctively she held onto the strap as the thief tried to tear her grip away.

"Let go woman or I'll hit you!" he yelled threateningly.

"NO!" she screamed back hysterically as the rain poured down on her.

The thief shoved her roughly in an attempt to push her off balance. He succeeded and Ahlia stumbled, losing her hold on her bag. Not looking to see if she was hurt or not, the thief darted away with her bag, leaving Ahlia prostrate on the cold wet ground. All her groceries were gone and though her purse was safe in her pocket, there would have been little in it worth stealing anyway. With effort, she sat up, but remained there for some moments, gathering her strength. Passers by, huddled inside their cloaks, did not seem to notice the young woman sitting on the ground. More likely they did not care to interfere. That was the nature of Avor. Everyone was faceless here. No one stopped to ask if she was alright. It was as if she was invisible. Ahlia smashed her fist on the ground and yelled in rage. Anger was an emotion she seldom allowed herself to indulge in. As she opened herself to her emotions, the hidden part of her that had been writhing in fury, leaped at the chance of freedom. Unbeknown to Ahlia wrapped in blind rage, the atmosphere about her began to fill with an increasingly powerful vibration. Along the street, the shop-windows rattled violently in their panes. Steam rose off her body as the raindrops evaporated instantly on hitting her. Streets away, Ahlia's attacker found himself bombarded by splinters of broken glass as the shop windows next to him shattered and exploded outwards. He threw himself to the floor and covered his face in terror. Oblivious to what she had done, Ahlia felt her anger begin to dissipate. She rose to her feet and tried to dust herself off, but she was soaked through, and the dirt was ingrained into her skirts. She sighed heavily, and pulling her bedraggled hair back from her face, she began to walk. The sooner she got home the better.

From the shelter of a shop doorway across the street, Mora followed Ahlia's steps with keen eyes. The old woman looked up at the grey clouds above her. As the girl walked away Mora cast her hand over the air in front of her. "Hidden she has been until now. Hidden let her remain."

* * *

Viad sat in his warm study before a roaring fire while outside the snow fell softly to the ground. Sebastian was sitting at the desk by the window staring out at the white landscape, a book on the history of Sorcery that lay before him, open, but unread.

"Master, how was it that Mora came to hold the Oracle?"

He had been pondering over what made one Sorcerer more powerful than another and had yet to come to a definite conclusion on the matter.

"Mora has always been a formidable Sorceress," replied Viad simply as he chewed on his pipe.

"Has she always been more powerful than you? Was she born powerful?"

"It is not as simple as that Sebastian. Mora has qualities that make her a dangerous adversary, with or without the Oracle."

"What qualities are they?"

Viad blew out a great cloud of smoke.

"Well, determination for one, strength for another, astuteness, cunning, and an insatiable desire for power that overrides everything else."

Sebastian's brow arched. "I see."

"But do not think that by emulating such qualities you are guaranteed the Oracle," warned Viad, "for there are many Sorcerers who have such attributes. No, the thing that separates Mora from the rest of us cannot be defined in words, but if you were to stand in her presence, you would soon understand."

"She sounds ruthless," remarked Sebastian.

Viad mulled the comment over. "Not ruthless," he corrected, "relentless. She is utterly relentless, as if directed by some invisible force."

"The Oracle."

Viad nodded.

"But this tells me nothing. She is powerful because she holds the Oracle and she holds the Oracle because she is powerful. I am none the wiser."

Viad smiled. "No, nor am I," he confided. "In my youth, I

was sure I would be the one to wield the Oracle. I was wrong and to this day, I am not sure how or why I failed."

Suddenly, Viad started in his chair.

"What is it?" asked Sebastian.

Viad was silent for a moment. Then he shook his head.

"For a moment, I thought I sensed…. ah," he finished dismissively, "but it is gone. It was too short and weak to be of importance, probably a child trying out their power for the first time. I am no longer interested in such matters."

* * *

Ahlia had not been home long when Chara knocked on her door.

"Come in," she called, without getting up.

Chara poked her head round the door to see Ahlia sitting alone at the table holding her head in her hands.

"Business still slow then?"

Ahlia felt exhausted. She couldn't face telling her friend about the thief stealing her precious groceries.

"Nothing all week!" she wailed. "Not a single client and last week all I had were the regular few. How am I going to pay the rent?"

"It's just a lull. Things will pick up. You'll see," consoled Chara. She put her arm around her friend.

"You're all wet and your skirt is filthy!" she remarked. "Been out, I take it."

"Shopping," replied Ahlia morosely.

'Get anything nice?" asked Chara brightly.

"Don't ask."

Chara hugged Ahlia tightly.

"Things will turn your way soon. You'll see!"

Ahlia had never been very good at being optimistic. She was always too aware of all the horrendous possibilities lurking around the corner, waiting for a chance to become reality. She nevertheless forced herself to accept her friend's reassurances. Perhaps Chara was right after all and things would get better.

She tried to cheer herself up with thoughts of the coming evening. She was meeting Risan at the Three Tons. He had been there to meet her almost every evening. She looked at the clock. She had time to rest for an hour before then. Who knew, perhaps tonight everything might change. She was already smiling again.

* * *

Thousands of miles away in the Wylderlands across the sea, a man tossed and turned in his bed as he slept, creasing and ruffling the delicate silk sheets under him. Beads of sweat rolled down his temples. His breathing was heavy and laboured, as if he were struggling against the entire world in his dreams. He shouted incoherent words at invisible people and his body tensed as it followed the actions of his mind. Suddenly, he let out a gasp as he was released from whatever realm he had been in. His eyes opened. Gradually his breathing became slower and more shallow. He lifted himself up and looked about the room. Enough moonlight streamed in from the large open balcony doors for him to see that he was alone. There was nobody there. He reached out to open a small, ornate chest that sat on the bedside table and from it plucked out a glass vial with a stopper in the shape of a dragon's head. With great care, he allowed a single drop of dark, thick liquid to fall onto his tongue. The properties of the liquid entered his bloodstream and merged with his organs, imparting a momentary sense of exhilaration. He sank back thankfully into his soft pillows and closed his eyes, but sleep would not come. Sighing heavily, he threw on a robe and rose out of his bed. He casually pointed a finger at the fireplace, which burst into life at his command. The crackling sound might sooth another, but to him it spoke of things, important things. He leaned over and rested a muscular hand on the mantelpiece in order to listen more closely.

* * *

The tavern was busy and it took Ahlia a few minutes to fight her way through the crowds to get to her friends.

"Where's Risan?" she asked.

Brynan made some unusually vague reply about him being busy that evening.

Chara was definitely quieter than usual. Ahlia waited for one of them to tell her, what she had already guessed. The conversation got more and more painful and awkward as they tiptoed around it until she could bear it no more.

"Is there something I ought to know?"

They didn't need to say anything. Their apologetic looks spoke volumes. In fact, she didn't think she could bear to hear. She put her hand up to stop Chara who was about to say something.

"I don't want to know," she said rising from her chair. She glanced back at her friends when she reached the door. Chara was clearly having heated words with Brynan about something, but Ahlia did not at that moment care. She wrapped her shawl about her and braced herself for the cold evening air.

She had not gone far when she heard the sound of hurried footsteps behind her.

"Ahlia!" It was Chara. "Listen Ahlia, I know you're upset, but he's not worth it, really he isn't."

"No, I'm fine. I feel a bit foolish, but it's hardly the first time."

"An old flame, apparently. I didn't know about her, honestly Ahlia. I have just had severe words with Brynan for not telling me about her sooner, but he swears that he did. I just don't remember. I must be losing my touch. First, I can't place that old woman of yours for the life of me and now I overlook something like this! It is just not like me."

Ahlia shook her head. "I know you both meant well, but forget it. Let's be honest, I'm not most people's cup of ale."

Chara squeezed her friend's arm. "Well, you're my cup of ale, Ahlia Dorag. There's not one in a million like you."

"I think that's the problem," replied Ahlia sadly and began to walk home. Chara started to follow her, but Ahlia stopped her.

"I'm very tired, Chara. I just feel like keeping my own

company for a while. Say goodnight to Brynan for me. I'll see you tomorrow."

"You're sure?"

"I'm sure. Really I am. I just need to get some rest."

Chara gave her friend a hug and ran back towards the tavern, leaving Ahlia the space she craved.

Tears rolled slowly down her cheeks as she walked home. She hardly noticed the people that passed her. At least here she was anonymous. In the village where she was born, there would have been stares and hushed whispers. Sometimes she thought she missed her childhood home, but she knew herself well enough to realise it was the idea of home that she missed rather than the reality. As she strained her memory to recall the truth, images returned to her of angry neighbours shouting at her parents each time a crop had failed or an animal had died and pointing accusing fingers in her direction. She remembered the village Elder's stern eye and as she grew, how hard she had tried to avert displeasure and gain acceptance. Her spirit would not be bound, however, nor would it play by the rules of those about her. She had come to realise that her mind worked differently and the older she became, the further apart she had grown from those about her. Coming to Avor was supposed to have been the start of a new life, but even in the city she felt like an outcast and had taken to living on the fringes of respectable society, reading people's fortunes for a living. She had come to the realisation that something was seriously amiss, and she deeply suspected that the problem was her.

* * *

Ahlia barely ventured out over the next few weeks. Her exposure to the Avor rain had left her with a nasty cold. She also felt incredibly tired and no amount of sleep seemed to lift her energy levels. She assumed that her tiredness was due to illness, but deep down, she was not entirely satisfied with the explanation. She had never experienced such a drained sensation before, as though her energy had poured right out of her and left her empty.

When there was a knock on her door one afternoon, she expected it to be Chara coming to try and drag her out of bed as she had attempted to do repeatedly. Clutching a well-used handkerchief, she climbed out of bed to answer the door. To her dismay, she found her landlord standing there.

"You owe me rent." He smiled at her, displaying tobacco stained teeth.

"But I paid my rent the week before last did I not?" she protested before sneezing loudly.

"Yes, but rent has gone up. I've had an offer from a potential tenant, double what you pay. I have mouths to feed, you know. I simply cannot turn down this sort of an offer, you understand I'm sure. Of course," he added, "if you can match it, you can keep the room."

Ahlia buried her nose in her handkerchief and blew hard. She didn't bother arguing. There was clearly no point.

"How much and how long have I got?" she asked wiping her nose.

"Two silvers by the end of the week."

"But that's today!"

"I'm not entirely heartless you know. I'll give you a couple of days to sort something out. Good day to you."

Ahlia watched him in disbelief, slamming the door shut when he was out of sight.

Within moments, there was another knock on the door.

"What now!" she yelled. "If it's bad news, go away!"

There was a long pause. Then just as Ahlia thought the person had gone, there came another knock. "I give up," she groaned as she opened the door. There stood Mora.

"May I come in for a moment?"

Ahlia made an exaggerated beckoning gesture with her hand. "Just what I need, come right in!"

Mora appeared not to notice the sarcastic tone of voice. She sat herself down at the reading table and gave Ahlia a long hard stare. The girl's anger had triggered and fuelled her dormant power. The Knowing was active. With her Sorceress' eyes, Mora could see it writhing about, desperate to escape the prison that

38

Ahlia had subconsciously built for it. Time was running out.

"I was wondering if you had given my proposition any further thought," she asked.

"If you are really a Sorceress, perhaps you can help me," replied Ahlia, bringing her finger up to her nose to stifle a sneeze. "I have had problem after problem since I saw you last. Not that that is so unusual, mind, at least no one here is accusing me of causing the death of their cat or blighting their crops."

Mora looked at her inquisitively.

"But even by usual standards, the last few weeks have been ridiculous! If I was true to my village birthing, I'd think you cast a spell upon me. That would be proof enough of you being a Witch at least, if not a Sorceress, I suppose. Everything is going wrong," she ranted. "Everything! And I'm fed up with it!"

Mora remained calm and soon her calmness pervaded Ahlia's trembling form. Ahlia felt her breath deepen once again and her emotions subside.

"I cannot fix your troubles for you, Ahlia. It wouldn't mean anything. In any case, if you were to come with me, you'd have to leave all this behind. Perhaps it is a blessing that there is less to sacrifice than you thought there might be."

Suspicion began to form a thought in Ahlia's mind.

"You aren't responsible for all this, are you?" she asked, waving her handkerchief at the old woman. "Your idea of convincing me, perhaps?"

Mora said nothing. Then she leaned over to the side, lifted her wide buttock and scratched her thigh. Ahlia stared at her in disbelief.

"You meddled with my life! You did, didn't you!"

Mora shook her head. "I may have squashed time a little, brought things to a head a bit faster, but I have not changed sequence or event. I don't do that sort of thing. It brings nothing but trouble. Magic is a very tricky business. People don't realise."

"This isn't magic!"

"On the contrary, controlling the circumstances and events of life is a very important part of magic, but if you really want a silly display…"

Mora gestured to Ahlia's cold fireplace. It had been weeks since she had been able to afford coal and a small charred block of wood was all that graced the hearth. Mora pointed her index finger at the hearth and within seconds it had blazed to life. She softly dabbed her finger at the dead candles on the mantelpiece and each sprang to light.

"Happy now? Was that the proof you sought? A pathetic show? Is that what you think magic is? Consider this your first lesson Ahlia. How has lighting that fire changed the course of history? How has it bettered existence? To waste power in such a way is stupid and dangerous. Magic is not the thing seen. It is the thing unseen. It is the invisible hand that turns the wheel of life. It is the very thing we take for granted. That is true magic. True magic happens within, not without."

Ahlia did not know how to reply. She was staring at the fire in disbelief. Mora watched her for a moment to see if Ahlia had understood her words, then continued, "Either way child, I'm offering you an alternative. If you hate it, you can always come back. I won't keep you against your will."

Ahlia sniffed loudly.

"Nasty cold you've got there," commented Mora.

"I feel so tired too. No amount of rest seems to help."

Mora's eyes narrowed, "Hmm…." was all she said.

Ahlia crouched down to warm herself by the fire. She shuddered in pleasure as waves of warmth permeated her body. She was far too distracted to notice Mora pointing a finger in her direction. Nor did she see the strange particles that travelled from Mora's fingers in a thin glittering stream.

Ahlia yawned despite herself.

"I must go and you must rest," said Mora. Think on what I have said. You lose nothing and stand to gain everything. Sleep on it. I'll be waiting for you by the clock tower at the marketplace tomorrow. Come if you want to. Only, if you want to."

She made her way towards the door, but stopped a moment to say as an afterthought. "I suppose I should, in all fairness, warn you that some doors, once open are difficult to close and once closed are difficult to open."

As if to make her point clear, Mora left, leaving the door behind her ajar and creaking on its hinges.

Once alone, Ahlia sat deep in thought for hour after hour. She had one night to decide what course her life should take. Should she risk everything? She looked about her rented room, her empty purse, her single bed. Then she opened the door of her small wardrobe and fished out a big material bag. She opened it up and peered inside to check it for size. Yes, she thought wryly to herself, her entire life should fit in there, with room to spare.

Chapter 4

After two weeks of rain, the sun had finally reappeared and the day had turned out warm and bright. The square was full of busy shoppers and people who had simply come out for an airing and to exchange local news. It was market day and as if to mirror the weather, the inhabitants of Avor were wearing their brightest colours and their warmest smiles. Young girls giggled amongst themselves as they paraded about the fountain area trying to catch the attention of the young men of the town. Wives tried to out-do each other in terms of quality and style of dress. Men too stood about smoking and talking, or ambled slowly, soaking up the precious rays of sun on their way to the taverns, gratefully appreciating every second of their day off. Shopkeepers called out over each other, adding to the cacophony of sound, in an effort to sell their wares to passers-by. Amid the bustling sea of people, as still as a rock, Mora waited patiently, utterly absorbed in her own thoughts. She would come. She had to. Anyway, if she didn't, then there was always the alternative plan. Mora was considering what the alternative plan might entail when through the crowds she caught sight of a young woman carrying a heavy looking bag. She smiled to herself as Ahlia's small frame was buffeted and shoved about by the shoppers like a rowing boat in a storm.

"Oh have I got my work cut out for me," she mumbled to herself, as Ahlia put her bag down and bade her good day.

"So you've decided to take up my offer then."

"Yes. I could do with a fresh start anyway."

Mora smirked at the comment. "You'll not be back this way for a while, you know."

"I thought as much. All my belongings are in this bag."

"Say your goodbyes, did you?"

Ahlia nodded.

"Who to?" asked Mora feigning idle curiosity.

"My friend Chara and her husband."

"Know about me, do they?"

"Chara does, but I don't think she believes you are what you say you are. She thinks at most you might be a witch."

Ahlia winced in anticipation of Mora's displeasure at not being taken seriously, but there was no reprisal.

"Would that I were..." Mora muttered under her breath, "...for then..." she tailed off for a moment before abruptly changing the subject.

"How's your cold?"

"Much better, thank you. I had a good night's sleep too, which seems to have helped."

Mora smiled to herself. "Right then, let's be off."

"To where? Where are we going?"

"You'll see soon enough."

"Very well, how are we getting there then?"

As if in answer, Mora started walking.

"But, I thought you said you live far away?" Ahlia called after her.

"I do," was the reply.

When Ahlia realised that Mora was serious and not about to stop, she hurriedly hoisted her bag over her shoulder and rushed after her.

Avor was for the most part a maze of tall, stone buildings connected together via a system of ill-kept streets and alleyways. There was little to distinguish one cobbled street from another, but Mora seemed to know exactly where she was going. With expert ease she weaved through the crowds in the main square, the waves of people seeming to part before her as she walked. Without warning, she veered sharply to the left, ducking into a backstreet. She walked remarkably quickly for such an old woman and it was all Ahlia could do to keep up.

"I hate crowds," remarked Mora, "but sometimes they can be useful. Sometimes that which is in plain view can be the easiest thing to miss. Remind me to teach you about that at some point," she said, wagging her finger at Ahlia.

They moved further and further away until the bustle of the crowded market place was barely audible. They had passed Cilnad Street lined with rows of small bookshops, where Ahlia often went to browse and were heading towards Farsher Street. Mora veered off, taking a series of smaller and smaller alleyways that grew increasingly quiet and empty until they reached an area of Avor that Ahlia would never normally have dared to walk through, for fear of being robbed. More than once she thought to question Mora's chosen route, but there was something about being with Mora that seemed to put aside her personal intent and bend it towards whatever it was that Mora happened to be doing or saying. It was the strangest sensation and it left no room for doubt or contention. Ahlia's anxiety heightened when they passed a group of sinister-looking men, hovering by an unmarked doorway. The men fell silent as the two women walked past. They followed Ahlia and Mora with their eyes until the women were out of earshot, before resuming their discussions.

"Ah, don't mind them," Mora whispered. "Racketeers is all they are, the least of our worries."

In time, they reached the edge of town. The dilapidated walls of Avor had completely crumbled in this impoverished district. There had been no war in the region for hundreds of years and funds for maintenance on the wall had, for the most part, been diverted into the pockets of politicians. As they clambered over the rubble and put Avor behind them, a rush of exhilaration seized Ahlia. She was really doing this. She had no idea what tomorrow might be like and although she felt a little afraid, she realised that she also felt good. Excitement surged through her body at the prospect of the unknown and she began to feel more alive than she had in years.

Mora trod on unwaveringly and spoke very little, ignoring any questions that Ahlia asked, telling her to save her energy for the journey. They were walking on the edge of the wide dirt track that served as the route out to the Fleger Forests that lay between Avor and the next big town of Darech, a good week's journey away. About them, the landscape was becoming increasingly green and grassy and the air was sweet and filled with the soft sound of bird song. Ahlia looked about her in delight. Though she had grown up in a farming village, she had not left the town in years and the experience of having such space about her filled her with pleasure. Her breathing seemed to deepen and she could feel her shoulders dropping a notch as she relaxed. Her aesthetic appreciation was shattered, however, by Mora declaring that she needed to empty her bowels and disappearing behind some nearby shrubs. Ahlia was silently grateful that she hadn't eaten all that much as the thought of using leaves as privy paper was less than appealing to her. When Mora reappeared, she peered up at the sky, shielding her eyes from the sun with her hand. She pursed her lips.

"At this rate we'll never make it before dark," she murmured to herself. She looked over at Ahlia who was sitting on a small boulder by the side of the track, resting her tired legs. She had propped her head in her hands, her elbows balanced on her lap, her eyes closed for a few moments respite. Mora pulled at a small dark drawstring bag that was tied to her belt. The knot untied itself and the bag purse came free in her hand. She rummaged around inside it and took out a pinch of a yellow grainy powder with her thumb and forefinger. Smiling to herself, she softly walked over to Ahlia and dropped some of the powder on each of the tips of Ahlia's shoes as they peeped out from under her dress. The powder seemed to dissolve into nothingness, but Mora could see it as plainly as firelight glowing on each shoe.

"That should speed us up a bit," she mumbled softly to herself. "Seeing as we've miles to go yet."

Ahlia started at the sound of a voice so close to her.

"Where did you appear from? I didn't hear you coming."

"That's because, unlike you, my dear, I don't blunder about like a Wylderboar when I walk."

"A what?" asked Ahlia.

"A Wylderboar... oh never mind. It's an animal, a large, clumsy animal that thumps about in the Wylderlands."

"The Wylderlands? Where in Spirits name are they?"

Mora turned her back to Ahlia and started walking.

"Far from here. It's where I came from. Come on. No time to waste," she called behind her.

Ahlia's expression turned to one of panic.

"We're not walking all the way to the Wylderlands are we?"

Mora stopped walking and chuckled as she turned to answer. "No. Not even I would be so foolish or arrogant as to attempt that! For one thing, there's a sea between us and the Wylderlands, and for another, they're not the same as they used to be. There is nothing there for me now."

Her tone was strangely sombre for a moment before it resumes its accustomed curtness.

"Now start walking!" she ordered.

Ahlia had never walked so far in the whole of her life. Every few hours or so, she had to beg Mora to stop for a rest. Each time Mora huffed in disapproval repeating they were wasting time. Morning turned into afternoon. After several hours, they took a detour off the main road into the leafy awning of the forest. It seemed to Ahlia that they often seemed to be taking two steps forward and one step back, winding and even backtracking as they walked, but Mora assured her that this was in fact, a short cut to her cottage.

"Oh. I was beginning to think you might be covering our tracks or something."

Mora was genuinely impressed. "Not entirely wet behind the ears then."

"But who would want to follow us?"

Mora shrugged, "I don't like uninvited guests, whoever they might be and you can't be too careful."

The afternoon light began to fade as evening set in and still they walked on. Finally, as the skyline was beginning to change into a dusky mauve, they came to a clearing in which someone had built a small stone hut with a thatched roof. It looked abandoned from the outside. Mora came to a sudden halt and sighed happily as they neared it.

"Here it is, home."

She turned in time to witness Ahlia's shocked face. "Oh don't worry, I know it's a bit rough on the outside, but it's much better on the inside. Come on."

Mora had lied. The inside of the 'cottage', as she called it was definitely as bad as the outside. The place was a hovel. Spirit alone knew what manner of insects called it home too. The room was arranged around a large fireplace, above which, on a hook, hung all manner of cooking implements. A large clay cooking pot sat to the side, next to a small pile of firewood. The floor was bare and dusty. Various pots and jars filled the room, stacked precariously on narrow wooden shelves. There was a wind chime made of old animal bones that hung from one of the windows. Under the window was a thin straw-filled mattress on a row of wooden slats that probably served as a bed. The mere thought of sleeping on it was enough to send Ahlia's back into spasms. On the other side of the room there was a small wooden table and two chairs. Ahlia noted that there was not one book in the whole place. Nor was there a doorway to another room. She groaned to herself. That meant the small wooden shack outside, which she had passed on her way in, was the privy. There was no way she was going out there at night, she thought to herself, absolutely no way.

She dumped her bag of belongings on the floor and dropped herself beside them and the bundle of firewood that Mora had insisted they collect on the way. They had been walking the best part of a day and she was utterly exhausted. Every bone in her body ached and her feet were covered in blisters. The noises emanating from her stomach made her aware that she must be hungry too, but she was just too tired to be bothered about that.

Mora grumbled in disgust, as she went about laying the wood in the hearth.

"That's the trouble with the young, too soft in the body, too soft in the head."

Ahlia felt utterly forlorn. "Why am I here?" she thought miserably.

Mora gave her a sharp look. "I'll have to teach you not to think so loudly," she said sharply, but she could see the comment was lost on Ahlia, whose brain was too occupied with generating self-pity to take anything else on board at that moment. Mora made a mental note that this pathetic tendency would also have to be stamped out as quickly as possible. Then she pointed a finger at the wood and sighed contentedly as a tiny spark turned into the beginnings of a glowing fire. She turned round to see if this too had been lost on her new apprentice. Apparently, it had not. Ahlia's eyes had grown as wide as saucers.

"How do you do that!" she gasped, her voice full of awe.

"You'll learn. That is why you are here," she replied, "but first things first."

Mora cast a predatory eye towards Ahlia's bag. Without knowing why, Ahlia tightened the grip on the handle. It was to no avail. With surprising strength and speed, Mora yanked it away and opened it. She began making a pile of the contents.

"Well you won't be needing any of this stuff for a start. No need for books. No need for writing material. Soaps and oils? Perhaps you thought I lived in a palace? No need for those. We have plenty of water and that is all you need."

She poked an accusing finger at her new apprentice. "Soft is dangerous. Soft is weak and soft is dead. There is only one place for softness to live and be safe and that is here." She thumped her chest.

"Be hard of character, but tender of heart and you'll never go wrong. Trust me," she cackled.

Ahlia placed one hand on her hip in indignation.

"If you knew I didn't need anything, then why did you let me carry my bag all the way here?"

Mora gazed intently into her apprentice's eyes. "Lesson two, my young apprentice. Lesson two," she chided.

"You could have rid yourself of your baggage at any time, but you didn't. Remember that no one else but you is responsible for your choices."

Ahlia opened her mouth to say something, but did not get a chance to voice her anger.

"You'd better close that before something decides to make a home out of it," snapped Mora.

"Your bed is there," she pointed to the mattress on the floor, "you'll have noticed the privy on the way in. Your duties include keeping it clean. You will also be responsible for keeping the fire going. That will be the most important of your jobs. Whenever I'm home, I must always have a fire going. You'll have to collect firewood and bring water in from the well too. I do the cooking. You sweep the floor every morning and every evening. Oh and you'll be helping me tend the garden, of course."

"There's a garden?"

"I always have a garden to grow my vegetables. I can't be doing with markets."

"And what about my study? You've taken my notebook and pen away. How will I write things down?"

Mora guffawed derisively. "Oh don't you worry, you'll learn plenty and you will commit it all to memory. First, you learn your way about the natural world. I can tell you're all soft and citified. You learn what nature can offer you. You don't need pen and paper for that. Then you'll learn the other stuff."

Ahlia envisioned days on end of housework. She was beginning to have second thoughts. "What about my cards?"

"Spirits, you haven't brought those things with you have you? You definitely won't be needing those anymore."

Mora's voice became stern.

"I won't lie to you. I shall push you hard. We have much to do and little time. You must trust that I will teach you all you need to know and more importantly, I will help you to form a mind that will be ever open to learning more. People are not the only teachers, nor are they always the best. My Master did teach me a great deal, but the greatest gift he gave me was an open mind to learn from the world about me."

Ahlia was surprised. "Your teacher was a man?"

Mora shook her head. "Not just a man, a great Sorcerer. He chose to teach me over a hundred others. I was truly honoured. In those days few women became apprentices."

"How did he pick you?"

"Every teacher has their reason. Sometimes it makes no sense to anyone else. Perhaps he knew I'd make a terrible wife!" she guffawed again, this time with self-amusement.

Then she suddenly scrunched her nose up. "Phew, what is that smell? It's been around here as long as you have."

Ahlia looked at her in shock. "What do you mean?" she pulled open the front of her smock and stuck her nose in to check that the hours of walking had not left their mark offensively.

Mora glared at her and thrust an open hand out. "Hand it over."

Ahlia's eyebrows shot up in alarm. "What?" she asked in apparent confusion, though she had by now realized what Mora meant.

"The perfume," Mora demanded sternly.

"But why? It's got nothing to do with..."

"With what? It has everything to do with everything."

Ahlia had never seen Mora this angry and she definitely did not like it. Reluctantly, she rummaged in her pocket and fished out the little bottle. She sheepishly handed it over to Mora who closed her fingers over the offending object and squeezed so tightly that Ahlia was sure the fragile bottle must have smashed under the pressure of such a grip. Then Mora opened her hand and flung the contents at Ahlia who tried to shield herself from the shards of glass she expected to be flying towards her. To her surprise, she felt nothing but a spray of liquid. The glass from the bottle had disappeared. Mora was still glaring at her. For the first time, Ahlia registered that the old woman's hump had all but vanished and she now stood taller than Ahlia.

"Vanity betrays the presence of a weak mind. There is no place for vanity here," she said angrily.

"Mora, don't you think you're over-reacting just a little bit?" ventured Ahlia, though she immediately wished she could swallow her words.

Mora looked furiously at her. "Vanity has caused the downfall of more than one and the suffering of more than many. Vanity leads to self-preoccupation, which leads to selfishness, which leads to greed and which leads to an ever downward stairway. I know what I speak of."

Ahlia bowed her head at her Mistress's tirade. She did not know what to say. About her the smell of roses was getting stronger and stronger.

"Roses you shall smell of until you are sick of it!" hissed Mora.

"Though knowing you, it will be months before you are bored of it, and I meanwhile shall be the one enduring the reeking stench and I shall be reminded."

"Reminded of what? Of my weakness?" asked Ahlia meekly.

"No. Of mine!" she replied storming out.

Mora left Ahlia in the cottage alone for over an hour. When she returned, she found Ahlia sitting quietly on the floor by the fire, her legs tucked underneath her. The girl lacked tenacity, thought Mora to herself. It was a problem. Looking at Ahlia now, any Sorcerer would be hard pushed to note anything extraordinary at all about the girl, but Mora was not any Sorcerer. She quietly laid down the mushrooms she had picked.

"Been thinking have we? Thinking of going home?"

Ahlia looked at her sullenly. "Why did you pick me, Mora?"

Mora looked her squarely in the eye. "Because you are the absolute opposite of everything that I was at your age."

Ahlia wasn't sure if she should feel flattered or insulted.

"...and," Mora continued, "...because you have the Knowing. It speaks for you though you refuse to understand its voice and it tells me that you want this."

"What do you mean, the Knowing? I don't know what you are talking about. I don't 'know' anything."

"This is not the time for such talk," Mora replied abruptly, "Now to bed with you. Tomorrow you rise with the dawn!"

Ahlia was exhausted. Without even taking her shoes off, she threw herself onto her bare mattress and flung the thin blanket over herself. In seconds, she was fast asleep, leaving Mora to watch the fire as intently as a scholar might read a book.

"How could I make her understand," she mumbled seemingly to herself, "that it was nothing to do with me. Not my choice, but the Oracle's."

* * *

51

Ahlia was not destined to get a full night's sleep. When Mora woke her, it was moonlight that streamed through the curtainless window.

"Full moon. Time for herb picking."

Ahlia rubbed sleep from her eyes and sat up. She arched her back, wincing as her spine cracked loudly. Hardly conscious of where she was going, she stumbled after Mora into the forest. Soon the sounds about her and the nip of the cool night air had awakened all her senses and she felt uncannily elated. Things seemed sharper and strangely beautiful in this silver light. The ordinary forest had been transformed into a place of true wonder.

"I see you like the night and I sense the night likes you. This is a good time for you. Remember that."

Ahlia's eyes were full of excitement. "Why? What does it mean?"

"Nothing..." Mora mused, "...and something. For today you just observe, anyway." She was preoccupied with the variety of plants that covered the ground. Every few moments or so, she paused and fingered the leaves of a plant very gently as if afraid of hurting it. Ahlia noticed that the old woman trod very carefully also, moving between the plants rather than over them. She left no trace of a path behind her and when she plucked leaves, she did so with extreme care. Some plants she uprooted entirely, but with the softness and dexterity of a mother caring for her young. The soil seemed barely disturbed when she was done, the hole refilling itself with earth. Ahlia could hear her murmuring to herself, or perhaps to the plants, it was impossible to tell.

"Mora, why do we have to pick the herbs at night?" she asked tentatively, almost afraid to interrupt.

Mora stood up straight and stretched her back. "I just like the night."

"And the full moon? Is that special?"

"The moon is always special. Can't pick herbs very well without it."

"Why not?"

"Because you won't be able to see a damned thing, is why. I should have thought that was obvious! Course, that's more true for you than me. I can pick herbs blind-folded, I'll wager."

Mora stood dead still and motioned for Ahlia to do the same. She put her hand to her ear. Ahlia listened intently. She could hear the rustle of the trees, the sounds of small animals, of insects even, but she did not know what she was listening for.

"Eventually, when you are ready, you will hear their music. Each one sings a different melody. It's very soft and your mind must be very still to hear it." Mora paused. "Come. We are done here."

It seemed to Ahlia that they walked in silence for at least an hour, until they came to a small opening among some rocks by which Mora had left a lantern on her previous visit. Mora pointed to it and the candle behind the glass burst into a bright flame. She picked the lantern up and called for Ahlia to follow her. "Come, I want to show you something."

Ahlia followed her through a narrow passageway, occasionally squeezing herself past rocks that jutted out here and there. Ahlia's heart was in her throat from fear as Mora led the way downward. Mora began to sing softly and Ahlia's fear gradually faded as the melody Mora crooned, washed over her. It seemed to bounce off the rocks, creating a hum that hung in the air even when she was not singing. Ahlia strained to hear the words, but they were in a language that she could not understand. Soon, they came to a wider cave. The air was cool and the rocks were colder still to touch at first, though the longer her hand remained upon them, the more they seemed to warm as if absorbing her body heat. Under her hand, Ahlia thought she could feel a gentle vibration coming from within the rock. The sensation was incredibly soothing and Ahlia was loath to remove her hand. Mora had pointed to the corners of the cave and lanterns had come to life, lighting up the beautiful walls. Seams of crystal sparkled in the light and waves of ochre and sandstone created fascinating patterns. It was all Ahlia could do to pull her eyes away. Mora smiled in satisfaction.

"It is quite something, eh?"

Ahlia nodded, awestruck.

"People used to live here eons ago, you know," said Mora gesturing about her.

"And down there…" she pointed to a passageway that led further downwards, "…is water. We are under a hill here and deeper in the rock is the source of a spring that grows to become a river. The water collects a little in these caves. You can drink it. It is clear as crystal, but cold mind!"

Mora turned to lead the way down the passage, but Ahlia held back for a moment to savor the beauty of the cave. The atmosphere of the place was so serene and quiet that time itself seemed to stand still. She could understand easily how people might have once sought sanctuary down here. She was about to walk on, when an abrupt and strange sensation rippled through her chest causing her to start. It was as if something had moved through and past her. She thought she saw something flit past her out of the corner of her eye, but even though she turned swiftly to catch sight of what it might be, she could see nothing there. She hurriedly left the cave and followed Mora's fast disappearing lantern, down another tunnel until they arrived at an even bigger cave. By one wall and flowing through into another cave deeper underground, was a small pool of water, so clear that she could see the sand and rocks at the bottom in the flickering lantern light. Ahlia gasped in amazement. It was the most beautiful place she had ever encountered. Mora was smiling to herself and breathing deeply and slowly as if to absorb something of the place into her. For a moment she cocked her head towards Ahlia and gave her a strange look.

"You alright?"

"Oh yes. It's truly wonderful."

Ahlia's cheeks were flushed and her eyes gleamed with delight.

Mora held her gaze for a moment and opened her mouth as if to say something, but seemed to think better of it. She closed her mouth again and returned her attention to the cave. Her smile broadened.

She was watching the Devas playing. They shimmered against

the rocks, transparent, yet visible, flitting and swirling about, their forms ever changing as they moved. Those of the Green path had come here seeking knowledge and Spirit for eons, until the mind of man changed in these parts and the Green ways were all but forgotten. Now the Devas seldom had visitors, and most who ventured into caves such as these came to damage the rocks by mining for gems. The Devas had little time for humans who would destroy their home, though it seemed they were fascinated by Ahlia; this girl who could feel them, but at the same time, not acknowledge them.

"She does not know what you are. You are outside her range of understanding. She can feel you, but she cannot accept you yet. You must give her time," Mora mumbled softly in her native tongue.

She called over to Ahlia who was lost in rapture. "Come. Let's get you to bed or you'll be good for nothing in the morning. Tomorrow I'll teach you a little bit about herb-lore."

"Do we have to go yet? It is so beautiful down here, so peaceful."

Ahlia's voice had taken on a dreamy quality. Mora gave her a long hard look.

"Ahlia!" she called sharply, deliberately shattering the tranquility. "It is time to go."

She led her apprentice out of the caves, the lanterns snuffing themselves out behind them, leaving the Devas to play in natural darkness.

Chapter 5

They returned to the cottage with a few hours left before dawn. Still fully clothed, Ahlia lay down to get what sleep she could before daybreak. She had not nearly had enough rest when her slumber was disturbed by a strange scraping sound. It took her foggy mind a few moments to realise that it was Mora, sweeping the bare floor with a hard broom. Trying to ignore the noise, Ahlia turned over, hoping to drift back to sleep, but the sweeping got louder as it came closer. Something hard knocked into Ahlia's back, making her call out in pain.

"Ouch!" Ahlia sat up and rubbed her back.

"Oh, did I catch you with the broom?" asked Mora innocently.

Ahlia scowled through the locks of her dishevelled hair. The old woman knew full well what she had done.

"Well seeing as you're up, you can go and fetch in some water from the well. The bucket's over there by the door."

Mora gave her apprentice a wide, toothless grin as she watched Ahlia reluctantly haul herself out of bed. Still half asleep and stiff from the previous day's exercise, Ahlia winced as she bent over and groped for the bucket handle. The old Sorceress chuckled to herself as she listened to Ahlia grumbling as she trudged to the well.

"Anger is good, anger is very good," she said, "Anger, we can use."

Ahlia returned to find Mora seated at the table. She had laid out a number of herb specimens on the table. She gestured for Ahlia to put the bucket down and take a seat at the table next to her.

"We will begin with herb-lore. By the end of the day, you will be able to identify and use all the herbs that you see before you."

Ahlia looked at the table. There were at least twenty separate bundles on the table. Mora launched into the lesson.

"This is Vera root. Now see how its colour differs from the other roots you see on the table. It is much darker, now…"

After listening to Mora for about ten minutes, Ahlia's head began to hurt. "Mora, I need to write some of this down. I need parchment and ink."

Mora looked at her and huffed loudly. "Why? What's wrong with your memory?"

"Nothing, but…"

"Well then, that's settled," said Mora in a no nonsense tone.

"But…"

"But what?" snapped Mora, pushing an invisible part of herself out so that it filled the space between them. Ahlia responded instinctively by retreating back into her chair and pursing her lip.

"But what?" repeated Mora more loudly in an attempt to stir Ahlia's fighting spirit, but it was to no avail. Ahlia visibly retreated further into herself, though she was fuming inwardly. Mora's keen eye took it all in and made a mental note. Emotions were often a good guide to the direction of a person's power. Ahlia's was moving the wrong way. If Ahlia didn't learn to turn the direction of her power outwards soon, she would not survive long.

*　*　*

It had been a long day. Ahlia's brain was addled with snippets of information about roots and leaves and names she had never heard of before. Mora had refused to let her get up until she could name every herb on the table and list its uses. Then they had travelled into the woods so that Ahlia could see the herbs in their habitat and learn to listen for each plant's distinct melody. Ahlia had strained her ears in vain. She had heard nothing but the sounds of rustling leaves and the birds in the trees. At dusk they returned to the cottage. All she wanted to do now was sleep. So tired that she could hardly stand up, she threw herself onto her mattress and in minutes was lost in a deep, dreamless slumber.

Mora smiled in satisfaction as she assessed the day's progress. The girl had done well. Perhaps there was hope yet. Outside, the pregnant moon sat heavy between the velvet clouds. She looked wistfully through the open window towards the forest. Tiptoeing past her sleeping apprentice, Mora closed the door quietly behind her and disappeared into the trees.

That night, Ahlia was roused by the feel of someone or something pulling at her arm as it rested over her blanket. Still only partly conscious, she assumed it must be Mora, but terror gripped her as she realised that these fingers did not belong to any person. They were sinking through her arms pulling at some part of her that was not flesh and blood, but had substance and form to it nevertheless. On sensing Ahlia's resistance, the ethereal hands retreated, just as Ahlia's terror was beginning to be replaced by the most exquisite sense of elation. There was something almost painfully beautiful about the presence that had been around her. Like a child disturbed from their slumber by a well-meaning parent, Ahlia let out a whimper and turned over before sinking back into unconsciousness.

That morning, she awoke in confusion and with a haunting memory of that exquisite feeling, coupled with an unexplainable sense of loss at its absence.

"A Deva. It wanted to contact you, but you were too scared. It is a pity," Mora told her when Ahlia asked for advice.

"The Devas are the shining ones. They are Spirits of nature. You were foolish to be so terrified. You will be lucky if it comes back. It made great effort and travelled some way to seek you out."

Ahlia felt forlorn. She thought to go back to the caves, but as if reading her thoughts, Mora warned, "Don't you dare go in there alone. You aren't strong enough to come back out. I told you people lived in those caves. They lived and died there and did not venture from them much. They could not bear to. You know what I mean, Ahlia."

Ahlia recalled the bliss, and the loss. She nodded. "Mora how do you know if they are good or bad? Or whether they mean you harm or not?"

Mora looked at her incredulously. She laughed loudly.

"I don't know about bad Spirits. I only know about bad people. People foolishly taint the world about them with their own inadequacies. What does a bird know of badness, or a rock or a plant? The forces of nature are not bound by our notions. They exist outside of the reality we dictate. There is no good and bad in it. The Devas just are. How they affect us is our choice and therefore our responsibility."

Ahlia looked thoughtful. Something was clearly bothering her. Mora waited patiently for her apprentice to speak.

"But Mora, I have never told anyone this before, but since I was a child I have had all sorts of frightening dreams and when I grew older, I heard voices in my sleep, voices that terrified me. There have been nights where I have awoken and was afraid to return to sleep."

Mora listened intently. "Ah, child. spirits will take on the shape of the energy you give them. If you only give them fear to work with, then that is what they must use. It is not the spirits you must banish, but the fear with which you meet them. What have they to gain by scaring you?"

"What you say makes sense, Mora, but in my sleep I have no control. I cannot stop being afraid and the voices sound so..."

"Deep? Old? Powerful? Inhuman?" suggested Mora softly.

Ahlia nodded in amazement at Mora's understanding.

"Give it time child, give it time. It will come. I will push you in many ways, but on this I will not rush. Such channels must be opened gently and carefully, lest you fail to cope. These are not human voices that you are hearing, nor are they the voices of the dead that have passed over. These are the voices of much older things. For now, do not dwell on it. Why don't you fetch us some water from the well and I shall brew some tea."

As she watched Ahlia leave, realisation spread through Mora like a wave of warmth from a fire. Ahlia was hearing the Ancient voices. This was going to be more complicated than she realised. As if the Oracle was not enough for a lifetime's worth of complication.

"Hear me Old Ones," she uttered in a voice that vibrated through the air. "You cannot use her as your voice. You will burst her head. She is not ready. Besides, the Oracle has laid claim to her. There will be one of her line that will honour your calling, but not yet. Not for years to come."

*   *   *

Hundreds of miles from Mora's cottage, on the snow-capped mountain range of Islan, Sebastian stood as motionless as marble. His skin was as pale as the snow that surrounded him. Only the visible mist of his warm breath as it reached the frosty air indicated that he was a living thing. Far above him, a white bird circled. Sebastian's eyes flickered behind his closed lids, mirroring the motion of the bird's eyes. As the bird let out a cry, Sebastian's own throat moved, though he made no sound. He had mastered the skill of merging years ago, but he could merge with no other creature as closely as with his ally, Nacor, a snow hawk. At this moment, he was looking down upon the terrain from the sky, feeling a freedom that he relished because it was in such contrast to his normal need for restraint. Since the day he had become an apprentice, he had known few moments as free as this. He was a servant of magic, bound to his path with unrelenting dedication even if that path should lead to his destruction. However, for this short moment, he could be Nacor, whose only concern was where he could find his next meal.

Back in the house, Viad used the long nail of his index finger to ripple the surface of water before him. He had been searching for Mora in his stone scrying bowl for so long that he had lost count of the years. Always, she managed to elude him, leaving him a step behind her each time. Recently, however, his efforts had been more fruitful. As the film of the water gradually stilled once more, Viad glimpsed something that made his eyes widen.

"The trees! Of course!"

He pulled his mind back from the image and blinked a few times to regain his normal focus. As he turned away from the bowl, his first instinct was to call for Sebastian and share what he had discovered, but something made him hold back. He knew that if he told his impatient apprentice of Mora's whereabouts, the boy would be off without another moment's thought. If he reached Mora too early, she would destroy him. The power of the Supreme Sorceress did not wane with time, it only grew stronger. Sebastian would not stand a chance.

"No, not yet," murmured Viad to himself. "Not yet," as he watched his apprentice from the window. Behind him, the water in the bowl rippled of its own accord as an image flickered across the surface; the image of a man dressed in black and red armour brandishing a knife. It remained only for a second, before falling back into the invisible depths of the water once more.

* * *

It was a fresh spring night and Mora had left Ahlia sleeping soundly in the cottage to walk in the forest alone as she so often did. From her smock she fished out a pipe. It sparked alight as she put it to her lips and puffed on it, sending whirls of grey green smoke into the air.

"So Viad, I see you have been busy," she said to herself as she watched the smoke intently.

"Unfortunately, you and your cocky apprentice are the least of my worries."

She tapped the pipe against the bark of a tree and its glow faded. When she was sure it was lifeless, she returned the pipe to her smock. Mora walked on in silence until she came to a small clearing in the forest. She had never brought Ahlia here, for good reason. Under a large shrub, discreetly placed, there was a small marker that had been there for over eighty years.

"Daughter in all, but blood," Mora called out softly into the night air over the grave.

"You who were better than me and should have become more than me: how your light shone!"

Mora sat quietly by the grave of her first apprentice. Tears rolled down the furrows of her wrinkled cheek as she relived for the thousandth time what had happened all those years ago.

Ahlia was awakened in the morning by a rough shove.

"Time to get up, softy."

She rubbed her eyes, but did not get up immediately. She knew it would be another day of trying hard and getting nowhere. She felt particularly morose today. All her efforts seemed to come to no avail. She didn't feel like she had changed at all. She accomplished nothing new. She poked at the beans Mora had given her for breakfast and picked at the bread. Mora controlled her irritation as a pile of crumbs began to form on the floor.

"Spit it out then."

"What?"

"The lemon you're sucking. Or whatever else it is that is making you look so sour."

"I'm just frustrated Mora, I don't feel like I'm getting anywhere. Maybe I'm too... maybe I'm too old to learn."

"Devils nipping at your self-confidence again I see. A bit of a habit with you, isn't it!"

"Well, I have doubts."

"Congratulations! And you say you haven't learned anything."

"Huh?"

"Most apprentices think they can run before they can walk. Some have been known to slip a knife between their teacher's ribs while they slept in order to claim their power. I can see with you I have nothing to worry about on that score."

Ahlia didn't know what to say next. Mora always knew exactly how to cast her into further confusion. She always answered every question that Ahlia asked, but that was the problem. Her answers, while seeming to make sense, never really satisfied Ahlia. The old woman looked at her with eyes that seemed to bore right through her.

"It's not answers you're after, its reassurance. That's why my answers don't appease you."

Mora threw her another piece of bread.

"If you must know, I was late in starting myself."

Ahlia's face brightened. "How old were you?"

Mora looked sheepish for a moment. It was an unusual sight. "Well I was thirteen."

"Thirteen! I'm near thirty! You, yourself said that most Sorcerers take on child apprentices. Perhaps it is just too late for me after all."

"You are missing the point," said Mora. "It's not how long or how early. It's not even how fast. It is how well. Although," she added, "fast is good, given the circumstances, fast is definitely good."

"What circumstances?" asked Ahlia. "You are always talking about time and running out of time and saying things like 'too much is at stake', but what is the rush?"

"I'm not going to live forever and I can't take my power with me!" Mora shouted, causing Ahlia to jump.

She returned to the subject matter swiftly, not giving Ahlia a chance to pursue any potentially dangerous lines of thought.

"When all is said and done there is only how well."

"And so how do I get to how well?" Ahlia asked meekly.

Mora beamed at her. "That's my girl. You see, you do know what to ask when pushed hard enough. That's exactly the right question."

She paused. "It all depends on motive, on intent."

"Intent?"

Mora nodded happily, as if sharing a wondrous secret that she had been dying to reveal. "Intent!" she repeated.

"Oh. That makes it clear. Clear as MUD!" complained Ahlia in exasperation.

Mora threw another piece of bread, this time at Ahlia's head.

"You have an advantage. Your character was formed without being corrupted by the potential of power. That makes your intent purer because you remember what it is like to feel helpless and you know that you can survive it. Those who grasp at power do so out of fear. Underneath there is always fear. Think on it. Think on it hard."

"But I have fear too. I'm afraid," said Ahlia. "I've always been afraid of things."

"Then conquer it. Don't make me waste any more good bread!" Mora yelled.

Ahlia jumped up in fright and ran towards the door. Mora raised her forefinger casually and pointed it at her apprentice. Ahlia found herself forced to stop dead in her tracks. She could not move another step forward, no matter how hard she tried.

"The difference between you and others is that you know you are afraid. They think they are not. To know a thing is the route to understanding it and to understand it is to wield its true power. Now go and think on it and don't come back till nightfall!"

She made a pushing gesture with her fingertips. An invisible force propelled Ahlia roughly out of the door sending her tumbling down the porch steps. Ahlia quickly got up and ran into the woods before the old Sorceress really lost her temper. Inside Mora cackled to herself and gnashed her worn gums together.

"Good to know I've still got my teeth!"

She let out a sigh as she watched Ahlia running into the trees.

"As if I had time to train a child. Besides, a child is exactly what they'll all be looking for!"

She looked at the crumbs on the floor and shook her head.

"A childish adult won't cross their minds in a million years, I hope."

She pursed her lips and made a whistling sound. Two sparrows fluttered down from a nearby tree and perched on the window-sill.

"Look what she's made you," crooned Mora softly, pointing to the crumbs. The birds hopped along the floor to the crumbs and began to peck at them. Soon the floor was clear once more and the sparrows were on their way back to the trees, their stomachs full.

* * *

Viad was in the library, a dusty room whose walls were lined with manuscripts and scrolls. He pulled out a large hand-bound book and was carefully turning the parchment pages. Finally, he paused as he found what he had been looking for. The page was covered in ornate script and on the edge of the page there was a detailed drawing of a talisman. It was oval in shape and formed out of a silver metal. A dark red stone had been set in the centre. Viad's index finger lingered over the picture for a few moments. Then he placed a book-mark in the book and closed it again, but neglected to replace it on the shelf. He left it instead on the large wooden table for Sebastian to find when the time was right.

"May he be wiser than I was," murmured Viad to the silent walls, "though my heart doubts it."

* * *

"Mora, why is it that no one ever comes to visit?" Ahlia asked in an effort to distract herself from the monotony of the task that Mora had set her. She had, to her dismay, been instructed to weed the entire garden. Mora, meanwhile, seemed entirely absorbed in inspecting her bean plants, but in truth was keeping a watchful eye on her apprentice's progress.

"I told you before. I don't like uninvited visitors," she said slapping Ahlia's hand away and preventing her from pulling out a valuable bean shoot.

"Ouch, that hurt!"

Ahlia rubbed her earth-stained hand and grimaced as she noticed how much dirt had lodged under her now ragged fingernails. She sat back on her heels in irritation.

"But you don't ever invite anyone either do you."

"I invited you."

"Yes, but what about other people?" demanded Ahlia, trying hard not to let frustration get the better of her.

"What of them?"

"Why is it that no one ever comes here? Witches often get people coming to consult them."

"I thought I made it clear that I was a Sorceress. The way of a witch is a noble one, but it is different. Though," she conceded, "sorcerers could benefit greatly from taking a leaf out of the

Green path. Our worlds are not as different as some might think. You will find that out for yourself in good time."

Mora seemed to mull over this last thought in her mind, but Ahlia's interest lay elsewhere.

"And what about these certain Sorcerers. What about other Sorcerers?"

"We steer clear of other magic workers," Mora said curtly as if reciting a rule.

"But why?"

"Because the world is too small as it is. No need to make it smaller. Magic workers need space, a lot of space. I, in particular, need an awful lot of space."

"But why?"

"Because I do," she said gruffly, but she knew this would not appease Ahlia's curiosity. By way of explanation she continued, "There is a place inside each worker of magic. Some describe it as a twist in the fabric of the very soul of a person. We call it the Knowing. It begins as a small thing, squashed by everything else. Like a muscle, as we use it, it grows in size. After time, it is no longer a thing merely inside us, it surrounds us too. It needs space."

"I don't understand. How can something inside us become outside us as well?" asked Ahlia.

"Even when small, the Knowing can influence our outside world without us even realising. A person can use it to work magic without consciously being aware that they are doing it. Of course, the effects appear to be random unless a person is truly gifted. It manifests as a kind of luck to the ignorant observer."

Ahlia smirked. "Then I definitely don't have the Knowing."

"Oh, yes you do," insisted Mora. "But you are different. Even children with the Knowing usually learn to control it quickly to achieve their desires. For some reason, you have not. That reason is your destiny."

"Why am I so different?" asked Ahlia.

Mora folded her arms and gave her apprentice an unwavering stare.

"You tell me," she said. "You and you alone chose to split

66

yourself in two, one part of you working hard to suppress, forcing the other part of you to resort to increasingly devious methods of expression. Of course, one can never suppress the Knowing entirely. It always leaks out."

"What do you mean?"

Mora wagged her finger at her apprentice. "Don't give me that. You know exactly what I mean. All that card reading business!"

Ahlia looked at the old woman incredulously, but Mora was right. A small part of Ahlia's mind that she had become very good at ignoring, knew exactly what the old Sorceress was insinuating.

"You were changing the threads of reality for the people who came to you," said Mora accusingly. "People acted on what you told them and their actions changed their futures. You were creating subtle changes in the Great Map, not for yourself, but for those who consulted you. If that isn't magic then I don't know what is, and you are just very lucky you didn't make too much of a mess. The doing of magic is a curious affair. The magic of the unseen, of the subtle, is a powerful form of magic. It doesn't have to be all fireworks and earthquakes. Any fool can do those if what they seek is to draw attention to themselves. Of course, the last thing *you* wanted to do was to draw attention to yourself. You just wanted to be like everybody else."

Ahlia's face flushed as the comment hit home.

"I cannot imagine why else anyone would try to shrink it," continued Mora. "In fact, I did not think it was even possible. The natural direction of the Knowing is outward. The Knowing in you moves inward as if you are trying to quash it. It is a most abnormal trait, most abnormal!" she shook her head, "Usually Sorcerers drive themselves to the brink of insanity by trying to expand it as much as possible, as quickly as possible. Even when they know the risks, they remain relentless."

"Why?" asked Ahlia.

"There is an unfortunate side effect to our work. It's called power. As we pursue knowledge, we accumulate power. Knowledge is only useful if it brings understanding and a truly powerful person knows that power is a ruse if used on anything except the self. Our universe is in the hands of the Spirits. To become great Sorcerers, we should slip through the waters of the world without causing so much as a ripple. Unfortunately, some Sorcerers perceive things differently. Instead of learning to control themselves and the demons within them they try to control others and the world around them. Some time ago there was a particularly big..." Mora searched for an appropriate word, "...problem in that way. That is why Ahlia, you must never pursue power for its own sake, never."

"A problem? What kind of a problem?"

"An argument."

"An argument between Sorcerers?"

"Well, more of a war really."

Ahlia looked at her teacher in disbelief. "I thought such things were the stuff of myth and legend! A war between Sorcerers?"

Mora shifted in her seat uncomfortably. "Of sorts," she answered. "But we digress. As I said, in most, the Knowing explodes out of them like a beacon. In your case, the Knowing implodes, burying itself ever deeper in you. You should be dead," Mora paused a moment, "or at least insane," she added. "It is a wonder you are not."

Of course, thought Mora to herself, it was also paradoxically the reason why Ahlia was still alive. Ahlia's use of magic was near to invisible and incredibly difficult to detect. Thus she had unwittingly been kept safe from the prying eyes of other Sorcerers, Sorcerers who would benefit greatly from killing her. Out aloud Mora simply said,

"It is why no other Sorcerer or Sorceress has noticed you. Think Ahlia. You told me once that you could not find a teacher – or it would be more accurate to say that a teacher could not find you. Even I with all my knowledge had become set in my ways. It took me a while to reverse my thinking in order to see you."

"You were watching me before I met you?" asked Ahlia.

"In a manner of speaking. I wasn't lurking in the shadows

outside your house, but it was hard not to notice you, even from a considerable distance, once I had been directed in what to look for."

"Directed by whom?"

Mora's expression darkened and her eyes narrowed. "Never you mind."

"But, how was it that you could find me then when you say other Sorcerers could not?"

Mora inhaled deeply. "It's complicated. All you need to know is, I'm better than most."

* * *

Across the seas, trumpets sounded a fanfare heralding the arrival of the rider. He pulled tightly on the reigns bringing his black steed to a rough halt, causing the animal's lips to curl in pain as the bit tore into its flesh. Blood trickled down the side of its jaw. The rider dismounted, heavy black boots thudded against the stone floor. He did not take off the dragon shaped helmet that obscured his face. He did not need to. All here knew who he was. Before him were the wide white marble steps of the palace entrance. The great bronze doors opened to allow him entrance. Heads bowed in reverence and fear. He knew there was only one thing that could be important enough for him to be called to the palace so urgently. It was time.

* * *

Ahlia had been practising being still. Sitting in the garden had been pleasant at first, but the sun had grown warm and she had become hungry and thirsty. Finally, she could stand it no more. On returning to the cottage, she poked her head around the door to find Mora dishing food into two bowls.

"Just in time!" remarked Mora, handing her a bowl.

As she ate, Ahlia mulled over something that had been bothering her. "Mora, tell me more about the war you spoke of, the war between Sorcerers."

"No, there is nothing to say."

"But what started it?"

"The same thing that starts everything. Power."

"Yes, but why were the two sides fighting?"

"I've just told you, power," she replied irritably. "Power objects to be precise, tools of power."

It was clearly something she did not wish to discuss, but Ahlia's curiosity was aroused and so she risked Mora's ire.

"Tell me about these tools of power then."

Mora looked as if torn in some way. "You aren't ready," she said finally. "It's too dangerous. Some things you are better off not knowing. You'll just have to trust me."

"But Mora..."

"Back to practise," Mora instructed. "Stilling the mind is vital to controlling the entire self, not just the mind. Meditate with your whole body, not just with your head. When you are done, I want you to watch the clouds."

"What for?"

"You are going to try to move them, but start by trying to part them."

"What for?"

"To see how difficult it is to control the world around you!" Mora snapped.

After an unsuccessful day of attempting to part and move clouds, Ahlia risked facing Mora's wrath and returned to the cottage. She prayed that Mora would not question her as to how she had fared and thanked her lucky starts when Mora seemed to have moved on to a new form of instruction.

"Ahlia, come here. Sit."

Ahlia did as she was told.

"Look into the fire. Concentrate. Don't let your head fill with romantic notions. Relaxed, but focused concentration. Look without looking, think without thinking, do without doing. Now, what do you hear?"

"Hear?"

"Yes, hear. Close you eyes if you have to. Listen with your mind."

Ahlia closed her eyes. She could hear the crackling of the woods and so she said this. Mora buffeted her about the head.

"Ouch!"

"Listen more carefully."

"I'm trying to."

Mora groaned. "Yes, that right there is the problem. You are trying instead of doing."

She sighed in exasperation. "Can you hear the roar of the flames?"

"It's only a hearth fire Mora, not a forest fire."

"Don't get smart. Can you hear its voice? This fire is all fires. It speaks the language of fire. It can tell you things if you listen." Mora pulled hard on Ahlia's earlobe. "Not with this." Then she jabbed her finger in the space between Ahlia's brows, "With this!"

They sat in silence for the whole evening. Mora would not let Ahlia get up until she felt satisfied that some progress had been made.

"Every evening you will learn to better understand fire."

"In order to master it? To read it? What am I aiming for?"

"There is no Master in this Ahlia and that is where many in our craft go wrong. This work is about partnership, not dictatorship. You start telling things what to do and nothing good will follow. If you make friends, however, friends help each other. There is mutual respect. If you care about fire, then fire will care about you. If you try to rule fire, well, don't be surprised if eventually your house burns down. You have only to look at history to see the folly of mankind. We think we have tamed the elements; that we rule the seas and own the land, but few of us heed the warnings. The flash floods, the sudden failed crops, the earthquakes, these things should remind us that all things are equal and no person or thing rules another. Approach the fire as a friend. Offer friendship; respect its power and it will speak to you and, in time, help you."

"Mora, what does the fire say to you?"

Mora tapped her bony finger on the side of her nose. "If I tell you, then you will have no incentive to find out for yourself.

71

Fire is my particular friend. That is why, when my time is come and I die, I wish my body to be honoured in fire. My body and everything I am wearing or have worn. All my personal belongings should be given as an offering to the Spirit of Fire. It will be your task to oversee, to be sure that my friend has reached every part of my corporeal self. Be sure Ahlia, that you take a keepsake from my ashes. It is important. Yes, Fire will release me into the next world."

Her tone was alarmingly serious. Ahlia suddenly realised how fond she was becoming of this old woman. She could not bear the thought of her dying.

"Mora, you are a Sorceress. Surely you will live to be at least two hundred years old."

Mora smiled. "I'm sure I will. Off to bed with you now."

Ahlia grinned. She was exhausted and glad to get to bed. Moments later she was fast asleep. Mora watched her as she slept.

"Poor child, may the Spirits be kind to you and deal you a happier lot than mine." The fire crackled loudly. "Not to say it hasn't been a wondrous adventure because it has, my friend. Oh, it has. Two hundred and six years of non-stop wonder, worth all the sacrifice, worth every bit."

*   *   *

Across the seas in the place once known as Wylderlands a resounding roar emanated from deep in the maze of caves underground causing the hills to tremble. Something inhuman was stirring.

Chapter 6

Ahlia lay on her mattress and looked out at the stars. It was a wonderful view. The soothing sounds of the life around them drifted in through the open window serving as a natural lullaby to ease her into sleep, but she wanted to savour for a while the feeling she had right now. What could she call it? Bliss, she was sure it had to be bliss

The weeks had faded into months and Mora's dilapidated cottage had become Ahlia's home. It no longer seemed like a hovel to her. It was simple, uncluttered and conducive to the life they led. The forest was mere yards away and the sound of birds filled the trees. Avor might well have been a million miles away. She missed Chara at times, but there was something immensely satisfying about being here with Mora. Yes, she had to admit she had hated the chores in the beginning, and it had taken a while to adjust to such a basic existence. Mora had buckled over in hysterical laughter many a time at the sight of Ahlia running screaming out of the privy on having encountered a hairy spider or earwig. It had taken time for Ahlia to overcome what Mora termed her "citification" and feel comfortable in more natural surroundings, but little by little she learned to appreciate the peace, to admire the beauty, and to wonder at the magnificence of the habitat she dwelt in. So many things that she had taken for granted, she now cherished. Simple things took on a deeper significance.

And then there was Mora. Mora was a wonderful mystery. Ahlia never knew what she might say or do next and she loved that, because though Mora had often shouted at her and threatened her, she knew the old woman would never hurt her. It was frustrating sometimes how reluctant Mora seemed to be to teach her "real magic" as Ahlia perceived it, but Ahlia knew that only when she was ready and had truly harnessed herself, would Mora teach her how to harness the power of magic. It was only now in retrospect that she could feel that she how different she was. She was so much more in command of herself. It was as if she had begun to move from her centre. Things felt right. Of course Mora never hesitated to find fault and remind her how much she needed to learn and improve, but that was to be expected. Mora, Ahlia had come to realise, despite all evidence to the contrary, was a fanatical perfectionist who made every attempt to impress on Ahlia two things in particular; that time was never to be wasted and that second chances were rare luxuries. Ahlia vaguely remembered the things Mora had told her on first describing the apprenticeship to her, but danger and loneliness and all those other awful things she had mentioned seemed pretty far removed at present. She had no doubt, however, that Mora had lived a hard life. She had often tried to question Mora regarding her past, but on this topic, Mora refused to divulge a single thing, insisting that they concentrate on the here and now and leave the past where it belonged. Ahlia tried to imagine what it would be like to be a powerful Sorceress and know the things that Mora knew. Fantastic images floated about in her head.

The sounds of the night worked their own hypnotic magic on her eyelids and weaved their way into her thoughts, gently breaking them apart and replacing them with sweet stillness. Before she knew it, she was fast asleep.

* * *

The next morning Mora did not awaken her and as a result she had slept until much later than usual. The sun was already high when she came out to the garden still bleary eyed, even after dowsing her face with cold water from the well. Mora cringed as Ahlia blundered through the house and then the garden.

"When will you learn to move more quietly!"

There were some things Ahlia just couldn't understand about the tasks Mora set her. This was one such task. Mora insisted that Ahlia move about as quietly and carefully as possible without disturbing her environment, whatever that may be. Ahlia was by nature not a neat or careful person when it came to such things. She often picked things up and put them in different places or knocked things over. Mora often accused her of leaving a trail like a Wylderbeast for all and sundry to see.

"Mora, there's only you and me in the house. In fact, there's only you and me for miles around. It's not like I'm being hunted down or anything."

Mora's knuckles turned white over her walking staff as she intensified her grip upon it to control her ire.

"It's about respect as well. You could be disturbing valuable signs with your reckless movements. Sometimes, you know, you have the grace of a swan gliding through water. I suggest you cultivate it. That is your priority today. Stealth and grace in everything you do. Watch every step."

Ahlia knew that everything Mora said or did was with good reason and even if that reason was unfathomable at present, she knew it would later become apparent. She had come to trust Mora implicitly without even being sure why. The old woman was just so charismatic, and she had a way of saying things that forced Ahlia to stop dead in her tracks and rearrange her perception of the world. She loved it and she loved Mora. Ahlia had never been close to her grandparents, and they had died while she was still young. Mora had become the grandmother she had never had.

"I'm sorry Mora, you're right."

Mora maintained her stern teaching face, but smiled inwardly. "Off you go. Firewood. While you're out there you can revise your herb knowledge and don't you dare come back until you are certain that you can tell the difference between every herb that grows in that forest and bring me specimens too, and don't forget stealth and grace in every step."

"But that will take an age!" Ahlia protested, though she knew it would be to no avail.

"That's the plan," Mora muttered to herself as she watched her young apprentice leave. She turned to watch her apprentice as she walked into the woods.

"Take care Ahlia," she whispered softly.

Mora was still in the garden when she became certain. Ahlia had been gone for almostt an hour. The hairs on the back of her neck stood on end as she listened to the message on the winds. She could feel the approach in the ground's vibrations. She let out a heartfelt sigh and kissed the leaves of the plant she had been tending. Then searching with her inner sense, she located Ahlia deep in the forest. Mora knelt to the ground and collected a handful of earth in her left hand.

"My power for her protection." She whispered her spell-casting over the mound in her hand, and made a strange gesture with her right hand, finally flinging the soil with all her might into the air in an arc. It seemed to keep that shape, suspended for a split second, before the particles dispersed and fell. It was done. Now all she could do was wait.

In the forest, Ahlia was absorbed in her surroundings. She had gathered some firewood and was now trying to learn the music of the world about her, as Mora had instructed so many times. In an effort to hear the silent music of the forest, she stood absolutely still, poised in earnest. The bolt of Mora's power hit her like lightening, knocking her off her feet and throwing her headfirst into the thick undergrowth where she lay hidden from sight, unable to get up. Inside her body, her nerve endings twitched uncontrollably, but she could not lift her limbs. A multitude of colours burst into her mind making it impossible to focus on anything. She gritted her teeth in an effort to endure the myriad of explosive sensations taking place inside her, but it was too much for her. She felt her consciousness drift away from her until everything was a haze of green shades. Finally, all became darkness as she passed out.

Back at the cottage, Mora sat quietly and patiently on the old upturned tree stump outside her door. Another hour passed before the sound of hooves became audible in the distance. The sound grew louder and louder and the tremors upon the earth under her feet more violent until a black stallion appeared from the trees and thundered towards the cottage, rearing up on its hind legs just a few feet away from Mora. She did not move a muscle. Her facial expression did not change in any part. She was the perfect image of composure. The rider dismounted landing his heavy boot-clad feet squarely on the ground. Mora looked up into the rider's face and stared him squarely in the eye. She showed no surprise.

"I have been expecting you," she said quietly.

* * *

When Ahlia had finally regained consciousness, she found herself entangled in a heap of brambles. She ached all over.

"What in Spirits name was that?" she asked as she disentangled herself from the undergrowth. She wondered how much time had passed. Mora would be cursing by now and thinking up some impossible task by way of punishment for her dawdling. She picked up her bundle of firewood and headed for the place she had begun to call home.

As she caught sight of the cottage, Ahlia was gripped by a sudden unexplainable knot of terror. She dropped the firewood where she stood as she saw that the ground before her was trampled up by horse hooves. She ran towards the cottage. The door had been knocked off its hinges. Inside, the place had been ransacked. Mora was nowhere to be seen. Ahlia called out, searching the gardens and even the privy. She finally found her by the well. She was dead. Her throat had been slit. Her faded smock was caked in blood mingled with dirt. Ahlia opened her mouth to scream, but no sound would come out. She looked about her, but there was no one there. Tears began to roll down her cheeks, precursors to the heart wrenching sob that finally made its way out from her very soul. Weeping she clasped Mora's blood soaked body to hers and rocked her as though she were a living child. Who had done this and why? Somewhere in the back of her mind, she registered, that the leather cord that Mora had always worn about her neck was no longer there.

The sky turned in colour and twilight set in. Ahlia had spent hours thinking on what to do. Then it had come to her, the recollection of a conversation months before. She returned to collect the firewood she had gathered and arranged it in the clearing in front of the house. With great care she laid Mora's body and her spare smocks onto the bed of branches. She took one slender branch into the house where the hearth fire was, as always, still lit. She thrust it into the flames until it was alight and carried the flame back outside to Mora's body. She wanted to say something, but words did not seem big enough to encompass the magnitude of this event. The passing of a Sorceress: a great Sorceress. Surely the world should stop. Surely the universe should take note, she thought to herself full of grief, but the wind still moved through the trees and the birds still flitted through the branches. In silence she lit the pyre and sat through the night as it burned, carrying Mora's soul into the next world. For the first time, she felt she could hear the language of fire as it roared. Somehow she felt it not as words but as sensations. She felt it was comforting her and sharing in her grief. Silently she thanked it for being there, for at that moment she felt as though she were the only living soul upon the earth. She felt totally alone.

She did not remember falling asleep, but she must have done towards the early hours of the morning. The fire had done its work and there was nothing but ash in front of her and a few remnants of the body that was once Mora. Tears sprang forth anew as she stood there. She was about to turn away when she thought she caught sight of something in the ashes. It was glinting in the early morning sun. There among the ashes was a small amulet, like that made for a child. Was it this amulet that Mora had worn about her neck upon that old cord? Ahlia had come to the conclusion that Mora had been killed by bandits who had ransacked the cottage looking for something of value, though how and why Mora had not defended herself was a mystery to Ahlia. Why had they not taken the amulet? Perhaps the killer had been unable to find it. Where could Mora have hidden it?

As she gazed at the small silvery object a thought struck her. Mora was not one for idle possessions. If she owned jewellery, it would be of significance. Was this what the killer had been looking for? Had Mora died because she had refused to give it up? She lifted the amulet out of the ash with an unused branch and carried it into the house. She laid it on the table and stared at it. It was of crude design and yet, there was something about it that made it hard to take your eyes off it. Right at the centre, there was a small red stone. Strange markings were carved into the oval metal back. She remembered Mora's words about the keepsake. She had said it was important. Tentatively she touched the amulet, but pulled her fingers away in haste. It was still very hot, almost unnaturally hot. She wrapped it in a piece of cloth and put it in her pocket. The hearth fire began to crackle loudly as if to get her attention. She focused on the fire. Within seconds, she could understand it. It was clearly telling her to leave and to leave now. One sensation there was no mistaking. Danger! The ground beneath her feet too seemed to be vibrating. Was the killer returning? She was not going to wait to find out. Fire was Mora's special friend. If Fire said leave, then leave she would. Within minutes, she had left behind her, her life as the apprentice of a Sorceress.

*   *   *

"Master?"

There was no answer. Viad had not left his chamber for two days. He had for the first time in years denied his apprentice access.

"Master, I beg of you, please let me in!" cried Sebastian plaintively.

A bolt drew back and the heavy door slowly pulled open, but Viad was not by it. He was sitting with his face to the fire in his leather chair. The fruit bowl was untouched and the water jug still full. His beloved pipe lay in two pieces on the floor. Sebastian knelt by his Master's knee.

"Master you have not eaten in two days."

Sebastian's voice was full of concern, but Viad remained oblivious and seemed not to have heard him.

"Did you read the book I left out for you?"

Sebastian nodded. "I did. I know what to look for at least, though it said nothing of how to use it once I have it."

"Such a thing would never be written down," said Viad gravely. Sebastian looked at the old man intently.

"Master, you must eat something."

"It is over," Viad whispered.

"Over?"

"My love is dead."

"I don't understand what do you mean?"

"The Oracle has moved on. She has passed."

"The Sorceress?"

"My reason for living is gone. Only now in the emptiness of old age, do I realise my mistake."

Sebastian was beginning to think the old man was feverish. He wasn't making any sense.

"But now is the time to take the Oracle as you instructed me."

Viad sighed. "So I thought, oh, so I thought."

As Viad turned to look at Sebastian, his eyes were brimming with tears. Sebastian had never seen his Master cry in all his time with him. It made him feel horribly uncomfortable, and even a little scared.

"We shared this world between us, she and I, but she was Supreme. She was the keeper of the Oracle. My foolish pride could not tolerate it... would not tolerate it and so I turned my back on her and as a consequence led this barren life."

He let out a doleful groan.

"Sebastian, let me tell you this. It is my last lesson to you. You may take a hundred women to your bed, but the woman you love, though you never touch even a hair on her head, will sit in your soul and haunt your dying thoughts. In your last breath, it will be her name you call out. She will be all your regret."

Sebastian was growing more alarmed by the minute. "When exactly did the Sorceress pass?"

"This morning. Someone has ended her time sooner than was

natural in order to gain an edge. I waited for my ambition to power me, but it did not. All I could think of was her, not the Oracle, but her. The flames taunt me."

Panic gripped Sebastian.

"The Oracle!"

"That is my legacy to you, your journey now. Mine is over. I will not stay long."

Sebastian bowed his head in reverence to the man that was his teacher. Viad made the sacred symbol in the air over Sebastian's head with his hand, acknowledging him as a fully-fledged Sorcerer.

"With my blessing, Sebastian, with my blessing."

"Master, where is the Oracle now? Who has it?"

"The Oracle is cloaked by powerful magic. I cannot see it. Whoever has it has not used it yet, for no cloak could hide that. I can tell you, however, that Mora was hiding in the Fleger Forests, using the natural energy of the trees as a shield."

"The Fleger Forests, of course! Evergreens would be the perfect physical and magical material from which to construct a cloak," remarked Sebastian.

Viad nodded sadly. "Though, it seems, it was not enough. Someone was able to tear through the cloak and kill her. The Oracle has changed hands."

"Then I must make haste. Journey well, Viad," said Sebastian, addressing his former Master now as an equal for the first time.

Viad nodded. "Journey well, Sebastian."

When he was alone once again, Viad sat back into his chair, to watch with his last moments, the flames dance.

Chapter 7

Ahlia had expected it to be no more than a day's walk back to Avor. To her astonishment, she discovered that by nightfall, she had only just emerged from the forest to find herself in a patch of long wild grass. In front of her on the other side of the grass, she could see the wide road that led back to the town. As she waded through the long grass, carefully picking her way through the hidden potholes in the uneven ground, she supposed to herself that she had wandered in circles in the forest. At least, she thought, from now on the route would be straight. There was no fear of losing her way. She turned onto the road, welcoming the solid, even surface under her feet, grateful that the hardest part of her journey was probably over. It couldn't be far to Avor now.

Ahlia walked through the night and when the sky began to gradually lighten as the sun crept over the horizon, Avor was still not in sight. Her legs were so tired, she could hardly feel them. Her tiredness seemed to rekindle her grief. Utterly worn out, both physically and emotionally, Ahlia allowed her legs to crumple beneath her and she half fell, half flung herself down onto the ground by the side of the road. Now that the weight had been taken off them, her feet were beginning to throb. Looking down at them triggered the memory of the last time she had walked this route in these shoes. She smiled as, in the growing light of the approaching day, she noticed a faint glow coming off her left shoe. She took the shoe off and inspected it. Embedded in the material was a tiny fleck of yellow.

"Ah!" she exclaimed to herself as understanding struck her, "Mora you..."

Her words tailed off as she remembered that she would never have the chance to argue with Mora again. As she replaced her shoe, her attention was caught by the sound of someone approaching. She looked down the road, with both eagerness and fear. Her fear quelled when she spied a horse and cart coming towards her. As it neared her, Ahlia could see a man wearing a broad rimmed farmer's hat at the reigns. The cart was full of vegetable produce. The farmer brought the cart to a halt as she waved him down.

"Are you headed for Avor?" she asked the man.

"Yes. It's market day."

Market day, Ahlia had not heard the phrase for a long time.

"Might I ride with you?"

"Surely," the man replied good-naturedly.

Ahlia quickly clambered into the back of the cart, arranging herself so that she did not squash any of the man's precious load.

"You've no need to sit back there!" The man called out to her in surprise, "There's plenty of room by me."

Somewhat reluctantly, Ahlia jumped off the back of the cart and walked round. The farmer smiled warmly and held out his hand to help her climb up next to him. Ahlia hesitated. It had suddenly occurred to her that she had not had contact with another soul other than Mora for many months. She felt awkward and shy. What if he started to ask questions? What in Spirits name could she offer the man by way of conversation?

"That's better," remarked the farmer, putting her reluctance down to a young woman's modesty. He gave the reigns a flick and after an initial jerk, they were soon on their way.

Ahlia scrutinised the man from the corner of her eye. He had a gentle, paternal air about him and his face was creased with the expression lines that all people who greet hardship with laughter have. Long crow's feet spread from the corners of his eyes and folds appeared on his broad ruddy cheeks as he smiled. Suddenly a thought struck her.

"I've no money," she said apologetically before breaking out into a grin. "But, if you like, I can tell you your fortune!"

"Well young Miss!" exclaimed the farmer smiling, but not taking his eyes off the road. "That would be payment enough indeed."

* * *

The farmer had dropped Ahlia off in the market square, just a short walk away from the building she had once called home. To Ahlia's surprise, it was all as she had left it. Chara was the same as ever and had welcomed her back with open arms. Even her room was there empty and ready to move back into. On Ahlia's questioning, Chara had told her that the other tenant had had a sudden change of heart the very day Ahlia had left. She also told Ahlia that many of her old clients had come around hoping to book readings and to top it all, Risan had showed up asking after her just weeks after she had gone. Risan. She had forgotten all about him. Ahlia had smiled wryly and could not say that she was surprised by any of it. She was not surprised at all. What she might once have perceived as meddling she now understood as a touch of grace. Mora had touched her life and everything had changed. Though she had thought she had cried herself dry, on remembering what had happened, fresh tears welled up in Ahlia's eyes.

Ahlia tried to settle into her old life it and for a short time, it appeared to her as though she had never left it. Well, almost as though she had never left it. Something was different. She was different and of course, there was the pendant. She had threaded it onto a silver chain, but was far too afraid to wear an object that had belonged to Mora. Who knew what kind of power it had. It also bothered her that Mora had never mentioned it. Perhaps it really was just a keepsake from a former lover or family member. Maybe it was an heirloom or of sentimental value. Ahlia entertained the notion for all of three seconds. Mora held no store by material objects. She would have kept her sentiments purely in her head if she kept any at all. Ahlia felt sure that Mora had died for that pendant. Perhaps it was the source of her power. Perhaps that was why it was worth killing for.

The metal had taken an uncanny amount of time to cool down and even then, it remained warmer than any metal Ahlia had ever before encountered. To the eye it seemed ordinary enough, but Ahlia remained reluctant to keep it anywhere visible or show it to anyone. After careful thought, she decided to sew a secret pocket into her smock and keep the amulet there, out if sight. She desperately hoped that whoever had ransacked the cottage and murdered Mora would not come looking for her.

* * *

Since her return to Avor, Ahlia had felt disinclined to venture out. She was in part still grieving for Mora, but there was also something else. She felt uneasy in the city and longed for the cover of trees. Her breathing, she realised, had once again become shallow and at times difficult. There didn't seem to be nearly enough space in any and every sense of the word. The constant flux of people about her was driving her to distraction. She could feel them all around her, pressing in on her relentlessly. Finally, however, she gave in to Chara's incessant nagging and agreed to meet her and her husband at the Three Tons for dinner one evening. She arrived to find Chara sitting by herself.

"Is it alright to wait a while for Brynan? He won't be long."

"Surely," replied Ahlia distantly, sliding herself into the seat opposite her friend. Her mind was miles away. In the secret pocket she had sewed, the mysterious pendant radiated an unnatural warmth through the material of her smock, as if warning her not to forget about it. Chara gave her friend a sharp glance.

Ahlia had given Chara a brief explanation of what had happened, though she had been careful not to mention the pendant. The less people knew about that, the safer everyone would be she had decided. Chara, however, was far too astute not to know that Ahlia was holding back something. Trying to read her thoughts, Chara asked, "You still have no idea who killed her? Or why?"

"On the surface of it, had it been anyone else but Mora, I would have said robbers, but it just doesn't make any sense. It was obvious she had nothing and she valued nothing by way of possession. I doubt she'd think to even stop a robber. More importantly, the woman was a Sorceress."

"She claimed she was a Sorceress Ahlia. Did you actually ever see her, you know, shoot out bolts of lightening or something."

"She had power," said Ahlia softly.

Chara smiled sadly at her poor misguided friend.

"She did," Ahlia insisted adamantly. "It's just hard to explain to you. She knew things."

"Ahl I'm not saying she wasn't gifted, but a Sorceress? Maybe she was just a Witch. It doesn't detract from what she meant to you."

Ahlia searched her memory to think of some momentous display of power that Mora had showed her. She could think of nothing concrete that would serve as proof. Then her eyes lit up. "She lit fires with her finger, just by pointing at the wood."

"That could have been a trick. If she was a Sorceress, why wasn't she using magic all the time? Why was she living like a pauper in a hut, wearing ragged smocks?"

Ahlia felt frustrated. The more she tried to explain, the more doubtful her explanations seemed to become.

"She didn't care for the things we do. She said that power was used too liberally and too frequently by too many, without consideration for the consequences. She believed that the true power was to abstain from meddling in things that were better left alone."

Chara made a face. "She would say that. Look, I'm just saying that maybe she over-rated her powers a little? If she was so powerful, how was it that she could not save herself Ahlia? Maybe it was a straightforward robbery or maybe she upset someone, we might never know for sure. What I do know, is that life goes on."

Ahlia sighed. "You're right of course. It does. So let's change the subject please. Speaking of life, when were you going to tell me about the baby?"

Chara looked at her in surprise.

"What do you mean?"

"You're not with child?"

"No! What in Spirits name made you think I was?"

Ahlia's brow wrinkled in confusion. "I don't know. I must have dreamed it. I haven't been sleeping very well."

She drummed her fingers on the table top absent-mindedly.

"And my fingers feel really strange, sort of tingly."

"Ah, you're just on edge after all that's happened to you," Chara said sympathetically. Then she chuckled, "With child indeed! Really Ahlia!"

"Hello ladies, might we join you?" a familiar voice greeted them. Brynan had arrived and he had brought someone with him.

"Hello Risan," said Ahlia flatly. A few months ago she would have been brimming over with excitement at seeing him. Now she could hardly muster up the enthusiasm to greet him. He seemed less handsome than she remembered, and smaller somehow despite his height. She leaned over to Chara.

"Spirits! How he's changed."

"Ahl what are you talking about? He looks better than ever," Chara replied giving her friend a conspiratorial nudge, her eyes gleaming mischievously.

"It is of no consequence now. He may not have changed, but everything else has," muttered Ahlia to herself. She took a swig of ale. She was barely half way through her first beaker, but to her surprise she had begun to feel very light headed, almost tipsy. She raised her beaker to Risan.

"Congratulations on your promotion."

Bemused, Risan shook his head. "Ahlia you are jesting surely? Or are they teasing you? I haven't been promoted."

It was Ahlia's turn to look confused.

"Oh, I'm sorry... I don't..." she looked at Chara, "I thought you said..."

On seeing Chara's blank expression, Ahlia realised that no one had the faintest idea what she was talking about and in truth, neither did she. Suddenly, the room was spinning. She tried to concentrate harder on the faces around her as they became increasingly blurred. She blinked rapidly a few times to regain her focus and for a moment it seemed to work, but there was something very wrong with what she was now seeing. Brynan was holding a baby girl in his arms whilst Risan's hair had grown longer, and he was wearing a thick beard. There was a wedding ring on his finger. She blinked again and everything had returned to normal once again. Her friends were looking at her strangely.

"Excuse me," she stammered. "I feel unwell. I think I should go."

Hurriedly she got up before anyone could say anything, and left.

"What is wrong with Ahlia?" Brynan asked his wife, his voice full of concern. Chara wasn't listening. A thought had struck her and she was counting out something on her fingers. Her brow knotted.

*　　*　　*

Sebastian knelt by the darkened patch on the ground. He pinched at some of the earth and rolled it between his fingers before bringing them to his nose. He pursed his lips at the faint pungent smell. He took in the surroundings, the door flung off its hinges, the mess inside, the dried blood stains by the well. He took it all in before letting out a long sigh. He was too late. He walked into the cottage. There was a powerful cloak over the place, but it was not of Mora's making. Mora's original cloak, that had been designed to conceal her whereabouts, had been torn apart at her death. That did not bode well. Someone had had the ability to find her even while she had been cloaked. The intruder had then covered their identity by magic, powerful magic. He pushed his senses out into the surrounding area. Was there another yet another cloak? With so much magical debris, it was difficult to separate the layers and the qualities. He brought his senses down notch by notch until he was in the almost in the material realm once again. It was here, in the last place he would have thought to look, that he found it. There was another energy residue more discernable and more recent. He could hear the echoes of heartfelt tears, female; the very faint almost imperceptible scent of roses. She had burned Mora's body in reverence. She must have cared greatly for the old woman.

Who was this girl? A relative? He let his senses linger over the quality of the energy she had unwittingly left behind. There was no distinctive trace of magic there, but the more he thought about it, the more certain he became. He could definitely sense something he knew very well indeed; an open mind, a very open mind, and a burning desire to learn. Mora had an apprentice after all! Why had his master not told him? Could it be that Mora had fooled them all, even the great Viad? Mora must have cloaked her. Cloaks within cloaks within cloaks, no wonder the energy of the place was a veritable mess. Mora had been the order that held it all together and she was no more. Whoever this apprentice was, she could not be too powerful yet. At least, she did not feel particularly powerful. The energy of a powerful Sorcerer lit a place like a shining torch especially when they used it. This girl had left nothing behind her, but her tears and the ash of a fire started by manual means. That meant she was either brilliant and knew exactly how to conceal herself from Sorcerers or had absolutely no knowledge of spell-casting. A faint glimmer of hope fluttered about his heart. This girl might have the Oracle. He would find the girl and if she possessed the Oracle, he would take it from her.

*   *   *

Ahlia tried her best to avoid Chara over the next few weeks and concentrated on getting rent money together. Some of her old regular clients had returned and even a few new ones had found their way to her. In fact, business had never been so good. A new client was sitting in front of her waiting patiently, but Ahlia was miles away. Her mind had drifted off to memories of Mora and thoughts of the pendant, as it did so often these days. Today she was feeling particularly uneasy and her gaze kept wandering to the door as if she expected someone to burst through. Her dreams were full of cloaked figures pursuing her, but she had no idea who they might be. She hoped the dreams were indeed simply dreams.

Her client gave a polite cough, bringing her back to reality.

89

"Oh I am sorry Madame I was lost in thought."

"Oh, that's quite alright. I understand. I know you diviners must search through the mists of the future and so forth. Take your time," the client said reassuringly.

As she shuffled, Ahlia smiled at the woman. "You are married."

"Why yes!" replied the woman in astonishment.

Ahlia smiled and pointed to the substantial ring on her third finger. It was hard to miss.

"Oh." The woman was clearly disappointed. Ahlia continued to shuffle. Without thinking, she said "...and your husband, no... your lover is stealing money from you."

The woman's mouth dropped in amazement.

"How did you know I have a lover?"

"Didn't you tell me? Wasn't that why you came? To find out if your lover was stealing money from you, and if so to find out why?"

"Well yes. I mean yes that's why I came, but I didn't tell you that. I didn't tell you anything!"

Ahlia shrugged, "I must be having a good day. I've been having quite a few of those recently. I'd best warn you he has an accomplice: A woman. It can all be seen in the cards you know."

The woman opened her mouth as if to say something, but no sound came out. She pointed at Ahlia's hands. It was at that point that Ahlia realised she was still shuffling the cards and had yet to spread them upon the table.

"Oh. Um... yes. Well. There you have it, your answer."

"Who is she? You must tell me who!" the woman demanded with urgency.

Ahlia shrugged her shoulders. "I don't know." An image popped into her head.

"Blonde woman, big bust, big curls, an annoying laugh." She shrugged again. "Does that make any sense to you?"

The woman's eyes narrowed. Cynthia. That harlot! And all the time claiming to be my friend! I confided in her!" she screamed and thumped her fists on the tabletop in anger.

"I suggest you save your ire for your lover or go back to your husband," advised Ahlia, realising that she had succeeded in creating what Mora would have termed, "a mess".

I think we'd best conclude the reading there. I hope it has been of some help," she said trying to hide her rising anxiety.

The woman was not listening. She was screaming lewd insults and death threats at the top of her voice. Ahlia heaved the woman up off her chair, and gently, but assertively escorted her through the door, closing it quickly. A moment later, there was a knock. Ahlia opened the door. It was the same woman.

"I didn't pay you," she said distractedly.

She grabbed Ahlia's hand and thrust a bag of coins into it, then turned and rushed down the stairs at neck-breaking speed.

"Yes thanks, call again, tell your friends, etc. Farewell," Ahlia called after her before hurriedly closing the door. She was still leaning against it, staring at the full bag of coins in her hand, when there was another knock.

"I'm closed!" she shouted.

"Not to me you're not!" called Chara.

"Chara, am I glad to see you. I believe I have just given the most accurate reading of my life. I'm still in shock. I don't understand. I've been getting really lucky lately, but I'm not certain it's a good thing. I really don't know if I should be telling…"

"Ahlia…"

"I mean it was quite astounding. I thought she'd told me but hadn't and…"

"Ahlia listen to me…" she said a bit louder, but to no avail.

"Spirits! I hope I was accurate I mean what if I wasn't? She's probably going to castrate her lover from what she said. I mean what have done? It's just all too …"

"Ahlia I'm pregnant!" Chara yelled in an effort to get her friend's undivided attention.

Ahlia stopped as if in a daze. "What?"

Chara sat down. "The very evening you mentioned me being with child, I started to feel unwell. It didn't resolve, so I paid a visit to the apothecary who then referred me to the midwife. I am indeed with child, though it is early days."

Chara looked at her friend. "Moreover, Brynan has just come home and announced that the Duke has just this morning given Risan an increase in income and the title of overseer."

Astonished silence filled the room for minutes on end.

Chara was the first to speak. "It is a small thing and at the same time it is a big thing and I suspect it might be the beginning of an even bigger thing."

Ahlia remained silent.

"There is something more. I don't want to worry you, but there have been a few people poking about town asking questions about your friend Mora."

"What sort of questions?"

"All sorts really, when she was last in town, where she went and so on. The ones that concern me most are about whether she had any friends or companions. I only came to hear about it recently and I didn't want to worry you. You've been so anxious lately. As far as I know, the first one turned up this week asking questions at the Spear Head inn. Don't ask me how I found out."

Chara had a complicated network through which she gleamed various bits of gossip and information about people. To call it a grapevine would be to belittle a highly complex networking machine.

"I am scared for you Ahlia."

Wheels were turning in Ahlia's mind. "What sort of people. Men, women?"

"Men, from what I've heard, some of them are throwing money about for information; strange money, foreign coins, some even gold. It's a matter of time before someone remembers and talks or puts two and two together, especially with your new found 'gift' beginning to draw attention. I've never seen you so busy."

It was true that Ahlia was not short of clients, but she was all too aware that she wasn't entirely in control these days of the words that were coming out of her mouth. She rubbed her palm against her secret pocket. She could feel the pendant through the material. It was warm enough for her to feel the heat against her skin. Was it to blame? As if it had spoken to her, she became sure.

"I have to pack." She hesitated. "Chara, I hate to ask, but can you loan me some money? I mean I do have some coin, but I suspect I'm going to need more."

Chara smiled and pulled out her purse. She put it in her friend's hand. "Here. Consider it a sorry for ever doubting you present." Her face became grave. "I should have taken things more seriously. I could have put you in danger."

"Hush now. I willingly opened a door that cannot be shut. This isn't your doing. You are my dearest friend Chara."

As an automatic reflex, she put her hand over Chara's belly.

"Healthy. She'll have brown hair, blue eyes, just like her father, but with her mother's temperament. Yes definitely her mother's temperament. Buy her a flute. She'll be musical."

Ahlia hugged her friend tightly, and ushered her out so that she could pack and get away as soon as possible. It was beginning to dawn on her why Mora had been so preoccupied with time.

Half an hour later, she was staring at a heavy bag that she had packed. The room about her was bare. She was just about to squeeze another smock in, when she suddenly stopped what she was doing. Something seemed very familiar about this picture. Despite her anxiety, she smirked to herself. "I never learn, do I Mora."

Moments later, she had emptied out nearly all the contents and was testing the bag's weight. It was almost empty, and she threw it over her shoulder easily with satisfaction.

"Much better!"

Chapter 8

He chuckled gleefully to himself, as he watched her leave the building. They had thought they were cleverer than him, but he would have the last laugh. While his old doddering Master, who was growing more senile with every hour, chose to scrutinise the fire and listen to hollow whispers in the wind, he had taken his own initiative. He had cast a potent scrying spell. It had required him to use up a lot of power and had left him dangerously vulnerable for a day, but power could be replenished in time.

Fate had smiled on him. He had thought long and hard about where to direct the spell. He couldn't afford to waste either time or power on getting it wrong more than once. His first effort had failed. Then he had thought to himself. Sorcerers need space, but a Sorcerer in hiding would surely choose the very place that other Sorcerers would be least likely to feel comfortable in. A crowd! Where better to hide than in a crowd? On his second attempt, he had cast his scrying spell over three towns, including Avor. Within seconds, the result was clear. There existed in Avor, an energy signature unlike any he had ever seen before. It must be the Oracle. He had cast another spell on reaching the town itself, which had brought him to this vicinity, but where was she exactly? He had waited and scanned for days, but it was a chance conversation with a group of men at an inn that had been the turning point. They had remembered the old woman because of the young, pretty woman who had sat with her. None of them had seen her in there before or since, but the barmaid was sure that she lived locally because she had seen her at the market many a time. Thus he realised that Mora must have handed down the Oracle to another woman. His gamble had paid off. All he had needed to do was to wait for this woman to expose herself.

It had been that easy. Here he was now watching her. Judging by the bag she was carrying and her hurried gait, she obviously knew someone was after her and was intending to leave town. It was the early hours of the morning and the streets were all but empty. Perfect! He thought to himself. He followed her at a safe distance. She glanced behind her every few paces it seemed, but he had cloaked himself carefully. He couldn't believe his fortune. She was turning into back street after back street moving further and further away from the town's busy centre. Then she turned into a street that was completely bereft of houses or people. Now was the opportune moment. He must strike now!

Ahlia gasped in shock as the tall figure of a man appeared out of nowhere in front of her. Her first thought was that he was a thief or an attacker. She thought to scream for help, but the street was empty and windowless warehouses lined either side.

"Look, I've no money and if you come near me, I swear by the Spirits, I'll kill you. I'm a lot stronger than I look!"

She dropped her bag and from inside her cloak pulled out a small sharp knife.

"Oh I'm sure you are. Of that I have no doubt," replied her assailant.

Something didn't quite fit. This man was far too well groomed and very well spoken for a street criminal. The cloak he wore, was well kept and of a thick material, as if made to shield him from a far harsher climate than that of Avor. Ahlia turned and made a run for the other end of the street, only to find him in front of her again. This was definitely not good, she thought to herself, as senses she barely knew she possessed kicked into action. Her nose curled involuntarily, reacting to an invisible stimulus. This man smelled of magic.

"Hand it over if you please," he said simply.

"I told you I've no money," she replied clinging stubbornly to her rapidly dissolving belief that money was what the man wanted.

He rolled his eyes upwards. "Do I look like a common thief to you?"

"You want me to give you something that isn't yours. I

would say that makes you a thief whether you be common or not," she answered defiantly.

"Hand over the Oracle. I know you have it," he said.

"The what? Are you mad? What are you talking about? You've got the wrong person."

The man made a sweeping motion about her with his forefinger. "No mistake. Mora gave the Oracle to you. I can sense it."

At the mention of Mora's name, Ahlia started. Goosebumps formed all over her skin and a shiver ran down her spine as ideas began to click into place in her head. Had this man killed Mora?

"Look," she said with as much confidence as she could muster. "I don't know what this 'Oracle' that you talk about, is. If you tell me, maybe then I can help you."

"Don't play games with me woman," he said impatiently, "The Oracle, the talisman, the eye of the Spirits."

"A talisman? I don't know what you are talking about," replied Ahlia feigning ignorance, wondering at the same time what kind of ghastly mess Mora had plunged her into.

He looked at her with contempt. "I can sense your limited skill. You may have the Oracle, but you are not worthy to hold it. Even if I hadn't found you, someone else would have. You wouldn't have lasted long. Trust me when I tell you that you are no match for me," he warned, taking a step forward.

Ahlia's desperation was growing by the second. She could think to do nothing, but stall her assailant for as long as possible, so that she might think of some way out.

"And why do you want this 'Oracle' so badly? From what you say, you're pretty powerful without it."

The man shot her another look of contempt. "I told you not to play games with me. To wield the Oracle is to be Supreme Sorcerer. You know that. You know how powerful it is."

"Oh I see," she said, as a plan formed in her mind, "you want to be Supreme. Of course, that means you know how to use it. The Oracle I mean. You know what it can do. Surely as I am the wielder, that makes me Supreme. Doesn't that mean I'm dangerous?"

Her voice wavered very slightly. She hoped it made her sound more unhinged than scared, but she doubted it.

"Just hand it over," he replied impatiently. "You can't have figured out how to use it yet or I would already be dead."

"But are you sure of that?" said Ahlia with more confidence than she felt.

The man thought for a moment. Then a flicker of a smile crossed his face.

"Yes. I'm sure. Hand it over to me or prepare yourself for combat."

Spirits! Ahlia cursed inwardly. It hadn't worked. "Very well," she answered. "I'll hand it over."

After all, didn't she just want to go home and be safe? If she handed the talisman over to him, then she could start again. Even if she could escape from this man, she suspected there would be others after Mora's talisman, and she couldn't rely on luck to save her from all of them. Her assailant was right. She felt anything but powerful and she had no idea how to use this 'Oracle', as he called it. She should just hand it over and be on her way. At least, that was what her head said, but at the same time, there was another place inside her that spoke. It was getting more and more insistent with each passing moment, and the more she tried to reason with it the more earnest it became. The man was getting visibly irritated at her seemingly illogical and foolish efforts to stall the inevitable.

"Actually," said a voice that she could not believe was her own. "Actually, on second thoughts, I think I'll keep it."

The man's face instantly contorted in fury at her words. "Then prepare for combat."

He made a gathering motion with his hands and thrust them in Ahlia's direction. She screamed and leaped for her life, narrowly avoiding his blast of mage-fire and jumped behind the cover of the pile of empty baskets that she had landed on. After taking a minute to catch her breath, she risked a quick peek to see where her opponent was. To her surprise he seemed much further away than she expected. Had he moved back or had she jumped much further than she thought? The man made a sweeping gesture and the baskets were flung aside by an invisible hand, exposing Ahlia. She pressed herself into the half cover of the shallow doorway nearby that she had scuttled into. Her attacker was in the middle of another strange gesture when a second figure appeared to the other side of Ahlia, hemming her in. Her heart almost seized up in terror. This person was also tall and their face was obscured by the hood of their cloak, but Ahlia felt sure it was another man.

Ahlia's first opponent did not seem ruffled. He even stopped to make a small bow by way of greeting, saying, "Hello Sebastian, I might have known you'd turn up."

"My hat off to you Marcus, for finding her first. It must have cost you some considerable power."

Marcus smiled. "Oh, I've enough left for this."

Sebastian stepped towards Marcus and made a pushing motion with his hand. Marcus' chest caved in slightly as he was moved backwards. He struggled to maintain his balance.

Sebastian raised an eyebrow.

"My, but you are still weak Marcus. Let this go. It's mine."

"No… it's… not!" yelled Marcus as he struggled to thrust out both his hands towards Sebastian.

Meanwhile, Ahlia had taken the opportunity to drop to the floor and crawl out of harm's way. The first man, Marcus, seemed to be more engaged in the fight and definitely weaker than the other and so she considered that route, but then this new arrival called Sebastian would probably spot her, and he still had one hand free. She prayed to the Spirits that she might be able to squeeze past him.

"Don't see me, please don't see me," she repeated over in her head as she crawled along the edge of the street.

Marcus advanced pouring all his power into the attack, until Sebastian finally was compelled to use a large amount of power to ward him off. Using both his hands, he gave one final mighty thrust forward, sending Marcus off balance and breaking his attack stream. In those seconds of respite, he noticed Ahlia making her escape. He immediately turned his free focus onto her. Marcus, however, had regained his balance just in time to see

Sebastian preparing to attack Ahlia and claim the Oracle.

"No! It's mine!" he screamed, and also aimed towards Ahlia.

Ahlia who had been crawling backwards along the floor with her face to them, froze in panic as she realised both men were aiming at her. She let out a piercing scream; a scream that seemed to stop time itself. She was vaguely conscious of bringing her arms up in a seemingly futile effort to shield her face from the harmful light that was about to stream towards her, her palms facing outward as if to push the danger away. There was a deafening sound like a loud crack of thunder, a bright light and then all was quiet darkness. Ahlia regained consciousness seconds later, face down on the ground. She was alive! She jumped up and looked around. Both men were lying motionless on the floor. She ran for her life as fast as her legs could take her.

Sebastian opened his eyes minutes after Ahlia had fled the scene. He flung the hood of his cloak back and looked about him. The woman was gone, and so was the Oracle. He cursed to himself. He stood up slowly and carefully. His cloak was ripped in places and he could feel a few cuts and bruises here and there, but he was not hurt too badly. Marcus, on the other hand, was another matter. He had used up all his power to attack, and had left none for defence. His body was torn open at the chest, his legs crumpled beneath him. The blast of mage-fire from the woman had killed him instantly.

Sebastian solemnly made a sign over his body.

"Journey well, Marcus," he said with gravity.

*　*　*

Ahlia, propelled by sheer terror, ran like the wind not even stopping to think. She had no idea what had happened. Perhaps the men had at the last minute changed their minds and aimed at each other. She hoped they were both dead. At least then she would be safe. She ran on and on not even knowing which direction she was taking. She had left Avor behind her hours ago, but she did not stop. The morning came and went, then the afternoon, the scenery around her changed becoming wilder and more desolate, but she could not bring herself to stop. At twilight, her legs suddenly gave way beneath her and she fell to the ground, her chest heaving from exhaustion. She remained where she fell for some time, waiting for her strength to gather once more and her breathing to regulate itself. When she finally felt some strength returning to her, a crescent moon was high in the sky, and the dimly lit surrounding landscape had turned into a world of eerie shadows. There was not a sound about her, except the low whistle of the wind. She trudged along the empty road for what seemed like hours, until eventually, she saw lights in the distance. They were coming from a solitary building that stood by the roadside. It had to be an inn, Ahlia thought. Hopefully they could provide her with a bed for the night. Her nerves were shot, and she didn't care to sleep outside in the darkness where anyone could creep up on her from any direction. She pushed open the door, and was grateful to be bathed once more in light and noise, though after walking in the dark for so long, her eyes took a few moments to adjust to the brightness of the room. She made her way to the counter, behind which stood a man and a woman of middling age. As she approached, the man leaned over the counter so as to be able to hear her above the noise of the room when she spoke.

"I'd like a bed for the night please."

The innkeeper grinned at her. "Why surely, Miss, if you can pay for it. Nine Silvers for a night. Food's extra."

She felt in her cloak pocket and produced two gold coins. "Food would be good and a warm drink too, if possible."

The innkeeper seemed satisfied. "I think you've bought yourself breakfast there, too."

He took a key off a hook behind the counter and handed it over to her. "Rooms are upstairs. Yours is second on the left."

"Thank you. Can you tell me, which is the nearest town to us?"

He scratched his head. "Well, we're not really near anywhere. Avor is about forty miles or so Westwards and over that way," he said pointing North-East, "about twenty or so miles, is Daresh."

Ahlia tried to hide her surprise. She could not have travelled so far in one day could she? Surely that was impossible.

"Thank you," she stammered. "I'll take my food upstairs I think. It's a bit noisy down hear and I'm very tired."

"As you like Miss."

"Oh, one more thing. I don't know if you could offer me some advice, but if a person was looking for er… a hired hand, who would a person approach?"

The innkeeper closed the distance between them and lowered his voice.

"That would depend on what kind of 'hired hand' the person wants. Are we talking simple farm hand, or…" he paused, "other services."

He gave her a conspiratorial wink.

"Protection," she said quickly, before he got the wrong idea.

The man pulled away.

"Ah well, that's easy. Take your pick. They're all here for what they're worth. The cheaper they are, the more filled with drink they are. Most of them are sat over in the corner taking up valuable space, the vagabonds."

She looked over to where he was pointing. To her dismay it was the corner where a lot of the noise was emanating from.

"A word of advice Miss. Be hard or they'll play you."

"Would you recommend anyone in particular?" she asked. Just looking at the unsightly rabble made her nervous. They all looked equally frightening and equally inebriated.

The innkeeper rolled his eyes.

"Depends on your budget and on their mood."

She gave him a pleading look and he took pity on her.

"Well, I'd avoid Faldon, he's not very good at keeping his hands to himself, if you catch my meaning, but there's not much between the others. Whatever they ask for, give them no more than half their price and for Spirits' sake don't pay them in advance or come morning you won't see them for dust."

As Ahlia looked over again at the men in the corner and thought about approaching them, her stomach turned with anxiety. She started to walk towards them, but half way there she lost her nerve, and changed direction to go upstairs to her room. As she did so, she knocked the arm of a stocky dark haired man who was carrying two beakers of ale to a table. Cursing, the man examined the beakers and his clothes to assess the damage. He had managed to save one drink by moving his arm out of the way, but the other had spilled all down him. He looked up to shout at whoever it was that had cost him a drink, his hazel eyes flashing angrily, but the culprit was already gone.

"Typical," he growled as he returned to the bar to get a refill.

"Fill 'em up Jon."

The innkeeper looked at him in surprise. "But you were just here a second ago. You can't have drunk them already! Not even you Lex!"

"Had a bit of an accident, some woman in a cloak bumped into me and caused spillage."

"Oh her, she's staying here."

"Well, you can put the drinks on her tab then."

Jon looked at the beakers. "This one's still almost full."

Lex picked up the beaker and downed its contents, wiping his dripping beard dry with his sleeve.

"Not any more it isn't."

John shook his head in mock despair as he put the beaker under a tap to fill it. Lex leaned heavily on the bar.

"Staying here, you say. Maybe I should pay her a visit. Explain to her the importance of manners. Maybe…" he rubbed his stubbly chin, "convince her to make it up to me."

Jon shook a threatening finger at him.

"Don't you dare! This is a reputable establishment."

Lex laughed out loud.

"No it isn't!"

"Well it would be, if you ruffians hadn't made it your drinking haunt."

He pointed an accusatory finger at Lex and then at the men in the corner of the room.

"Then again, business has never been so good, but she's not your type and you are definitely not hers. Mark me on that."

"Jon how can you say that? I'm a man in my prime."

Lex thumped his chest with his fist and succeeded in almost winding himself.

"I can see!" laughed Jon. "As it happens, she is looking for a man."

Lex's eyes lit up.

"Not that sort of a man you lecherous dog, she's looking for protection and I think she can pay for it too. Interested?"

"Maybe."

"Well, she didn't say much, and I haven't mentioned it to anyone else yet. I doubt she'll be down again tonight. I'll keep it under my hat till morning, if you like, while you think it over."

Lex looked at him suspiciously. "My thanks, I think."

Jon handed him over two full beakers and he returned with them to his table. Jon's wife pulled at his sleeve. "What did you tell him for? He's the most saturated of the lot of 'em! The poor gel could do better than him. He hasn't lifted a sword in months."

"Now Marta, he once had quite a reputation you know. Some work will do him good. Besides, he owes me a heap of coin. Perhaps this way, I'll get it out of him."

* * *

The bed was comfortable enough, but Ahlia slept fitfully despite her exhaustion. She awoke in a start more than once to check that the chair she had place under the door handle and the heavy chest she had pushed against the door were still in place. When she finally did manage to sleep a stretch, she began to dream.

Mora was tugging at her hand and mouthing something to her. She tried to pull away out of fear, but Mora would not release her grip. There was the thundering of hooves. She looked up to see a rider on a black stallion rushing towards them. Blood dripped from the knife in his hand. She tried to focus on his face, but she could not. Mora was desperately trying to say something to her, but knew that Ahlia could not understand her words. She forced Ahlia's hand open and spelled something out with her finger on Ahlia's open palm. Then she squeezed Ahlia's hand closed and let go of her. The thundering of the hooves was getting louder and louder as the rider approached. Any second now he would be upon her. She shrieked as her mind was filled with the image of the symbol embossed on the rider's armour of a black winged creature on a blood red disc.

When she opened her eyes, she was sitting bolt upright in bed, dripping with sweat, panting as if she had just run up a flight of stairs. She padded over to the wash basin to splash cold water on her face. It soothed her a little. She had no intention of going back to sleep. She could not bear to dream again. Luckily it was almost day break. Her breakfast would be ready soon. Food would ground her.

Lex had made up his mind. He had spent some time thinking about it and he decided that he simply had to do it. He needed the money. He owed money everywhere. Jon's inn was the only place still open to him and even here he was fast outspending his welcome. He had spent the last few months dodging debt collection squads sent out to find him and break his bones. He had therefore invested in a bath and brushed his clothes down, hanging them out of the window to air them while he shaved. The result was quite a sight and Jon had almost died of the shock. After seeing Lex go to so much effort, he promised to wake him as soon as the woman came down. Ahlia had come downstairs at the crack of dawn. Jon told her it would be at least half an hour before breakfast could be served, but he offered her a warm mug of fresh milk laced with honey, on the house, to sip while she waited. Then he popped upstairs to Lex's room and gave the sleeping man a firm shove.

"Wake up!" he hissed. "She's downstairs."

Lex rubbed his eyes and looked at the clock on the wall.

"What already? Spirits! Alright, alright, I'm coming."

Moments later he had come downstairs and followed Jon's discreet head jerking in the direction of Ahlia's table, though Jon could have saved himself the trouble as Ahlia was the only person down there at that time of the morning. Lex sauntered over as casually as he could and stood in what he hoped to be an impressively imposing manner over her.

"You're up early, Miss!"

She looked up to see who was addressing her and fixed a pair of big dark eyes on him; eyes that a man could lose himself in, he thought somewhere in the back of his mind.

"Er... Jon the innkeeper here's a friend of mine. I often stay here," he told her.

She was still looking at him, although it seemed as if her mind was elsewhere.

"Breakfast should be ready soon, I think. Mind if I join you?"

He looked familiar somehow, but she couldn't place him. Had he been there last night? She couldn't remember. Her head was still full of the horrible images from her dream.

Lex tried to smile as charmingly as he could. The effect was quite frightening and it was all Jon could do to keep a straight face as he came over to their table with a hot plate in each hand.

"Ah, I see you have met my friend Lex."

He put the plates down on the table. "Mind the plates, they're hot. Enjoy your breakfast."

Ahlia would have been happier eating on her own. Still, he seemed to be a friend of the innkeeper and maybe she could get some useful information out of him.

"Take a seat," she said reluctantly.

Needing no second invitation, Lex jumped into the seat and began shovelling his breakfast down his throat. Ahlia had never seen anyone eat so quickly or so messily.

"Travelling are you?" Lex asked in between mouthfuls of griddled meat and egg.

"Yes."

"Where to?"

"I haven't decided yet."

"On your own?"

"I haven't decided that yet either."

"Trader are you? What's you trade?"

It was too early in the morning to think up a lie. "Fortune teller," she replied.

Lex stopped eating and gave her a strange look. "What's you're real trade?"

105

Ahlia pointed to his plate. "Your breakfast is getting cold."

"Why, you have a point there," he said and resumed eating. "I'm a mercenary myself."

Ahlia shot a glance in the direction of Jon who had done a good job of making himself look utterly absorbed in washing some beakers. "Are you now."

This was the point where she was supposed to offer him work. She didn't seem to have taken the hint. Perhaps she was a bit slow in the head, he thought. After all, women were a bit dizzy by nature, especially women with money.

"You know, hire my sword out for a price. The right price of course, protection, that sort of thing," he said helpfully.

"And what is the right price?" she asked.

Lex felt happier. She was playing along nicely.

"Well depends on the job of course, and the time involved."

"And the danger?" she asked. "What price do you put on the danger?"

Lex almost choked on his food. He didn't like the way she had said that. It sounded serious.

"I mean," Ahlia continued, "I don't want to hire someone who leaves me stranded at the first sign of trouble."

Lex pushed his empty plate away and leaned back in his chair. He gave her a long searching look. He took in her complexion, her clothes, her manner and most of all her eyes. Her eyes spoke volumes and they belied her seemingly confident air. She was afraid.

"Who are you running from?" he asked.

"I thought men like you fight first and ask questions later," was the curt reply.

"Only if we want to end up in a casket! Who are you running from?" he repeated his question.

"No one!" she said innocently.

"Don't give me that. Rest assured if the trouble you're in is as serious as I suspect it is, no one else will touch you with a bargepole."

He was telling the truth. Lex had a reputation for being as mad as madness gets and moreover he was now desperate too.

No one could match that combination.

"You'd better tell me everything," he said.

"I can't do that."

"Then I can't help you," he got up to leave.

"Alright!" she conceded, "but I don't know much myself and what I do know, you won't believe anyway."

Lex took his seat again and patiently waited for her to continue.

"I really am a fortune-teller. Well, I was anyway. Now, it seems I am more than that. People are after me and I'm not sure why. It has something to do with a woman I knew. She's dead now. She was murdered. They think she passed something on to me, something that they want."

"And did she?" Lex asked.

"I don't know because I don't know what it is that they want," she lied.

"And this something is valuable is it?"

"Not in terms of money."

"In terms of what then?"

She knew she couldn't stall forever. She took a deep breath. "Power, magical power to be exact, Sorcery."

He knew it had been too good to be true. When he first sat at the table, he had been hoping for an easy ride. He had foreseen a pretty woman, afraid of robbers and such, who needed an escort to the next town or further perhaps. Easy money, but no, he should have known. He cast a filthy look in Jon's direction and mumbled something about favours followed by a few obscenities, before resuming the conversation.

"And these people who are after you are…"

"Sorcerers, yes."

He looked at her incredulously.

"There are no Sorcerers in these parts. There haven't been for hundreds of years. If they ever existed at all that is."

"That is what you think," Ahlia hissed venomously. I can personally assure you that you are wrong."

Either she was mad, or she was telling the truth and had really encountered Sorcerers. She did not look mad to him. He had heard stories about Sorcerers when he was a young mercenary serving merchants who needed protection from bandits, as they journeyed to and from the ports. The taverns in those port towns had been full of foreign folk with wild tales. What he had gleamed from those stories was one certain fact. Sorcerers were bad news.

"Forget it Lady. If what you say is true, I can't help you. No one can help you. I suggest you get rid of this thing you claim you don't know anything about and maybe they'll spare you."

"It's not all bad, there is an up side!" she said before he could try to leave again.

"I'm a Sorceress myself; Supreme Sorceress to be exact."

After all she said to herself. That's what her opponent had implied.

Lex leaned across the table. "If that is so, why do you need the likes of me then?"

"Because I can't use a sword, and they can, and I have to sleep sometimes, and I need someone to buy me some time, and help me come up with a plan," she explained, the words tumbling out a little more clumsily than she would have liked.

Lex scratched his head. Supreme Sorceress? She was probably lying, but if she wasn't, he really didn't want to upset a Sorceress. Spirits, he didn't even want to upset a fortune-teller. Who know what hex she might put on him. His luck was bad enough as it was.

"Look, lady…" he began.

"I'll pay you in gold," she interrupted, placing a single gold coin on the table and pushing it towards him. It was, in fact, the only one she had left. "I'll give you as much as you want, within reason of course. I'll make you rich beyond your wildest dreams!"

Desperation had hit. She had to convince him to come with her. The thought of being alone in the world amongst an unknown number of enemies, filled her with terror. The money issue could be figured out later, she reasoned to herself. Assuming she was still alive later.

Lex had in fact not heard much after the word gold. It was his special word, a magic word that lifted his spirits made him feel happy when he thought of it. After all if this woman was truly a Sorceress, then she was probably wealthy and if she wasn't a Sorceress, then it was unlikely that Sorcerers were following her and there would be even less to worry about. He'd get at least a few dozen Silvers out of her. What had he to lose, he thought. If he didn't like it, he'd just leave. There was nothing to stop him.

"You've got your man," he said picking up the coin. "Be ready to leave in half an hour sharpish."

Ahlia gave him a radiant smile that almost stopped his heart.

"I'm ready now," she replied sweetly.

Chapter 9

Ahlia parted with some more coin and purchased one of the innkeeper's horses from him. She was sure she was being at least mildly cheated, but she had little choice and this was the price of convenience. She had never ridden a horse more than once or twice in her life, and Lex took some amusement at the few hiccoughs she initially encountered, though even he was impressed at how quickly she mastered the skill.

Ahlia had insisted that they take a route along as desolate and unpopulated a trail as possible, but she had no idea which direction to take. Thus it was up to Lex, who to Ahlia's relief seemed to know the terrain well, to determine which way they would head. They rode through the morning and late into the afternoon until they reached the bank of a river. Lex dismounted. "There's a bridge over that way," he said pointing to the right. "You can't see it from here because this part of the bank forms an alcove that's hidden by the trees. It's a good place to camp and consider our options."

They were in the final weeks of summer, and the day was warm and sunny. Lex pulled his shirt off and knelt down to soak it in the river. When it was wet, he began to use it to wash his chest and under his arms.

"I hope you've got another shirt," called Ahlia disdainfully, from where she was sitting.

"No," he answered, but she wasn't listening. She was staring at the crisscross mesh of scars across his back.

"Lex, what happened! Are those battle wounds?"

"Eh? Oh my, back. Not exactly, I've had those since I was a child. My father used to beat the Spirits out of me on a regular basis. I was a handful and I probably deserved some of it, but not all. Not all."

He splashed water over himself while Ahlia tried to imagine what Lex as a child had done to deserve such a beating. Short of really hurting someone, she could think of nothing. He glanced back at her. From the look on her face he could tell what she was wondering.

"He was a drinker..." he said, as if that explained everything.

"Spirits! I'm sorry Lex," replied Ahlia, her voice full of sincere sympathy. Lex winced at the sound.

"Why? He did me a favour," he said grimly as he started to wring his shirt out. "Because of him I learned how to fight, how to protect myself. It was him pushed me over the edge. He gave me cause. Without cause, I'd not have amounted to any more than him, a drunkard farmhand, taking orders off some bastard Duke and working my hands to the bone for pewter pennies. Anyway, he paid in the end. He picked a fight in a tavern with someone meaner than him, got himself stabbed, and died of his wounds. Taught me though, taught me that there's always someone meaner and stronger no matter how mean and strong you think you are."

Ahlia didn't dare offer her sympathies again, but she couldn't resist her curiosity. "What of your mother, your siblings?"

"Mother remarried, I heard. I'd gone by then to try and make something of myself. I've a sister somewhere. Don't have much to do with her, she married young and moved away."

He put his damp shirt back on.

"And you?" he asked.

"My parents are farmhands back in the Dryn Country."

"The Dryn Country!" he exclaimed. "I thought your complexion was a bit green for a local."

He wondered if all the women in land had eyes like hers, but said nothing. Ahlia gave him a nasty look.

"It's from a lack of sun. My land is much hotter. If I was at home, my skin would be dark."

"Whatever, you're pale enough now with a definite green tinge," he said smugly, "and do they know about the trouble you're in?"

Ahlia looked away.

111

"No. Actually, they think I'm a shop hand. Secretly, I think they're all a little relieved I've made a life for myself elsewhere. I think I have always seemed a little odd to them."

Lex laughed. He watched her for a moment as she sat on the grass, carefully braiding her hair to keep it out of her way. Curiosity got the better of him.

"No husband? No lover?"

"That is none of your business!" she glared at him.

"Just making conversation and it helps to know what loose ends you might have left behind. The fewer people you care about, the less leverage your enemies have on you."

Ahlia thought of Chara, but said nothing.

Soon, the light began to turn as the sun started thinking about its descent. Lex announced he was going to take a quick look around. Ahlia stoked the campfire before settling to sleep. Her thoughts were full of Mora. Fire had been Mora's special friend. "For Spirits sake, Mora," she complained into the fire as though her teacher were there. "What kind of a mess am I in? I wish you were here to advise me. I have no idea what to do, no idea where to go."

A notion flickered through her mind. She remembered her exercises with fire. Perhaps fire would speak to her now. She tried to still her mind and open it, but Lex's arrival broke her concentration.

"Seems safe enough, no one appears to be following. You must have given them the slip when you left Avor."

Ahlia had told Lex that she had been followed by two men in Avor, and had managed to escape while the two fought each other. She decided against elaborating on the other minor details of what had actually occurred. This was, she inwardly argued in her defence, partly because she really did not know what had actually happened. It was all a blur in her mind, obscured by the fact that it had all happened so fast in such a dark place, and she had been so very afraid. Besides, she did not know how much she could trust this man and it always paid to be cautious.

Lex groaned wearily as his body hit the hard earth. "Let's get some sleep we've been up since the crack of dawn, and it's not like I got much sleep the night before either. An early night is just what I need. Do you some good too by the looks of you. A good sleep might lift those dark circles under your eyes."

Unexplainably irritated by his comment, Ahlia flung herself down onto her makeshift bed and threw her blanket over her. She hated to admit it, but Lex was right. The events of the past two days had drained her profoundly in a way that did not feel like ordinary fatigue. In a few moments she had fallen into a deep slumber.

Ahlia should have anticipated that her night would be disturbed. She was holding Mora's blood soaked body again, but this time she did not wake in fright. The dream shifted and she found herself walking across a wooden bridge. The landscape moved by her faster than it should, though she could not understand why. There were rows and rows of fields. By a cornfield, she could see a small house. There was a little boy sitting on the steps playing. She could not see his face, but his hair was the colour of straw. There was a brown dog sleeping nearby. Then the scene began to fade gradually and she was plunged into a dreamless sleep.

She awoke early. The scene was still clear in her mind. It was as vivid as if she had been there, but she did not know that place or the boy. She was, however, filled with a certainty that she could not explain. She knew she had to go there and she knew it was important. She also had a strange feeling that danger was not far off. Not her general fear given her circumstances, but more of a clear knowing that someone or something dangerous was following her. She looked over at Lex. She called over to him softly, but he didn't answer. He was still asleep. She got up and walked away from the campsite. She pulled out the Oracle from its secret pocket. It really did look like a strange eye. It was as if it was staring up at her.

"What is it about you that is so important?" Taking a deep breath, she threaded the talisman onto a piece of string she was purposely carrying in her pocket, put the necklace on and braced herself for what might come. Absolutely nothing happened.

She didn't know whether to be thankful or disappointed. She

replaced the talisman back in her secret pocket for safe keeping.

Again, she had a feeling of danger. She looked around her, but there was nothing. She tried to imagine where the danger could be and in the process, her mind seemed to click into a spontaneous automatic movement. It reached out invisible fingers further and further over the landscape to the North where they had ridden from. She was just wallowing in the wonder of what she was able to do when the fingers hit an invisible wall. She poked at it with her mind. It did not give. Suddenly, there was a sensation that she could only describe as having her invisible fingers severed. She clasped her head as a sharp slicing sensation gripped her mind. It was not like any pain she had felt before. Her stomach turned in a wave of nausea. The surrounding landscape began to spin. She sat down to steady herself, focusing on her breath as much as she could until it was deep and even once more. As her panic subsided, so did the nausea. She scolded herself mentally for being such a coward. Once fear was out of the way, excitement took over. How far had she been able to reach out with her mind? How had she been able to do that? It had happened without her thinking to do it, as if she had done it a hundred times before. Was it the talisman? It couldn't have been because she had taken it off. Perhaps Mora's tuition was kicking in at last. What else could she do she wondered. Out here in the wilderness, she felt as if anything might be possible. She was so far removed from her old life and all the things that defined her, limited her. Out here she could be anyone and anything. She could become who she wanted to be.

She focused on a rock and with her hand mimed picking it up. It didn't budge. What was she doing wrong? She analysed her thought processes and her actions. She was focusing her intent on the rock and telling it to rise. She tried again. The rock shook unsteadily, but did not rise from the ground. She thought about what it was she did when she ignited wood to make fire with her finger. How was that different? She cast her mind back to one of her lessons with Mora. The memory was still fresh in her mind.

"Today you learn to call fire like I do," said Mora with a glint in her eye.

Ahlia looked up from her sweeping with excitement.

"In this task is the essence of all magic. You learn to do this Ahlia and you have learned to do everything, so pay close attention."

She beckoned Ahlia to the fire. With a sweep of her hand she had put out the flames. "Now, you know that the wood can burn, and that knowledge makes things easier. All you have to do is get it to burn again. Use you finger to point your intent. Try."

Mora sat back while Ahlia focused and pointed, and pointed and focused, but not a single spark ignited. After a while Ahlia stopped trying.

"Don't you dare stop at the first sign of failure. That's a terrible habit to get into! Persevere! Persevere!"

Ahlia resumed her attempts, but nothing happened. "What am I supposed to be thinking when I point? What am I supposed to feel?"

Mora gave a wide toothless smile. "That is a wonderful question, a wonderful question. Tell me what are you thinking, what are you feeling when you point?"

Ahlia thought for a moment. "At first I was visualising fire. I was thinking of flames, but that didn't work, so I changed to intending wood to burn."

"And how are you doing that exactly?"

"Um... I'm saying in my head, 'wood, burn!'"

"Ah, I see," said Mora. "Tell me are you saying, or are you commanding?"

"Commanding I suppose, except it's not working."

"How do you feel Ahlia, when you are commanded to do something. Do you just do it immediately?"

"It all depends doesn't it?"

"On what?" asked Mora innocently.

"On who is doing the commanding, what they are commanding me to do and whether I agree with them."

"Agree with them?"

"Yes, whether I see the sense in what they are saying. If I think they are right, then I would probably do it."

"Ah, how interesting," said Mora in a cryptically meaningful way.

"Mora I don't understand what this has to do with the fire," said Ahlia.

"Do you like being commanded to do things?" asked Mora

"Not really," replied Ahlia

"Why not?"

"Because I don't like being told what to do. I never have."

"Why is that?"

"I don't know. My personality I suppose."

"How do you feel if someone asks you to do something? A favour, for example."

"Oh Mora, I don't know. If it's reasonable, I do it."

"Ah reasonable, so you think about it, who is asking, what they are asking, why they are asking, that sort of thing."

"Yes."

"You prefer people to ask things of you than command you."

"Yes, definitely. Wouldn't anyone?"

"But, of course, asking does not guarantee that you will do what the person asks."

"No, but nor does commanding."

"Even if the person threatens your life? 'Do this or I'll destroy you,' then what?"

"Then I am more likely to do what the person says, but I won't like it."

"And given the chance would you exact your revenge on the person or see that person brought to justice for threatening you?"

"Yes, I would."

"In a minute, I am going to ask you to try again, but first understand this. There are many different ways of magic, as many ways as there are personalities. In general, it is good policy, and to be honest, it is the natural result, to manifest magic in harmony with your character. You are a person who does not like being told what to do. In fact you resent it. You feel your intelligence is being insulted. That, by the way, is because you have a sense of your own power, your own ability. If someone gives you good reason, however, or you like them, you are more likely to do as they ask."

Mora's eyes glistened with an almost unnatural brightness as she spoke to her young apprentice. She had been waiting patiently for this opportunity to share with another person the things that she had learned over the long years, and she was enjoying herself immensely.

"The world is made up of things. We call them objects. We are wrong in that limited definition. Everything has power, whether it be rock, tree, cloud, bird or even the dust under your feet. Everything is a thing of power. Now, listen because this is important. If you coerce a thing of power – and remember, everything is a thing of power – do not expect it to like you very much, and don't be surprised if it gets its own back on you when you're not looking. If you command a thing of power to do something, it will probably do as you command if your personal power is strong enough, but don't expect it to respect you, and don't ever bother even attempting to befriend it because it won't listen. On the other hand, if you ask a thing of power to do something, then, you are opening up a dialogue and offering a partnership. However, do not be surprised if it wants to know why, and maybe decides it would rather not."

"So, demanding is more likely to meet success than asking? That cannot be right," interrupted Ahlia, shaking her head. "It cannot be right."

Mora gave her troubled apprentice a radiant smile. "I agree. It cannot."

Mora picked up a stick and pointed to it with the forefinger of her free hand. A flame appeared on her fingertip. She used her fingertip to light the wood. Ahlia marvelled at the effortlessness of Mora's action, her face had remained serene throughout.

"Of course, if a thing of power has a special liking for you, then you can work with it like no one else, except those it perhaps likes better than you, and if a thing of power likes you best, well... let's just say you are lucky indeed."

She winked at Ahlia. "There are some Sorcerers who choose to control and command. It works for them, but they pay a price. They must be ever vigilant. Some Sorcerers coerce. They must be even more vigilant. The thing they coerce most easily is usually the thing that destroys them eventually. Make no doubt about it, to coerce anything is to commit harm, and there will always be repercussions. It is the natural law of the universe we dwell in. Some Sorcerers choose to ask and must then accept a yes or a no. they are of limited power in some ways, but are unlimited in others, especially if a thing of power likes them best. Finally, there are Sorcerers who ask and give reason. If they work for the good of things, they are likely to get more yes's than no's from things. Bear in mind, if you are asking a thing to destroy itself or consume itself, you had better have good reason. If I ask you to jump off a cliff, you'll say no, but if I tell you it's the only way to save someone's life, you might think about it at least, no?"

"Mora what kind of Sorceress are you?" asked Ahlia with curiosity.

"For most of my life I have been akin to the latter kind. I don't tell things what to do, I ask. I put forward a good argument and if a thing says no, I ask why. More often than not, I am satisfied with its answer and gain in wisdom, which is its own power in itself."

"Am I like that Mora?" asked Ahlia.

"Yes Ahlia, I think you are. I would have little to show you otherwise."

Ahlia breathed a sigh of relief. "I'm glad. I feel comfortable with that way."

Mora beamed at her as she put out the burning stick with a wave of her hand. "Now in the light of what we have discussed, try again."

Ahlia looked at the wood. "But Mora from what you've told me, I am asking the wood to allow itself to be consumed by fire."

"Yes," said Mora. "So you had better develop very good reasoning skills! Although things of power are open to transformation, and do not cling to particular physical states with the same insistence we do. Nothing is ever really destroyed. Nothing ever really dies, it merely changes."

"What reason do you give?"

"Fire is my special friend. It manifests easily for me. As for the wood, I have explained how important it is that my special friend is near me many times over the years. It has stopped asking now. When I was younger, I planted many a sapling to thank wood for its use and I never squandered or took for granted its preciousness. In this instance, however, I have explained how important it is that you learn Sorcery and it agrees, as does fire."

"Right, so I am actually talking to both fire and wood."

"Exactly so, now do you understand why some magic is easy and some magic is hard?"

"I'm getting there, I think," replied Ahlia tentatively.

"One more piece of advice Ahlia, you must understand a thing's language to talk to it and that takes time. You have practised talking in other ways. Now you must bring a set of separate skills and ideas together. That will take time. Be patient and persevere."

Ahlia had practised for hours and hours over the time she spent with Mora. She had once succeeded in lighting the fire, but was then unable to do it again. About a month later, she found herself able to do it once again, but this success too was followed by weeks of failure. Mora had not seemed in the least bit dissatisfied with her progress, and had explained that Sorcerers spent power when they did magic, and that power took time to replenish. The stronger the Sorcerer, the larger their power capacity, the less frequently they needed replenishment and the faster they replenished. Mora had assured Ahlia that as her understanding and skills grew, so too would her power capacity.

Now Mora's words echoed in her head. Mora had always insisted that magic was a partnership between powers. When Ahlia pointed her finger at wood, she didn't tell it to burn. Nor did she simply ask it. It was more like discussing whether it would be open to burning. Sometimes, the wood said no and Mora had made it clear that to insist against the wishes of an object or element was to harm, and to harm brought repercussions. There was also the matter of asking fire to manifest. The simple task of making fire required her to speak with, and get the approval of both wood and fire. In theory then, she thought it should be easier to get a small rock to move. Once again, she focused her intent on the rock, but not with the hard energy of a demand. Instead, she channelled her concentration gently towards the rock until there came a moment that she could not be sure that she herself was not, in fact, the rock. This time, the rock's movement mirrored the motion of her hand, and rose off the ground. She lowered it and tried a heavier rock, much heavier than she could physically carry. It rose almost as easily. Excitement surged through her. What else could she do?

With her intent, she picked up a stone, and propelled it into the water. She did this exercise again and again until she could control the speed, direction and distance of the stone's movement. She tried to elevate herself off the ground. That was much harder and she could only manage a few inches. It was possible to move a few inches in each direction too. Ahlia tried over and over, but instead of getting better, she noticed she was getting worse. Perturbed, she went back to the rock lifting, but found she could barely do it! It took her a moment to realise what had happened. She had exhausted her power. Never mind, at least now she could test how long it took her power to replenish of its own accord.

If only she had had more time with Mora. Oh, how she missed her. She sat down to think over all the things that that old Sorceress had told her during their time together. Mora had always said she would teach Ahlia all she needed to know. Had she known how their time would be cut short? Ahlia tried to recall her lessons. There was the listening to and watching of the elements, fire in particular. There was the insistence of stealth, which she now all too easily appreciated the importance of. The emphasis on care in movement made sense too, if she was to direct magic through her body movements. Of course, there were the mental exercises, clearing the mind, focusing in order to speak with things. Now it all made sense.

She made her way back to Lex. He was still fast asleep.

"Some guard!" she muttered under her breath.

"And where have you been?" His voice startled her.

"The bushes," she lied.

He turned over to face her. "Must have been quite a bowel movement."

"Sorry?" she asked sharply.

"You've been gone over an hour."

"Oh. I went for a wander too."

Then she realised his meaning. "Next time, I shall let you know where I'm going."

"That would be a good idea," he said curtly without opening his eyes. "After all, you are paying me to protect you and I can't very well do that if I don't know where you are."

Ahlia nodded.

"Point taken, Lex."

At least he seemed to be taking the job seriously. She supposed that she ought to be thankful. Her attention wandered over to the campfire. It had gone out. One small flame shouldn't be hard to muster, surely? Had she replenished enough for that? It hadn't been very long. There was still a small pile of unused firewood on the side. Ahlia threw a couple of small branches onto the dead embers. She pointed her finger at them and focused with all her intent. A spark! She saw a spark! Sure enough a minute later, they had a campfire burning once again.

"Well," said Lex, his eyes wide open now. "I suppose you really are a Sorceress."

Ahlia beamed with delight.

"Of course," he continued nonchalantly. "I knew as much, when I saw you levitating rocks."

"You were spying on me!" exclaimed Ahlia indignantly. She made a mental note to in the future, when scanning, make sure she scanned the landscape in all directions.

"Lady, as I said before, I'm just doing my job, the job you are paying me to do," he said simply. He sat up and stretched.

"Come on then. Let's make a move in case anyone else saw your little display."

"I know where I have to go," she said.

"Oh? Where?"

"I don't know the name, or the exact location. It's a house by a cornfield. There's a boy there."

"A boy?" Lex looked at her in disbelief.

"Yes with straw coloured hair and a dog, a brown dog."

"Oh, I see, that narrows it down doesn't it!"

His sarcasm was lost on her as she tried to recall every detail of her dream. "It is across the bridge and past some fields."

"Oh, that's very helpful. We'll find it easily with that information!"

Even she had to acknowledge it was not much to go on. She looked downcast.

"This a vision of yours?" ventured Lex.

"Yes. How did you know?"

"Oh, let's say I had a feeling from your description."

He sighed heavily, "Very well, tell me exactly, and I mean exactly what you saw. Every detail mind, leave nothing out."

Ahlia related the things she had seem on the way. As she revisited the journey, she remembered other details and potential landmarks. Finally, she knotted her brow in concentration as she began to realise that somehow, although she did not know the place of her vision, she knew how to get there.

"It is that way," she said decisively pointing east. "I don't know how I know that, but I am sure it is."

She braced herself for Lex's argumentative reply, but to her surprise, he fell quiet and stroked his chin thoughtfully, as he looked at her.

"Right then, let's get moving."

Ahlia heaved a sigh of relief and hastily climbed on to her horse.

Chapter 10

Guided by Ahlia's new found inner sense of direction, they had managed to find the place in her dream. As they approached, they made out the figure of a man standing outside the house. He was pointing a crossbow in their direction, but Ahlia remained remarkably unperturbed.

She nudged Lex. "Look, a brown dog."

As if sensing Ahlia's interest, the dog, who had been lying under a stationary cart, got up and ambled over.

"I think you should look for more substantial confirmation before you jump to conclusions, don't you?" Lex replied eyeing both the armed man and the dog warily.

Ahlia disagreed. She knew this was the place. She dismounted and knelt to greet the dog who, despite Lex's scepticism, seemed to revel in her attentions, nuzzling its greying snout into her hands.

A chestnut haired woman of middling age came out of the house and approached the man to whisper something into his ear, but he did not lower the crossbow. The woman gently put a hand on his arm and he began to lower his weapon slowly and reluctantly. Ahlia took this gesture as an invitation to approach and walked up to the couple, Lex and the dog following closely behind.

"Greetings to you."

The woman looked Ahlia up and down, then turned to scrutinise Lex. When her eyes fell upon his sword, they rested there some moments.

"Mora sent you I suppose," the woman spoke finally.

Ahlia was taken by surprise. "Yes. I suppose she did, in a manner of speaking."

The woman huffed.

"Typical. The hag's dead and she's still interfering in my life."

Ahlia's mouth dropped at the severity of the woman's comment. On seeing her response, the woman smiled despite herself.

"Oh, no need to look so shocked! Mora and I were blood. She was my kin, but she was also much more than that, as you probably know."

"How do you know that she's dead?" Ahlia exclaimed in surprise.

"You wouldn't be here if she wasn't," was the curt reply.

"Anyway," she gestured to the dog. "Mora's dog, Deeb. She left him with me last time she passed through these parts. He's been whining relentlessly these past few weeks. It wasn't hard to figure out why."

Ahlia cast her eyes down at the scrawny looking hound. His fur was unkempt and in tufts, and the hair of his tail was bedraggled and matted, but he looked up at her with huge warm brown eyes that would have melted the hardest of hearts.

"Don't let that soppy look fool you. He's a vicious thing when he's angry and don't think we don't feed him either. He eats anything he comes across and still looks like he's half starved," the woman's tone was hard, but not cruel.

Ahlia smiled warmly at the woman who had obviously inherited her dead relative's sharp manner of communication.

"Who's your friend?" asked the woman gesturing with her eyes at Lex.

"Oh, forgive me. This is Lex. He has been helping me."

"Protecting you, you mean."

"Yes. I had some er… unwanted visitors a few weeks ago and…"

"You'd better come inside," the woman interrupted, looking out beyond them as if checking the horizon for something.

She pointed with her thumb towards her husband who was still watching them with suspicion.

"Don't mind Eric. We've had a few unwelcome visits of our own in recent weeks."

Ahlia and Lex followed her into the house. Inside, in one

corner sitting on a colourful rug, a little boy was playing. It was
the boy from her dream. She nudged Lex and pointed to the boy,
but he was far more interested in what the woman was doing.
She was ladling stew out of a big pot and dishing it into bowls.

"Hungry?" she asked.

"Famished!" replied Lex heartily.

Ahlia looked at him in disgust and interjected, "but we can
eat on the way, please don't trouble yourself."

"It's no trouble. I cooked plenty. Can I ask your friend to
take a bowl out to my husband? You'll find him in the workshop
behind the house. He'll welcome the company, though he may
not show it at first. Don't mind our sour dispositions. It has been
a hard year and this recent turn of events has complicated things
further for us, but that is no fault of yours."

She handed Lex two bowels of stew and a loaf of bread and
looked at him meaningfully. He took the hint and went off to
find the woman's husband almost tripping on the way out, over
Deeb, who had positioned himself on the threshold.

Once they were alone, the woman gestured for Ahlia to sit.
She roughly rolled up her work worn sleeve to show Ahlia a
strange star shaped birthmark on her tanned inner wrist. The
sight triggered off a memory in Ahlia's mind. She had seen such
a mark before on Mora's arm in almost the same place. She had
noticed it during her first week with Mora, when the old woman
had rolled up her sleeves to stir a pot over the hearth fire. Ahlia
remembered how dark the mark had been against Mora's
shrivelled, alabaster skin.

"Just for proof's sake, you need to start being more careful
who you trust from now on. Mora was my kin through my
mother's blood line. What's your name?"

Ahlia gulped, "Ahlia," she blurted out.

"Ahlia, that is a strange name."

"I'm from Dryn country."

"Ah. I am Lera. I too am from a different place. My family is
from the Wylderlands originally, but then you probably know
that. I was born in these parts, but my blood just can't get
accustomed somehow. It is all so... ordinary."

It seemed a strange comment and Ahlia did not know how to respond.

"Course, the Wylderlands are not what they used to be." Lera's expression darkened. "Not at all what they used to be."

Ahlia was about to ask her what she meant, when Lera began to speak again.

"You've got it then? The Oracle? Can I see it? See what all the fuss is over?"

Ahlia hesitated for a moment. Did Mora intend for Ahlia to hand the Oracle over to this woman? Lera was her kin after all.

She fished about under her cloak and pulled the talisman out from its secret pocket.

"Here," she said holding it out. "Mora probably sent me here to give it to you."

She couldn't help feeling loath to part with it, though she could not understand why. The object had caused her nothing but trouble so far.

Lera held her hands up in horror. "Not likely. Spirits! I don't want it. That thing brings nothing, but danger. I've a family to think of."

They both looked at the boy who was playing happily on the floor with his toys.

"But I thought..."

"Well you thought wrong. I was checking to be sure you had it, is all. I'm no Sorceress. I just happen to be related to one, that's all. Yes, I have the odd strange dream such as one where I see a raven haired woman I've never met before, and I sense danger behind her and before her, but those sorts of dreams are few and far between, and that's the way I like it. I have made my choices, and magic has no place in them. The pull in my blood is there, but weak enough for me to suppress. It is like that for some of us. I only hope my son will be as lucky," she said looking over to where her son was playing happily. Her brow creased with tension.

"Quite a few characters have passed through here lately, sniffing around to see no doubt if she'd given that thing to me," she said pointing at the talisman as if it were cursed.

"That's why Eric's so jumpy. He feels he has to protect me and Jani. Course, it is residual energy they pick up on, from the last time she was here, though that was years ago. You can't sweep a presence like hers away too easily. Believe me, I've tried. There isn't enough clearing herb in all the world."

Ahlia looked alarmed, "I shouldn't be here. I'm putting your family in danger."

"Oh, don't worry about us, it's not us they're after. There is a particular etiquette about the whole business that Sorcerers follow," she paused, "for the most part anyway. There are 'rules'. You'll understand though, why I can't offer you lodging tonight. Eric wouldn't have it."

"Of course, of course."

"Anyway, it's for your sake as much as mine. As I said, residual power is like a signature. They can detect it. So far I've acted as a useful red herring. No doubt what Mora intended, to take the scent off you for a bit. I'm glad to see you're not on your own though. Your companion looks sturdy enough. Good with a sword is he?"

"Would Mora do that? Put your family in danger like that?" asked Ahlia in horror, ignoring the question that had been put to her.

The woman shrugged, "The Oracle is more important, but do not misjudge her. Mora never did anything without due consideration and foresight. She was a great Sorceress remember. You cannot, but trust her."

"If she was such a great Sorceress, how is it that she allowed herself to be killed?" questioned Ahlia choking back involuntarily emotion as an all too vivid memory of a blood soaked face flit across her mind.

"I rather suspect she decided to use her power for something else," replied the woman pointedly, staring Ahlia meaningfully in the eye, but the meaning was lost on her.

"What could be more important than saving her own life?"

Lera appeared surprised at the question.

"As I said, the Oracle. If you have the Oracle, it's because you are meant to have it. Your apprenticeship was officially over the day that thing found its way to you."

"But I'd only been living with Mora not even six months. I know hardly anything about being a Sorceress, and I don't know anything at all about the Oracle. She never mentioned it. I never saw it before I picked it out of the ashes of her pyre."

The woman raised her brow. "Well Sorcery must run in your family."

Ahlia shook her head. "I doubt it somehow. I come from farming people. Even fortune-telling is frowned upon where I come from."

"Ah, but it will be there. The seam will be there, buried deep, hidden, travelling across the generations waiting for someone to discover it and mine it. If Mora chose you to be her successor, and I'm assuming she did given your current predicament, then she did so with reason. Mora wasn't in the habit of making mistakes. Mora was the second woman in two thousand years to hold the Oracle. She held onto it for over a hundred years waiting for her successor to come along and take its responsibility from her. Sorcery is mostly man's business. They are more easily attracted by the prospect of power. They are willing to trade everything else, sometimes even their consciences. Not that there aren't plenty of women like that too, mind. To become a Sorcerer you need more than the gift. You need to have the lust, the lust for power. Mora had it. She was, they say, a fearsome thing in her youth. Then without warning, she changed. Not that she was less frightening, but she was somehow less detached. She cared about things. She cared about people too, not that she'd suffer them near her for long, mind. I don't know what part the Oracle played in all that. I only know fragments of the story from my mother and grandmother and my own brief moments with her. She had a habit of appearing now and again as if checking up on us. Yes... you must have wanted to become a Sorceress even if you weren't prepared to admit it to yourself."

"Can you tell me anything about the talisman?"

"The Oracle is a power object. No one knows from where. Some say it fell to this world from the stars, eons ago. There is

128

something very special about it. No one knows exactly what though. The holder never tells anyone, as far as I know. Over the centuries, it came to pass that the Sorcerer who wielded the Oracle was revered and considered Supreme among his or her kind. Now, I don't know if that was because a person needed to be extremely powerful to hold onto it and use it, or if the very wielding of it made one Supreme. Of course, everybody believes the latter to be true, though it is well understood that to wield the Oracle is a very difficult thing, and I doubt just anyone could do it. Nevertheless, Sorcerers always want more power. So, of course, the holder of the Oracle is constantly vigilant, ever watching their back, and when they are nearing death, the scavengers swoop in hoping to claim the Oracle for themselves."

She looked deep into Ahlia's eyes.

"To hold the Oracle is to be in constant danger," she said finally.

Ahlia swallowed hard in an attempt to suppress her increasing anxiety. "Isn't it ever just handed down? What if I gave it away?" she ventured.

The woman laughed. "I don't think that has ever, or will ever, happen. No one ever wants to give up the Oracle once they have it. It is a curious thing. No, the Oracle only parts with its owner in death, and not before."

"But someone might just steal it from me."

"Doubtful. You'd defend yourself in whatever way was necessary, and you'd either succeed in fending them off, or die trying," Lera replied gravely.

Ahlia remembered how she had felt when the Sorcerer named Marcus had demanded her to give the Oracle to him. She had risked death by refusing him, though she had been certain it was sheer madness.

"But I was going to give it to you," she argued.

"That's what you might think. I doubt if you would have been able to. Something huge must over-ride your desire to keep the Oracle before you can give it away, something far greater than simple fear or a shallow sense of appropriateness."

"So, in brief, every Sorcerer existing knows I have this

talisman and will try to take it from me."

"More or less. They all know the Oracle has moved to someone else and it won't be long before the better ones track you down. By better, I mean more powerful, not kind hearted. The easiest way to take the Oracle from you is to kill you. That ensures you will not come after them some time later to claim it back. A Sorcerer takes no risks. It is their way. It will become your way."

"And what if someone gets lucky and bumps into me by chance. Could a Sorcerer who wasn't very powerful take it off me?"

"In theory yes, but that would never happen. There is no such thing as chance for one, and secondly they'd have to have more power than you to take the Oracle from you against your will. As I said before, you will find yourself doing whatever it takes to keep the Oracle. Whatever it takes," she repeated for emphasis.

Ahlia put her head in her hands in dismay. "But I don't have much experience at all, and I would hardly consider myself very powerful. I know nothing about spells and such and what power I have seems to drain very quickly."

"Spell-casting is just one facet of power and of the art of Sorcery. It takes power to act, power to make decisions, power to draw people to you, to endure, to persevere, to keep faith, to follow your heart. All these things are reflections of your personal power. I can sense that you have more than most. You just direct it differently. Try to direct it into your spell-casting if you wish to improve it."

"I wouldn't even know where to begin."

"Spirits! You really have a confidence problem!" exclaimed the woman, "Get over it. You don't have time to self indulge. Mora left the Oracle with you for a very good reason. You must remember that. I can tell you no more than that. I do have something for you, however."

Lera went into the pantry and returned carrying something covered in an old piece of rag. She handed over the bundle to Ahlia who opened it to find a thin book of handwritten pages.

There was no title on the leather cover.

"She said you were a book lover, and you'd probably need this for comfort more than use. It's not in her handwriting, it is in mine. She dictated it to me the year of the floods, when she left Deeb here. That's why they couldn't detect it. Sorcerers are arrogant creatures. It isn't what they would consider a power object, and so they think it has no value. Of course, that is what she intended them to think."

Ahlia opened it at the front and was started to read, but the woman slammed her hand down on the page.

"Not here please. The moment you read it, you pour power into it, and you might as well light a beacon for all to follow."

Ahlia made her apologies, but the woman brushed them off. Outside, they could hear Lex's voice as he and the woman's husband approached the house. The woman went into the pantry once more, this time returning with a bundle of provisions in a canvas bag. She handed it over to Ahlia, thus communicating that the visit had come to an end.

Ahlia nodded to indicate that she understood, but something was bothering her.

"Can I ask one last question? When did you say Mora was last here?"

"The year of the floods." Then realising that this meant nothing to Ahlia, explained, "About a year and a half ago, perhaps closer to two. Why?"

"You said that Mora told you that I was a book lover, but I met her for the first time less than a year ago. It doesn't make sense."

The woman gave a wry smile. "She really kept you in the dark didn't she, but that's Mora way. Everything has to be a challenge no matter who you are or what the circumstance."

They could hear Lex approaching. Lera bowed her head in a strangely formal fashion and said, "If we should not meet again, journey well Ahlia."

Lex entered the house only to be ushered straight back out again by Ahlia. Deeb rose to attention at the sight of Ahlia moving, and quietly tailed behind her without her realising.

131

They mounted their horses and waving a quick farewell, they left, in what Lex felt to be unnecessary haste. The home cooked stew had reminded him of the comforts he was missing. He had hoped that the family would provide them with lodging for the night, and had been looking forward to a soft bed and a warm breakfast. As he looked back disappointedly at the farmhouse, he noticed something.

"That flea bitten hound is following us. Go home!" he waved ineffectually at the dog who clearly only had eyes for Ahlia, and had no intention of listening to the musty smelling man.

Ahlia chuckled.

"He was my teacher's dog, and now I suppose he thinks he is mine."

Lex looked at her then at the dog, who was happily trailing, in disbelief.

"Fine," he said in gruff resignation, "but he's your responsibility."

Chapter 11

In order to put as much distance between them and Lera's family, Ahlia insisted that they ride on late into the night. She and Lex had also agreed that a moving target was more difficult to find and hit than a stationary one, and to stay in any one place for too long would be dangerous. However, eventually, fatigue set in and they decided to look for somewhere to stop and make camp. When the flat open fields of the farming landscape gave way to forest, Lex chose a secluded spot. As soon as they had gathered some firewood, Ahlia ignited a fire by magic, and smiled in satisfaction as the wood burst into flame. Fire had been Mora's special friend. Perhaps it would be hers too.

After they had eaten some of the provisions given to them by Lera, Ahlia insisted that Lex get some sleep and she take first watch.

"I just don't feel sleepy and I want to read some of this book. Maybe it will help me decide what to do next."

"Whatever you say Sorceress, but wake me if you want to. I sleep light."

He thumped the bag he intended to use as a pillow, into a comfortable looking shape and threw himself down. After a few choice curses regarding the hardness of the ground, he fell silent, and Ahlia was left in the soft, dark stillness of the night. She huddled closer to the fire, craving its light as much as its heat. A dry twig gave a loud crackle as it burned, causing her to almost jump out of her skin. She looked over at Lex, but he had not stirred.

"Light sleeper indeed!" she muttered.

She felt remarkably on edge, and her fear seemed to be making her senses almost painfully sharp. Her head turned at every sound or sensation. With invisible fingers she probed into the darkness in all directions. She could feel animal life, but nothing human for what was about a fifteen mile radius, she guessed. She ruffled the fur on the back of Deeb's neck, and relaxed a little as she watched him settle down for the night beside her. She would just have a quick skim over the pages. That should be safe enough. By the light of the fire, she opened the book and began to read.

The first few pages contained recipes. There were lists of herbs she knew well. A few recipes looked like more elaborate versions of formulae Mora had used in healing tonics, but there was another recipe she could not be sure about the use of. She had never heard of putting those particular herbs together in that way. The list of ingredients had a curious instruction; 'To use when all is spent'. All what? She wondered.

The next chapter was a brief version of a very well known folk tale about a dog and a scorpion:

'There was once a dog. One day after heavy rains, he was on his way home, when he saw a scorpion by the bank of a river.

"Please help me get back to my home over on the other side. The river has flooded and the wooden log I usually use to cross over is under water. I cannot swim. Help me!" the scorpion pleaded.

Now, the dog knew all about scorpions, and how dangerous they were.

"If I touch you, you will sting me," he said.

The scorpion insisted that this would not be the case.

"Why would I do that? If I sting you while you are carrying me, I will drown myself."

On hearing this, the dog agreed. He let the scorpion climb on his back and he began to swim to the other side of the riverbank. They had almost reached the other side when the dog let out a painful yelp, for the scorpion had stung him.

"Why did you do that? Now we will both die."

"I could not help it," replied the scorpion as both animals began to sink under the water. "It is my nature."…..'

It was a story that every child knew. Why, in Spirits name, had Mora included that old tale? Ahlia quickly flicked through the rest of the book. There was an intricate hand drawn picture of the Oracle. The red stone had been coloured in so well that it fixed Ahlia's gaze for a few moments as if she was looking into the real stone. The writing under it read thus;

> *'The stone is not of this world, having hurtled through the otherworld universe to land here. It plagues us, enticing us with the potential of being otherworldly, when to be truly so is an impossibility. Abandon it if you have the strength to, for it brings with it the most horrific of paradoxes; the miserable responsibility of power, and the frightening realisation that we cannot control our universe. Those who seek it for its power, are nothing more than fools, for the lesson of the Oracle is that power is a mere illusion.'*

Ahlia desperately wanted to read on, but the writing was simply too small to read by the fading firelight. Her eyes were sore from trying. What she could manage to read was so cryptic that it made her head hurt from confusion. She flicked through the book until she came to the last page where something caught her eye.

There was a note scrawled diagonally across the page in writing that was different to the rest of the book. It said, *'It is the universe, not the talisman that is the Oracle,'* and was signed, *'for A from M.'*

A low growl from Deeb broke her concentration. The fire was just still burning. Closing the book and tucking it away in her bag, she wondered how much time had passed. She made another mental sweep of the areas. Seconds later she was shaking Lex.

"Wake up. Someone's coming."

Lex jumped up, hand on scabbard. "What? where?"

"That way." She pointed to the direction in which they had been heading.

"A mile or so, less now, they are travelling really fast, I mean really fast. They'll be here in minutes."

Lex stamped out the last embers of the fire quickly, and pulled Ahlia into the dark cover of the trees. Deeb remained standing to attention by the fire his alert eyes staring out into the darkness, ears cocked, his snout quivering in the night air. He only relinquished his post at a sharp call from Ahlia to join them where they were hiding.

Almost instinctively, Ahlia began to repeat in her head, "Don't see me, don't see me, don't see me."

A figure appeared out of the night. It was a man. He kneeled for a moment and pointed a finger at the dead campfire. It burst into life. He stood in clear visibility as if completely unconcerned. Perhaps he did not know that they were there. Ahlia peeked through the trees to catch a glimpse of her potential opponent.

"There is no point in delaying the inevitable," he called out.

Before she could stop him, Lex had walked out to the fire.

"I was just being careful, just avoiding being robbed. You know what these roads are like."

The man looked at him quizzically. "You are not what I expected to find here," he said in a condescending tone.

"What do you mean?" asked Lex innocently.

"Are you alone?" the man peered into the trees.

Ahlia was still repeating over and over in her mind, "don't see me, don't see me."

"Yes."

There was a faint rustle in the darkness, and the stranger's head whipped instantly in the direction of the sound. Lex held his breath a moment, then exhaled quietly as Deeb padded out from the trees. The stranger did not relax at the sight of the dog, instead looking past him in the direction he had come from.

"You're welcome to join me, if you want," Lex offered in the hope of distracting the man's attention.

The man ignored his offer. "You have two horses," he commented, his voice full of suspicion.

"One's my pack horse. It's not for sale I'm afraid, but then, if you give me a good price..."

"No. I don't ride... and no one else has passed through here?" he asked as if not convinced that all was as innocent as it appeared.

"Well, when I first got here to make camp there was a traveller passed by, and sat for a while. Quite antisocial they were. They didn't speak, and they kept their hood up so I couldn't even tell if they were woman or man. I thought they might be from some religious sect or something. You know the sort, sworn to silence and all that. They sat for a bit, warming themselves by the fire no doubt. Then they suddenly got up in a panic and ran off into the darkness. It was most odd, I can tell you. I thought you might be them, coming back."

The man seemed to be thinking. He looked about him again. "And you couldn't tell which direction they went?"

Lex scratched his head, then pointed out to the horizon. "Oh, I'd guess that way, but I couldn't be sure. Very odd they were. Very odd," he repeated for effect.

The man's mouth curled into a small smile. "Yes, I can imagine. Thank you," he said, and disappeared into the darkness.

Lex resumed his place by the fire, but did not sleep. After ten minutes or so, Ahlia crept out from the trees. Neither of them said anything, and for a long while they just listened to the sounds of the night. Eventually, Ahlia hazarded another mental sweep. She could just about detect the man moving away from them at remarkable speed. He had covered an uncanny distance already.

"It must have been the book that attracted him. Lera warned me about the potential danger of opening it. It leaks power or something."

"So you opened it anyway," said Lex in a strained voice.

Ahlia nodded. "I couldn't help myself. I was dying to know what was in it."

Lex tried to contain his fury. "Leaks power?"

"Magical power acts like a beacon by which Sorcerers can detect each other."

"Nice of you to tell me."

"Oh did I forget to mention that?" she said continuing on hastily before Lex had time to say anything scathing.

"He was probably doing a sweep of the area, and picked up the power signature. Or it could be the talisman itself he picked up on, or my sweep. I swept the area when we arrived, but I couldn't detect anyone. He wasn't within my range yet, I suppose. He can move incredibly fast."

A memory flickered in the back of her mind of the unbelievable distance she had covered after her encounter in the alleyway in Avor.

"Sorcerers can move faster than humans and horses?" Lex ventured recalling how the man had said he didn't ride."

"Yes," said Ahlia with much more conviction than she felt. She had in reality very little idea as to what Sorcerers could and could not do. She recalled how exhausted she had felt after running from Avor to the inn.

"It can be very tiring though," she added.

"If Sorcerers can detect each other, what just happened here then? He didn't know you were here. He came here, but he couldn't detect you. Did you cast a spell or something? An invisibility cloak?"

"A what? No!" At least she did not think so, though the idea of an invisibility cloak sounded good. It sounded plausible. It sounded somehow 'right'.

Well maybe the night likes you," said Lex simply. His words sounded familiar, as if she had heard them before, but Ahlia could not place them at that moment.

"Look, you need to explain this magic thing to me. I need to know what Sorcerers can do, and what they can't, if I'm going to protect you," demanded Lex.

She had known it would be a matter of time before she was going to have to tell him the truth about her. She had delayed it as much as possible, for fear he would leave.

"There's a bit of a problem with that, I'm afraid."

"Don't give me any 'only for the initiated' rubbish or I'll leave you here to fend for yourself," he warned, misunderstanding her.

"No, it's not like that. Or maybe it is, but I'm almost as much in the dark as you."

He looked at her quizzically. Then his look changed to one of suspicion. "You are a Sorceress aren't you? I mean, you must be. I saw you do the fire thing like that man did, and I saw you moving rocks about without touching them."

"Yes, but I'm a bit inexperienced."

Lex did not like the turn this conversation was taking. "How inexperienced?"

"Well, a lot inexperienced. The truth is I don't know why he couldn't see me. I do know that I really, really didn't want him to. Perhaps that had something to do with it; my intent. I'm very new to Sorcery, well, more of an apprentice, in reality. My Mistress was murdered before I had a chance to really get to grips with magic and... and such stuff."

There was a sharp intake of breath. "Such stuff!" Lex rolled his eyes in dismay, "So the other morning, wasn't you just doing some warm up exercises, and being a bit groggy."

"No. That was me testing my power out for almost the first time."

Lex cursed under his breath. "Well what by the Spirits does the book that woman gave you say?"

"Regarding how to use my ability? Not much, I'm afraid."

He cursed again.

"Don't open that book again unless you have to. Come on. We're leaving."

He sounded curse after bitter curse at Jon the innkeeper, at his mother for birthing him, at Ahlia, at Sorcerers, and at the world in general as his frustrations mounted. "We're going to be slaughtered," he thought despondently to himself.

After an hour or so riding in silence, Ahlia felt brave enough to try and say something. Lex still looked stern and uninviting of any conversation, but she couldn't bear it any longer.

"Lex, I'm sorry I wasn't more honest with you. I really am."

"Save it," he said brusquely. "Just tell me one thing. Were you lying about the gold too?"

"No!" she exclaimed. He looked at her piercingly.

"Well not entirely," she said, folding under such a scrutinising stare, "I have money. Well, some money."

"Let me recall, what was it you were going to make me? Ah yes, rich beyond my wildest dreams, that was it."

He couldn't believe the gall of the woman. What was it she had called herself? Supreme Sorceress no less. He should have smelled the rat then.

"You're going to leave me aren't you." Ahlia tried to conceal her dismay. The thought of being left alone was almost unbearable.

"Oh yes. As soon as we get to the next village, you are on your own," he told her firmly.

They rode all night and through the dawn in silence until they reached the outskirts of a village. The place was just beginning to come to life, and a couple of shopkeepers had already lifted their shutters and opened their doors. The sight of a wooden sign with a frothing cup of ale on it seemed to cheer Lex up immensely.

"Ah! Civilisation," he held out his hand. "My fee, if you please, or even if you don't please for that matter."

Ahlia pulled out her pouch of money and placed it in Lex's open palm. He tested the weight of it.

"Better than nothing, I suppose. Well, have a good life. If not a long one," he called as he rode away.

Ahlia watched him dismount and tether his horse outside the tavern. It clearly wasn't open yet, but that wasn't going to stop a man like Lex. He banged loudly on the door with his fists and yelled loudly enough to wake the whole village, including the animals in the surrounding fields. It seemed to work, however. The door opened and Lex disappeared from view. Deeb looked up at his mistress expectantly.

"Stay with him will you?" she asked.

Deeb's grey snout wrinkled in reluctance.

"Please. That way you can stop him leaving." She knelt down

140

and looked deep into the dog's eyes. "I don't want him to leave."

Deeb let out a short gruff bark to indicate he understood, and went to keep sentry at the door of the tavern.

The sun was getting brighter by the minute and Ahlia moved across the street to where there was some shade. Once she had tethered her horse, she dropped herself heavily onto some full sacks of grain that were propped up against a wall outside a shop front, and rubbed her back. After days of running, falling, riding, and sleeping on the ground, it ached terribly. To think she used to complain about the mattress Mora had given her to use. She was lost in memories of Mora, when someone tapped her on the shoulder. She hastily got up assuming a shopkeeper was upset with her for using their produce as a seat, but when she turned to face the person who had interrupted her thoughts, she realised that he was definitely no villager.

The man in front of her was in his mid twenties. He was dressed in a fine deep blue tunic and long soft leather boots. His face was clean shaven and his stare as cold as ice. Ahlia's heart sank at the sight of him as she realised who he must be.

"Prepare yourself for combat," the Sorcerer said sternly.

"No," replied Ahlia sulkily.

"What?" he asked in apparent confusion.

"I said no. I'm not fighting you."

"I want the Oracle, and you have it. I can sense it. Prepare yourself," he insisted unperturbed.

"What are you doing? Aren't there rules about this sort of thing? Look about you! There are people all about us. You can't attack me in broad daylight, in public!" Ahlia reasoned.

"Why not?" he asked nonchalantly, "They are nothing to me. If they get caught in the crossfire, then so be it."

"How can you be so callous?"

He seemed indifferent to her criticism. "Give me the Oracle," he demanded.

"No." The word came out of her mouth, but she had no idea why she was saying it. She didn't want to die. She definitely didn't want to die, but she knew she would rather die than relinquish the talisman.

"The Oracle," he said menacingly.

"No!" she said more forcefully, meeting his stare with equal intensity.

He took a step towards her and started making a sweeping gesture with his hand. Ahlia instinctively put her hand out to ward him off.

"Keep away from me," she shrieked hysterically.

To her surprise, the man was thrown on his back. Without hesitation, she ran off heading out of the village. She was moving faster than she believed possible. The ground was a blur beneath her feet as she tried to make as much distance as she could, but she could sense that her opponent was closing in on her. Fear gripped her as she felt him gaining on her. Soon he would be upon her. She was surrounded by open fields with no cover. She had no choice. She turned to face her attacker as he approached. In a fit of panic, she screamed at him incoherently whilst flailing her arms about wildly, her eyes tightly shut from sheer terror. She was mildly aware of the surroundings getting brighter, even through her eyelids, but was too busy being hysterical to give it much thought. Her breathing became more and more laboured, until she could barely catch a breath. Sudden darkness set in as she lost consciousness. I'm dying, she thought. I'm dying.

Chapter 12

Ahlia awoke in a strange bed. All her muscles ached and she winced as she tried to turn her head to look about her. Lex was standing in the doorway.

"So, you're alive then."

She tried to collect her thoughts. "There was a Sorcerer..."

"Yes there was... past tense."

"Did you kill him?" she asked.

Lex pointed to his chest in surprise. "Me? No. I didn't kill him." He gave her a long stare, and soon realised that she had no recollection of what she had done.

"You did. You burst him open like a melon. It wasn't a pretty sight, I can tell you."

The room was beginning to spin. She sank back onto her pillow.

"I thought he was going to kill me."

"He probably was," said Lex matter-of-factly. "Just as well you beat him to it, quite impressive for a novice. Not sure you even needed the likes of me protecting you. Remind me never to upset you."

A tear rolled down her face. "I don't even know what I did or how," she cried. "I feel awful!"

"Well it's no small thing to kill a man."

"I don't mean that, I mean I feel like a cart has run me over, or as if I've got the fever. I feel physically awful," she wailed.

Lex was beginning to feel out of his depth. He called out to an old woman who came in with a bowel of soup-like liquid, and mopped cold perspiration off Ahlia's brow.

"This will make you feel better dear. An old recipe, handed down from healer to healer in the village. We use it to replenish after strong fevers, and childbirth when a person's energy is low and they feel weak and such."

The brew smelt awful and Ahlia held her breath as she quickly gulped a mouthful down. Her face contorted in disgust at the taste.

"What's in it?"

As the woman listed the ingredients, Ahlia realised that she recognised many of them. It was one of the recipes from Mora's book. Had Mora taken the recipe from these people or had she taught it to them? She wondered, as she endeavoured to drink the contents without tasting too much. Then she lay back, exhausted by her efforts. Within minutes, she was fast asleep.

"Works every time, but give her a day or so," the woman said to Lex. "Goes back generations, this recipe does. They say a witch woman turned up at the village, passing through while my great grandmother was in labour. Baby needed turning, but it lay awkwardly, and the midwife thought she'd lose them both. It's said the witch woman helped with the delivery. No one knows why she chose to come here of all places and why she chose to interfere, but there you go. 'Twas her made this broth, and left the recipe with my great grandmother with instructions to use it wisely and freely to anyone that needed it, and never to forget to hand it down. That was the only recompense she asked for, and that's what has happened. Saved many a life, it has, for sure I reckon."

Lex stroked his stubbly chin thoughtfully. "Uncannily handy that," he mused to himself.

To everyone's surprise, within a couple of hours Ahlia was up and about. She felt much better. Even the old woman remarked she had never seen the broth act that quickly before.

"Mind yourself miss, you're probably weaker than you think."

The woman had a point. Ahlia felt better in her body, but something felt not quite right. It was as though her body was tired, but her mind was fresh, or the other way round, only she was sure it wasn't her mind that felt drained, or her body, but some third part of herself that she had no name for. It was an odd sensation. She wandered off into the empty room she had been resting in and pointed her finger at a candle. Nothing happened.

The tonic had restored her body, but it had not replenished her power. She wondered if one of the other recipes in Mora's book could.

"Drained yourself have you?" she had been so busy focusing on the candle she hadn't heard Lex come in.

"What are you still doing here? I thought you quit," she said testily.

"Yes, well, I've been thinking about that, re-evaluating the situation, so to speak."

"Oh? And suppose I no longer require your services?"

He said nothing, but pointed at the candle.

"It will come back. It just takes a bit of time," Ahlia retorted.

"Why don't you have another go? Let's see how much time. Let's see how long you are vulnerable for, when your power is spent."

He had a point, though she was loath to admit it while he was being so smug.

"You abandoned me once. Who is to say you won't again, when I really need you?" she countered.

"I can't see anyone else queuing up for the job, but if you feel like that..." he turned to go.

"What would be in it for you?" she asked, curiosity getting the better of her. "You know I've no gold."

Lex turned to face her again. He seemed to think long and hard before he spoke.

"Things are slowly beginning to add up. Seems to me, your Mistress entrusted you with whatever it is she entrusted you with, after no small consideration. You are more powerful than you know: that much is apparent. Stands to reason you are probably able to do all sorts of things you just don't know about yet. Gold might feature there. No doubt, you'll also be doing a lot of killing, and I'm thinking gold might feature there too."

"What? How?"

He pulled out a big black material pouch. "You burst his head, but thankfully not his purse. It seems that Sorcerers, present company excepted, tend to carry a fair amount of coin on them."

Ahlia looked at him with disdain.

"And I thought my enemy had no morals."

Lex grinned undaunted by her disapproval. "Well he wasn't going to use it was he?"

Ahlia didn't want to be on her own, and at least, she thought to herself, she had already done the groundwork with Lex. She doubted she could trust him, but she couldn't face the ordeal of looking for someone else, and explaining the whole story from the beginning again. Besides, she might not find anyone to replace him. She had nothing to offer them. Lex on the other hand, would be content to rob corpses for payment. It was grisly, but at least she wouldn't have to worry about paying him. It seemed he was assuming that she would be leaving quite a few corpses behind her. Perhaps she would, if she was lucky.

"Is this what I've become?" she murmured to herself. "I barely recognise myself."

Her brow knotted momentarily in anguish before she forced herself to regain her composure. She did not want to appear weak in front of Lex. She fixed her dark eyes on him.

"Very well, Lex. Let the deal stand. Just make sure you prove useful. I've yet to see you wield a sword. You could be awful for all I know."

He seemed affronted. "You may not have seen me fight yet, but who the Spirits do you think it was that followed you to that field after hearing you scream half the village down? Glasses broke you know, by the way, a whole shelf of them in the tavern. Who found you and carried back here? Maybe I should have left you between the intestines and the cattle dung!"

"Oh," she whispered shamefacedly, "Thank you."

"Besides, you must value me else you wouldn't have sent your hound to stalk me. He's been sticking to me like honey to a bear's paw, and I know it isn't for the love of me. Now, I suggest we move on before any of you friends home in on your 'signature' or whatever it is you call it, though the display you left in the field might serve to deter the more weak-stomached of them from following too closely."

Half an hour later, they were on the move again and Ahlia

had to admit, that she was glad of the company.

*   *   *

In the recesses of the Palace across the sea, there was a bloodcurdling scream of rage.

"This is not it! This is not the Oracle. Again, I have been fooled by that wretched hag!"

Uttering a string of curses, the man dressed in robes of black and red, trembled with rage. It was all he could do to calm himself. With all his strength, he squeezed the pendant that he held tightly in his angry fist, muttering under his breath, releasing his grip only to let a stream of fine dust escape through his fingers. He kept his back to the soldier, the Captain of his Dragon guard, who knelt at his feet.

"Go back and find it, and this time…" he said, giving his Captain a look frightening enough to curdle the blood of a lesser man. "Do not fail me!"

The Captain of the Dragon Guard, unflinching under his master's wrathful eye, thumped his gloved fist to his chest, and rose without hesitation to do his master's bidding.

*   *   *

After yet another day of riding to nowhere in particular except as far away as possible from where they had come, Ahlia was thankful when Lex suggested stopping for a short while to stretch their legs and rest. The weather was turning much cooler as they moved further away from the warm Southern districts, up towards the Northern Heath regions. The scenery about them was becoming more wild and barren. Trees were replaced by hardy shrubs, and they had not seen any sign of human settlement since they had left the village. As she dismounted, Ahlia's breath was visible in the air before her, and the cold tips of her finger fumbled with her horse's reigns as she tried to tether the creature safely to a bush.

"I think it's as safe as it is ever going to be," said Lex. "After all, distance isn't a problem for them is it! So are you going to tell me what it is they're all after then?"

"It's a talisman. They call it the Oracle."

"Is it made of gold?"

"No Lex, it isn't made of gold or silver, for that matter. It does have a stone in it, but don't get any ideas, I don't think it's precious in your sense of the word. See for yourself."

She rummaged under her cloak and pulled the Oracle out. It sat passively in her flat palm as Lex examined it warily from a distance. Just looking at the stone made him feel nauseous, though he could not understand why. He took a step back to put more distance between him and the strange object.

"So what does it do?" he asked.

"I have no idea. I haven't had a chance to think much about it. Mora never mentioned it to me. She didn't even give it to me really. I found it among her ashes. It doesn't make sense. Everyone wants this thing because they believe it makes the wielder a Supreme Sorcerer. That means Mora was Supreme, and yet her killer was still powerful enough to find her and kill her."

"But not smart enough to find the Oracle."

"No, and I cannot understand why not."

"She obviously hid it very carefully with spells and such," Lex said confidently. He felt he was getting the hang of this Sorcery idea.

"Why didn't she save herself and the Oracle? Why did she have to die?"

"She obviously had a tough choice to make. You miss her don't you," he observed.

She nodded, trying to fight back tears.

"She must have been quite something."

"She was a squat, smelly, old woman with a fierce temper and terrible manners. She was wonderful," Ahlia said wistfully.

Images flashed through her mind of that fateful day, the house, Mora's body, the blood, the pyre, the Oracle amid the embers and the ashes.

"What I need," she said hastily changing the subject and biting back her tears, "is to find a Sorcerer who doesn't want to kill me, who doesn't want the Oracle, and who can help me understand about power."

"But didn't that Mora teach you anything? What did you do all that time you were with her?"

"A lot of the time she was explaining things about the world, about herbs and plants, about the nature of things." Her mind wandered back to the fable in the book.

"No magic at all?"

"Well she taught me how to light fire, and I can lift rocks as you know."

"Yes, very handy if you're a woods guide, but what else did she teach you?"

"We talked a lot about understanding things. Mora believed everything in the world has power and a voice of sorts. She could talk to the wind and the fire, and she could see things. She talked about the future and the present and the past all being linked in a Great Map. All of us have our place. None of us is random. I was just a fortune-teller when she met me. She taught me many things, but you could say in some ways, it appears to have been more theory than practical. It's as if she wanted me to understand certain things that she considered important. More important than magic I guess."

"Judging by what I saw out there this morning, she probably thought she could rely on your raw talent to do the rest."

Ahlia looked downcast.

"I feel like a monster. It can't be good for me either, what I did. When I do something… like that, it exhausts me. I can't do anything for hours after. Even now, I think I could just about lift a pebble. Some part of me, that I can't quite locate, is desperately tired."

"Judging by the light display and the end result, I'd hazard a guess that you used a bit more magic than was required to do the job. You need to learn how to hold back a little, if anything. I mean you just need to kill 'em not splatter 'em all over the countryside."

Ahlia winced as her conscience was pricked. "Please, Lex. Don't remind me. I panicked. I didn't know what I was doing."

After some thought Lex said, "It seems to me that they haven't been too bright so far, your opponents."

"What do you mean?"

"Well I can't comment on what happened in Avor, but the first one we encountered didn't even sense you. So you must have been powerful enough to dupe him, or he was just not very good – though he could move fast, I'll give him that, and this second one jumps right in to attack you in broad daylight obviously without an inkling of what you might be capable of. That's just plain stupid. Shows lack of foresight. I thought Sorcerers were supposed to be intelligent?"

"You think they should want to know what I am capable of first before they attack?"

"Absolutely, I would."

"But I don't even know what I'm capable of."

"Yes and I'm beginning to wonder if that isn't all part of Mora's plan. If you don't know what you're capable of, how can they? Maybe she deliberately avoided the display of magic for a reason. You told me about power signatures. When you do magic, other Sorcerers can more easily detect you. Perhaps not your exact location, but roughly, like when you were reading the book for example."

Ahlia shot him a look of new respect. She was beginning to realise she had underestimated his intelligence. Yes, he thought as he caught her glance, he was really beginning to get the hang of this Sorcery thing.

"The Sorcerer in the village told me he could sense I had the Oracle, but no one else came to the village looking for us. Why do you think that was?" asked Ahlia.

"He was probably in the vicinity, and picked up on the Oracle. I don't know, perhaps he had some special spell or something to detect it, that the others don't have. Anyway, my guess is if there are any smart ones out there, they'll be wary now that they've seen you in action – assuming of course there's a Sorcerer's grapevine, which I have no doubt there is. Even Sorcerers are people underneath, for the most part."

"How many am I going to have to kill to protect myself?" she asked dejectedly.

"My guess is many," Lex said calmly.

Ahlia shivered as a cool gust of wind blew through her. She wrapped her cloak more tightly about her.

"It's strange," Lex remarked as he threw her some bread and cheese that he had pulled out of his bag, "there's a part of me that's getting a bit pulled in by all this. You know, there was an old man at a tavern I used to drink at a few years back. He was a good warrior in his day, not many in our trade live to old age, and he was gone eighty. He used to tell stories when he was drunk, which was more often than not. He claimed he'd survived an encounter with a Sorcerer. Said he knew for a fact that there were Sorcerers all over the place, but they were choosing to keep out of the way of human folk. Said it was a matter of time before one of them got 'ideas'. Course, no one wanted to listen to the ramblings of an old drunk. I wish I'd paid more attention to him now."

Ahlia bit hungrily into her piece of cheese, thinking that perhaps she had succeeded in finding just the right mercenary for the job, after all.

*　*　*

Far, far away, waves crashed against the side of a mighty ship as it ploughed through the dark and treacherous night seas, making its way from the land that had once been the Wylderlands, to the continent of Arinthia where Avor lay. Safe in its bow, sat ten soldiers, their faces hidden by visors. The neighing of their horses could be heard above the sound of the waves. Their hooves smashed against the wooden stalls, their animal eyes huge and rolling half mad with fear as their masters sat motionless patiently waiting for them to reach their destination. A small distance away from his soldiers, the Captain of the Dragon guard sat by himself, deep in thought.

Chapter 13

The inn was filled to the brim. It appeared to be the only place for miles that weary travellers could find sanctuary from the cold and bitter night. Outside the wind had begun to howl over the rolling Heathlands, and thick, heavy clouds were just visible in the dark sky. A few intermittent drops of rain had begun to fall and by the looks of things, more promised to follow. There would be few brave enough to camp outside on such a night. Both Ahlia and Lex had breathed a sigh of relief when they had come upon the inn.

"The dog will have to stay outside in the stables," insisted the innkeeper, "and I've only the one room left, and it costs nine Silvers."

"Very well," said Lex.

"No, not very well," contradicted Ahlia.

"Look, I shall be the perfect gentleman, I assure you!" said Lex, acting affronted, though he did not feel it, "and Deeb will make himself nice and warm under some straw."

"I mean, I don't have four Silvers. I've run out of money," she whispered, pulling him out of the innkeeper's earshot.

"Well, have you at least got enough for an ale?" he whined.

She muttered something that Lex suspected was rather less than lady-like under her breath as she slapped a coin down on the table. Then a smile spread across her face lighting up her features like the sun coming out from behind a cloud.

"Order me an ale too. I think I may have an idea," she said cryptically, and went to speak with the innkeeper who, after a few moments, nodded his head as if in agreement over something.

"I do believe I have solved our financial problems, for the moment," she said on returning to Lex, and pulled out a pack of well worn cards from her bag. "Just give me a wide berth."

Ahlia moved through the room from table to table brandishing her cards and offering to tell people their fortunes. Lex watched in amazement as person after person handed coins over. Over two hours passed before she returned to him and picked up the ale he had ordered her. She gulped it down with remarkable finesse and sighed heartily. She dug into her pockets and put a handful of coins down in front of him.

"Pay for the room, and the rest is yours to use as you want. Think of it as your wage for the day," she smiled. "I'm exhausted though, it must be easily past midnight."

"You go upstairs and sleep. I'm not tired, and it's nice and lively down here. I'm going to stay a while and make some friends who might be kind enough to share a beaker or three with me."

Ahlia rolled her eyes towards the ceiling in mock despair, and bade him goodnight.

Lex moved to the nearest table to join in a lively card game, thinking perhaps he could double his wages. An hour later, he had lost his last coin, but the winner of the game had kindly bought him a drink to appease his loss.

"Your ale, Sir."

A pretty barmaid leaned over him seductively giving him ample view of the contents of her tightly packed bodice as she placed the beaker on the table. "Mind, it's brimming over."

"Mmm, yes I can see," remarked Lex, and gave her a lascivious wink.

She giggled. A drunken man staggered across the room, bumping into her. She fell forward over Lex, who caught her deftly.

"My, well caught Sir! Thank you. Old Borvey's always doing that to me. Good thing I'd set the beaker down already or I'd have soaked you. My, but you're just rippling with muscle. A soldier are you?"

Lex grinned wantonly, not removing his hands from her waist. "Something like that. Why don't you sit here a while and keep me company," he asked her sweetly.

"Well, my shift is coming to an end and I live upstairs, so it's not as though I've far to walk home…"

"How very convenient," he commented, grinning from ear to ear. Perhaps, he thought, he'd get to bed tonight after all.

"It has been a bit of a dull week, in all honesty. She moved closer to his ear and whispered. "I could do with a little fun!"

A few ales later, Lex was in the barmaid's room. She drew him near and kissed him with fervour, while pulling at his shirt. He clumsily manoeuvred her towards the bed. For some reason at that moment, Ahlia jumped into his mind. Oh, she would be alright for a few hours, he reasoned. She was surely asleep by now. The girl, sensing his hesitation, put her hand on his groin encouragingly and then started to unbuckle his belt. Lex needed no further encouragement. He grabbed her and kissed her, knocking her off her feet and they toppled over onto the bed in a fit of laughter.

* * *

It was late, but the hubbub from downstairs continued on and drowned all subtler noises. Ahlia had paced about for a while, cursing at the drunken noise-mongers below who were interrupting her precious rest, but then it had begun to rain heavily outside, and the sound of water against the window pane had finally soothed her to sleep. Her peace was not to last, however. She had not been asleep for more than an hour when the door to her room, despite having been locked by her hours before, was opening very slowly. In the darkness, her eyes opened abruptly in response to what she could not see, but could definitely sense. She had felt a tingling sensation in her fingers all evening, but now it was close to unbearable, and had awoken her. She surmised that it must have something to do with her present uninvited company. She pointed to the candle next to her bed and it lit up with enough uncanny brightness to illuminate her guest.

"Let me guess," she said grimly to the figure in front of her. "Prepare myself for combat."

*   *   *

Something was not quite right. Lex was severely off his game, and it wasn't like him. He just couldn't concentrate. Something was bothering him. He'd never felt anything like it before, but he had a horrible suspicion that it was guilt that he was feeling. After struggling with it for a bit, he realised he would have to do something about it before he could enjoy himself.

"I've just got to check something and I'll be back," he said pulling away. "Just a few minutes."

The girl was more than reluctant to let him go. She clung to him tightly, and covered him with kisses. Lex groaned as he was torn between pleasure and an uncharacteristic sense of duty. He wrestled with himself, but it was no good. It was no good. He needed to check that Ahlia was safe.

"I'll just be a minute," he promised ignoring the maid's pleas for him to stay. He untangled himself from her tight embrace. "A minute," he promised her again, grabbing his sword on his way out. He was barely out the door when he heard a scream so piercing it seemed to tear open his head.

He ran over to Ahlia's room. The door was ajar. He tentatively pushed it open and a flood of light streamed out, causing him to shield his eyes with his hand as he entered the room. Inside, Ahlia and the Sorcerer she was fighting seemed to be locked in some kind of stale-mate. They had each other held in some kind of power exchange and neither was giving way, though blood was streaming out of Ahlia's nose. They were both too busy to even notice that Lex had entered the room. Without hesitation, he lifted his sword and brought it down heavily on Ahlia's opponent, slicing him across the back. As the Sorcerer turned to see who had struck him, Lex thrust the sword for good measure into the man's belly. The stranger flopped onto the floor, dead. Ahlia had fallen back onto the bed, blood still oozing out of her nose. She was as pale as the sheet she was lying on, and she was panting with exhaustion.

"Takes... so much out... of... me..." she said between shallow breaths, but I'm... alright," she insisted. However,

155

seconds later, she had lost consciousness.

Aware of a new presence, Lex looked up to find the barmaid at the door. Her mouth was open as if to scream, but shock had robbed her of her voice.

"Paid you did he, to keep me busy? Or let me guess, it's just a coincidence?"

"I didn't know he meant... he said he owed you a favour. You have to believe me," she said earnestly.

"Well you can make yourself useful, and get me some hot water in a jug."

The girl didn't move. "Now!" he shouted.

With the water came a concerned innkeeper. He slowed down on his way in to inspect the door.

"Nice establishment you have here. A woman can't even safely go to sleep in a room she's paid for," complained Lex angrily.

"But, I gave her the key. We've only the one," said the man, clearly confused as to how the intruder got in without damaging the door.

"Well obviously someone else had one too. I suggest you get him out of here, he said pointing to the corpse."

When he was alone again, he pulled out a bag that the old woman from the village had given him. She had prepared some herbs in little bundles for Ahlia, in case she should need them. He pulled one out and dropped it into the jug, and waited for the herbs to infuse the water. Ahlia's nose was still bleeding even in her sleep. He gave her a gentle shake.

"Ahlia, you have to drink some of this tonic. It helped you before, remember? I think it's cool enough to sip now."

He helped her raise herself and drink.

"My head really hurts," she whimpered in a childlike fashion.

She dabbed at her nose with her finger. On seeing the blood she gasped, "Oh no!"

"Don't be such a woman. It's just a bit of blood," said Lex.

"I am a woman you oaf and as one, I'll warrant I've seen more blood than you. We bleed every moon you know!" she answered tetchily.

"All right, all right," he said, "settle down. I'm sorry."

He tipped out some of the jug's contents onto the cloth and gently held it to her nose.

"Can't hurt can it?" he said as she looked at him in surprise. "Here hold it there for a while."

When her nose finally stopped bleeding, Lex let her go back to sleep. She slept until morning and awoke to find him sitting in a chair by the window, but half turned to face the door. The sound of footsteps approaching caused him to immediately reach for his sword, but it was only the innkeeper bringing up some breakfast.

"I thought she could do with some food," he told Lex, "On the house, of course," he added. Lex nodded his thanks and took the tray from the innkeeper. Ahlia watched him as he carefully laid the tray over her lap. She had never seen his face so serious since she had known him.

"I'm feeling much better," she told him, "We can be off soon."

"Are you sure you want me to come with you?" he asked morosely.

"Um... let me see... after the events of last night I would think my answer would have to be... YES."

"Aren't you even a little bit annoyed that I never seem to be there when you get attacked?"

"But you do a great job of patching me up in the aftermath, and last night I would say you saved my life so don't sell yourself too short. Look, the first one passed us by, the second one, well, you had officially quit, so I cannot blame you for that, and last night... "

"Last night, I fell for the oldest trick of all. He paid a barmaid to keep me busy so he could get to you," he growled full of anger at himself.

Ahlia fell silent.

"Exactly," said Lex, imagining what she must be thinking.

After a long pause, Ahlia said in as strong an authoritative voice as she could muster. "You are forgetting an important point."

"And what is that?"

"If Sorcerers are going to that much trouble to ensure that you are out of the way, then they must see you as a threat. A threat to them is protection to me. Now, let me eat this before it gets cold, I'm starving!"

Lex fell silent as Ahlia attacked her breakfast with heart.

"Anyway, in all fairness," she said in between mouthfuls. "I sort of gave you the night off. I mean I expected you'd get drunk or something."

She was trying to make him feel better, but she realised too late that she had made matters worse.

"You expected right, it seems," Lex said in a dangerously calm voice that belied what he was feeling.

"Look, you killed the bastard," she said with surprising vehemence. "Accept that you saved my life. We don't have time for self indulgence."

Saying the last phrase made her jump internally. It could have been Mora speaking.

"See what you're doing? You're making me sound like Mora. Mora was always telling me off for indulging in self pity," she complained.

Despite himself, Lex's mouth curled into a faint smile.

"Did you get a look at him?" Ahlia asked to change the subject as she mopped her dish clean with some bread, "Spirits! This tastes good! He wasn't from around here. I wonder where these Sorcerers are coming from? I know it'll sound callous, and I can't believe I'm saying this, but was he carrying any money? Did you check?"

Lex looked at her with surprise.

"As a matter of fact, I did relieve him of his purse as well as his life," he admitted. "He was carrying a fair sum."

"Good," said Ahlia as she munched. "Consider that a small down payment for the coming week. Now if you don't mind, I'd like to get washed and dressed. I'll see you downstairs."

She waited until he had closed the door behind him before slowly easing herself out of bed. Her legs buckled under her as she tried to stand. She still felt terrible. Her head was pounding

158

and her whole body was sore all over, but she knew they had to leave this place. The power surge from last night would attract Sorcerers to them like a swarm of bees to a flowerbed. The sooner they were on the move, the better.

*   *   *

She used the banister to hold herself up as she walked slowly downstairs, putting on as much of an appearance of health as she could to meet Lex with. She did not want him to know how weak she felt. She did not want anyone to know. The herbal brew was helping her, but it was not far reaching enough, and it did not replenish her power. She needed something that worked faster and deeper. She would have to take a closer look at the recipes in Mora's book. One of those had to be a power replenisher. Lex was sitting in an armchair, staring into the fire, a plate of food lay untouched on the floor beside him. Ahlia eased herself into the chair opposite him.

"Lex, you shouldn't waste good food," she chided in what she intended to be a light hearted manner, but he wasn't listening. His attention was on the man who was approaching. His hand was already on the hilt of his sword in anticipation of trouble. The man smiled brightly at them, and if he noticed Lex's agitation, he chose to politely ignore it.

"Might I be so bold as to interrupt? Allow me to introduce myself. My name is Simon Larius. I am a bard, a storyteller, a collector of stories and song. Perhaps you have heard of me?"

"Afraid not Sir Storyteller," said Lex, mocking the man's aristocratic accent.

"Should we have?" asked Ahlia.

"No, no," Simon conceded. "It's just that some have. I am quite well known in certain circles. Most of my sponsors are Dukes, nobles and so forth. They pay very well, but it often means I have to travel considerable distances at times to honour appointments."

"You do seem a bit familiar," she said trying desperately to place him in her head. She did not think she had seen his face before and yet she felt almost certain that she knew him somehow.

"You have probably seen me perform somewhere or other. I work everywhere you know. So many towns so many places. Such is the life of a wanderer like me."

"Oh. Yes. That's probably it," said Ahlia politely for want of anything else to say, though somewhere in the recesses of her mind something was trying to fight its way through.

"Can we help you in some way?" asked Lex trying to get to the point. His words were polite, but his tone concealed nothing of how much this man was beginning to irritate him.

"I heard you both had quite an adventure last night."

"Sort of," replied Lex. "What of it?"

Simon turned to Ahlia, and addressed her in the hope of more a civilised conversation. "They say your husband here killed the intruder. Is that true?"

"Ahlia laughed. "Lex isn't my husband, but yes he killed the intruder."

"You are lucky to have such a brave, noble warrior for a travelling companion."

Lex was feeling more uncomfortable by the minute. The man had given him a complement, but he somehow felt as if he was being patronised or mocked.

"Especially in these parts," Simon continued. "The area is riddled with bands of cut-throat robbers. Your intruder may well have been such one."

"He may well have," said Ahlia, giving nothing away.

"If you're travelling further north, I wonder if you and your brave friend might come to my aid. I'd feel safer travelling in company for a while. This is my first time in these parts without a party to travel with. Usually I have an escort, of course, but the man they sent this time was a useless drunken oaf, and I dismissed him. I do so hate putting my life in the hands of people who shirk their responsibilities, and debauch themselves at the slightest opportunity, regardless of the safety of their charge."

Lex shifted uncomfortably in his seat. He was fast coming to the conclusion that he did not like this man.

160

"Oh, I don't know." Ahlia looked tentatively at Lex. "We are a bit eccentric in our travel plans."

Simon put a full purse on arm of Lex's chair. "I'd pay, of course. My safety is worth the price to me. If this is not enough, I could send more on to you at a later date if you give me a place of contact."

The purse was not small. Lex pulled it open and looked inside. There was enough coin inside to tide them over for a week or more. Then again, the man was already annoying him, and he didn't know how much he could tolerate before he indulged his inclination to hit him in the head. He also still had the purse of the dead Sorcerer. Nevertheless, you could never have too much coin, and who knew what might be facing them in the days ahead. On the other hand, they would be lumbering themselves with a total stranger who might get in the way. Of course, he might also come in useful, if he could be trusted or help to disguise them at the very least. As he looked at the man, his mind swayed back and forth in argument. Why couldn't they just take the purse and leave him behind after a day or so? Ah! The perfect solution.

Simon smiled at Ahlia and she smiled back. There was something very soothing about his presence and Ahlia liked him. She supposed that he had to have been blessed with a certain amount of charisma to be a successful performer. Of course, it helped that he was very handsome. He had silky blond hair that he wore tied back and his face was clean shaven. His hands looked well cared for, and he looked as if he had taken great care over his dress. She noticed that Lex also seemed to be scrutinising him and weighing something over in his mind.

"You can travel with us, but I can't guarantee your safety. If we should decide to change direction, you're on your own. Oh, and no refunds for any reason whatsoever," said Lex gruffly.

"That is more than fair," replied Simon graciously. "I shall just make ready my horse."

When Simon had gone, Lex turned to Ahlia. "We rid ourselves of him as soon as possible," he said in a tone that made it clear the subject was not open to debate.

Chapter 14

The journey had thus far that day been uneventful, with only the blustering wind to contend with, and Ahlia was deeply thankful. She noted with some amusement that Lex was giving Simon a remarkably wide berth, contributing no more than the occasional grunt to the conversation. Deeb too seemed less than impressed with the new addition to their group, and had taken to trailing Lex's horse, though all the while keeping a close eye on Simon's every move, particularly when Simon ventured near Ahlia.

Simon appeared to be a font of knowledge. He had travelled widely and visited many places. He talked gaily of his adventures, and on one occasion tried to lift their spirits with a song, until Lex growled at him to cease his droning lest he bring trouble upon them. Simon rebelled by continuing to hum quietly to himself. Ahlia allowed herself to fall back a little, and fished the Oracle out of its secret pocket. She turned the talisman over in her fingers, and scraped at the metal with her nail. Something caught her attention. This was no simple decorative design. She brought the Oracle nearer to her face to look more closely, catching her breath in wonder at her discovery. Later when they stopped for a much needed rest, she shared what she had found with Lex.

"There are tiny runes etched into the silver!" she said excitedly.

"What do they mean?" asked Lex.

"I'm not sure, but perhaps that is why the Oracle is always so warm. Here, feel."

Lex backed away, though his gaze was transfixed by the object in Ahlia's hands.

"No, no. I have no desire to touch that thing. The stone is

eerie. I have coveted my fair share of jewels, granted they always happened to belong to someone other than myself, but that thing is unlike any stone I have seen. It looks like an orange eye."

Ahlia made a face and examined the stone more closely.

"So it does! I hadn't thought of it like that. It seemed redder before too, but now its colour is lighter than I remembered. I wonder how it works. I have tried wearing it, but absolutely nothing happens. Perhaps I have to decipher the runes?"

"Are you sure it is not just a token, an emblem, you know like a crown signifies who is king."

"I don't think even Sorcerers would be so foolish as to risk their lives over a trinket. No, the Oracle does something: something important. I have to find out what that something is, if I want to stay alive. Lex, I need to open that book again."

"Well not now!" hissed Lex gesturing towards Simon who, to all intents and purposes, appeared to be snoozing.

"Simon!" he called out loudly, "Don't make yourself too comfortable. We are moving on shortly."

Simon moaned from under his cloak. He had wrapped his head in the hood in order to get some respite from the wind and warm his nose and ears. Tentatively, he poked his face out, and shivered as the wind greeted him. Lex watched him in disgust.

"Soft as fresh dung," he said under his breath, spitting on the cold hard ground.

*   *   *

The Captain of the Dragon Guard dug his spurs deep into his steed's flanks for the umpteenth time causing the animal to speed up yet again. The horse neighed in pain, but its rider took no heed. For fear of feeling the spur a second time, it strained every muscle in an effort to produce more speed. The pace picked up, and his soldiers followed suit. They had much ground to cover, but they were getting closer with each second, he thought with satisfaction. Soon they would be upon her.

*   *   *

There was a pulsing in Ahlia's head. It had started about ten minutes before, and it was getting worse with each passing minute. She had no idea what it meant. It wasn't painful, but it was getting impossible to ignore. Deeb watched his mistress intently, acutely aware that something was wrong, but unable to sense what as yet. His old Mistress had confused him in such a way many a time. Most humans could not smell or sense things that were right under their noses, but Deeb served Mistresses whose senses were far sharper than his.

"Stop a minute," she called to the others as she reigned in her horse and brought it to a standstill. Feeling a burning need to feel the floor under her feet, she dismounted. As soon as her feet hit the floor, she knew. She could feel the vibrations travelling through the earth to her soles. Walking towards Lex, she glared at him meaningfully. He was quick to take the hint, and bent his head to listen as she said in a lowered voice,

"There are riders approaching." She pointed her finger outward. "From there. I think they know where we are because they are riding directly towards us and at some speed."

"How many?" asked Lex.

Ahlia pushed her mind out, like an extended hand it brushed across the landscape until it hit a boundary as solid as steel that blocked from sensing any further.

"I'm not sure, about ten I think. I don't know why that number comes to me, but it does."

"Ten Sorcerers?" asked Lex with a sharp intake of breath.

"I'm not sure. I hope not. Spirits, I hope not!"

She pushed her mind out again. "Wait! They're slowing down. Now they're changing course. They're not coming towards us anymore."

Lex breathed a hearty sigh of relief. "Maybe they weren't after you."

"Maybe," said Ahlia unconvinced. Still, she was glad the threat was gone, for now at least. She mounted her horse once again and spurred it on.

* * *

The Captain of the Dragon guard had heeded his Master's warning.

"Not too close you fool, not too close or she will be upon you and you have no idea of what she may be capable of. We must test her strength carefully."

He had buried his outrage at the rebuke, and veered his soldiers away from the target. Horses neighed in agony as they were viciously reigned in. Their hooves clattered and scraped across the ground as they adhered to their riders' instructions, leaving a trail of dust behind them as they sped away.

* * *

The cold barren Heathlands had begun to give way to more fertile territory, though the climate was still chilly. Hills topped with tall evergreen trees undulated before them. The sight of trees was enough to lift Ahlia's low spirits. She smiled as she watched birds in flight, circling round the treetops. She had come to appreciate trees as much for their magical sanctuary as for their physical cover. Evergreens in particular, had a potent energy of their own which served to obscure other energy sources. She realised that this was in part at least why Mora had chosen to live in such a thick area of the forest, and she suspected that hiding between the trees had helped her to remain undetected at least once before. Of course, she thought to herself unhappily, she might not be the only one making use of the cover that such trees afforded. She would have to be vigilant, though at present, she was glad to be free of the awful exposure of the Heathlands, where the wind had buffeted her and her companions until they could not hear themselves think. She had tried to listen to the wind, but its voice was so cold and harsh that she had been unable to tolerate the connection for long. All she had sensed was that they should press on at all costs. Though the mystery pursuers had disappeared, Ahlia's anxiety had not quelled, and she remained alert. As her inner senses became more acute, so did her outer ones. Even the light of a grey overcast day seemed overwhelmingly bright, and the rustling of the trees almost drowned out the sound of Simon's voice as he chattered about a wealthy Prince he had once performed for. From under his bushy brow, Lex watched her carefully. She had wavered more than once on her horse, as if she might fall from her saddle, and her knuckles were white upon the reigns. Her brow was knotted, and her face pale, making her dark hair seem even darker than it was. Her bottom lip became redder and fuller as she bit into it almost hard enough to draw blood, utterly absorbed by her thoughts. Once in a while, he called to her asking if she was alright, making a circling gesture with his finger. At his request, she swept the area with her inner sense, but always gave the same reply, shaking her head in vain. All seemed clear and yet she knew at the same time that something was wrong. She looked at Simon, who appeared oblivious to their concerns. He had started complaining about saddle-sore. Lex glared at him with poorly veiled murderous intent, and muttered something scathing about putting Simon out of his misery for once and for all. Simon arched his brow delicately, but the rebuke did not deter his chatter for long. They rode on through denser and denser forest until the trees became so compacted that it was almost impossible to get through on horseback.

"We are in a thicket," remarked Simon as they dismounted.

"Well noted Simon," commented Lex sarcastically.

"Now, now," chided Ahlia, intervening to keep the peace. "We can lead the horses through. It gets easier after a few metres or so. I can see breaks between the trees. It is my fault, I was in front, and I am afraid my mind was elsewhere."

"I do not see why you should blame yourself Ahlia when your hired scout should be the one to proffer his apologies," said Simon in a deceivingly sweet tone. He shot a malicious glance at Lex who was only too happy to return the look with equal venom.

"I'm getting tired of your banter. If you have an issue with me then I suggest you out with it," snarled Lex.

To Lex's surprise, Simon turned, his normally peevish expression transformed to one of sharp, hard hatred. He stood fixed for a moment, his body full of tension in a way that was enough to concern Ahlia.

"Enough!" she shouted. "We are all tired and tense, and the last thing we can afford to do is take it out on each other," she pleaded, her voice breaking into a tired sob. Simon kept his gaze fixed on Lex for an instant longer before suddenly releasing it and walking up to Ahlia.

"Lady Ahlia, forgive our selfishness. The last thing that I would wish to do is cause you distress." Simon took her cold hand and brought it to his lips.

"Forgive me."

She nodded shyly, in surprise. "Very well then," she said awkwardly. "We should press on, and put this behind us."

She pulled on her horse's reigns to lead it through the trees. When Ahlia was at a safe distance, Simon moved closer to Lex once again.

"Do you really for one moment think I would demean myself by sullying my sword with your filthy blood?" he asked in a provocatively mocking tone.

To Simon's surprise Lex laughed heartily, causing Ahlia to turn back her head momentarily and wonder what was going on.

"Ah Simon. I like this side of you!" he laughed again as he followed Ahlia through the trees, leaving Simon in no small state of confusion.

Ahlia was right. Soon the trees began to thin out, and small chinks of light streamed down from between the branches once again. The mood seemed to lift too and Lex even broke out into a strange chuckle on one or two occasions. Ahlia and Simon exchanged questioning glances, but Ahlia was more thankful that the tension had eased between her companions, than curious as to how or why. As they stumbled into a small clearing, she suddenly noticed that her hands had changed from being ice cold to unnaturally warm, and they were beginning to throb as they had done back at the inn. As she heard a soft growl begin to emanate from Deeb, her heart filled with dread at what she knew she must anticipate.

Sure enough, within less than a minute, an armed figure

emerged from behind a tree. Another followed suit, then another until they were surrounded.

"The riders!" gasped Ahlia. "But how?"

Lex did not answer, but instinctively drew his sword. He knew an enemy when he saw one. Simon calmly looked at the tall figures before them. They were well armoured, too well for simple bandits, too well even for mercenaries. Each was wearing red and black, and their uniforms bore a crest on them unlike any he had ever seen before. Their faces were covered by visors, and each soldier brandished a long gleaming sword.

Lex turned to see Ahlia raising her hands, readying her aim at the soldiers. He could have sworn he could hear the air about her begin to crackle.

"Don't you dare!" he hissed. "If they're here, then there's probably a Sorcerer not far behind. Conserve your power until we're desperate."

Then in a louder voice, he called over to Simon. "Run. I'll keep them busy. This is what you paid me for."

Simon looked at Lex, then at the men, then back to Lex.

"There are ten of them and one of you."

"Not your concern," said Lex as he gripped his sword, and readied himself for the fight ahead. "You and Ahlia should get out of here. You'll only get in the way."

Simon turned to face the approaching men. He drew out his own sword. "I think I shall stay, actually. It's about time I put my fencing lessons to good use."

There was no time to argue.

"Fine, but don't expect me to look after you. You're on your own. It's Ahlia I'm concerned about."

"As am I, I will not let her fall into the hands of these men."

Lex did not hear him. He let out a bloodcurdling yell, and charged towards the nearest adversary bringing his sword down with all his might on the soldier. Simon was more wary in his approach. He skirted around the two approaching soldiers looking down the point of his sword at them. They were broad and trod heavily. That meant they would be clumsy fighters, relying on their strength rather than their skill. He tested the first, striking then parrying blow after blow. Their swordsmanship was good, and it was clear that someone had trained them well, but not well enough. He was not discouraged when the second soldier added his sword to the fight. Simon danced and whirled, and in no time had sliced his sword through both his opponents and was moving on to the next two whilst spearing through a third on route.

Meanwhile, Lex had aimed at the man he suspected of being the leader. He stood a head taller than the others, and his visor was bronze in colour compared to the silver of the others. Lex jumped forward rashly, narrowly avoiding a blow aimed at his head. He smashed his sword down upon his opponent in retaliation, but the soldier was too quick, and their blades locked. Lex struggled against the soldier's hefty push, gritting his teeth, willing the man's sword back. He mustered all his strength, and finally managed to knock the blade away, leaving his opponent open enough to receive a fatal death blow through the side gap of his breast plate. The soldier fell to the ground with a heavy thud.

Ahlia watched desperate to do something, but she knew Lex was right. Nevertheless, she could not let anything happen either to Lex or Simon. Her skin prickled, and the hairs stood up on the back of her neck as she watched the fight with mounting anxiety. Deeb had begun barking incessantly in an attempt to ward off these dangerous beings from his Mistress, and was standing guard between them and her. On one occasion, he seemed about to leap towards the fighting, but Ahlia's call pulled him reluctantly back. Ahlia's hands tingled with an unbearable intensity, and it took all her restraint not to use them. Her eyes flitted from Simon to Lex, making sure that neither of them was in difficulty. To her agitation, Simon was moving further and further away from her, finally disappearing from her sight as he followed two of their attackers into the trees. She thought to follow him, but Lex looked to be in trouble and she dared not leave him, just in case. She just had to hope that Simon would be alright.

Simon, as it happened, was more than alright. He was almost

enjoying himself. He rarely got to fight real opponents, and it felt good to put all his training into practice. One soldier already lay crumpled and bloodied on the floor, making Simon's tally four so far. He could have finished this one off already, but he was toying with him. He wanted to tire his enemy into submission. It did not take long for his opponent to fall to the floor exhausted and heavily wounded.

Simon held him by his mail shirt, tapped his blade on the crest on the soldier's arm band then put it to his throat, just under the visor.

"Is this a Sorcerer's Insignia? Who do you work for?"

The soldier said nothing. Simon peered into the eyehole of the visor. In the shadow, to his shock a pair of luminous green eyes flashed at him. He ripped the visor off to reveal a face of something that was almost a man, but not quite. It had sharp splinter like teeth and swarthy skin covered in pock marks. The chin was pointed, as was the tongue that lolled about in the wide mouth as Simon shook the creature.

"Who do you owe allegiance to?" he hissed through gritted teeth, so as not to be overheard.

The creature spat out sticky, yellow phlegm into his face causing Simon to shiver in disgust. For all he knew this Sorcerous monstrosity might not be able to speak. He wasn't going to get anywhere. He slid his blade across the creature's throat, and dropped it on the floor face down. He heard his name being called. Ahlia and Lex were looking for him. He disappeared into the trees, emerging to greet them from a different spot.

Lex walked over to him. "Listen, my thanks to you. I underestimated you."

Simon smiled faintly. "I do have certain hidden talents that often prove useful. Being with your good self, and the necessity of protecting the lady gave me the spur I needed."

His countenance clouded over as he contemplated the Insignia.

"Something wrong?" asked Lex interrupting his thoughts.

"What? No, not at all. I am not in the habit of killing people.

It is taking its toll on me mentally I fear, sending me into a morose frame of mind. My apologies."

"Don't let it worry you. Those weren't men. I don't know what they were, but they weren't men."

He pointed his sword at the nearest corpse that lay visorless on the floor. The inhuman face was exposed for all to see.

"Course, it's good to know that they can be killed," continued Lex. "It seems the throat is their weakest spot. Those visors are designed to protect the throat. Otherwise it takes quite a few good blows to bring them down."

Simon remained silent as he gazed at the lifeless corpse.

Ahlia had had little to do with the battle, but had watched for a Sorcerer to appear. To her surprise, none had. As Lex looked over at her and raised a questioning eyebrow, she gave a little shrug and pulled a face as she walked over to the men. "Something just doesn't smell right," she said.

"What in Spirits name are those things?" asked Lex. "I've never seen anything like them before. I mean I've heard many a tale about monsters, but I've never actually seen any. That old drunk I told you about Ahlia, he used to tell stories about monsters too, but said when he was a boy the last of them were forced away to uninhabited parts. Spirits! I wish I'd taken him a little more seriously."

Ahlia said nothing. The bodies around her were beginning to release something into the air, and the stench was making her feel queasy.

"Did you notice the symbol they all were wearing? A black winged lizard. They must be a clan or something," said Lex

"Yes, something," said Simon, his mind working furiously beneath his calm exterior.

"Look can we get out of here. Something doesn't smell right, and I mean that literally as well," stressed Ahlia.

She was right. The odour was easily detectable now, and it had a toxic quality to it. Who knew what properties it might have. They moved away before it overwhelmed them, though something kept causing Ahlia to turn to look behind her. She felt like she had forgotten something or had missed something obvious, but she could not for the life of her imagine what it might be. Perhaps it would come to her later.

In the shadows, the Captain of the Dragon Guard watched them leave the scene of carnage from where he had waited on horseback cloaked by his Master's power. His hidden eyes followed Ahlia's every step, until she was finally out of sight.

* * *

They were on the move once again. It seemed they were forever rushing away from places like criminals fleeing the scenes of their crimes, Ahlia mused grimly. Her nomadic existence was becoming almost natural to her, but this most recent encounter had disturbed her far more than any battle with a Sorcerer could. Despite the apparent victory, she was feeling uneasy. Her mind kept drifting back to those strange creatures. Where had they come from?

"I don't understand. Why did no sorcerer appear?" she finally asked Lex who was riding next to her. She spoke in a hushed tone to avoid Simon hearing.

"Maybe they were scouts, sent on ahead to test your strength, wear you out. Maybe when the Sorcerer realised you weren't going to use your magic he backed off."

Ahlia thought it over. It certainly seemed plausible. "You're probably right. A smart move, whoever it is they must be powerful though. Those were not natural creatures. I think they must have been created by some awful form of magic."

"Can Sorcerers do things like that?" asked Lex in wonder.

Ahlia gave him a look.

"Sorry, I keep forgetting you don't know," he continued swiftly to placate her.

"Well," sighed Ahlia. "No doubt whoever this lot worked for will be back and then we'll end up knowing more than we'd probably wish to."

She grinned at the sight of Lex wincing as he tested his shoulder gingerly. "For once it's not me who is the worse for wear," she commented. "Would you like some of that horrid

172

tasting brew you always make me drink?" she asked him wryly.

"I'd rather die of my wounds than suffer that!" he replied, making her laugh till she had to hold her sides to stop them hurting.

"What's the matter?" Simon called over.

"Oh just Lex being a big baby, that's all," laughed Ahlia.

Simon looked at them in a strange way for a moment.

"You two are the oddest pair I have ever met," he remarked which caused Ahlia to break into laughter once again.

"If you only knew us better!" she said between peals of much needed laughter.

* * *

In the palace over and across the seas, the King and Master of the Dragon Guard drummed his long nails against the side of his goblet of wine.

"I see," he said aloud to no one in particular. His voice was soft as the velvet robe he wore. "How inconvenient! I suppose I shall need more soldiers," he said casually. He beckoned a serving girl who was standing by to wait upon her Master and gestured for her to refill his goblet. He drank deeply as he wandered to the window and looked out upon his Kingdom. Seeing how much and how many belonged to him always cheered him in exasperating moments such as this.

"Let's see" he mused. "Fifty? A hundred?"

He took another sip of wine.

"Oh why take unnecessary risks."

He pulled a vial out from a chain around his neck, and held it up close to his eye so that he might better peer into its contents.

"A couple of hundred should suffice. It is only blood after all."

* * *

"I have to admit Simon, I was fairly impressed with the way you handled yourself the other day, even if you do dance about

173

the place like a girl when you fight," Lex said as he chewed on a piece of cured meat. They had come to a small stream and Lex, who was always hungry and thirsty, had broken into their provisions. He pulled out the stopper of his water flask, and took a series of large gulps. As he wiped the drops from his new sprung beard with his sleeve, his eyes clouded over as he daydreamed wistfully of a frothing beaker of ale.

Simon gave Lex a condescending look.

"I was schooled by a great Master. That is why I have poise and control as opposed to your preferred method of blunder in and smash as though you were a wounded bull."

Lex raised a shocked eyebrow at his complement being met with such as stinging rebuke.

"Is that so? I'll wager I have killed more men than you. I have been a fighter all my life," he replied sharply.

"Well done," said Simon, patronisingly, "hardly something to be proud of, though I think. In any case, I doubt you would survive an encounter with a true swordsman."

"Is that so?" asked Lex in a dangerous voice.

Ahlia could tell where this was heading, but she knew better than to appeal to them to stop behaving like such fools. They would never listen.

"Perhaps you ought to teach me how to be a better swordsman," he proffered standing up and drawing his sword.

"Perhaps I ought," replied Simon in a steady, even tone. He too rose from his cross legged position and pulled out his blade.

They both stood poised, almost hovering over the ground as each anticipated the other's move. They held their swords towards each other, Simon giving Lex's thick swords a tap to signal that they had begun. Lex burst into action at the cue lifting and smashing his sword down, but he was too slow and Simon had already withdrawn, and was circling about him like a bird playing with its prey. Lex took a deep breath before jumping in to engage Simon once again. Steel clashed with steel.

Ahlia had hoped that her companions would simply release a little tension and resume their composure, but she began to see that the so called 'practice' fight was becoming nastier with each

174

blow. Both had drawn blood and showed signs of being thirsty for more.

"That is enough!" shouted Ahlia at the top of her voice in order to be heard over the clash of swords. "I have never seen such a pair of idiots. If you both wound yourselves, who is going to protect me?" she reasoned.

Her comment gave the men food for thought. A second later, Lex was sheathing his sword. Simon followed suit. He bowed deeply. "I apologise for causing you distress yet again Ahlia. Rest assured I would not have harmed him."

Lex spat upon the floor as he listened, but kept the peace for Ahlia's sake.

"Perhaps we should press on then, seeing as we all have so much energy and no need of rest," said Ahlia crossly.

"No, no. You need to rest. Look at you, you can hardly stand," argued Lex.

Ahlia put her hand to her forehead. "I do need a rest. I need…" she picked up her bag. Staring meaningfully at Lex and patting her bag gently, she said quietly. "I'll be down by the stream."

Lex nodded in understanding. He shifted into a more upright position so that he might better reach for his sword should he need to.

"Where is she going? Does our company offend her so much?" asked Simon. The subtle surreptitiousness in their behaviour had not escaped him, though he did not show it.

"She just likes to be alone sometimes is all," replied Lex casually.

Ahlia followed the stream away from her companions until they were almost out of sight. She wanted to read the book again. As she opened it cautiously, she made a mental sweep of the area. At least this time, she knew that Lex too would be on guard. She flicked through the pages, until she came to where she had left off previously.

Much of the prose seemed to be written in a very cryptic fashion. Much was written on how cumbersome a burden the Oracle was.

'The stone's density is that of the entire universe. It contains the universe. It places the burden of the universe upon the shoulders of the wielder. One false step upon the path, and the wielder will stumble and fall endlessly.'

Another passage said something that Ahlia felt to be all too true:

'The Oracle is the colour of blood because it has been bathed in blood. It can turn men into murderers, and drive the soberest to insanity.'

She searched for information about the runes that were inscribed on the silver, but there was nothing. Instead she read:

'The Oracle is the eye that sees and it weeps with what it sees. There is no shielding the eye from the pains of unlimited sorrow and joy. It is more than mortals were meant to bear.'

"Very well, so it is awful, but how do I use it?" Ahlia asked out aloud in exasperation.

"I am lumbered with it, and you knew I would be Mora. So why tell me all of this, but not tell me how to use it?"

She pulled the talisman out of her pocket and holding it tightly in her fist, waited for something to happen. Nothing. She tried to push her intent into the stone, to probe it. Nothing. She recalled what the book had said about the stone having the weight of the universe inside it. She held the amulet in her open palm, and stared into the stone. How could a small stone contain the entire universe? Peering into the stone, she gradually began to sense a strange kind of force, pulling at her mind. Unable to lift her gaze, she found herself drawn ever inward into an amber luminescence that sent her consciousness spiralling down deeper and deeper. All sense of time and space disappeared until finally she reached a point where could not be sure whether the stone was in the world, or the world was in the stone. Where did she end and the stone begin? She could no longer be sure. Her head began to swim. Saliva began to rush into her mouth as a strong nausea set in. Finally, though it took an incredible feat of will, she forced herself to break her gaze, and leaned to the side to be sick.

"I see you've made progress, but I think that's enough for one day."

Lex knelt by her to hold her hair out of her face as she retched. She had been gone over an hour, and he had come to see if she was alright.

Simon appeared, just in time to see Ahlia slap her hand over an object that she had dropped on the ground in the hope of easing her nausea. His ever watchful eyes took in the book that lay open beside her. He watched Lex rush to close it with his free hand as if every second counted.

"What's going on?" Simon asked suspiciously.

"She is being sick," said Lex bluntly.

"I can see that plainly for myself, but why? Is she ill?"

Lex wracked his brains for an excuse. "Woman's thing," he said finally. "You know what I mean."

Simon raised an eyebrow. "Of course," he replied demurely.

Ahlia's retching was coming to an end and with each breath, she was feeling less nauseous.

"We should move on," insisted Lex.

"Are you entirely heartless? Ahlia is obviously not well. She is no fit state to ride," snapped Simon.

"We... should... move," Ahlia insisted between breaths, "I'll... be... fine."

She was as white as a sheet, but she made herself rise to her feet and smile weakly.

"I'm fine," she repeated as convincingly as she could. She still held the Oracle tightly in her closed fist, but she had wrenched her intent away from it in the hope that it would resume its more customary inert state.

Lex knelt down to fill his leather water skin from the river before they moved on.

"Simon please ready the horses," directed Ahlia. Simon hesitated as if reluctant to go, but then turned and disappeared behind the trees.

Ahlia's leg trembled with the effort of standing. Her hand too trembled as she held out her hand to accept the flask of water that Lex had filled for her to drink from. Lex watched her intently as he helped her to drink. With a sudden ferocity of emotion, he told her, "I would, that you would throw that accursed thing away."

Tears welled up in Ahlia's eyes. "I cannot. I just cannot."

Lex pursed his lips.

"Then let us get as far as we can from this place, because they will all be upon us if we don't," he said as he helped her to her horse.

Chapter 15

On the outskirts of the town of Fagras, two burly men stood waiting at their designated rendezvous point. Their attire and weaponry made clear their trade and those few people unfortunate to pass by this particular alleyway, hastily crossed over to the other side of the road making sure their head was turned in the other direction in the firm knowledge that sometimes it was best to see as little as possible in order to remain in good health.

"She's late," complained the taller of the two men, who had become bored of picking at his teeth with his dagger.

"She'll be here," assured the other, then sniffing the air like a hunting dog continued. "If she's not already."

A slender figure stepped out of the shadows. "Well done. I see your reputation as a tracker is clearly earned, though it took you a few moments to notice my presence."

The tracker sniffed as is unperturbed.

"I'm as good as you'll get. There's not many out there as will be so willing or able as me to track down a Sorceress for you. They say my great grandmother had the Knowing. It's in my blood. It's how I can track so well."

The figure stepped closer and pulled back the deep hood they were wearing, to reveal the face of a woman who, to the eye, appeared to be in her late thirties. Lines had begun to form along the contours of her face heralding the onset of middle age, though she was in fact in her early twenties. She had often noted the lines in dismay as she looked into her mirror, but they were the price that the pursuit of power had exacted from her, and she bore them with dignity. Accepting that beauty was lost to her, she had cut her dark hair short and put vanity firmly to sleep for ever, for power was everything.

"This statement is meant as a justification of your price, I suppose," she said.

The tracker nodded in affirmation. The woman clicked her teeth.

"Very well, you find her for me and I shall reward you handsomely. Double of what you ask for. As for your friend, I trust he will be more than able to take care of her companion, who is, by all accounts, little to contend with. However, if you can muster up a willing other it would not hurt."

The taller man nodded.

"Good," said the woman contentedly, "be ready here at dawn."

She replaced her hood and slipped back into the shadows.

The tracker waited until he was sure that she had gone, and then waited a few cautious moments longer before speaking.

"You sure you want to do this, Gark?"

Gark raised an eyebrow in surprise at the question. "Didn't you hear? Double she said."

The tracker rubbed his stubbly chin. "Can't trust those folk. We're expendable to them. I shouldn't have let greed cloud my judgement. I suppose there's nothing for it now. She'll kill us if we back out. Dead if we do and dead if we don't."

Gark gulped. "That bad?" He trusted his friend's instincts implicitly. The tracker had made a formidable reputation for himself due to those very instincts. The tracker said nothing for a moment. Then in a flippant tone said,

"Ah who knows, we may get lucky. She may be as good as she thinks she is. Might as well go home and get some sleep. Tomorrow will come soon enough, eh?"

*　*　*

Simon was singing quietly to himself by the camp fire. It was a ballad about a warrior prince and the noble feats that he had accomplished. The lovely melody soothed Ahlia's sad spirit.

"That was a beautiful song," she said when he had finished.

"It is more of a story than a song," he smiled at her warmly.

180

"However, I thank you for the compliment. Might I say, Ahlia, that you look lovely by firelight."

Ahlia had been braiding her dark hair as she listened to him sing. She blushed deeply at the compliment. There was something about the way Simon looked at her that made her feel special. Sometimes, she could tell he was watching her, but whenever she met his gaze, he would just smile and nod. He was certainly brave too. She had watched him cut through his opponents with unbelievable ease. She could not help but be impressed.

"I suppose you know an awful lot about... things," she finished the sentence lamely and cringed inwardly at the thought of how ignorant she must sound.

"I know a little," he answered.

She was eager to ask him what he thought about those creatures they had encountered. He had said very little since then. Perhaps he was still in shock. Ahlia doubted that anyone in these parts could have encountered such monsters before.

"Where do you think those creatures came from?" she asked as innocently as she could.

Simon mulled something over in his mind. He fixed his gaze on her intently for a moment before resuming his soft smile.

"I am no expert, but I suspect that they were Sorcerous creatures, produced by magic."

Ahlia's heart jumped into her throat.

"Sorcerous?"

"Yes. Sorcerers are capable of producing such creatures if they are powerful enough."

"You know about Sorcerers then Simon?"

Simon smiled to himself. "Of course I do. I am a Bard. Many good tales have Sorcerers in them."

"But those are just stories aren't they?"

"Ahlia, a Bard's business is to preserve history in as beautiful a way as he can. The stories I tell have their roots in real events, just as all great legends have their roots in real events. Take for example the great tales of the Sorcerer's Wars."

Ahlia's eyes widened.

"Can you tell me that story?" she asked.

Simon chuckled. "I can tell you some. The song cycles are very long."

"Can you tell me a short version?" she pleaded.

"Well, it is not my custom to dishonour the song cycles by cutting corners, but I cannot refuse a lady."

He paused dramatically for effect.

"Imagine a time when Sorcerers and other wielders of magic moved openly and freely about the world of ordinary folk. Imagine too that there were two kinds of Sorcerers; those that followed the path of inner power and those that followed the path of outer power. Those who followed inner power, had very little to do with ordinary folk, often choosing to seclude themselves. They concentrated on learning all there was to learn about existence. They desired to understand the universe, and through their efforts they amassed great personal power. Then there were those Sorcerers who followed the path of outer power because they desired to rule the universe, and through their efforts they too amassed great personal power. It came to be that there was not enough room for the two groups to live in peace, as their principles made it impossible for them to be compatible. The songs tell of the many battles fought over territory and principles. The most obscure and the most beautiful of all the songs, tells the tale of the objects of power and the battles fought over them."

Ahlia drew in a sharp intake of breath, and waited for Simon to continue. As if deliberately tantalising her, he held a pregnant pause. Then he softly began to sing;

"Steel and grail and staff and stone
Where powers unearthly make their home
The sword of incomparable might
Shall be the one empowered to smite
The grail of mystics covered in runes
Shall be the one to heal all wounds
The staff of ash is the one to guide
And the stone sees where the others reside"

Ahlia, awestruck, carefully listened to every word.

"It's a beautiful song," she remarked, "but what does it mean?"

"I must be honest and tell you that I do not know. I sing the songs, but I cannot say that I understand them all. Few people ever ask to tell you the truth. They just listen to the music for the most part."

"Please go on," pleaded Ahlia. "It is so lovely."

"That is where that particular song ends, I am afraid."

Ahlia fell silent for a few moments. The Oracle burned in its secret pocket. She could feel the heat through the cloth of her skirt. Was the Oracle the stone that Simon sang of? But how could a stone see? And what were these other objects that the ballad had recorded the existence of. She cast her mind back to her conversation with Mora about objects of power. Surely these items in the ballad were such objects. How ironic she thought to herself, that she had sought to find information from Sorcerers, when a simple Bard's song held at least one vital, all be it small, part of what she needed to know.

"So you believe in Sorcerers then," she said finally.

"I surely do and those creatures were the creations of a Sorcerer, I'll wager."

Ahlia shivered involuntarily.

"Do not be afraid, Ahlia. It was simply our misfortune to meet with them. Who knows where they were headed and what their intention was. Your friend Lex did not think to try diplomacy before rushing into a fight," he said scathingly then paused for a moment. "Though I am loath to admit it, he was probably right to assume that they were bent on hostility."

Ahlia looked at the ground directly in front of her.

"Why do you travel with that oaf? He is coarse and a drunkard too I'll warrant," remarked Simon.

"Lex and I have experienced much together."

"I see," replied Simon archly. "I would have thought you to have better taste. You could have the pick of any man surely."

"That is not what I meant. I just feel comfortable around him."

Simon gently shuffled over to be closer to her. He was watching her so intently that she could not bring herself to meet his gaze without risking a deep blush.

"Where are you travelling to?" he asked softly.

"I'm not sure yet," she said truthfully. "I had to leave where I was. Things didn't work out there. It's too complicated to explain."

"Try me. You'd be surprised at what I might understand," he said persuasively.

Ahlia gave a long drawn out sigh.

"You are all alone aren't you. That is why in desperation you cling to Lex. You think you have no choice."

She said nothing. His voice washed over her like warm water. He took her hand in his.

"You have no idea how special you are."

Ahlia jerked back a little as she exclaimed laughing. "Oh I have some idea. Believe me."

Simon drew her towards him in a way that was both gentle and compelling. She felt her inhibitions melt away as to her surprise he brought the palm of her hand up to his lips and kissed it. In a voice that seemed to echo in her very being, he sang:

> "You are the stuff of which tales are spun,
> Radiant as the sun.
> You are the glory that men fight and die for,
> Cry out in the night for
> And that to which all men aspire,
> Fanning the flames of their desire,
> Ever higher,
> Until they reach you, and burn in your fire."

Ahlia's breath quickened despite herself, as Simon's song came to an end and she felt his grip tighten upon her hand.

"Am I interrupting something?" a voice asked loudly, spoiling the moment. Simon did not take his gaze off Ahlia immediately, but let it linger a moment before turning to Lex who had reappeared from his wander in the bushes, carrying a limp dead rabbit in his hand.

"Ah, I see you have caught us an evening meal, Lex."

The two men locked stares for an uncomfortably long space of time, until Ahlia could bear it no more.

"Good, I'm starving. The sooner we eat the better." She picked up a branch from the firewood they had collected and nervously began stoking the fire.

Reluctantly, Lex averted his eyes, and began skinning the rabbit with a little more force than was needed. The corner of Simon's mouth curled into a slight wry smile. He surprised himself at how much he thoroughly enjoyed being a thorn in Lex's side.

They watched the meat slowly roast over the fire in silence. When it was cooked, Lex used his fingers to tear off strips and hand them roughly to the others. Simon accepted his portion with obvious disgust for Lex's lack of etiquette. Lex appeared oblivious, and crunched on the bones with satisfaction. Ahlia picked at the flesh with little relish. The warm meat nourished her body, but it could do little to reach the other form of fatigue she was experiencing. No one seemed disposed to conversation. After he had picked the bones of his portion clean, Lex declared he was going to take a short nap. Roughly pulling his blanket over himself, he turned over and settled to sleep with his back to the fire. Simon, for once, announced he was in agreement with Lex, and would also be grateful for some sleep. Ahlia agreed to take first watch. She knew that sleep would not ease her fatigue. Once she was sure that Simon was fast asleep, she took the opportunity to reach into her bag and retrieve Mora's book. With her back to the men so that she had some privacy, she poured over the pages until she found what she was looking for. Since her encounter with the Oracle the previous day, she was suffering from intermittent bouts of nausea and dizziness. She was concerned that the Oracle had somehow drained her power and she realised to her dismay that each time she felt her power leave her, she became increasingly anxious to restore it once again. After having lived for thirty years with no power that she knew of, in a few weeks, she found herself unwilling to exist without it for even a few hours. She was beginning to understand why Mora had taken such great pains to explain the trappings and temptations of power, but she argued with herself that she had no choice. She had to maintain her power or perish at the hand of another more powerful than her. She flicked through the pages until a phrase caught her eye and made her stop.

"To use when all is spent," she read to herself.

She would need to search out the necessary herbs and there was an incantation to be chanted. She tapped her finger against the list of ingredients on the page. Some of the herbs she already had been given by the old woman in the village, but there were other herbs she would need to gather. As she stared at the names on the page, she began to become increasingly sure that if she got up and looked for what she needed, she would meet with success. Closing down her outer senses, she sat very still and allowed her breath to deepen. Gradually, she felt herself being pulled towards a clump of bushes to her right. Just behind them, she could sense, she would find the herbs she was looking for. She pushed her senses out to better judge the distance. To her surprise, she realised that what she has thought to be a matter of yards, was in fact a matter of miles, but there they were, the roots she needed.

She closed the book, and returned it to her bag. Twilight was looming as the setting sun cast its last rays about the sky. Rising to her feet and brushing her skirts down, she slung her bag over her shoulder. She looked over at Lex who appeared to be still fast asleep. She walked up to him and nudged him firmly with her foot.

"Eh?" he started, sitting up quickly in anticipation of trouble. "What's wrong?"

"Nothing," replied Ahlia.

Lex was clearly un-amused at being woken without good reason, but Ahlia seemed utterly indifferent.

"Come on, there's still an hour or so left until nightfall," she said, trudging towards her horse.

Lex looked at her in surprise. "You want to ride on?" he

asked as she roughly nudged Simon to wake. Lex noticed, to his satisfaction, that at least Simon was receiving the same brusque treatment from Ahlia that he had.

"Yes, for a few while at least," she said, swinging herself into her saddle.

"This way," she called as she trotted off, leaving Lex and Simon to quickly gather their things and follow.

*　*　*

Ahlia led the way, often turning abruptly in one direction then in another, until Lex could hardly contain his irritation. He couldn't begin to fathom what it was she might be doing. Simon was being remarkably passive, simply following Ahlia dutifully without saying a word. There was something eerie in the way Simon was so accepting of all that happened. He had never once complained that he was being taken out of his way. In fact, Lex realised, Simon had never actually clearly stated which direction was supposed to be his way.

"Look Ahlia, the moon's rising and the horses need their rest. We can't ride much further," complained Lex.

Ahlia's horse halted abruptly. "Yes, of course. Here is fine," she replied as if in a daze, without really taking in her surroundings. They had arrived at a patch of open land that had absolutely no shelter. Lex looked at her in disbelief.

"Well, not exactly here. I mean anywhere around here that's appropriate," she added when her focus returned and she realised where she had stopped. Lex surveyed the landscape. In the distance, he could make out a clump of brush and some rocks that might provide them with some shelter.

"There. We'll camp there," he said leading the way. "And this time, we're staying put."

Soon, they had settled themselves down for yet another night sleeping on the hard ground, when Lex stood up and began to saunter towards the bushes.

"Where are you going?" Ahlia asked with more sharpness than she intended.

Lex cast a less than friendly glance over at Simon. "I'd tell you, but that would be 'uncouth'," he said in a sarcastic tone and gestured towards the clump of bushes.

"Not that way you're not," she warned.

"Why not?" he asked in bewilderment.

"Because I'm going that way. You go over there," she pointed in the opposite direction, "or you can wait until I get back. I may be some time though."

In her mind's ear, she could hear the music of the herbs she needed for Mora's recipe. Above her, the moon was full and bright. It was the perfect time. Lex opened his mouth to argue, but shut it again when she gave him what he secretly called her 'agree with me or I'll turn you into a toad' look.

"Fine!" he snapped sulkily as she disappeared into the bushes with Deeb close behind her. "Women!"

Simon laughed. "Go on, I'll keep watch."

"Thank you," said Lex disappearing in the other direction.

When he was sure they were both gone, Simon directed his attention to Ahlia's bag which was conveniently lying not far from him. He crept across the ground with the stealth of a practised thief, lifted the flap and foraged about. His searching hand came across a book. The same book he had seen her peeking into when they had stopped earlier for a rest. He had, at that time, felt the power surge so strongly, it had been all he could do to contain himself. Power had wrought that book. He must know what was in it. He pulled it out and looked at the cover. There was no title. He desperately wanted to open it, but he knew that if he did Ahlia would probably detect him immediately. Then of course, there may be others lurking in the darkness who would feel the power too. He would have to cloak himself then cast a cloak over the book, to be absolutely safe. He placed his hand over the book and murmured quietly. Then, very tentatively, he opened it.

"That does not belong to you," came a threatening voice from behind him. This, the most obvious problem, he had not counted on. Cursing himself inwardly and dropping the book, Simon spun round.

"Ah, Lex, yes... I know... I was just... curious... you know?"

"No. I don't," replied Lex.

"I would have put it back."

Simon noticed Lex had his hand on his sword handle.

"I think, Simon, you should leave before I get angry and kill you."

A strange and dangerous look flickered across Simon's face. "You know, Lex, I've never liked you. You are coarse, base, degenerate, and, all in all, a pathetic wretch of a man."

Simon watched with controlled animosity as Lex's rising temper coloured his cheeks red, and engorged the vein above his brow. Simon calmly drew his sword and pointed it steadily at Lex.

"You have no idea what you're dealing with."

Lex laughed pulling his own sword out with much less finesse.

"Let's see you put your sword where your mouth is."

At the same time and with equal force, they leapt towards each other and clashed swords ferociously. Neither seemed inclined to give way, but reinforcing his stance with all his body weight, Lex managed to thrust Simon's sword back. Simon, realising he was losing ground, lithely leaped back and to the side just out of the reach of Lex's blade. Lex spat on the ground in frustration before plunging towards Simon once more. Steel clashed against steel over and over as they fought, blow after parry after blow, Simon's technical expertise seemed perfectly pitted against Lex's experience and strength, and he scored a slash, slicing through Lex's sleeve and drawing blood. Like an enraged wounded animal, Lex fought back with even more fervour. It was fire against ice, Lex's passionate lunges against Simon's cool calculated jabs. Soon, both of them were beginning to breathe heavily. Simon was surprised at his opponent's stamina. He had expected a much easier fight. Lex had been abusing his body all his life, but with his sword in his hand, he felt nothing but bloodlust. Without a hint of a warning, Lex smashed his sword down against Simon's sending it hurling out of his hand onto the ground a few yards away. Instinctively, Simon thrust out his sword arm, palm open towards the sword. To Lex's astonishment, the sword trembled on the ground slightly then sped handle first towards Simon's open hand, as if connected by an invisible thread. It landed neatly in Simon's hand, ready to be used. Simon had not even given the matter a second thought until he saw Lex standing practically immobilised by sheer shock. He suddenly became aware at the same time that they were no longer alone. Ahlia had reappeared and was standing on the other side of the fire. The roots she had been holding were lying strewn on the floor, her hand open and limp, her face deathly pale in the firelight. Her dark eyes were wide and gripped with terrible realisation. She had seen. The moment seemed to last an age, until Ahlia suddenly thrust her hand out, palm outwards, releasing a bolt of power that hit Simon in the centre of his chest and sent him hurtling in a blaze of crackling mage-fire, out of sight into the nearby bushes. Coming to his senses, Lex made to go after him, but Ahlia stopped him.

"He's already gone and you won't be able to catch up with him," she said gravely.

She followed Simon with her mind. He was running at a tremendous pace away from them. Then she lost him. He must have blocked her or cloaked himself. She went over to the fire and stared into the depths of the flames. From somewhere deep in her throat a curious soft droning noise manifested and began to sound.

"He won't be back tonight," she said finally after some moments. "He won't be back until he is ready."

"I am surprised you did not kill him Ahlia. You don't usually leave them alive," said Lex reproachfully, "and him of all of them, right under our noses, the conniving..."

A number of curses escaped his lips before he was done. He looked across to Ahlia for an answer, but there was none. Crushing the plants she had picked underfoot, as if they were not there, she walked over to where Simon had dropped the book. She picked it up with great care and returned it to her bag.

"Perhaps you are finally gaining control over your power. Still you probably should have killed him you know," continued Lex as Ahlia lay down on her blanket. She appeared dazed.

"I cannot believe we didn't see it coming," he kicked at the ground in anger.

"You did. You never really liked him," she said in a detached voice.

"Yes, but it didn't cross my mind he might be a Sorcerer himself. Even when he went for your book, I thought he was just looking to steal it. Those creatures the other day, you don't think they were his creations do you?"

"They might well have been. He might have been hoping to drain me and then strike. It would explain why no other Sorcerer turned up," she replied bleakly.

"I'm so angry with myself. I mean, yes, I thought he was an arrogant bastard, and I suppose I never quite trusted him, but it never crossed my mind that..." his sentence tailed off as he saw the look on Ahlia's face. She was terribly upset. His look turned to one of concern. He had never seen her look so sombre. As she put her hand up to her brow, Lex noticed that her fingers were trembling. Deeb, who was sitting quietly by his mistress, let out a sympathetic whimper.

"I need to rest," she said, her voice faltering as she spoke. She turned away from the fire with her back towards Lex so that he could not see the tears as they rolled down her cheeks.

Chapter 16

Days had passed and Ahlia's mood had not lifted. She remained strangely sullen and her eyes appeared glazed over as if some part of her spirit had left her. Her jaw was set firmly in an expression that was neither frown nor smile. Lex found it hard to get any meaningful conversation out of her and soon stopped trying.

She had spent hours grinding between two stones, the herbs she had rescued from the ground where she had dropped them on the night of Simon's betrayal. After chanting over them for what seemed like hours, she finally added them to spring water heated over an open fire. The result was a pungent brew that she carefully poured into an empty water gourd once it had cooled down. The task tired her out, though in some ways it had given her some respite from her torment. Something was happening to her, and she could not understand it. She fluctuated between feeling unbearably fragile, and incredibly hard, and the hardness brought with it a cold numbness that terrified her. Those moments where she felt nothing, separated her from all existence. It was all she could do to fight her way back to make a connection once again with the world around her. Sometimes she deliberately gripped hold of objects to feel the physical sensation of them and thus remind herself of who and where she was. Lex watched her silently from the corner of his eye with unceasing concern, but he had no idea what to do for her.

"I always thought that it would be the thing that you carry that would change you, but I see that is not the case, for you say you have yet to fathom its use," he said finally.

Ahlia looked downcast.

"It is your own power that changes you then?" he asked softly.

"So it would seem Lex or perhaps what I am forced to do with it. Damage and destroy is all I am able to do when all I truly wish for is…" her voice tailed off.

Lex awkwardly busied himself sharpening his blade as tears spilled over the rims of her lids and plunged down like rainfall from her face onto the ground. She cried silently and shamelessly, not bothering to wipe the tears away, but letting them clear streaky paths down her grime smeared cheeks.

Lex's strokes became more and more disjointed until he could continue on no more.

"Tell me what I can do for you Ahlia and I shall do it. Whatever you need fetching or wherever you need going…" he could hear the impotence of his words in his inept attempt at consolation. Internally he burned with frustration, knowing that there was surely something he could do, but not knowing what that might be.

Ahlia limply shook her head. She longed for someone to reach into the dark place that grew ever larger within her and wash it away with tenderness, but she knew none could reach there. Despair was filling her like a black wave and as it passed, it left behind it a cold resolve. She gathered her skirts and pulled her cloak to her.

"Let us see this to its end, for there is no alternative," she said finally, her words hard as stone as she wilfully stamped out the last remnants of pain.

The sun was slowly turning westward as the day waned. Ahlia's stone set features did not alter until a strong gust of wind whipped about her ear and penetrated her mind speaking in a tongue only she could hear. She reigned in her horse and motioned to Lex. He unclasped his sword in response, his hand poised over the handle. Ahlia considered changing direction for a split second, of attempting to avoid what was to cross their path, but then what was the point, she thought with resignation. There would only be others elsewhere. Spurring her horse on, she consciously concentrated on gathering her power to her, feeling with a strange and novel satisfaction, her hands begin to tingle and her hair begin to raise slightly from its ends as the energy surged through her. She felt their presence well before they were visible. It was hardly difficult and she was not surprised when two tall burly men rode out from the cover of trees to block their path. Both were wearing makeshift armour that seemed to be comprised of pieces from unrelated sets, taken as tokens from the men they had defeated in previous battles. Each brandished a large sword.

"Ahlia run!" yelled Lex rearing his horse protectively in front of her to shield her from the approaching men, his sword already drawn.

"Let me take care of this," she shouted back.

"Don't be a fool. If they're here, then there's a Sorcerer here too. Save your energy for that."

Sure enough, a woman jumped down from the tree behind them, landing deftly on her feet. She looked older than many of Ahlia's previous opponents and was dressed in a plain brown tunic and trousers. Her dark hair was cropped short. As she had dropped down from the tree, she had lowered her magic cloak and the proximity and sheer strength of her intent was enough to send a chill down Ahlia's spine. This was no novice or ex-apprentice. Slowly and with the grace of a queen, Ahlia dismounted to meet her foe.

Lex had charged and engaged the two men, fighting for all he was worth. Although the men were larger than he was, he was taking advantage of the fact that this slowed them down. He hated to admit it, but his sparring sessions with Simon had opened his eyes to new techniques that were proving very useful indeed. Lex used the men's own force against them. One man lunged at him only to find himself pulled off balance by the propulsion of his thrust as Lex stepped neatly aside in a way that Simon might have been proud of. Lex thrust his sword, aiming to place a blow between the plates of the chest armour of his opponent. The blow was stopped from penetrating as deeply as he would have liked, when the other mercenary's sword came crashing down upon his own, forcing Lex's sword to the ground and placing him once more in a defensive position rather than on the attack. He jumped from his horse to retrieve his blade and fearlessly grabbed his opponent to pull him down off his mount.

The Sorceress had cast a cold examining eye over towards the fighting for a moment as if unsure whether her mercenaries could contain such a fierce opponent, but her thoughts were interrupted by Ahlia's battle cry.

"It's me you want isn't it? Prepare for combat!" she yelled as she thrust her hand out to fire a bolt of energy. As the woman countered, Ahlia created a block that appeared about her like a luminous bubble, and she ran as far as she could away from Lex with incredible speed. Her opponent followed. Ahlia could not afford to expend too much energy on maintaining her shield while she prepared to attack, and the moment her opponent noticed the bubble flicker and being to fade, she took immediate advantage. A shower of razor sharp stones pelted Ahlia from behind sending her running, looking for cover. The woman had mentally seized them and hurled them at her, but only a few small ones had broken through Ahlia's fast fading block. Ahlia called to the wind, it blew the dust up from the ground and swirled about the Sorceress, blinding her and buffeting her in every direction, giving Ahlia time to find cover behind a tree and gather herself. Her opponent was strong, stronger than she had before encountered in combat. She had broken away from the wind trap, quelling the dust storm and was preparing to attack again. The Sorceress summoned the power of Fire and thrust a flaming ball towards the tree that Ahlia was standing behind. The tree burst into flames and a heavy branch came crashing down, but Fire refused its command and fell short of Ahlia who silently gave her thanks to Mora's special friend. The Sorceress was taken aback for a moment, but quickly recovered. She aimed her raw personal power at Ahlia, releasing bolt after bolt. It was all Ahlia could do to deflect each onslaught. Somewhere in the back of her mind, she wondered who would last longer, the attacker or the defender. The blows seemed equally strong in their consistency. There was no sign of the Sorceress weakening. Ahlia meanwhile, felt the energy draining out of her with each tirade of blows. A strangely calm part of her could feel that there was more power deep in her somewhere, but she just could not access it. Something was in the way, though she had no idea what. Meanwhile, the energy reserve that she had come to gauge well would soon be completely depleted, and she guessed she had enough in her for one last attack.

Finally, seizing upon a tiny window in the array of attacks, she raised a small rock and flung it towards the woman using her senses to aim the rock well so as to use the minimum power possible. It hit the Sorceress squarely in the chest and knocked her off her feet causing her to land heavily on her back. She thrust her open hand out in Ahlia's general direction as she fell. A bolt escaped from the Sorceress' outstretched fingers. Ahlia stepped aside to try to evade the blast but it tore through her dress ripping into the soft flesh of her thigh. She screamed in agonising pain and fell to the ground as her leg gave way underneath her. Blood began to pour from the wound. At the sight of his mistress in distress, Deeb leapt at the Sorceress with all the ferocity of a tiger, sinking his sharp teeth deep into her arm, but the woman shook him off, flinging him aside like a rag doll.

Ahlia forced herself into a sitting position facing her opponent who was still on the ground unable to get up. Ahlia looked about her desperately. She was feeling weaker by second, and she had no idea how much power her opponent still had left. She spied another rock and seized it with her mind, lifting it high above her opponent. Then she let it go. It hurtled downwards towards the Sorceress' head, but the woman saw it in time, and threw it off course so that it landed a few feet away from her. Ahlia cursed inwardly. Then her Sorcerous-mind registered the sound of rushing water. The river! With all her might she formed as strong a mental grip as she could muster. Invisible hands seized hold of her opponent's body as one might a heavy bag, and dragged her kicking and fighting across the bumpy ground towards the river. At the same time Ahlia called out to the Spirits of Water to help save her and carry this threat far away. On reaching the bank, the invisible hands flung the live load into the water. The river accepted the task and swirled about the Sorceress, making it impossible for her to make it back to the bank. It was all she could do to keep her head above water to breath.

"Away, away," insisted Ahlia in her mind and Water agreed. The current sped up and the Sorceress was carried downstream faster than imaginable. Ahlia followed her further and further downstream with her mind. "Away, away," she chanted. The Sorceress was expending her last remnants of energy fighting against the river's magically enhanced current. Soon she would be spent. The world around Ahlia was becoming more blurred by the minute. She could feel that her nose was bleeding again. Her dress too was soaked in blood from the deep tear in her leg. She leaned over to her side and vomited.

"Lex!" she called out mentally with her last dregs of power. "Lex!"

By the time Lex had defeated the two men and found her, she was lying in a sticky dark pool of her own blood which was fast mingling with a smaller pool of vomit. He felt her neck for a pulse. It was frighteningly faint, but she was alive. He had no idea how. Judging by the amount of blood she had lost she should have been dead. He picked her up, and carried her to a grassy spot. He tore away part of her skirt to see the full extent of the damage. The blow had ripped her leg open. The wound was longer than it was deep spanning from the inner side of her upper thigh down past her knee into her calf. Her opponent must have caught her mid stride as she tried to step out of the way. The bleeding strangely seemed to have slowed down of its own accord. He looked around. In the distance he could see the lights of a settlement. He wrapped her leg up as tightly as he could with a piece of material that he tore from her undersmock. Then as carefully as he could, he put her over his horse's back. He climbed on behind her and headed for the lights as fast as he could.

*   *   *

Ahlia's opponent was swept along by the fast current of the river for miles. The water was alive with magic, and she could not compete with its energy. To keep afloat she had used the last remnants of her power for a buoyancy spell, but it had cost her her consciousness. She regained her senses to find herself bobbing face up by the river bank.

A large hand encased in a thick leather glove reached down in front of her face offering assistance. Thankfully, she grabbed hold of it, and it pulled her out of the water with surprising ease. That was, unfortunately, where the civilities ended. The same huge hand shot towards her neck gripping it in a deadly vice and lifted her off the ground. She struggled for a few moments, her legs flailing helplessly in the air, desperately trying to reach the ground. After a few moments, her body became limp and still. The hand released its death grip, and let her lifeless body fall to the ground. Heavy boots stomped away, leaving the unburied corpse for the scavengers to feast upon.

*　*　*

Lex banged frantically on the door of the first house he came to. He had ridden to a small crop of cottages he had seen in the distance, desperate to get help for Ahlia.

A man opened the door ajar first, but on seeing Ahlia in Lex's arms he flung the door wide open and pulled them inside. The man's wife, who had come from the bedroom to see who was in her house, brought her hands to her face in dismay at the sight of Ahlia's condition, exclaiming that the village healer was away, visiting a relative. After a heated, but hushed discussion, the man rushed out. He returned not long after, bringing with him an older man.

Lex had not bothered to wait. He had plonked a bag of coins on the table and demanded a bowl and a jug of boiled water, a clean cloth, and a needle and thread. He put a bundle of herbs into the jug and the bowl. Carefully, he unwrapped the bandages to expose Ahlia's wound, and washed it with the cloth and herbal mixture. He was thankful that she was still unconscious and unable to feel any pain. He set about burning the needle in the fire to sterilize it. Then he rinsed it in the boiling water.

When he was satisfied, he began to sew Ahlia's wound. The villagers watched him in amazement.

"Are you a healer sir?" asked the older man.

"No, but I've had to sew myself up quite a few times so I know how it's best done."

"You cannot stay here," urged the man in a worried voice.

Lex pointed his head towards the money on the table. "Why not? I can pay."

"Whatever trouble you are in, you cannot bring it here. We have children to think about," the man said pleadingly.

Lex close his eyes and nodded wearily.

"I know and I'm sorry, but you have no idea how important this woman is. I don't even know, but judging by how many people are trying to kill her I'd say she was the rival of kings. For all I know she could be fighting for our very safety, the safety of those very children you are worried about."

"Sir you must leave," the man pleaded, obviously too afraid to event attempt to understand.

"Alright, alright!" Lex growled angrily, "Just give me time to clean her up and we'll be off. At least get me an empty bottle to put the tonic into and some food. Take what you want from the purse."

They brought him what he asked for. He refused to rush despite the villagers hovering over him uneasily. Eventually, when he felt content that there was nothing more he needed from them he announced that they were leaving. Ahlia was still unconscious. The two men helped him get Ahlia up onto the horse and he rode off. When the village was out of sight, he stopped and lay her down on the ground under the cover of some trees. He covered her with his jacket and felt her pulse again. It was still weak, but it was definitely stronger than it had been. He had to wake her to get her to drink the tonic. It wasn't easy. When he did manage to rouse her back into consciousness, she whimpered from the pain as it set in. He propped her up against him and forced her to drink the tonic.

"I thought I'd died," she murmured weakly.

"Yes well you nearly did. You should be dead. I can't

understand why you're not."

"My leg hurts!" she moaned.

"That's a good sign. Wiggle your toes for me."

She wiggled them weakly, her face creasing in pain as she did so.

"That's another good sign. Of course you won't be able to bend your leg or even walk probably for some time."

"I shall be a sitting target!" she exclaimed.

"Don't despair. You seem to heal faster than a normal person. Must be a Sorcery thing. The important thing is that you replenish your power as quickly as possible."

He handed her the bottle with tonic in it. "So drink up and then sleep!"

Ahlia put her hand over his. The warmth of her touch seemed to penetrate and travel up his arm into his chest. Despite the awfulness of the situation, a madly inappropriate sense of wellbeing enveloped him.

"What are you doing to me?" he asked in wonder, but she did not answer. She was already asleep.

*　　*　　*

Sebastian had used the cover of night to gain entry into the library. He would have preferred to access his old Master's volumes, but there was no time for such a journey, even with a Sorcerer's speed. Now that his time posing as Simon had come to an abrupt and untimely end, he was free to gather crucial information. There were things he needed to know fast. All was dark and lifeless inside. He guessed that the inhabitants had gone off in search of the Oracle. He doubted there would be a Sorcerer in existence who hadn't. In his mind's eye, there burned the memory of a crest of black and red. Since his encounter with the Sorcerous creatures that had attacked Ahlia, a strange foreboding had set up residence in his mind. There was someone else far more powerful than he, after the Oracle. Someone perhaps, so powerful that Ahlia would be unable to defeat them, though he had to admit, Ahlia was far more comfortable in her power than he had imagined, and she had a certain unpredictability that made her difficult to gauge. He could not understand why Ahlia had not killed him, for it was obvious that she could have easily destroyed him or at the very least wounded him gravely, but she had instead sent a thrust of energy propelling him several hundred yards away, merely winding him. She had allowed him to escape. Her actions had sent him into confusion.

With the stealth of an assassin, he moved from bookshelf to bookshelf, his inner eye perfectly able to see and guide him in the gloom. Finally his senses told him that he had found the book he was looking for. He pulled out a large dusty volume and he hastily bundled it into a bag he was carrying.

"My, my! What have we here? A sorcerer turned thief."

Sebastian slowly and carefully turned around.

"Lights!" the voice called and the lanterns in the room blazed to life on command to reveal two cloaked figures. They pulled back their hoods revealing their faces well enough for Sebastian to tell that one was a man and one a woman.

"What gives you the right to help yourself to our Master's library?" asked the man.

"In truth I did not think anyone would care," replied Sebastian by way of excuse. "How is it that you are not both seeking the Oracle?"

"We might ask you the same question," interjected the woman. "What is in that book that is of such importance?"

Sebastian scrutinized first the man and then the woman and quickly surmised that she was obviously the more powerful and intelligent of the two.

"I am not here to challenge. I am simply in need of information."

"By violating our Master's library, you have already challenged," replied the man menacingly.

The woman moved forward and was about to place an arresting hand on her comrade's shoulder, when something seemed to stop her and she stepped back abruptly. It was too late. Sebastian took in a sharp breath as he sensed the man's power surge in preparation. The man released his power in a single gesture, aiming not at Sebastian, but at the bookcases behind him. They instantly collapsed and would have buried Sebastian had he not swiftly stepped out of harm's way. With a wave of his hand, the Sorcerer sent a shower of books to pelt Sebastian from all sides and blind his vision, preventing him from focusing his aim. Blindly, Simon thrust a stream of mage-fire towards his opponent that ripped through bookcase after book case as it moved towards its target. The Sorcerer successfully fended off the attack and was about to retaliate, when Sebastian, relentless in his onslaught let out bolt of energy that found its home in the centre of the man's torso, sending an electrical current through his nervous system that convulsed his entire body. He twitched countless times before, finally falling lifeless upon the ground, the blood already draining from his once animated features, his finger that had been formed to point a bolt of energy towards his opponent, now forever fixed in that impotent gesture. Sebastian held his breath, anticipating the woman's retaliation at the death of her comrade, but it soon became evident that she had little intention of fighting him.

"I ought to kill you where you stand. He was my love," she said, her voice like cold water trickling down Sebastian's back.

"In name only I think," he retorted with the same iciness. "Your heart has long grown cold for him. He was not your equal therefore hardly worthy of you affections."

The woman raised an eyebrow in surprise. "Most astute, but must a person love only their equal?" she asked.

"Absolutely, power demands it regardless of what we personally might consider. You held yourself back for him. He did not have enough power to pursue the Oracle and you were holding yourself back." He gazed at her with eyes that seemed to bore right through her.

"Moreover you resented it. With each passing day you resented it more. You would have killed him yourself eventually."

The woman smirked partly to hide her shock at his statement, partly in contempt of his arrogant assumption.

"We are not all as cold blooded as you. Do not presume to understand a woman's mind or heart for it will undo you," she warned.

Sebastian bowed. "On that point I concede, though I wonder how long you could have fought the pull of the Oracle before it destroyed you."

"Again you presume! Not every Sorcerer or Sorceress feels the pull with equal strength. I see your thirst for power is particularly strong, so much so that it perhaps clouds your judgment."

Sebastian didn't believe her words. He could not conceive of anyone not wishing to possess the Oracle. The desire for the talisman tormented him unbearably every waking moment. It governed his every move.

"Even if by some strange happening you are immune to the Oracle's pull, you and all our kind should be concerned with what I may have discovered."

He opened the book upon a nearby desk and leafed through the pages. Suddenly he stopped abruptly and banged his hand upon an open page. The woman looked to see what it was that Sebastian had discovered.

"Surely not!" she exclaimed. "It is impossible. They are all dead. They have been dead for hundreds of years! Read for yourself right there!"

Sebastian looked at her gravely. "I hope more than you that I am wrong, but there is a vast and old source of power heading this way and it can only be the doing of an Adept. If I am right and he or she gets hold of the Oracle, we shall all be doomed to a grim fate. Not one of us shall survive except in slavery.

"They say the holder of the Oracle is once again a woman."

Sebastian nodded.

"You know of her?"

"I have spent time with her."

"And survived?"

"She did not know who I was. I deceived her."

The woman stared long and hard at Sebastian, taking in the handsome contours of his features.

"She must have wanted to be deceived," she commented finally in a tone of respect that Sebastian could not understand.

"That would make her fallible," he concluded after a moment's thought.

"Fallible? No! Human? Yes, human still. As yet neither her power, nor the power of the Oracle has changed her. She is in transition. She is still able to feel."

Sebastian was completely lost. "I do not understand what you are saying."

The woman looked at him almost pityingly. "How could you? You probably surrendered to your power years ago. For some of us, it is not so easy to give up our former selves."

"Her feelings will make her weak in the face of what is to come," argued Sebastian.

"Yet she holds onto the Oracle still, despite the efforts of those with seemingly more power and experience," she retorted wryly.

"If you are right and an Adept has somehow survived and comes for the Oracle, then none of us can win against this power. None but the wielder of the Oracle has more than a slim chance of survival. I do not have enough personal power to challenge either the holder of the Oracle or the Adept that comes to take it from her. Neither do you."

Sebastian's ego smarted at the affront to his abilities, though deep down, he worried that she was indeed correct.

The woman replaced her hood. "Do what you want with the book. I have no need of it. I am gone from this place."

"Might I ask the name of one who seemingly holds so much wisdom?" Sebastian called after her as she disappeared through the open doorway. He sensed her stop in her tracks.

"Rhianad. My name is Rhianad," came the echo of a reply from the corridor.

Sebastian had made it his business to inform himself about as many Sorcerers as he could, but her name was unfamiliar to him.

"My name is..." he began in an effort to introduce himself, but stopped in the realization that she did not care who he was. She had already gone.

Chapter 17

Ahlia had spent two days in a state of delirium. She alternately shivered and burned, murmuring incoherently all the while. Lex did all he could to keep her comfortable and every few hours endeavoured to squeeze a few drops of tonic between her cracked lips, but there were moments he feared he would lose her. She was too ill to be moved and it was probable that even if he did manage to get her to another village, they would be turned away. They needed to find a town, where they could melt into the crowds, where no questions would be asked. By the third morning, Ahlia's fever suddenly broke. She opened her eyes to find Lex hunched over beside her. He had fallen asleep from sheer exhaustion despite all his efforts to stay awake, his hand still upon the hilt of his blade. His shaggy matted hair was caked in dirt and framed a haggard visage. An unruly dark beard had sprouted from his chin and jaw line and in her still dreamy state, Ahlia thought he almost looked more like a bear than a man. She owed her life to him and it pained her to see how weary he looked. She licked her dry lips and would gladly have reached over to the gourd that lay beside her sleeping comrade, but she did not have the strength and she did not care to wake him just yet. Deeb, who had been resting quietly at the feet of his mistress cocked his head up. Ahlia put a finger to her lips to keep him silent and he returned his head to rest between his paws.

Despite her discomfort, she felt a strange sensation of peace. She knew it was a temporary illusion, but she savoured it none the less. Involuntary tears rolled down her cheeks, tears that she was too weak to suppress. She did not suffer them long, however. Mustering all her strength, she heaved herself upright. Tentatively and with a great deal of dread, she flicked open the blanket that covered her to reveal her wounded leg. It had been bandaged up and so, to her relief, she could not see the extent of the wound. She wiggled her toes. At least they seemed in working order. She had feared that her leg might be lost. She had dreamed that it was. As the cold morning air hit the bandages and wafted through them, Ahlia shuddered. The slight motion was enough to stir her sleeping guard. Lex started and looked about him with the urgency of one taken by surprise. Ahlia smiled. On seeing her awake, Lex looked shamefaced. He opened his mouth to say something, but Ahlia deliberately distracted him by reaching out for the gourd. On seeing her need, he rushed to help her drink.

"Careful now," he said as she began to drink in great gulps.

Refreshed, she lay back down. "Thank you!" she gasped.

"How do you feel?"

"Stiff!" she said. "How bad is my wound?"

Lex looked grave. "Bad. For an ordinary person, I would have said fatal. But here you are alive as yet."

Ahlia flicked the blanket open once again.

"Your handiwork?" she asked gesturing to the bandages.

Lex nodded. "Did what I could."

Ahlia cast her mind back to the battle.

"She was strong that one. The strongest yet I think."

"But you defeated her."

"Just."

"You can't think like that. You defeated her and that is all there is to it. I'm just amazed this is the first time you've been really wounded. It was a lucky blow on her part."

Ahlia lapped up his reassurances. She was in need of reassurance.

"How long have I been unconscious?"

"This is the third morning."

The news startled her. "Then we should move!"

Lex shook his head in disagreement.

"I don't think you are fit to travel yet Ahlia."

In defiance Ahlia began to pull herself upright forcing Lex to come to her aid. "I'm fine and I can surely ride if I can't walk."

There was no arguing with her.

"Very well, let's see about getting you onto your horse."

With painstaking care and much wincing on Ahlia's part, Lex helped her onto her saddle. She blanched visibly from the pain, but she made no utterance of complaint.

At the first village they came to, Lex asked for directions to the nearest town. To his relief, he was told that there was a small market town less than two day's ride from them. He told Ahlia of his plan to take her there where they might blend in amongst people. Ahlia was too weak to argue and allowed Lex to take command of the situation.

* * *

It was good to be among people again, even if they were strangers. Ahlia, who had begun to forget what it was like to be in a bustling marketplace, thought this single street was tiny by comparison with the winding roads and alleyways of Avor. Avor to her now was a distant memory. It was as if someone had described the place to her rather than she having actually lived there herself. She had, as time progressed, become increasingly preoccupied with her inner world. She could no longer suppress the strange twitches she was prone to as renegade streams of power coursed through her. It seemed that each time she used her power, though it drained her initially, it also served to open up her abilities further. So far, she was acutely aware that all she had used her power for was to kill. This was having dreadful effects on the human side of her personality. Her mind screamed self defence while her conscience was wracked with guilt. Her eyes had become more sunken in their sockets, and there was an uncanny stillness about them. Sometimes she wondered if she still needed to blink.

Lex noticed the changes, but said nothing. It was none of his business after all he reasoned. Yet there were moments where he was almost afraid for her. He was not a man who had much time for spiritual matters, but he fancied at times that she was fighting for her soul as the power that lived in her tried to engulf all that she had been. Some might have seen it as transformation. Lex felt in his heart that he was witnessing a systematic destruction.

"Hey!" he called to her. She had been wandering about the street aimlessly, not even looking at where she was going. He pulled her towards a shop door.

"Don't you think you could do with a new skirt?"

Ahlia looked down at her torn, bloodstained skirt and smiled weakly.

Lex pulled a pouch from his belt and shook it so the coins inside clinked against each other. He smiled.

"What's your favourite colour?" he asked almost shyly.

Ahlia tried hard to process the question. It was so simple and normal that she found it hard to focus on.

"Green," she said finally with some effort.

"Green it is then!" said Lex cheerfully and ushered her into the shop. He plonked the bag of coins on the table, and had a long talk with the woman behind the counter. The woman looked Ahlia up and down and frowned.

"I'm not letting you try anything on until you've bathed. A bath can be arranged, but it's extra, mind, as I shall have to send out for things," she warned.

"Yes, yes." agreed Lex impatiently and pulled a face at Ahlia. She found the corners of her mouth raise into a weak smile.

"A bath sounds good," she said wistfully.

"I shall leave you to it then," replied Lex nodding to the woman. "Look after her. I'll be back in an hour or so."

The feel of clean warm water against her skin was glorious. She had undressed and kicked the filthy stained rags that she had been wearing as far from her as she could as if to distance herself from more than just the clothes. Her leg was healing at a remarkable rate and she no longer needed a bandage, though it was obvious that the scar would never fade. It would have bothered her tremendously at one point in her life, but now, she hardly cared. For all she knew she would be dead soon enough. The dead were not troubled by vanity and did not mourn their scars.

She had finally settled on a simple green smock, much to the shop keeper's distress. The woman had hoped to sell her something far more costly, but Ahlia declined, choosing to invest instead in a new pair of boots to replace her worn old ones. As a final touch, she had helped herself to some scent from an open bottle on the counter. The familiar smell of roses filled the air as she pulled open the stopper.

"You hardy need that dear!" remarked the woman, "You already smell of roses. Your perfume clings to you something extraordinary. I noticed it when you walked in. That kind of perfume does not come cheap. From the east, if I'm not mistaken. 'Twas how I knew you must be a Lady despite your appearances. I'd not have served you otherwise."

Ahlia could not help but smile and in doing so she felt part of her ordinary self return to her. She replaced the stopper and thanking the woman, left the shop, her mind filled with memories of Mora.

Turning a corner on her way towards the tavern where she presumed she would find Lex, she came abruptly face to face with a blond man who had stepped out from a doorway to block her path.

"Simon!" she gasped and took a precautionary step back.

The man pursed his lip.

"My name is actually Sebastian and..." he added hastily, "before you do anything we both might regret, I've come to talk," he stressed.

"What could we possibly have to say to each other?" she said scornfully.

"I know I don't deserve a hearing, but I have come to warn you."

"And why would you do that?" she asked, her voice full of distrust.

"Will you at least spare me a moment and listen? What have you to lose?"

He motioned for her to follow him through the open doorway to the side of them into a bare storage room. The door shut behind them of its own accord.

"You are in grave danger," he began.

"Of that I am more aware than most I think," she interjected sarcastically. "I can take care of myself."

"I know what you are capable of," he explained, "I have known since that night in Avor when you killed my rival, Marcus for trying to take the Oracle from you. I was there and barely escaped with my life myself. I know that my Master, may his soul be at peace was in utter awe of your Mistress and I think he loved her too moreover."

"You were there in the alleyway?" she gasped. It seemed like years had passed between that night and now. Now she understood why he had seemed so familiar.

Sebastian nodded.

"Ahlia listen to me. There is a wave of magic moving towards us. You have been too distracted to notice, but if you'll only push your sense out far enough you will feel it right on the periphery of your inner vision. It is moving towards you, fast. I cannot tell what it brings with it. It is not human. It is a Sorcerous creation of some kind. Ahlia, I am the strongest Sorcerer I know of, this side of the sea, but someone else stalks you who is at least as strong as I am and far less restricted by ethics."

"Are you stronger than me?" Ahlia asked softly.

"We don't have time for that. Right now you have to listen to me. I'm trying to tell you…"

Ahlia didn't appear to be interested.

"Answer me Simon or Sebastian or whoever you are. Do you think you could defeat me?"

Sebastian paused before answering. "I do not know. You defeated the Sorceress Jian and she was one of the strongest that I know of, of our kind. What is it that you want me to say? Until I am certain that I know your limitations and find you at a disadvantage, I would not be so foolish as to engage in combat with you. There is of course that oaf Lex to contend with. Though I am loath to admit it, he is a fiend with the sword and he sleeps with one eye open, the eye that is permanently fixed on you. He seems to have made you his personal mission. No money could buy such dedication. Perhaps he hopes to redeem his miserable existence by saving you."

Sebastian had his suspicions about Lex's ulterior motives, but kept these to himself. Right now he needed to impress upon Ahlia how serious the coming threat was. Her refusal to react was making him increasingly frustrated.

"And are you afraid this unknown Sorcerer or Sorceress will steal the Oracle from under your nose?" asked Ahlia.

"This Sorcerer will kill you!" he replied, his voice full of urgency and something that Ahlia did not quite recognize.

"So would you to take the Oracle from me," she said flatly. It was something she had come to terms with some time ago. "What difference does it make to me who kills me? If I am to die, I am to die."

Sebastian searched frantically for something to say in reply, but he was torn internally between his burning desire for the Oracle, and a strong inclination to preserve Ahlia's life driven by the fact that he cared for her. Finally, his emotions overcame his senses.

"I do not want you dead. By the Spirits, I do not want you dead," he said, with such fervor that Ahlia looked at him in surprise. He rose and left swiftly before he had a chance to incriminate himself further.

* * *

Lex was beginning to worry. He had returned to the shop only to find that Ahlia was long gone. He had walked up and down the busy main street looking for her and searched in various shops, but to no avail. He was beginning to think the worst when he caught sight of her as she resurfaced from a small side alley.

"Where have you been?" he asked irritably.

"Nowhere. I was just looking around," she lied, "I didn't want to disturb your drink," added in a more scathing tone than she intended.

For the first time since she had met him, Lex looked visibly hurt by her words.

"I was eating not drinking," he said his eyes downcast. He

thrust a material bag at her.

"Here, provisions. There's bread and cheese and dried meat and some wine. The wine's for you not me. I thought it might put some colour back in your cheeks. You look so pale still."

She accepted the bag meekly, full of remorse for her harsh words.

"I'm sorry. It's just that I..." she began, but she could not finish.

"I know," said Lex simply, saving her the trouble.

There was an uncomfortable pause.

"Something bad is coming and I might not have the power to stop it Lex," Ahlia said dolefully, changing the subject.

She told him about her encounter with Sebastian and the danger he had warned her of.

Lex listened gravely. If what Sebastian had told her was true, they both knew that time was running out.

* * *

Sebastian had not long left the Ahlia when he picked up the unmistakable signatures of two Sorcerers heading towards the town, their focus fixed on Ahlia's own signature. A pained expression flitted across his face and he stopped dead in his tracks, torn between two courses of action. Finally, he made his decision and with the speed of a Sorcerer, ran to intercept Ahlia's attackers.

* * *

Ahlia was still terribly weak, despite all her efforts to display the contrary. All her energy was automatically diverting to healing her leg, but the wound seemed to be more than simply physical. It seemed to act as a leaking point for her power even though the flesh was healing well. She wondered if that was how Sebastian had found her, through the trail of power as it dripped like invisible blood from her wound. If Sebastian had found her, who else might? The thought of yet another fight sickened her to her stomach. Lex, who had been packing the provisions into the horses' packs, watched the colour drain from her face for the hundredth time.

"We're not going anywhere yet," he said firmly. "Not until you have had ample time to rest. This place is only as dangerous as any other for you, so what difference will it make?"

Ahlia nodded weakly. Her head was beginning to spin and her surroundings were becoming increasingly faint. Lex caught her just in time as her legs gave way. He hoisted her into his arms and carried her towards the nearby inn, muttering,

"Sorcery be hanged. If we are to die tomorrow, we might as well be comfortable today."

* * *

Sebastian was standing at some distance opposite the two Sorcerers that he had tracked down, barring their way into the town where Ahlia now lay sleeping fitfully.

"I cannot let you pass," he called to the hooded figures.

"This is no business of yours. Stand aside," was the reply in a female voice that was strangely familiar to him.

"The Oracle is my business," he retorted.

One of the figures came forward slowly and steadily until Sebastian could clearly make out her features.

"It seems that we are destined to cross paths for better or worse," the woman commented.

"Rhianad is it not? I thought you had chosen not to pursue the Oracle," he looked past her to her companion, "and I see that yet again you allow a lesser man to command you. How disappointing!"

Rhianad smiled.

"Are you going to kill this one too?" she asked.

"Only if he attacks me or insists on pursuing any route into the town."

"Why should he not? It is the right of every Sorcerer to pursue the Oracle. You are breaking the rules Sebastian."

Sebastian knew that this was true. He looked away into the

distance for a moment.

Rhianad let out a sigh of understanding. "Ah, I see. You are here not to attack, but to protect: to protect her."

She smiled wryly. "What power indeed this woman has."

She paused for a moment as she looked back to her companion.

"I shall convince him to turn back. He is no match for you."

"But I suspect you are," Sebastian replied knowingly.

Rhianad did not answer his question, but instead pointed in the direction they had come.

"Three more are coming and they will not be so..." she searched for the appropriate word, "understanding."

Sebastian nodded, "I shall be here to greet them."

"Of that, I have no doubt. Fare well Sebastian."

"Journey well Rhianad"

"Oh no Sebastian. Save that phrase a while yet, for such things come in threes, and we shall meet again. Of that I am confident."

Sebastian watched her return to the other Sorcerer. After a short exchange of words, they headed off returning along the road they had come from. He breathed a sigh of relief and sat down by the side of the road to wait for the three Sorcerers who would be approaching, if he was not mistaken, within the hour.

*   *   *

Ahlia slept fitfully as Sebastian stood up to meet the approaching Sorcerers. A cold perspiration broke upon her brow as he gathered his power and without waiting launched straight into attack killing one of his foe instantly, mage-fire ripping a gaping hole in the Sorcerer's chest. She tossed and turned upon her sweat soaked pillow as he turned upon the other two, deflecting their blows with the ease of a child flicking a fly away. He smashed his power down upon them, unleashing all the power of the turbulent emotions he could not voice to anyone. Without concern, he scorched the earth about him, leaving trails of flickering mage-fire. Power clashed with power, but even combined, the two Sorcerers were no match for him. He was fresh and intent on stopping them. Deep in her slumber, Ahlia's breath quickened as pooling their energy, the Sorcerers aimed a single deadly stream of power at his head. He pushed it away with all his might, forcing it to remain just feet away from him. The Sorcerers intensified their efforts to push the stream forward yet again. Drops of blood began to fall from Sebastian's nose as he drew increasingly upon his power reservoir. He broke one hand away to slash blindly across the ground. The stream of energy that left his fingers crept across the ground severing the leg of one of his opponents just below the knee. The Sorcerer screamed in agony and fell to the ground, withdrawing his power from the attack. In the short lull, Sebastian used the last dregs of his power to deflect the attacking stream of power back, returning it whence it came. Ahlia called out incoherently in her sleep as: not so very far away from where she lay: the Sorcerer who was still standing, disappeared screaming into a haze of mage-fire, his burning body falling to the ground with a thud. Sebastian turned swiftly to the surviving Sorcerer who lay whimpering on the ground, his life blood oozing from his amputated limb. The Sorcerer made an impotent attempt to shield himself from the inevitable, but it was to no avail. Sebastian drew his sword and plunged it down into the chest of his foe. The man's eyes bulged wide open for an instant, before he fell backwards, the sword coming away cleanly from the death blow. Sebastian, panting heavily, wiped the blood from his nose and sheathed his sword. It was done. She was safe: for now.

*　*　*

Ahlia arose some hours later, refreshed and oblivious to the events that had taken place on the outskirts of the town. Lex was pleased to hear her ask for food and urged her to eat as much as she could. He had brewed some fresh tonic for her. She sipped the now familiar tasting liquid, sighing deeply as she felt her energy gradually returning to her.

"I dreamed of blood," she said quietly as she sat by the

215

roaring fire, a blanket wrapped around her.

"That is no wonder," replied Lex. "Your days have been filled with blood."

"No. This was different."

She tried to formulate sentences to describe her sensations, but it was impossible.

"No use dwelling on it now. Rest a while longer and when you feel strong enough, we shall rid ourselves of this place." Lex stared into the fire gravely, hoping in his mind that her dream was merely a dream and not an omen.

*   *   *

The soldiers of the Dragon Guard had long since landed and had marched day and night from the port their ship had docked at towards their objective. Their captain urged them on relentlessly, knowing that they were creatures of Sorcery and would not tire. The few men that were interspersed between the monsters his master had created rode, like himself, on horseback. The sooner they reached the Sorceress and took that which was in her possession, the sooner his Master would be satisfied. Nothing else mattered.

Chapter 18

They had been riding in silence for hours when Ahlia finally announced wearily, "I don't want to do this anymore. I don't want the Oracle. I'm tired."

Lex had known this was coming. Ever since the encounter with Sebastian, he had known this was coming.

"But you should consider that Mora entrusted the Oracle to you for a good reason. She managed to live a long enough life and hold onto it," he insisted, though he privately wished he could fling the cursed talisman into the deepest abyss.

"Yes, but at what cost Lex? I never got the chance to ask her. How much did she have to give up? How many people?"

"From what you've told me of her, she seemed to think it was worth it. She doesn't sound like the sort of woman to have any regrets."

"I don't want to end up alone," she said, "if I manage to stay alive that is," she added bitterly.

"Don't do this to yourself. No good will come of it," Lex said with unexpected softness. He was surprised at how strongly he felt the need to console her. A part of him, admittedly a part he barely recognised, wanted to hug her and tell her that everything was going to be alright, but he did not know that it would be, and he would not lie to her.

"You told me once to throw it away. Have you forgotten?" she asked accusingly.

"And I wish at that moment that you had," he said woefully.

"And now you change your mind. Now you tell me to keep it."

"I thought I could see a simple end to this, but the only simple thing was my thinking. There is no easy end to this. I thought the best chance you had of surviving would be to give

217

up the talisman. Now I realise, especially if what Sebastian told you is true, that holding on to the Oracle is your only chance of surviving."

She fell silent, lost deep in thought. After some time, she said abruptly, "I know what to do. I must contact Sebastian."

Lex's expression darkened as he guessed what she had in mind.

"You think I am making a mistake," she accused.

"It is your choice Ahlia," he replied.

"I don't know. Is it? Is any of it? Mora said I could not avoid my destiny, but I might try anyway."

She formed a picture of Sebastian in her mind and concentrated as hard as she could, calling him to her.

Lex watched in awe as a soft glow began to emanate from her body. Despite himself he found an image of Sebastian forming in his head which he could not rid himself of. Ahlia was calling him to them. Eventually, the glow about her faded and she opened her eyes.

"It is done," she whispered.

An uneasy feeling began to form in the pit of Lex's stomach, but the decision was Ahlia's to make and there was nothing he could do.

* * *

Lex was not happy. He had just listened to Ahlia's plan, and did not like it at all except the part about them waiting in a tavern. That part he could live with. The rest of the plan he did not like one bit, but there was no arguing with Ahlia. That much he had learned the hard way.

"Why? Are you sure you want to do this? What if he turns on you?"

"He won't, He won't have cause to."

Lex raised his hands up in dismay.

"I'm not even going to ask what you mean by that."

"Good. It's my business," Ahlia snapped.

"Oh, I see, fine. Well Miss Sorceress I'd hate to interfere in your business. I mean, who am I to interfere when you're doing so well making an idiot out of yourself, not to mention putting us both in danger!" he said angrily.

"You don't have to stay Lex."

"Well maybe I won't!"

"I'll understand if you don't."

He was getting more annoyed by the minute. He hated it when she was being all understanding. It irritated him beyond belief, but he knew he'd lost. If he went she'd win, and if he stayed she'd win. Either way he was doomed to being predictable: him, a man who had built his life and reputation on being free and impulsive. Look at what she had reduced him to! Well let her look after herself then Miss Supreme Sorceress. Let her fight her own battles!

"I'll be over there by the bar if you need me," he growled as she walked away.

Grumpily he threw a coin upon the bar, and ordered an ale from the innkeeper who presented him with a frothy beaker. Staring at the foaming liquid would once have filled him great satisfaction, but now his once pleasantly carefree mind was clouded with worry. He cast his eye over to where Ahlia sat by herself at a table deep in contemplation, the hubbub of the people around her barely registering. He wanted more than anything to go and sit with her, but there was something about her demeanour that stopped him. He knew could not help her this time, though he was loath to admit it. Nevertheless, an army of men would not have succeeded in uprooting him from his vantage point at the bar. Whatever was to happen, Lex fully intended to be there and do what little he could.

It was half an hour at least before Sebastian arrived. Ahlia thought he looked almost regal. He was wearing a dark silk suit covered by a heavy black cloak. His long blond hair was braided. A wide silver band covered the first phalange of his index finger. He greeted her with a nod of his head before taking a seat opposite her.

"Well," he said "I am here under truce as your message said."

"Thank you for coming."

She pulled out a small pouch from her pocket and placed it on the table.

"Here. If you want it so badly, you can have it. It's yours."

Sebastian looked first at her then at the pouch. He was torn between suspicion and desire.

Ahlia slowly opened the pouch and tipped it upside down. Out fell the Oracle.

Sebastian's eyes grew wide with wonder.

"Is that what I think it is?"

"It's yours. Take it."

"It's so small. I had no idea it would be so small."

"Yes. Well, it is."

Sebastian shook his head as if suddenly coming to his senses.

"Wait a minute. You cannot just give it to me."

"Why not?"

"Because you can't. No one gives away the Oracle."

"Why not?"

"It's the Oracle for Spirits sake!"

Ahlia was beginning to lose her temper. She didn't have time for this.

"I know what it is Sebastian."

"You expect me to believe you're handing over your power just like that."

"I didn't say anything about my power. I'm just giving you the Oracle."

But to be the wielder of the Oracle is... is..." he was lost for words.

Ahlia shrugged. "I wouldn't know I've never wielded it."

"What?"

"You heard," she hissed. "I've never used it. I don't know how to."

Sebastian gripped his head in his hands in sheer disbelief. "You mean you've survived all this time on your own abilities."

"As far as I know, with a little help from Lex and on one occasion yourself."

"It is true what they say about the Oracle affecting the mind. You have lost your sanity!" he remarked.

"Whatever, Sebastian, just take the thing and get as far away as you can."

"You can't mean it. You can't! I just cannot understand. You are giving up Supremacy!"

Ahlia was losing her patience fast. She shook her fists at his in exasperation.

"Trust me it's over-rated."

The dam that held her emotions back was crumbling fast.

"Let me tell you about Supremacy," she hissed across the table. "Supremacy is an old toothless spinster in a tatty grey smock living in a run down cottage waiting to get her throat sliced."

She breathed deeply to calm herself down before continuing, "Supremacy is having the power to change anything, and at the same time knowing that nothing should be changed."

She looked at him with pleading eyes. "It doesn't mean anything Sebastian," she said her voice full of earnest, her heart pouring out into her voice. "There is more to life. There is love."

It didn't take much to see he wasn't listening. He was hearing, but not listening. His hand was hovering over the Oracle. For a moment time seemed to stop. She had the strange feeling that there were shadows overlaying them, as though this whole scene had taken place before. Suddenly, he whipped his hand back. He looked at her his eyes full of contempt and anger.

"Temptation: the ultimate trick of a Sorceress. There is no glory in this. I will win the Oracle by my power and my ability or not at all," he said furiously, his face wracked with emotion.

Lex could stand it no more. As he made his way over to the table, he saw Sebastian rise swiftly, knocking a beaker of ale off the table. He turned as Lex approached with Deeb.

He gestured to them with scorn.

"I can't say much about the company you choose for yourself: A flea bitten hound and a soulless mercenary: hardly befitting a Sorceress."

Lex could feel his blood begin to boil.

"I've no love for you either 'Simon'."

Sebastian's lip pursed. His nose twitched, but from the corner of his eye he noticed that Ahlia's finger was raised.

"I think we're done here," she said in an even, steady but definitely no nonsense tone. The air about her crackled ever so slightly, charging the atmosphere with a threatening tension. Without another word Sebastian left. Lex sat down in his place and looked at Ahlia.

"You gave him the Oracle didn't you."

She did not look up at him. "I tried to."

"And he turned it down? Perhaps he is smarter than I thought. Maybe he realised it wasn't really the Oracle you were giving him."

"What do you mean?" she asked sharply.

Lex knew he was treading on dangerous ground.

"Nothing," he said dryly. "I wish you had taken that wretched trinket and shoved it down his throat."

Ahlia let out a long sighed. She got up and went outside not even looking behind to see if Lex was following. Deeb, who had been waiting outside patiently, jumped to his paws at the sight of his Mistress and padded over to catch her up as she walked. Then suddenly Ahlia stopped. She took a deep breath as if to inhale the very colour of the night and then said, "I'm going on, on my own."

"Don't be ridiculous," replied Lex who was two steps behind her.

"I'm going on, on my own," she repeated.

She was frighteningly calm. Her voice was without intonation, her face without expression. It was too late that Lex realised that this was merely the calm before the storm.

"You can't be serious."

There was no answer.

"I mean you expected him to turn you down didn't you really. You knew there was no way… you did know."

"Leave me be."

"Now don't get upset."

"Leave me be!" she said in a voice akin to thunder, to raging sea.

She wasn't upset. No, 'upset' did not even begin to cover the myriad of sensations that coursed through her. Her heart pounded in her chest and her hands trembled under the strain of her attempts to contain what she was feeling. Involuntary tears welled in her eyes, but she refused to let them fall and so they remained trapped there on the rims of her eyelids, glistening like dew on petals. She thought of all the set backs, the disappointments, the betrayals, the heartache. She thought long and hard about the heartache. She thought about the loneliness, the isolation, the burden of having a power that was entirely inappropriate for the world around her. She thought about being supreme and the part of her that had desired it. Even now she cursed herself, for being unable to let that part of her go entirely. Was she a victim of her own soul's desire? Why was it that her heart and soul seemed to wish so earnestly for two so very different things? She blamed herself and she blamed the world. She blamed everyone and everything. She blamed herself for the wanting, she blamed Mora for the giving, she blamed Sebastian for the denying, she blamed the Sorcerers for the trying, but most of all she blamed the Oracle for being.

To anyone who gazed upon her in that moment, they would have beheld a woman consumed by the power of her very own glory, her very own intensity, her very own ability. A woman, who without even trying, overshadowed all who dared stand near her. She was unapproachable, her field of energy radiating out far from her body, her eyes seeing what others could not, her mind probing what others should not, her heart daring what other would not, her soul transcending what other might not. She was frustrated fury, and she was unbearable pain all merged. She stood, rooted to the earth in a desperate effort to maintain grounding, to maintain sanity. She knew that she stood on a sword's edge, but she could not, at that precise moment be sure which way she would leap. She looked away from Lex into the gloom of the unlit road saying in a tone cold enough to freeze a man's soul with fear,

"Anyone who comes near me tonight... anyone... will not live to regret it."

Lex stood transfixed by a mixture of awe and fear, unable to move as she set off into the shadows, with Deeb faithfully tailing a step behind his Mistress. After a few feet there was a short sharp command and Deeb followed no more.

* * *

Lex sat on an upturned barrel. He had half a mind to go back into the tavern and forget all about her. After all, she had caused him nothing but trouble since the day he had met her. She obviously didn't want him around anyway. Alright, so he wasn't rich as he'd hoped, but he did have a purse full of coin, enough to pay off some of his debts. Anyway, she had made it clear she didn't want anyone around, not even the dog. She was a powerful Sorceress. She didn't need anybody. She certainly didn't need him. Deeb sat in front of him with eyes full of expectation.

"What!" yelled Lex. "You heard her!"

Deeb gave a short sharp bark then shot a look towards the direction Ahlia had gone.

"She said she'd kill anyone who followed and don't think she didn't mean it. You saw the look in her eye!"

Deeb cocked his head, put his snout in the air and turned his back on Lex, looking sorrowfully towards the path his Mistress had taken.

"Oh come on, don't be like that!" exclaimed Lex. Then he stopped himself.

"I can't believe I'm talking to a dog... a dog! See what she has reduced me to! See! That's it! I'm going in for a drink." He pointed a threatening finger at Deeb. "And don't expect me to feed you either."

Lex aggressively pushed the door of the tavern open and went inside only to come back out again almost immediately.

"Alright! Alright!" he yelled at the dog, who had not moved and was still waiting patiently.

* * *

Sebastian had already put miles between himself and Ahlia. This

224

was not how he had envisioned things to happen. He had assumed that by now he would have the Oracle in his hands and be close to deciphering its mysteries. Instead, the Oracle lay in the possession of a naïve and inexperienced woman who had hardly the ability to control her own power let alone that of the Oracle. He could not understand how it was possible that she was always able to defeat her opponents. Her lack of training certainly made her unpredictable and that seemed to operate to her advantage, but there had to be more to it than that. What was it that had led Mora to choose Ahlia as her successor? Sebastian suspected that the one quality she had that no other could mirror was her untarnishable innocence. She had killed many and yet she somehow remained vulnerable. Instead of wallowing in her power as another might, she endeavoured to control it and hold on to her humanity. Of course, she would lose the struggle. No Sorcerer could remain human. Even those that worked to protect humanity did not interact with it. There would come a point when she would cease to see people as people and herself as human, and then she would embrace her power for better or worse. Then of course there was the Oracle. If Ahlia managed to tap into its secret and unleash its power, then it would all be over. There would be another two hundred or so years of peace in the world of Sorcery. Sebastian had no doubt in his mind that Ahlia would follow in Mora's footsteps, and disappear from the world for all accounts and purposes. However, there was the threat from across the sea. Sebastian sensed an old and strong power. One he suspected to be as malefic as Ahlia was benific. There was always balance in the world. This must have been the force that Mora had defeated and kept at bay for so many years. How was it that Master Viad had never spoken of it? Sebastian moved from riddle to riddle, answering one question with another until his mind could take it no more.

* * *

Lex followed at what he hoped was a fair distance. He was sure she would detect him and then turn on him perhaps, but he could not stop himself. Yes, she was turning into something unfathomably powerful, but he also knew the other side of her. He knew she cared too much, and that would be her undoing. It would destroy her if she expressed it, and it would destroy her if she suppressed it. She was caught in a vice. A part of him was telling him to get out of the whole situation before he wound up dead, but another part of him just could not let go. As he walked, he cursed inwardly over and over at his own stupidity. He had no way of knowing how far she had gone. If she had broken into a run she could be miles away already. Even on horseback he might not be able to catch her up. He hoped her wisdom would overcome her emotion, and she would conserve her power in case she needed it. He wondered what would happen if she used up all her energy in a fight. She'd be a sitting target at the mercy of the most ordinary bandit. His stomach turned as he imagined possible scenarios. In her angry state she wasn't likely to think straight. He had to find her before she got herself into trouble. Still, she could be anywhere by now. Luckily, Deeb was also more than reluctant to leave his Mistress, despite whatever she might have to say on the matter. It was all Lex could do to hold the dog back.

A few hours later they spied an ethereal glow over the trees in the distance. Someone was using magic. The glow intensified, then faded, only to reappear a few hundred yards further away. Someone had found her first. Deeb growled and darted off into the bushes. Lex followed behind and found him standing over a prostrate body. It was the body of a mercenary, at least what was left of him. There were remnants of a chain mail shirt and a clean weapon lay just out of reach on the floor. He hadn't stood a chance. Ahlia had aimed for his face, but most of the top half of his body had taken the blast too, and was torn open by the force of her power. Lex and Deeb continued on, leaving one gory sight only to find another a few hundred yards further. There at the site where they had seen the second glow over the trees, lay three more bodies littering the ground like broken dolls. Lex inspected them. All had been killed by magic, but none looked like a Sorcerer to him. Then he noticed a leg poking out from behind a tree trunk. Cautiously he dismounted and with sword in hand went over to see who the leg belonged to. No one apparently, it had been seared clean off in a manner that no blade could match. A few yards further still between the trees, Lex found the owner of the leg and beside him the cloaked body of what he guessed to be the Sorcerer. Blood caked the Sorcerer's face but Lex could find no wound. What was visible of his face was unnaturally pale even for a corpse. It was as if the blood had simply poured out of his nose and ears and mouth, draining him of life. So, she had defeated her foes, but at what price he wondered. How much power had she used up? Was she hurt? He had to find her.

"Come Deeb," he beckoned, "let's find your Mistress."

She had not gone too far. On catching her scent, Deeb began to whine in earnest, pulling at the mental leash Lex had curbed him with, which consisted largely of warnings of what Ahlia might do to the dog if she caught sight of him following her. Very cautiously, they approached a small clearing between the trees. There sat Ahlia. Deeb was quiet, but cast a sorrowful eye towards his Mistress. Too afraid to go over himself after listening to hours of Lex's warnings of how Ahlia might act, he nudged Lex in the thigh with his wet nose. She was sitting with her back to them, leaning against an old tree stump. She was very still. Perhaps she had fallen asleep. Then again, perhaps she was hurt, or worse. She had let them get this close without stopping them. Lex took a tentative step forward, deliberately letting a twig crack under foot so that she might hear someone was there. He was certain she must know it was him. To his surprise and concern she did not turn around or even flinch.

"Ahlia," he called out softly. There was no answer. He continued to edge his way closer to her. It was only when he was almost upon her that he saw that she was crying. Tears streamed down her face, but no sound came from her. For a moment his tough calloused heart softened.

"Hey now," he said crouching next to her, "crying isn't going to change anything."

She tried to speak between soft sobs, "He... doesn't..." her sentence dissolved into a fresh stream of tears.

227

"I know," said Lex. He wasn't good at this sort of thing. He didn't know what else to say. Deeb had, on seeing that his Mistress seemed to have not killed Lex and so would probably not kill him, had followed in Lex's footsteps. When he saw the state Ahlia was in, he began whining quietly. He sat by Ahlia's legs and put his big head on her lap.

"Look now you're upsetting the dog!" said Lex.

He put his arm around her to comfort her. She burrowed her head into his shirt and sobbed loudly. "You er...stay right there until you're done," he said awkwardly. "You sleep right there. Deeb and I will take watch."

She had finally fallen asleep in the early hours of the morning. Lex looked up at the sky. Time was pushing on. They needed to get moving. His shoulder had gone numb. He shook it gently hoping to wake Ahlia at the same time. She did not move. He nudged her head with his stubbly chin. This time she moved her head, but did not wake. Her braid had come undone. He could smell her hair. It was sweet and warm. For a brief moment he forgot she was a Sorceress. As she rested in his arms she was just a beautiful, sad woman. On an impulse, he kissed her forehead.

"Ahlia," he whispered. "We have to move on."

She moaned to let him know she had heard him and rubbed her face with her hand.

As she came to, she remembered the events of the day before.

"Oh I have felt better," she murmured. "But at the same time I feel better too."

She raised her face up to smile her thanks at Lex, her eyes still sticky from sleep and dried tears. She could feel his face near hers. There was a thought, more like a knowing that the distance between them was slowly closing. She felt his lips on hers. There was a split second of panic before she allowed herself to plunge into the kiss. She was not sure if it was seconds, minutes or hours when they finally broke apart. She opened her eyes. Lex was wearing a somewhat shocked expression on his face.

"Um... we should be moving on," he mumbled sheepishly, "It's not safe to er....hang about."

The morning was cold and still. Ahlia's head however, was

whirling. Had she kissed him? She was sure he had kissed her. Well she thought he had kissed her. Oh Spirits had she kissed him? His face was a picture of shock. Even now he was avoiding looking at her. Spirits she had kissed him hadn't she! Why had she done that? Simple, she was insane that was why, completely insane. She cast a furtive glance in his direction. He appeared entirely focused on the road ahead. Oh what had she done!

They rode on for hours with only hunger pangs from Ahlia's stomach breaking the silence. Finally she could take it no more.

"Lex can we stop to eat?" she asked.

He had cocked his head to the side in trepidation at hearing his name and seemed somewhat relieved when he realised what she was saying.

"Of course, surely, I'll catch us something."

A little later they were picking meat off rabbit bones in front of a small fire. Ahlia felt she was about to explode from the awkwardness. She had just made up her mind to say something when Lex beat her to it.

"Listen Ahlia I… I er…" he paused as if trying to find the right words, "I hope you're not angry with me. I mean I'm an impulsive person. Well," he laughed nervously, "You know that better than anyone I guess… . What I'm trying to say is… I wasn't trying to… well you know… You were upset… and…" he gave up.

Ahlia was picking nervously at her leg of meat. She looked up briefly carefully avoiding catching his eye and nodded.

"It's alright, really, I'm not angry."

Why on earth did he think she was angry? Was it because he had kissed her back? Or did he think she might be angry because he hadn't kissed her back. Had it been him who broke off the kiss? It all seemed like a dream that she couldn't quite remember. Then she had a worrying thought.

"You're not angry with me are you?"

Lex raised a shaggy eyebrow in surprise "Me? No! Spirits! Why would I be?"

"Good. That's settled then I guess."

"It is?" asked Lex.

"Isn't it?" asked Ahlia anxiously.

"It is," Lex agreed firmly as if he couldn't believe his luck. "Just don't turn me into a toad or anything."

The tension was broken by laughter as Ahlia promised she wouldn't.

* * *

Brade, the Captain of the Dragon Guard rested his troops in preparation for the coming battle. The Sorceress was less than two days away now. As he looked about him, he noticed that the camp had divided itself into two parts, one human and one less human. They did not mix. While the men sat about smoking and playing dice games in the centre near the fires, his Master's creations sat on the periphery of the camp, deadly still. Eventually, over the course of the evening, the men one by one, lay down to sleep. The creatures remained alert and on watch. Fuelled by magic, they had no real need of rest.

Only when the last of his men had put his head down, did Brade follow suit. He was more mentally than physically tired. All day he had been listening to his Master's instructions as well as keeping track of his own thoughts. As he lay his weary head down, he wondered if there would ever come a time, when his Master's voice would no longer echo through his head.

Chapter 19

Ahlia awoke early the next morning and took great pleasure in watching the dawn break. It was a precious moment of peace where she could lose herself in the beauty of the world. How many times had she taken such a sight for granted, when she was certain in the knowledge that there would always be another one just one day ahead?

Lex kicked earth over the embers of the fire, and noted with relief the small smile on her face as she mounted. He thought he could even detect a rare sparkle in her eye. Neither of them suspected how effective a simple kiss had been in restoring part of Ahlia's humanity to her, and arresting the all consuming pull her power was having upon her.

Ahlia had refused to travel covertly anymore, and now they journeyed along a well worn dirt road much used by travellers and merchants. Ahlia's mind though more relaxed than it had been in many weeks, nevertheless was now automatically accustomed to scanning the path ahead and the terrain around them simultaneously. Suddenly, she let out an involuntary gasp, but she continued to ride on without comment thought her temporary ease was now clearly shattered. Lex strained his eyes to the crossroads that was coming up. A figure on horseback, clad in black sat waiting there by a worn wooden signpost.

"Sebastian," said Ahlia quietly. Lex's hand instinctively moved to his sword hilt. Ahlia halted her horse. She remained motionless for some moments as if transfixed. One thought filled her mind. Had he come to challenge her?

Sebastian waited patiently, careful not to make any sudden move that might be misinterpreted. He eventually risked making a slow bowing gesture in the hope that it would become evident that he wanted to talk. Ahlia's eyes never left him for an instant, but she could not move. She was afraid that the man she cared for had come to kill her and some part of her hoped that if she remained terribly still, she might stop time in its tracks and prevent the inevitable. Lex spurred his stationary horse into motion and began to trot towards Sebastian. Ahlia managed to let out a small cry of concern, but Lex staved her off with a wave of his hand.

"What?" he asked bluntly when he had ridden up close to the man that he had once called Simon.

Sebastian looked past him towards Ahlia.

"Don't even think about it," growled Lex. "She wants none of you and if you've come to hurt her, you'll have to go through me first."

"I don't doubt it," frowned Sebastian. "But as it happens, I am the least of your worries. In fact, I have come to help."

"Help!" Lex guffawed. "Go impale yourself."

Sebastian clenched his teeth as if to refrain from retorting. Lex pulled on his horses rein to head back, but Sebastian prevented him by moving his steed to cross Lex's path.

"She will die because of your arrogance. Is that what you want?"

Lex shot him venomous look.

"Is that what you want?" Sebastian repeated. "Even with me by her side, I do not know if she has little more than a fighting chance. The thing which comes for her is powerful. I cannot begin to tell you how powerful."

"And what's in it for you, eh? The Oracle is what. Don't tell me you're doing it for the love of her because you only care for yourself, and you have made that much clear even to her love-blinded perception of you."

The mention of love cut Sebastian to his core in a way that he was not prepared for, but he showed nothing of his discomfort.

"There is little point trying to hide that the Oracle is always in my mind. Whatever power seeks to take the Oracle from Ahlia, is a terrible and an ancient one. In truth, I know I would fare better with Ahlia as the holder of the Oracle than this other power which is as menacing and as cold as it is strong. Ahlia maintains the equilibrium as Mora did before her. There is a modicum of peace in the world as a result. I do not know what might happen if the power that hunts her should acquire the Oracle, but I suspect that its will is selfish and dominating. It would not go well for man or Sorcerer."

"Just as I thought," said Lex with satisfaction, "it is yourself you are concerned for."

He looked over to Ahlia. He knew she needed all the help she could get if she was to defeat the coming foe.

"You step one foot out of line and I shall crush you," he said threateningly.

"Believe me Lex. If either of us lives through what is to come, I shall be more than happy to let you try for the sport of it."

He looked past Lex once again to Ahlia, who unable to take the suspense no more, was riding up meet them.

"Ahlia," Sebastian said softly in greeting.

"Sebastian," she replied with a meekness that boiled Lex's blood.

"Will you accept the truce I proffer that we might together meet that which comes? I believe it is our only chance."

"Our?" she asked in surprise.

"What comes to crush you comes to crush all of us. It will stand for no competition."

"I see," replied Ahlia hiding her disappointment.

"It heads towards us from the Northwest."

"There is no avoiding it?" Ahlia asked, and though she already knew the answer a glimmer of hope still stubbornly remained.

"Not as long as you are in possession of the Oracle."

"Then I shall ride to meet it. It is time this was over. I am done hiding from fate," she said bitterly.

"Lex," her voice changed now to one of concern. "You need not be part of this. It is a matter for Sorcerers."

Lex stared hard at Sebastian and remained silent as if he had not heard her.

"Lex!" she said more loudly.

Still, he maintained a stubborn silence, his expression set as if in stone.

"He does not trust me Ahlia," Sebastian explained. "In fact, I suspect he is hoping for the chance to kill me. You will not succeed in turning him away."

Ahlia sighed heavily. Perhaps she would succeed in changing Lex's mind along the way. She was almost sure she was riding to face her death, and she wanted no company on her journey to the otherworld.

"What is it that comes for me?" she asked Sebastian, her brow knotted with concern.

"An Adept," he replied simply as if she should understand.

She looked at him questioningly.

"A Sorcerer of considerable age and notable power: not someone recently out of their apprenticeship like most of us, but someone who is practiced and determined," he explained.

"From where?"

Sebastian brought his horse close to hers and took hold of her hand.

"See with me," he instructed.

Ahlia first tentatively then more confidently allowed the boundaries of her perception to fall away in the union of their hands and minds. Power mingled with power to create a far reaching sense that skimmed over forest, rivers and villages for miles until she sensed a wall of such length that she could not move around it. She let out an involuntary gasp. What shield could be so huge, and what was it that lay behind it?

As if reading her thoughts, Sebastian uttered. "I do not know Ahlia, I do not know, but can you feel the power of it?"

Ahlia nodded.

"What is it?" asked Lex impatiently.

His question went unanswered. Sebastian let go of Ahlia's hand. He was looking at her strangely. In merging with her, he had tasted some of her power, and what he had discovered had amazed him mentally and sickened him physically. Fighting back the sensation of nausea and the saliva that was rushing to his mouth he commented,

"Your power is different to any I have encountered before. It is…" he searched for an appropriate word, "raw" he said finally.

"Is that good or bad?" asked Ahlia.

"We shall soon see," came his reply. "We shall soon see."

*   *   *

Sebastian led the way towards the Northeast, following the trail of power as it crept steadily towards them. The terrain about them changed to greener countryside, its beauty belying the danger of what was heading towards them. They left the road, cutting across the fresh green grass. Ahlia had pulled the Oracle from her pocket and was having one last desperate attempt at trying to understand how it might work. Sebastian had taken control of the reigns of her horse so she might concentrate better.

"I wish I could help you Ahlia, but in truth I know nothing of how the Oracle works. Those that do are long dead. Mora was the last to master it. Is there nothing she taught you that might help?" he asked.

Ahlia rolled the talisman over in her hand.

"I have tried over and over again, but I suspect that I am just not ready," she confided. "It is too strange in its power for me to grasp and it makes me feel nauseous even holding it sometimes."

Sebastian recalled how he had felt when he had merged with Ahlia and tasted her power.

"I understand some of what you say," he said.

"You do?" Ahlia asked in surprise.

"I know I cannot help you because your power is of an alien flavour to me. I do not know if it has always been so, or if Mora had something to do with transforming it, but the source of your power is unlike any other I have come across. If that is what is required to work the Oracle, I fear it would take me more than the time we have to understand its secret."

"Repulsive to you isn't it," she said accusingly.

Sebastian did not dare answer her.

"I feel it," she continued, "I feel it eating away at me, bent on being used, only being unleashed to destroy those who stand in my path. Sometimes I touch my face on waking, and half expect

235

myself to be disfigured or transformed beyond recognition. I feel I must somehow merge my power with the Oracle, but am tormented by the fact that I cannot. Whatever comes for me, I greet it happily, because at least it will end my dilemma."

Sebastian looked at her in shock.

"At least if I am dead, I can stop caring," she said in justification. She cocked her head to one side. "Ah, it comes," she said with uncanny relief.

Sebastian who had been distracted by listening to what Ahlia was telling him, scanned the horizon. He bit his lip with grave concern in a way which was uncustomary for him. Within moments what he had sensed was visible to the naked eye.

From over the hills before them, a dark thick cloud of soldiers swarmed over the countryside towards them.

"What are they? Man or creature?" asked Lex deferring to Sebastian's eyes which were keener.

"Both, a mixed infantry, by the Spirits there must be fifty of them at least!" gasped Sebastian.

More soldiers piled over the hill with every passing second.

"Closer to a hundred and fifty and more coming," said Lex gripping his sword all the more tightly, his jaw clenched in determination.

"We cannot win this," said Sebastian. "There are three of us and we dare not exhaust Ahlia's power."

Ahlia cast a dark eye at the approaching army.

"If I do not use my power, then we stand little chance."

"But there is a Sorcerer amongst them. I can sense the power, though it is strange as if it is both here and not here at the same time. I cannot understand it." Sebastian's smooth brow wrinkled in confusion.

"Perhaps this mighty Sorcerer is nothing but a coward, sending troops wrought by magic to do his bidding," Lex said with disgust. "He thinks like a strategist. How else might he test the power of that which he does not know the capacity of?"

Brade the Captain of the Dragon Guard, sent his soldiers before him. Normally, he would place himself before his men, but he had been given strict instructions. He was to let his men tire her out. Her companions would fall, and she would follow once her power was spent. From a safe vantage point, he watched his soldiers crashing down the hill.

Sebastian launched himself into the fray, his sword in one hand, his mage hand free to send destructive blasts of power out into the enemy. Lex pushed in after him slashing and stabbing with all his might. There were too many. Ahlia was gripped with terror as seemingly endless waves of soldiers appeared. She prayed to the Spirits that Sebastian would be able to hold his own while she used short bursts of her power to fend off the soldiers that were crowding about Lex. Sebastian pushed his senses through the bodies that pressed towards him and searched for the strongest source of energy.

"That one!" screamed Sebastian as he spied Brade on horseback in the distance.

Understanding his meaning perfectly, Lex nodded and gritted his teeth as he slashed through soldier after soldier to reach their leader. Perhaps if the leader fell, then the others would retreat.

Brade was watching the battle with little satisfaction. He was after all a soldier and disliked being forced to stand back from a battle, even one as ridiculously uneven as this one. Though he had to admit, the Sorcerer was something to contend with, and the woman had begun to use her power too. Nevertheless, all was going according to plan. Yet Brade was hardly happy. His soldiers were making adequate progress without him, but the smell of blood on the air made him hungry for the challenge of a hard fight. When he noticed Lex cutting a path through the soldiers towards him, Brade could not resist. Ignoring his Master's orders, he dismounted and walked to meet his challenger.

Lex thundered forward and smashed his sword upon the man's black helmet, but only succeeded in hacking off the crest that adorned it. They clashed swords over and over again, neither making any headway until a blast from Sebastian's hand knocked the Captain off his feet and turned his breast plate to solder. Before Lex could descend upon him, Brade vanished into thin air as his Master cloaked him from afar.

"Retreat!" his Master's voice commanded sternly from many miles away. "Retreat before you are undone."

Brade reluctantly heeded his Master, fleeing the scene, leaving his soldiers to their fate without a second thought. After all, more soldiers could always be created, but he was unique. He was angry at having been made to leave so obvious a victory and run like a coward, but the eyes that watched from a thousand miles away had seen the coming of something awesome that had caused them to give such a command. They had seen the vortex of power that was being created about Ahlia as wisps and strands of random aerial energy were called and fashioned into the shape of her intention. She had stood on the edge of the battle, using her power sparingly. She had waited for the Sorcerer to appear amidst the chaos and attack her, but no Sorcerer came. She realised her true foe would not come to face her until they could be sure of victory. They would send more and more monsters and soldiers and her days would be filled with death. Wandering into the fray, she released bigger and bigger blasts of power. She saw Lex, hopelessly outnumbered, get hewn down and trampled underfoot. She saw too that Sebastian's face was growing more haggard by the minute. Soon he would be drained of power and his sword would serve him little in the face of so many. He would fall. Ahlia looked about her with a deep spiritual weariness as all she saw about her was death and as her spirit ached so did her physical form in unison.

No more pain. I can stand it no longer, she thought. I can stand it no longer. She pushed all her intent inward and searched deep within her for a place that she did not until this moment know existed. It was a place of pure fury and cold will where she found nothing but a desire to destroy. All light fell away from her eyes until they were as black as the moon she was born under. Her face darkened as she tapped into this place of raw power, and from it cast a merciless hand over her opponents.

"No more!" Her thunderous voice echoed over the battle. Mage-fire of deepest purple sprang from her hands and moving centrifugally, obliterated everything in its path. Soldier after soldier fell and burned to crisp, then turned to dust in the relentless flame of her wrath. The grass despite its moistness, caught flame and turned into a sea of fire. The ground beneath trembled and shook causing all around her to stumble and falter, but she stood firm and resolute. The Oracle blazed in its secret pocket in response to the power that had been unleashed by its Mistress, the colour of the stone clouded over until it was jet black. Ahlia's eyes had become black orbs of infinite darkness, the whites utterly obscured.

"I am death!" she thundered in a voice that resounded over and above everything, "Fear me and perish!"

Waves of power lit the skies about her creating an effervescent glow that could be seen from miles away by the naked eye. All of Sorcery felt the impact of such terrifying power being unleashed. Under her hand even those soldiers who tried to run were disintegrated before they had taken more than two steps as the wave of mage-fire reached them. There were no prisoners. It was not until every one of her opponents was reduced to nothing more than a dry parchment version of their former being that, with incredible difficulty, Ahlia gradually curbed her power. The Purple flames drew back until all that was left of them was a glowing ember in the palm of her right hand, and the wisps of smoke that rose from the smouldering ashes about her.

As her cold fury subsided, the whites of her eyes became visible once again and she gradually returned to her senses. In absolute horror, she looked about at the damage she had done. The entire stretch of land before her was a mass of singed earth and charred bodies. Trees had turned to charcoal where they stood, and looked as if they would crumble to dust at any moment. Frantically, she searched the battle field, her eyes darting about in near madness as she looked for Lex and Sebastian. There, in a far corner, among the charred bodies, she made out two pale blue hazes of light. One, the brighter of the two, was moving towards the other which was fading fast.

Sebastian ran over to Lex who lay in a pool of his own blood. He was hanging on to life by a thread, but at least he was still alive. Most of Sebastian's power had gone into constructing a shield about himself to protect him from the wave of mage-fire that Ahlia had unleashed. He had just enough power left to seal up some of the wounds and stop further blood loss, but it would not be enough. He was astounded that Lex had not been burned to a crisp. A very faint shield had somehow automatically sprung up about the wounded mercenary. Sebastian had no idea where it could have come from.

Ahlia reached them, breathing heavily more from anxiety than fatigue and roughly pushing Sebastian out of the way with a strength that surprised him she poured all the power that she had left into the depleted body before her. Sparks of gold and green flickered about her as she rested her hands on Lex's chest. After some moments, when she had no more to give, the sparks spluttered and fizzled out.

"We must get him somewhere warm," she urged. "Help me Sebastian. I cannot carry him. My power is spent."

"You mean you didn't use the Oracle to do what you just did? The army? That was your own power?"

"Help me Sebastian," she begged ignoring his question. "He's badly hurt."

She stumbled as her legs buckled slightly beneath her from exhaustion and shock.

Sebastian stood transfixed for a moment. Here she stood. Powerless, the Oracle within his grasp. It was what he had always dreamed of. He could take it from her now by simple brute force. It was surely that easy and he would not even have to harm her. He could simply take it and run. As if reading his mind she stood upright to face him squarely with eyes that tore into his very being. In them, he saw two very different women. One pleaded with him not to destroy her faith in him, to help her save their comrade. The other looked at him from a place of unfathomable power that made his soul quake. This woman, he realised would not hesitate to tear him limb from limb with her bare hands before he was able to make a move towards her. Alone, either woman would have been compelling, but together, they were invincible. Abandoning any thought of confronting her, he hastily took up Lex in his arms and carried him to an abandoned horse, flinging him over the saddle as gently as he could so as not to re-open any of his wounds.

*   *   *

Over the seas, The Dragon Master smashed his fist upon the oak table before him in fury, and let out a bloodcurdling yell of rage. As the sound of his anger echoed through the room and faded, he composed himself. He had, after all, been careful to test her power, and it had paid off. Now at least, he knew what she was capable of. Unfortunately, he realised, now so did she. It was time for more drastic measures. He pulled at the vial which hung from the silver chain about his neck. It was nearly empty. He huffed in frustration. So much to control, it took so much effort. He could not simply leave his dominions to rule themselves, it would be too risky. His power seeped through this land, and made it his. He would have to bide his time, but return to this business, he would, for he would not be satisfied until the Oracle lay in his possession.

*   *   *

Lex opened his eyes many days later to find Ahlia by his side, the Oracle dangling from her hand. She had been examining it while she waited for him to regain consciousness.

"Welcome back," she greeted him as she replaced the talisman in its customary pocket.

"I have to say it feels strange being on this side of the healing process for once," she joked, though secretly she wished with all her heart that their roles were reversed. She had barely slept since the battle. She had feared she might close her eyes and wake to find him dead, and so had kept a constant vigil. The tiredness showed upon her face, but the dark circles under her eyes were due to more than fatigue and concern for her comrade.

"Very funny," Lex's voice cracked from a combination of disuse and a very dry throat. He pointed to the water that sat in a jug beside him. Ahlia poured out a glass and helped him sip from it.

"The worst is over. You are mending well. You will be good as new in a month or so."

"A month!" he must have been more seriously injured than he realised. Everything happened so fast and he had been mad with battle-fury. He had not felt a single blow, though now the memory of his wounds was becoming increasingly sharp.

"Just tell me one thing. That fop wasn't responsible for saving me was he? I think I'd rather die than suffer his gloating," said Lex falling back on his pillows.

"He helped seal some of your wounds, and the people here have been wonderful. I told them you were a battle hero and that you have saved my life many times."

Slowly fragments of memory pieced themselves more coherently in Lex's scrambled brain.

"But it was you who brought me back. After I had fallen, all became a dark haze, but I saw your face in the mist that surrounded me. It was your hand I took to find the way back."

Ahlia said nothing.

"That makes us even by my estimation," he continued trying to sound smug. "I've saved your life a few times, and now you have saved mine."

Ahlia could not help but smile. She nodded in affirmation. After a few moments silence she rose and turned her face away from him, busying herself with stirring the pot of stewed herbs on the table.

"I am glad you are mending well Lex," she said with more gravity than she intended. He looked over at her with the knowing of one who has been through much with another.

"Say it," he said. "Whatever it is, say it."

She bit her lip as she stirred.

"Now that I now you are going to be alright, I must thank you and bid you goodbye. I am leaving," she said as formally and with as little emotion as she could.

"Is that so?" he said grimly.

"I have given it much thought and I have reached a conclusion. I can take you with me no longer. I have no need of your sword, and I am tired of death."

The coldness of her words bit into him as sharply as any sword.

"What? But how will you protect yourself?" Lex asked weakly trying to prop himself up.

"I shall manage. A Sorceress has no place among ordinary people, Lex. A Sorceress such as I has no place even among her own kind. I must be alone," she rose to her feet.

"You hate being alone," he told her.

She did not answer, but turned her face aside so that he could not read her expression.

"You are leaving just like that! After all that has happened," he exclaimed bitterly.

"Because of all that has happened," she said, her voice cracking slightly, betraying her feelings.

"When are you going?" he asked.

"Now: you have been a noble comrade Lex. I am only sorry I could not make good my promise of payment to you. Rest assured, however, when I can, then I surely will."

"You will return to pay me?" he questioned, a glimmer of hope flickering in his eyes.

"I will have payment sent to you as quickly as I can," she answered.

"I see," he said, his voice loaded with unidentifiable emotion. He fell back upon his pillow, and with painful effort turned over to face away from her.

There was nothing more that she dared to say. She knew she had better leave now while her resolve was strong.

"Goodbye Lex."

Lex refused to answer her or even turn to look at her as she walked out of the room.

She had intended to pick up her bag, walk straight out and leave, but she was having trouble mustering up the necessary intent. Turning into the open doorway of the main room, she paused by the open fire and sighed heavily. As if in response the fire crackled loudly at her.

On hearing the noise, the lady of the house came out of the nearby kitchen where she had been washing dishes, to poke her

243

head around the door.

"I shall be leaving shortly," Ahlia said to her, though she was saying the words more as an affirmation for herself.

"Very good Miss," replied the woman.

"You have been a kind and generous hostess. I cannot thank you enough."

"Oh, think nothing of it," replied the woman bashfully, wiping her wet hands on her apron. After all, thought the woman, there had been more than enough incentive to be a good hostess: Ahlia had paid her most handsomely for her trouble.

"You will let him stay for as long as he needs, until he is recovered?" it was more a statement than a request.

"Of course! Do not worry yourself on that account," insisted the woman.

Ahlia nodded, pleased at the sureness of the answer.

"Then I shall partake of your warm fire a little, and then be on my way."

The woman nodded and took this as her cue to leave Ahlia to her thoughts. Once alone, Ahlia opened her bag and pulled out the battered book that Lera had given her. She needed to disappear without a trace, and the book might betray her with its power signature. After all, she thought bitterly, what had it taught her? Nothing, she was still none the wiser on how to use the Oracle. Without pausing to consider any further, she flung the book upon the burning logs in the hearth and watched with satisfaction as the flames fiery fingers probed the book, burning where they touched until the pages were curled and brown, then black, as paper slowly turned to ash. She gazed deeply into the fire, thinking to lose herself in stillness, but Fire had other plans for her. As her mind was drawn in to the flames they began to speak to her for they had read the book and they understood what she could not. She listened until they had finished speaking, her mind reeling with messages that were not communicated by words, but by energetic impressions. As if to indicate that the conversation was over, the fire died down in the hearth. The book was nowhere to be seen. Ahlia knew it was time to leave, though her heart wished to stay.

Outside, Sebastian was waiting for her with a horse.

"I think you are wrong in this," he said as she mounted the steed.

"There is no other way. This is best for all. You have seen what I am capable of."

She was racked with guilt over what she had done. She had unleashed her power in pure mindless fury and her only consolation was that somehow, Sebastian had managed to shield both himself and Lex from the force of her blast.

"I do not know myself anymore, and I have yet to even begin to fathom the Oracle. I have much to do. Do not concern yourself. I do not think anyone will bother me for a while after yesterday's display. I hope it will be a lasting deterrent to all who pursue the Oracle," she said making it clear that she included him in this statement.

Sebastian, fully understanding the weight of her words, nodded as he released the reigns of her horse and watched her ride off into the distance. He remained fixed to the spot, watching her until she was a speck on the horizon until, finally, he could see her no more. After standing alone absorbed in thought for some moments, he went to check on Lex.

"Not gone with her then," Lex said with malice.

"She did not ask me," replied Sebastian.

"I can at least take some comfort in that. She is better off alone than with the likes of you," Lex retorted.

"I take it you will not be heartbroken then to hear that I am returning to my home in the mountains, and that you are unlikely to see me again."

"Never would be too soon," growled Lex, wincing as he tried to sit up.

"Then I shall bid you farewell and leave you to resume your former occupation which I believe consisted of drinking ale, fornicating with barmaids and falling into debt."

Lex threw a string of unrepeatable oaths at him as he, laughing, walked out of the door.

It was over. Sebastian had only now to follow in his Master's footsteps, and be the best that he could be without the Oracle.

245

Strangely, he was, in a sense, relieved. He was looking forward to being in the mountains again. He too was tired of death and destruction. Perhaps now, they would all find some peace.

Part 2

Chapter 1

Over a year had passed since she had set eyes on a familiar soul or even exchanged more than a few words with a stranger. Sometimes she thought her heart would break from solitude, but there was no remedy. As the world of humans faded into the past, she immersed herself in the world of natural Sorcery, learning to master her connections with the elements and build upon her power. The Oracle now hung always about her neck, but though it remained ever warm, it never deviated from its inert state. Ahlia had come to perceive herself as the keeper rather than the wielder of the Oracle. She had stopped even trying to fathom its secrets and was simply grateful that she had managed over the year to recover part of her humanity once again. It had meant opening her heart once more to a myriad of emotions, and there had been many tears over the last four seasons and many lonely moments. With Deeb by her side the loneliness had seemed bearable, but he had passed away in the winter months, and the loss of him had grieved her deeply. She had cursed vehemently at the universe for giving her enough power to destroy hundreds, and not enough to prolong the life of the animal she cared for.

Time had passed and she'd waited for her opponents to find her, but strangely, no one came. She assumed that news had spread regarding her newfound capabilities. Potential rivals seemed to be giving her a wide berth, biding their time as they went about gathering their energies. It was purely a matter of when they would come rather than whether, and despite her abhorrence of violence, she was prepared for the inevitable fact that she would kill again in order to preserve her ownership of the Oracle. It was all she had now.

Unbeknown to her, the Oracle worked upon her despite not

being fully active, deepening her abilities, hardening her resolve, and gradually opening her mind to its language. The messages that she had gleamed from Fire the day she burned the book Lera had given her, had buried themselves deep in her mind, changing every thought pattern they touched. In her alienation from the world of humans, her mind formed new connections with the world around her. The trees became her kindred and the birds her companions. She learned to listen to the words of the wind and read images in the water. There were times she could not help herself and asked for news of Chara, Sebastian and Lex. To know that they were alive and well gave her great comfort though she missed them terribly. She often found her mind turning to them as she gazed into the fire. Was this the life that Mora had intended for her? Was this what it meant to be guardian of the Oracle? How long would it last?

Then the answer came. She heard it first on the Wind. Earth was still as was Water, but Fire crackled its warning. *He comes!*

Who comes? She asked, but she could not understand the answer.

She went outside to look out to the horizon throwing her senses out: Nothing.

Then the wind called to her. *Look up!*

She threw her senses up into the air. They hit something of colossal size and density. It was like nothing she had ever encountered before. Within seconds the sky began to darken and rain ash. Something was in the sky: something huge.

The darkness grew as a mighty black cloud descended from the sky. It landed a few hundred metres in front of her, sending violent tremors through the ground. The regal arch of its neck supported a head that was the stuff of nightmares. Long sharp teeth glinted in the sun. Two enormous yellow eyes fixed on her, pinning her down with their gaze. She was paralyzed with shock, completely unable to move. The creature smashed the ground with a mighty scaled claw, and opened its tooth spiked mouth to let out a blood curdling roar. Before her stood a thing out of legend, out of children's stories: a great black dragon. She tried to muster up her power to attack the beast, but could not draw upon it fast enough. The combination of shock and a year of peaceful living slowed her reflexes. Without touching her, the dragon lifted her off the ground. She tried to struggle against an invisible grip, but she found she could not move a single muscle in her body. It spun her round like a rag doll as it probed into her mind.

"He who commands me awaits you," its words boomed telepathically like thunder in her head. The dragon breathed blue steam out from its nostrils. Ahlia braced herself for being burnt to a crisp, but to her surprise the steam felt cool. Her wrists felt particularly cold. She cast her eyes down to see that they were bound by blue smoky manacles that seemed to be made from the dragon's breath. An invisible force propelled her forward towards the dragon's chest. As she got closer, she could see a thin chain around its neck. The manacles attached themselves to the chain, and the power that held her up suddenly vanished to leave her suspended like a human amulet around the dragon's neck.

"The bearer of the talisman, has become my talisman!"

The dragon's laugh boomed through her head as it pushed itself up from the ground and with a mighty lurch launched itself into the air with Ahlia dangling helplessly from its chain, screaming for all she was worth.

*　*　*

Hundreds of miles away, on a stretch of land outside his old deceased Master's house, Sebastian was practising his combat techniques. The shiny steel of his blade glinted in contrast to the pale snow covered surroundings. It was early spring in the mountains, but the snow had yet to melt. Sometimes it never did. Somehow, Sebastian felt it appropriate when it didn't. He had always felt more comfortable in the numbness of a seemingly eternal winter.

Suddenly, without warning, a searing pain hit him in his chest and caused him to drop his sword. He scanned the area about

251

him, his eyes wild with pain. He could see nothing. He threw his senses out; nothing. He put his hand over his chest to ease the pain as he struggled inside. From the area of the pain, an unbearable internal sensation of coldness was spreading. He stumbled into the house to find his Master's old room. Another needle of pain seized him and he leaned over the fire, supporting himself on the mantelpiece to let the flames warm him. Then as suddenly as it had come, it was gone, but this time it left behind it the sensation of a great vacuum; an emptiness. In that emptiness, as he tried to regain some of his body heat, he heard the sound of Fire's message and he knew.

* * *

It had not been hard to find Lex.

"It seems time hasn't changed you any Lex," he remarked, looking about him at the sordid décor of the tavern. He had slipped into the seat in front of Lex as the previous occupant got up to relieve himself.

"This place is a cesspit even by your standards. Do you know I actually had to step over an unconscious man to reach your table? He's just lying there on the ground in the dirt."

Lex, who had been peering into the depths of his beaker of ale, froze at the sound of the familiar voice.

"What in Spirits name are you doing here?" her growled without looking up.

Sebastian took a seat. "The Oracle," he said simply.

Lex rolled his eyes. "Oh no. I'm done with that."

"It's gone," Sebastian continued, utterly unconvinced by Lex's seeming lack of interest.

"Well maybe she finally came to her senses and threw the wretched thing away," Lex said reaching for his beaker and emptying the contents.

Sebastian's nostril curled slightly, but he maintained his cool countenance.

"You know she wouldn't do that. You know she couldn't. Ahlia is gone too."

"Rubbish, she's just cloaked herself. I don't have time for this," he said crossly as he gestured for the bar maid to bring him another beaker.

Sebastian slammed his fist on the table in irritation.

"I said she's gone. I found the remains of her cloak in Esher Valley."

Lex stopped what he was doing. "What do you mean the remains?"

"It had been shredded. It takes powerful magic to shred a cloak of that strength. I have only ever seen such a thing once before, when Ahlia's Mistress Mora was killed."

He knew he had caught Lex's attention when the mercenary waved away the bar maid who had come to refill his beaker. He knew the question that Lex wanted to ask, but could not bear to form. He answered it swiftly to put him out of his misery.

"She's not dead. I believe she has been captured."

"By who?"

Sebastian threw down a fragment of torn material that bore an insignia on it of a black dragon on a red background.

"Remember this?"

"Spirits!" Lex exclaimed. The insignia brought up a flood of memories that he had spent the last year drinking hard to forget.

"I took the liberty of holding on to it as a keepsake. I have searched all my old Master's texts and I can find only one mention of the Insignia. It is written that it belonged to a powerful Sorcerer sure enough, a Sorcerer who lived at least a thousand years ago during the time of the Wars of Sorcery.

"Wars?"

"Yes, too many Sorcerers and too little space. Sorcerers require a great deal of space."

"You mean territory."

"Whatever. Then to add fuel to the fire, there were the power objects such as the Oracle. To have the objects and wield them would…"

"Let me guess, make you Supreme?"

"Yes, and more. Some Sorcerers were not satisfied with the divide of power. It is a given fact that all Sorcerers always want more power."

Lex looked at him wryly.

"Really, I did not know that," he said with sarcasm.

Sebastian ignored him and continued.

"Some Sorcerers believed if they could have control of the objects of power, they could have control over everything, including ordinary men of no power, such as yourself and more importantly, other Sorcerers too."

Lex shot him an evil look.

"Because Sorcerers are far more important than ordinary folk aren't they Sebastian."

Sebastian sighed in frustration. Lex was not making things easy. Of course, he had anticipated that this would be the case, but there was no time to indulge him.

"The owner of this insignia was one such Sorcerer. This is the emblem of the line of the Dragon Master. What happened to the original Sorcerer is not documented except that he fled these lands and travelled across the sea after narrowly being defeated by Mazon the Wise during an attempt to gain possession of the Objects of Power. Mazon believed that the balance of power should remain as it was, separating man from Sorcerer and Sorcerer from power object. On realising the potential danger that the Objects of Power posed if in the wrong hands, he cast a spell of immense power that scattered the power objects through time and space, to keep them safe, and that is where the story ends. Except it appears that Mazon the Wise must have kept the Oracle himself, and handed it down to his apprentice and so forth until Mora finally gave it to Ahlia. Each time the Oracle changes hands, there is a window of opportunity to seize it before the new owner is able to wield it. However, once it has been used, its owner become far too powerful to overcome. Everyone retreats and waits for the next opportunity. We cannot help ourselves. We are drawn to the power of the Oracle like bears to honey. I do not know what the Oracle's particular power is, though I have my suspicions, but I can tell you that the desire for it is all consuming if a Sorcerer is not strong enough to fight it. Its pull is extraordinary."

"And yet she offered it to you and you refused it," said Lex.

Sebastian remained quiet, but his eyes spoke volumes.

"Ahlia has the Oracle. Surely she can defeat any of your kind that stand in her way?" asked Lex breaking the uneasy silence. His tone betrayed how desperate he was to be convinced that this was so.

Sebastian looked grave. "She has not wielded it yet."

"You saw what she did to all those soldiers," insisted Lex. She must have used to Oracle then.

"On the contrary, I think that it is exactly because of what she did to all those soldiers that she seems to have held herself back. I think she stopped trusting herself after what happened," said Sebastian.

"She's been holding on to that cursed stone all this time and not used it? After all she went through? After all she put us through?"

Lex ran his fingers through his shaggy hair, his eyes wide with disbelief.

"What in Spirits name was she doing in Esher valley?"

"I am not sure Lex. Growing, I suspect, learning to master her power, probably using the valley as a haven from other Sorcerers. The area is incredibly secluded. Not a soul for miles."

"Alone? She's been out there all this time alone?"

"Yes, it would seem so."

"But Ahlia doesn't like being alone," he said so softly, that he appeared to be talking more to himself than addressing Sebastian.

Sebastian did not understand the comment and felt embarrassed by it. It was moments like these that brought home the divide between Sorcerers and ordinary humans.

"It is quite customary for Sorcerers to spend the majority of their lives in solitude Lex. It ensures that they live longer for a start."

"All this time I assumed you, at least, would be in communication with her. If I had known she was on her own..." his words tailed off.

Sebastian grew impatient.

"Well she is not alone now. Someone has found her and has taken her and the Oracle. If we find the Sorcerer using this insignia, I wager we'll find Ahlia. Will you help me find her?" Sebastian asked in earnest.

"You're supposed to be a great Sorcerer. What's the use of all that magic if you can't even find one small woman!" Lex said venomously.

"Lex this isn't easy for me. I'm asking for your help. I cannot find her alone. Believe me I've already tried."

Lex looked at him incredulously.

"How long has she been missing?"

"A week, maybe two, I'm not sure."

He made no mention of the pain he had felt at his home in the mountains. The sensation, he suspected, of her screams.

Lex leaped up from the table in rage.

"And you come to me now when the trail is probably ice cold! I ought to kill you where you stand."

"There will be time enough for that later. Right now, Ahlia needs us."

"Don't insult my intelligence. You just smell a chance to grab the Oracle."

"Believe what you like."

Lex kicked the chair away and put his hand on his sword.

"If she's hurt, I'm holding you responsible."

"Fine, but right now we don't have time to lose. I believe Ahlia and the Oracle have been taken across the sea. It is several days ride to the nearest port. If Ahlia's captor activates the Oracle, it will not just be Ahlia who suffers."

He paused for a moment and looked Lex squarely in the eye.

"I've a fresh horse outside waiting. Will you come or not?" he asked in a tone that demanded an immediate answer.

"Of course I'm coming," replied Lex as though there had never been any doubt.

Lex stepped outside with Sebastian to find three horses waiting. One already had a cloaked rider on its back.

"And who is this?" asked Lex suspiciously.

The rider pulled back their hood. It was a young woman. Her

head was covered in soft sandy curls and her eyes were a piercing blue.

"This is Rhianad. She is a Sorceress, a friend of mine."

Lex arched his brow. "I didn't think Sorcerers made friends with one another."

"This is... different."

"I see."

Lex stared at Sebastian as if he had just crawled out from under a rock. It was a look that left no doubt that he wished Sebastian would crawl back under that same rock so that he could squash him under it.

* * *

They rode towards the shoreline, through the night and into the next day, mostly with Lex leading the way. Sebastian had to agree that Lex was the expert terrain man and had knowledge of the more pedantic things that a Sorcerer might easily over look. Thus he had acquiesced and allowed Lex to ride on slightly ahead while he and Rhianad followed behind.

Rhianad asked Sebastian again and again about Ahlia, but he always told her the same things. She was certain there was more to know and that Sebastian was concealing things from her. She made an excuse about checking on the route and rode ahead to catch up with Lex.

"You knew her well I understand," she said, "Ahlia, I mean."

"I know her well," he corrected her, "as well as anyone can."

"Sebastian often speaks of her."

"Does he now?" Lex spat the words out.

"She seems to be quite a woman."

Lex sighed. "Yes she is. Like no other I'll wager."

"The wielder of the Oracle, the Supreme among Sorcerers," Rhianad recited, her voice was filled with awe. "The second woman in a thousand years to hold the Oracle!"

"Hmm, she smells good too," he said wistfully, "sort of warm and a bit flowery."

Rhianad looked at him as though he had just blasphemed.

"I'll never understand why the idiot turned her down, but then I guess he just wasn't man enough," he continued oblivious to her disapproval.

She shot a startled glance back at Sebastian to see if he could hear. To her relief, he seemed oblivious enough.

"Yes that would be right," Lex murmured to himself, "only a small man like him would be intimidated by a woman's power."

"I take it you were not," she said archly.

Lex grew quiet for a minute. To Rhianad his silence spoke volumes.

"I'm not good enough for her. She deserves better," he said quietly.

"She told you that?"

"No. But it's a fact. You'd have to meet her to understand. She's a serious woman, a special woman. I've been a ...well, you know where you found me and I'm sure Sebastian has filled you in on the rest."

"He says you're a womanising wretch of a drunkard who sells his sword for a drink."

"Can't argue there I'm afraid. As I said, Ahlia deserves better."

"Sebastian doesn't drink or womanise," she mused.

"I said better, not stiffer! Sebastian is a selfish power hungry fool," he growled.

"Ah. Now I am beginning to understand," she said.

"Understand what?"

"Well," she said matter-of-factly, "It is obvious to me that you are both in love with her, but you are also both terrified of her. Neither of you has the courage to be with her, but neither of you wants the other to be with her either. Poor woman. No wonder she left."

"And what exactly is your part in this Miss Sorceress?" he asked hotly.

"Oh me? I've nothing to hide. I'm in love with Sebastian. I think I am at least. He wants to rescue Ahlia and the Oracle. I go where he goes."

"And it doesn't bother you that Sebastian might have feelings for Ahlia? Though I think you're wrong to imagine that Sebastian can feel deeply for anything except the Oracle."

Rhianad shrugged. "It is better that I know sooner rather than later," she said.

"Also," she added as an afterthought. "The more I hear about this woman, the more I want to meet her. Of course, there is also the Oracle itself."

Lex gave her a sharp look.

"I don't want it," she continued hurriedly to appease his concern. "Well, that's not true actually, I do. Every Sorcerer does. It's like a pull in the blood, but I know it is not for me. I just want to see it. To know what it is about."

"You mean you don't know either?"

"No one does really, though Sebastian knows more than most. His Master Viad was once a close friend of Mora's. Viad's Master was also a formidable Sorcerer and, it is said, was a lover of the written word. Very little is documented about the Oracle. Whatever it was the elder Sorcerers knew, they took the knowledge with them to the grave. It is as if to even write or speak about it was too dangerous."

"Yes fascinating," said Lex flatly. "I think the thing would be best off at the bottom of the sea."

"Why such animosity towards the Oracle?" asked Rhianad, although she suspected she already knew the answer.

"That thing nearly got me killed. Wherever it goes, trouble follows," he answered.

"Oh, is that so?" she answered innocently. "I thought you might hate it because Ahlia chose it over you."

Lex's lip stiffened. He opened his mouth as if to reply, but then seemed to think better of it and spurred his horse on to leave Rhianad behind once again.

They stopped briefly to catch and cook some lunch. Lex caught some fowl and skinned and cleaned the carcasses before throwing them onto the fire to roast. Rhianad found the process revolting. She seldom ate meat. As it cooked, she announced her intent to have a wander around the area to escape the smell of burning flesh. As soon as they were alone, Sebastian spoke.

"Lex you haven't had any strange dreams or sensations over the past year?"

"What do you mean strange?"

"I don't know exactly what I mean."

Lex gave him a weird look. "No. I haven't," he replied.

He shoved some more wood into the fire and turned the meat.

"I don't dream. Except…"

"Except what?"

"It's personal." He said gruffly.

Sebastian leaned forward in earnest. "I'm asking because it might be important."

"In my dreams I can smell her hair sometimes, is all. Ahlia's hair," he said reluctantly.

"I don't know why and I don't remember anything else. I mean it's not like I'm dreaming of being with her or anything, just the smell of her hair."

Lex braced himself for berating remarks, but to his surprise there were none. Sebastian rubbed his clean shaven chin in thought.

"When was the last time you dreamed that?"

"Well not for a while now you come to mention it."

"A few weeks or so?"

Lex could finally see where the line of questioning was going. "Yes a few weeks."

Sebastian nodded. "I thought it would be so. So a few weeks she was far enough for the link not to be broken, but since then has moved further away."

"What link?"

Sebastian did not hear him. He was lost in thought.

"Water, it must be water. Only a large stretch of water would diminish her power so. Her element is fire. He must use water as a shield. It has to be the sea. I'm sure we're going in the right direction."

"What link?" asked Lex again, loud enough this time to snap Sebastian out of his ruminations.

"I don't know. I think I shall probably spend my whole life

trying to work out that Lex, but a link there is: a bond between her and us. She created it I think. She may have left, but she never quite let us go."

"Or we her perhaps," added Lex.

Both were quiet for a while.

Then Sebastian said finally, "If you dream of her or any thoughts come to you about her as we travel let me know. I am sure that Ahlia has learned to dream journey by now. When she is able to, I think she will try to communicate with us."

"Dream journey?"

"Yes, travel in spirit through the dream world to covey a message. Doesn't she ever speak to you when you dream of her?"

"Yes sometimes. Sometimes she says I drink too much."

He jumped with realisation. "Are you saying she can put herself in my head?"

Sebastian grinned. "Not just yours. Not just yours. It would seem that she just cannot keep away from us."

Lex thought for a moment. "What does she say in your dreams?" he asked trying to hide his burning curiosity.

"Sometimes it's not what she says that is important," Sebastian said as with as much nonchalance as he could muster, but he could not resist quickly casting a furtive glance in Lex's direction. "It's more what she does!"

He got up and turned away before Lex could see his face break out into a sly grin, leaving Lex to violently poke at the cooking meat as if his was trying to kill it all over again.

When Rhianad returned with her harvest of strange looking mushrooms, some fat root vegetables and some shoots, she stopped dead in her tracks. The air about the fire crackled with tension and Lex's expression was dark and stormy.

"And what exactly have you boys been discussing?" she asked.

"We were considering Ahlia's whereabouts. I'm sure she's across the sea," Sebastian answered.

Rhianad went to sit by the fire. She pulled out a small knife and began to whittle a small stick.

"There are a lot of lands over the sea. We still are almost none the wiser."

She skewered the mushrooms one by one and placed them over the flames. The roots she placed directly into the fire to roast slowly.

"We will find her. I say we head for the closest land over the sea. Once I'm there I will probably be able to sense her," said Sebastian with confidence.

"And if you don't?" asked Rhianad.

Sebastian had no answer for her. He stared into the flames, his countenance as dark and stormy as Lex's.

Chapter 2

Four soldiers were ready and waiting when the dragon landed on an empty stretch of grassy ground. They were taller than ordinary men and each wore a bronze visor and ornate armour. On their arms they all bore the same crest of a black dragon against a red background.

She was still unconscious when the soldiers brought her to him. He had come out to meet them close to where the beast had landed. It had dutifully released its prey to the soldiers, and crawled into a rocky opening in the side of the hill, but not before booming in an ominous tone;

"Tell the Sorcerer who is Master of both you and I that I do not like this work. He cannot hold me forever. There will come a time when he can no longer use my blood against me to force me to do his bidding thus. I am dragon. With each year I age, I grow stronger. He will not hold me forever."

The Captain of the Dragon Guard said nothing to the beast from which his office took its name, but deep in the recesses of his heart he felt the dragon spoke the truth, not only of its situation, but of his own. For Brade too was growing stronger, he felt, with each year. Soon, he thought to himself, he would be strong enough; soon. He looked down at his prize as she lay in the arms of the soldier.

The altitude had all but frozen her and her lips had almost turned blue, but she was beautiful. Not in the same way that his Master's concubines were beautiful. Her beauty was raw. It spoke of open plains rather than lush quarters and natural smiles rather than false laughs. She smelt of freedom not servitude.

"Leave her with me. I shall take her in."

Bowing their heads in deference, the soldiers handed Ahlia's limp body over to him. When they were out of sight, he knelt down and lay her gently on the floor. He removed his large black studded gauntlet and stroked her cheek with his rough bare hand. Then he reached down beside her body and scraped up some wet earth from the ground. He carefully and gently smeared it over her face and clothes and caked her hair with it until she was filthy and her features barely discernable. When he was done, he picked her up and flung her across his horse, climbing into the saddle himself and setting off in the direction of the rooftops of the palace just visible in the distance.

* * *

They were approaching a crossroads. Rhianad overtook the two men and road on to the left before they had a chance to even read the signpost.

"Hey!" yelled Lex, "I thought Sebastian said she was across the sea. The port is to the right."

Rhianad stopped her horse.

"We travel this way. I have a stop to make."

She spurred her horse on again.

When Lex looked to Sebastian for an explanation, he shrugged and seemed equally baffled, but he knew better than to argue with Rhianad.

"She'll have a good reason. She usually does. Regardless of that, the matter is not up for discussion by the looks of things."

They spurred their horses on to catch up with her until they were each either side of her. Neither of them asked her anything out aloud, but she knew they wanted an explanation.

"I want to ask someone for their advice. Unlike you two foolish egotists I am not happy about travelling over the seas to a land I don't know, to fight Spirit knows only what army, and or Sorcerer who happens to be holding the Supreme Sorceress, who I have never met and may also have the Oracle, an object no one really knows much about."

"She's got a point," said Lex, as Rhianad took in a deep

breath after her tirade,

"I hadn't thought about it that way."

"True," agreed Sebastian, "although we should not forget that I am a pretty powerful Sorcerer and Lex here is a dab hand with a sword." he said in a tongue in cheek tone.

"Oh, please, this is no time for bragging," replied Rhianad un-amused.

After fifteen minutes or so, Rhianad indicated it was time to turn off the main road into a forest thicket. The trees became denser and denser and the sky became less and less visible until it was almost entirely obscured by a green canopy with only the occasional shaft of sunlight peeping through. The surroundings became gradually more and more eerie, and there was a definite chill in the air that had not been there before. For no apparent reason, the horses were becoming increasingly unsettled.

"There!" hissed Lex suddenly, his hand going for his sword. Sebastian followed his gaze to see a grey wolf watching them from a shadowy area through the trees. It was there and then it was gone. Rhianad did not appear in the least bit interested or distressed, but carried on walking.

"Where in Spirits name are you taking us?" asked Lex.

"Home," she answered pointing to a small wooden hut in a small roughly hewn clearing in front of them.

She walked up to the door and knocked. It opened and a woman came out to greet them.

It was hard to tell how old she was. Her eyes seemed bright and young, but her face was haggard and wrinkled, and her hair was as grey as the wolf they had seen.

"Welcome." She ushered them into her dwelling.

"It has been a long time," the woman said to Rhianad.

"Yes, it has," Rhianad answered.

"You require my advice I expect."

"I do."

"'Twill cost you."

"I know. The usual?"

"Why not!"

Rhianad gestured for Lex and Sebastian to sit.

"This is Samia. She is, if there was any doubt in your mind, a Witch, a powerful Witch." Samia nodded in agreement whilst chuckling at Sebastian who was endeavouring to find a less dirty spot on the floor, taking care to sit on his cloak rather than get his trousers dirty.

"That's right, a daughter of the Earth I am. Not a pompous Sorcerer who thinks to better the Mother of Nature." She spat into the fire.

"I take it she isn't fond of Sorcerers," ventured Sebastian.

"No," said Rhianad. "She is not."

"And what can a Witch tell us that we cannot find out for ourselves?" he asked.

Samia cackled.

"Ever the egotists, hence even the strongest of you is plucked from the ground like a worm by a giant bird and carried over the sea."

Sebastian fell silent while Lex perked up.

"Seems she can tell us a fair bit by the sounds of things so far. I'm not a Sorcerer by the way, so if you're turning anyone into toads, you can exempt me old mother."

The Witch looked at him with eyes that seemed to bore through him.

"Not a Sorcerer eh?" she smiled strangely in a way that made Lex uncomfortable.

"What more can you tell us?" he asked hastily.

Samia took a black iron pot from next to the fire and set it in front of her. From an earthenware jug she poured out some water until the pot was filled.

She took a deep breath, looked into the pot and concentrated.

"I see a scaled bird breathing fire, the colour of the void upon blood, a crest."

"Who does it belong to old mother?" Lex asked.

"Mighty he is, the drinker of the blood."

"I don't like the sound of that!" exclaimed Lex before the others hushed him into silence.

"You cannot defeat him. If she could not, you have no hope.

266

Not with your ways. He will see you. He sees me, but he does not care. I am but an old Witch and no threat to him. He has the arrogance of a King and a King he is."

"A King and a Sorcerer," reiterated Rhianad for clarification.

"Indeed, beyond your years and mine and my mother's, such is the power of the blood."

She stretched out her hand first towards Sebastian then towards Lex and smiled.

"She is alive, but unable to help herself. He has her in his grip. You must go to her."

She started in surprise as she looked into the pot once again. "She is young! Young to her power, but her power is old. It is and it is not of this plane. How strange. I cannot explain."

The woman pulled away from the water as if afraid she might fall into the pot head first.

"Enough. I can see no more without him becoming suspicious. Even a Witch he will tolerate only so far. It is to the Wylderlands that you must go. That is where he resides. That is where you shall find the woman you seek. Loved by the Old Gods she is, for she has heard their voice."

"Thank you," said Rhianad. "You two wait outside for me. I'll be out shortly," she told Lex and Sebastian. She waited until she and the Witch were alone before speaking.

"Now tell me the rest of what you saw. All of it."

The old Witch looked Rhianad straight in the eye with a confident and familiar knowing.

"I see you are heading against a very powerful enemy and your chances are slim."

"I know that."

"There will be difficult choices to make. There is division between you regarding your priorities, a division which goes to the root of things."

Rhianad sighed, "Sebastian."

"Hungry you were born into this world, and if you are not careful it will be hungry that you die. I knew the day I first put you to my breast, that my milk would never quench you. Insatiable is the appetite for power amongst your kind. You

Sorcerers will never have enough. You would have been better sticking with your birthright and the ways of the Earth Mother."

"You know sometimes mother, I think you may be right, but I have made my bed."

"For him to sleep in it?" hissed the old woman as she poked through the door towards Sebastian. "Tread carefully. He has a heart that is torn already in two directions. With you it will make three. Is that all you are worth? One third of a shallow heart? I think my daughter is worth more than that. I know she is."

"Alright mother, enough. You have exacted you price as usual. I have listened to your opinions on my life, and I promise I will consider what you say."

"The door of your home is always open. I would that you not go on this endeavour. I fear for you." She reached out towards Rhianad, but did not touch her.

"I must," Rhianad replied with resignation.

The old woman said nothing. She knew her daughter was right. This was her destiny.

"Then at least let me give you some things that might be of use to you if you don't turn your nose up at such Witches tools. For all his arrogance, that young fool out there has no true notion of the magnitude of the foe you face. He only thinks he does."

She spat into the fire again, and yanked a sack off a hook on the wall. She walked to a small cupboard and began to fill the sack with various things.

"Thinks he's very high and mighty. You've more power in your little finger. Does he know?"

Rhianad remained silent, but could not help smiling to herself at the comment.

"No, I thought not. You'd be better off with the other. His heart runs deep, and though the surface might be an almighty mess, the essence is true, but I suppose you'll end up being as foolish as I was. Your father was an arrogant fool, but he did look fine. Sorcerers always do. They wear their power well when all is said and done," the witch mused.

Finally, she handed her the sack when it was almost full.

Rhianad tested its weight. It was surprisingly light.

"Nothing in there you don't already know how to use. Unless you've forgotten, being as now you're a Sorceress and all."

Rhianad pushed through the invisible barrier that seemed to exist between them and taking the old woman's hand, she brought it to her forehead in reverence. She had not forgotten her roots despite the old woman's fears.

"Thank you mother."

The old woman's face softened and she leaned forward to embrace her beloved and only child.

"May the Goddess watch over you and protect you from those with hard hearts."

*   *   *

"About time!" remarked Lex as Rhianad reappeared from the hut. "We were beginning to think she'd put you in that pot of hers and eaten you!"

"Witches don't eat their daughters," said Rhianad bluntly as they mounted. She didn't have to see the look on Sebastian's face to picture it.

"And who were your parents Sebastian. Duke and Duchess I suppose?"

"As a matter of fact they were, I think."

"And how much of use did they ever teach you? I knew how to poison a man in five different ways before I was seven years old and how to heal him too. I cast my first spell at ten."

Lex sniggered as Sebastian squirmed visibly in his saddle. "I wouldn't upset her if were you!"

"I thought you were a Sorceress," said Sebastian frostily.

"No law against having two careers is there?"

"I can't imagine who in Spirits name took you on as an apprentice knowing you were the daughter of a Witch?"

"That would be my father Sebastian. He was quite a well known Sorcerer. Efanad. Perhaps you've heard of him, but of course you have. I caught you stealing from his library not so long ago if you recall."

Lex was struggling in vain to stop himself from laughing too loudly.

"Of course my parents never married," she added.

Sebastian could not believe his ears, matters were getting worse by the minute.

"Oh don't look so shocked Sebastian. Does knowing that you are bedding the illegitimate daughter sired by a Sorcerer off a Witch upset your delicate sensibilities so much?"

Sebastian swallowed hard as he took in all that she had said. He had never seen her act or speak in such a way before. She had always been quiet and deferent towards him. For the first time he realised how much he had underestimated her. He looked at her defiantly and said, "Beauty is beauty and power is power however it was begotten."

Rhianad nodded stiffly to display her approval of his answer.

"Well saved Sebastian" Lex winked at him.

*　*　*

They rode on until they reached the port of Sincar. Much to Lex's dismay, the witch had validated Sebastian's fears that Ahlia had been taken overseas and so a boat journey was inevitable. He eyed the vast expanse of the ocean with dread, much to Sebastian's amusement.

"Don't tell me you get sea sick Lex," he teased.

"I wouldn't know. I've never been on the sea before. I've always done my fighting and my drinking over this side on dry land, where I belong."

"Your remarkable lack of exposure to anything outside your small realm of existence never ceases to amaze me," commented Sebastian in mock fascination.

"Just choose a ship that will get us there in one piece," replied Lex curtly.

Sebastian laughed and walked towards the first of a series of ships that was moored on the quay.

"Not that one," shouted Lex after him, "It looks… old."

Sebastian held back his mirth as he bowed his head and conceding to Lex's wishes, abandoned that particular vessel.

Sebastian soon returned to announce that he had procured passage across the sea on a sturdy vessel. It was to be at least a day and a night before they reached the other shore and so he had negotiated with the captain for use of the two vacant cabins so they could get some rest. Rhianad insisted on having a cabin to herself. Sebastian had pulled her to one side after her announcement regarding the cabin arrangements.

"Don't give me that look," she had said archly. "You two need to bond. Besides, I'm not sure if I'm still angry with you or not. I need time to think," she said firmly, and disappeared into her cabin. As she eventually settled down to have a much needed sleep, she chuckled in amusement at the thought of Sebastian and Lex sharing a cabin together.

Both men had also decided to take full advantage of the soft cabin beds and had turned in early.

"Gone off you already has she?" Lex couldn't resist the dig.

"No, she just thought I should keep an eye on you. That is all," Sebastian replied.

"Of course she did."

Lex grinned to himself in the dark. To his surprise, the Sorcerer didn't rise to the bait. Lex was beginning to think Sebastian had fallen asleep when a boot came hurtling out of nowhere and hit him in the head.

"Oh a veritable feat of magic that was to be sure!" he yelled.

Sebastian sniggered in the darkness until he could hold back no longer and burst out laughing. Lex also began to laugh heartily despite himself. It was some time before the laughter died down.

"Oh, I needed that," chuckled Sebastian.

"Yes," agreed Lex. "So did I."

Soon they were both fast asleep.

The next morning Lex awoke early, but he did not rise. Instead, he lay in his bunk turning matters over in his mind. Sebastian eventually awoke some time after. Still half asleep, he groaned and swung his legs over the edge of the bunk, blindly groping around the floor to find his socks and boots.

"Sebastian, I've been meaning to ask you something."

"What?" Sebastian asked yawning loudly.

"That night when Ahlia offered you the Oracle. Why didn't you take it?"

Sebastian stopped what he was doing and sat still for a moment. Then he got up and splashed his face with cold water from a bowl. Lex got up too and pulled his boots on. He sat on his bunk waiting for Sebastian to say something. When Sebastian realised that Lex was in earnest, he said finally,

"It was humiliating. She was humiliating me. She was telling me that she knew I couldn't defeat her."

"How do you know she was doing that? How do you know that she wasn't simply saying that she knew to beat her you'd have to kill her and that she didn't want to die? She was giving you a way out. By rejecting it you were telling her you'd rather kill her," Lex argued.

"Rubbish. I have other proof of her pity. What about when she let me escape the time I drew swords with you. She could have killed me, but instead, she chose to let me know she did not consider me a threat by sparing my life. She knew I would return and it did not scare her. She knew I couldn't defeat her. She knew it in her soul."

"Did it not occur to you that maybe she just didn't want to kill you?"

"How would you feel if a woman offered you pity. Don't tell me you would accept it."

"Sebastian, she offered you the Oracle in good faith. She cried her heart out after you refused it."

Sebastian's features darkened.

"Well I was not in the best of moods myself that night I can assure you."

Lex grunted in frustration at Sebastian's self-centredness.

"It wasn't the first time she'd cried over your sorry self, you know 'Simon'. Moreover, it wasn't pity she was offering you."

The point Lex was making penetrated and registered. Sebastian sighed heavily.

"I know what she is worth, believe me, but she confuses me and scares me at the same time. She is a mass of contradictions. Hugely power and hugely vulnerable in a way that I just cannot fathom. Then there is the issue of the Oracle and that will never disappear. I do not expect you to understand Lex, but she is chosen as the wielder of the Oracle and as such will always stand apart. She is a sun whose heat is just too much for me. Her light is just too bright. She will always outshine me and I just cannot bear it."

"You are right. She will always outshine you, but not because she holds the Oracle. She outshines you because she was and is willing to do what you cannot, give everything up for the sake of love. She cares. She cares that much and because of that she deserves the Oracle. It's not the Oracle that makes her Supreme. She was always Supreme, and it is because of that she has ended up with the Oracle. It has chosen her because she has heart. I've seen none to come even close to competing with her on that score. None of your kind and none of mine."

In the back of Sebastian's mind, a faint memory stirred of a conversation he had once had a long time ago with his old Master, Viad.

"I know," he said quietly, "as I said, I know what she is worth. I suspect she will be all my regret."

"It's not too late," proffered Lex. The words were painful to speak and he almost choked on them, but he had to say them.

"You don't understand. I cannot change my nature. To be with her, I'd have to become someone else. You of all people should be able to understand that."

"What should I understand?"

"Oh please Lex! I overheard you talking to Rhianad, all that 'I don't deserve her' business. How weak an argument is that? According to your advice to me you should seize the opportunity and make a better man of yourself, change yourself to deserve her."

"It's not as simple as that," Lex said gruffly.

"It is for me apparently, why isn't it for you?" Sebastian asked sarcastically.

"Because she's never looked at me the way I've seen her look at you!" Lex erupted, his voice trembling with hurt.

There was an awkward silence before Lex found his voice again.

"I may seem the same on the outside, but it stops there. I couldn't help but change, from the moment I met her and every day since. Just knowing her changes a man, but loving her, loving her I think could transform him."

Sebastian was taken aback.

"I had no idea you love her that much."

"Well I find that I do," Lex said quietly, swallowing back the emotion he was feeling.

He didn't know exactly when he had realised. It had crept up on him. At first he thought his old sense of pride was kicking into action. He wanted to do his job and protect his charge, who just happened to be a beautiful, remarkable woman. Then out of nowhere the yearning had begun and he had ignored it. It had intensified with 'Simon's' arrival and he had called his feeling 'suspicion' and felt justified when 'Simon' had turned out to be Sebastian, but that had been a false diagnosis. His true ailment and reason for disliking 'Simon' had been jealousy. It was not until Ahlia had finally sent him away that he had begun to understand his feelings. He could not ignore the gradual comprehension brought on by an ache which grew daily. It made him aware that instead of fading into the back of his mind, the memory of her became more and more poignant and vivid with each passing day, and the unacceptability to him of her absence more apparent. Then there were the dreams, bitter sweet. He went to sleep in hope and dread; hope of seeing her once again and dread of waking to find it was just a dream. He no longer recognised himself. The things he had valued, he no longer relished, and things that he once had had no time for, now mattered to him beyond belief. He had become a man of principle. He had become a man who cared about things. He had become a man who suffered the anguish of unrequited love. He was a man haunted by the memory of a kiss. Not all the ale in the world could numb his agony.

"Can you understand now why a part of me hates you for what you do to her?" he spat the words out at Sebastian like daggers.

Without waiting for a reply, he walked out of the cabin, slamming the door behind him, leaving Sebastian alone with much to think about.

*   *   *

They reached land late that morning. They had made some enquiries and found that the port and all the territories for miles around were under the domain of a single King, but the outskirts such as the port itself were sub-ruled locally by the original Clan-Chiefs of the lands. Some Clan Chiefs were peaceable and friendly, while others guarded their territory jealously. Nevertheless despite any minor disputes between the Clan Chiefs, all owed allegiance to one man, Emperor Myron. They had learned that Myron's palace was far inland and they had set off in the direction as pointed out to them. As soon as they disembarked, Sebastian appeared ill at ease and the further they got away from shore, the more uneasy he became. Even the horses at seemed nervous initially, and though this could have been due to the ordeal of the boat trip, Sebastian was not convinced. After riding for a while, he called for the others to halt. He dismounted and looked about him warily. Then he knelt on the ground and pinched a handful of earth, rolling it between his fingers and closing his eyes. His wrinkled brow made clear the level of his concentration, and his concern.

"What is it?" asked Lex.

"Power, a lot of it and not elemental, but generated by sorcery. It seeps through the earth. If we use any magic, even to light a candle, he'll detect us. In fact, he might already know we are here."

He picked up a handful of earth and held it out to Rhianad, who dismounted in order to receive it into her hand. Her lip pursed.

Returning the earth to the ground and wiping her hands

clean, she pulled out a small sachet from the bag her mother had given her. With her fingers, she gathered what looked like dust and scattered it over Sebastian who looked up in surprise. His nose wrinkled as a pungent odour filled the air about him.

"What in Spirits name is that?" he asked.

"Witch's veil," she replied, "Mother used to use it to sneak up on father. It will mask us to an extent from other Sorcerers unless we are specifically being looked for."

She threw some over herself.

"Hey what about me?" asked Lex.

"You don't need it. A Sorcerer wouldn't dream of you being a threat."

"Thanks. I think."

Sebastian was looking at her with new respect. He was beginning to realise that there was much about Rhianad that he had taken for granted.

"What else have you got in that bag?" he asked cheekily.

"The stuff of Witches, you wouldn't understand it," she said patronisingly mounting her steed and riding on ahead.

"I like that girl," said Lex. "I like her a lot!"

Chapter 3

Ahlia came to her senses, to find herself surrounded by iron bars. She did not remember when she had lost consciousness. She remembered being hauled up into the air helplessly suspended from the dragon's neck. She remembered it being bitterly cold that high in the sky, cold and white, and she had imagined that they must be flying through clouds. Immediately, she felt about her neck for the Oracle, but as she had feared, it was gone. She looked at the cage about her and then out to the room beyond the cage. It was lusciously decorated in imperial reds and golds. There were guards standing to attention by the main door of the room. Daylight streamed in from long glass doors that were flung wide open to reveal a large balcony terrace. Silk curtains billowed in the breeze revealing as they occasionally parted, a man standing on the balcony, his back was to her as he looked out at the view. Like the room, he too was dressed in imperial red and gold.

As if sensing that she was once again conscious, he turned around. He was tall and broad shouldered, and a shock of black hair half covered his angular face and one of his eyes. The exposed eye gleamed like a green emerald as it took in the sight of his prisoner with obvious self satisfaction. Slowly and with all the grace of an emperor, he walked towards her to scrutinise her more closely until he was just a few feet away.

He paused, Ahlia suspected, for effect.

"Welcome to the Wylderlands. Allow me to introduce myself. I am Myron, King of these parts and…" he smiled "of course, I am a Sorcerer."

"A Sorcerer King?" she repeated his words in disbelief.

"Yes. Unusual I know for these times, but there you have it. Over the years I managed to amass enough wealth and troops and of course power, to conquer this place. It took some time, but in the end, I won. I always win… in the end," he said with poignant emphasis, as if to make her more keenly aware of her status as his prisoner.

He raised a gloved hand to show her the Oracle dangling from its silver chain.

"You and your Mistress between you led me on a merry chase. There is definitely no matching the cunning of a woman, especially a woman like Mora. Oh, I cannot tell you how good it is to finally be rid of her."

"You killed her!" she accused, her voice full of venom.

"Yes," he said clearly without remorse.

"Though admittedly, her time was at an end regardless of anything I personally did. We all have our time. She knew that. She didn't even struggle. I foolishly thought that was because she had no apprentice and knew that no one else could compete with me. I had it all carefully planned; to pre-empt the natural stopping of her heart by a few hours, or perhaps a day. The others would only detect her heart's final beat, but I would be first to reach her. The Oracle would fall to me."

"So you slit her throat," said Ahlia almost choking with emotion.

"Not personally. Brade my army captain took care of that for me. Really all he did was put the old hag out of her misery. She was going to die soon anyway. Hard to believe really what she had become," he reflected, "She used to be so beautiful, so powerful."

Myron looked to be in his late thirties at the oldest. He certainly didn't look old enough to have known Mora in her youth. He caught her confused gaze.

"A youth spell of course. Mora was at least, ah let me see, two hundred years or so. I am at least a hundred and fifty years older than her. I'll never understand why she didn't use one."

His eyes lost their focus for a moment as he mulled something over.

"Perhaps it has something to do with the ingredients."

Ahlia shivered involuntarily as she tried to imagine what

ingredients this man used that might be considered repulsive enough to turn Mora's cast iron stomach.

"I should, of course, have realised it was all too easy. I of all people should have known Mora better than to even entertain the thought that she would release the Oracle without fighting to the very last breath of her existence. It appears I was in retrospect slightly over confident: an unfortunate side effect of my general long term success. I did not even consider the possibility of failure."

"If you are truly so powerful, I do not understand why it has taken you so long to come after me when I have been beating other lesser Sorcerers away for some time."

Myron clearly did not take the rebuke well. His full lip tightened for an instant before he regained his composure.

"As I said, I was a victim of my own success and it seems it made me over confident. I was sure that I had amassed enough power to see through Mora's devious tricks, but I was mistaken. Mora was wearing a decoy. She wrapped a strong cloaking spell around an amulet she was wearing about her neck. When it was brought to me, of course I assumed it was the Oracle, but I was wrong. Who knows where or how she hid the true Oracle at the time."

"But you are a great Sorcerer. You must have realised you had the wrong amulet," said Ahlia in a deliberate attempt to test his patience.

"Not at first. You see the Oracle is renowned for many things including how difficult it is to master. For a while, I thought I was just having a few problems learning how to work it. It was quite some time before I started to suspect. The amulet was filled with an intense power for sure, but it was her power she had filled it with, as if filling a jug with water. It was nothing more than a decoy. How could I have anticipated that she would succeed in finding another apprentice and so late in the scheme of things. The chance of such an occurrence was so remote, that I had not bothered to contemplate it."

Ahlia looked at him in confusion.

"What do you mean another apprentice?"

279

Myron seemed surprised by the question.

"My, we are ignorant aren't we," was all he would say on the matter before swiftly returning to the subject at hand.

"Of course, when I redirected my attention over the sea once more, I couldn't help but notice you and the energy signature emanating from you."

"And from what was in my possession?"

"Ah no, not at first, I tracked you by your power alone, you are tainted with the flavour of your Mistress's energy. All I had to do was follow the brightest beacon. Who else would have the Oracle?"

"But you did not come yourself," remarked Ahlia with a clear, but veiled accusation in her voice."

"No," Myron answered unashamedly, "that would have been foolish. I sent Brade and my soldiers after you, but you know the rest."

She did indeed.

"It was at a high price indeed that I finally understood how powerful you really were, even though you were not using the Oracle yet."

He looked at her dirty, torn clothes with disdain.

"Though I must say it is hard to believe looking at you. You look more like a Hedge Witch than a Sorceress. Then again perhaps you were trying to emulate your hag of a Mistress."

Ahlia was aware that she must look a state. Her long hair had been buffeted by the wind and stood wildly raised about her head. She could feel the grime on her face and her well worn smocks were tattered and dirt ridden. Compared to this silk wrapped King she looked a veritable mess to be sure, but then Mora had always said that vanity was dangerous not because it was a vice, but because it betrayed a weakness and smallness of spirit that could be turned against a person. It was always good to be underestimated. Let him think she was not a threat. She would show him!

"Well don't ask me if the stone in your hand is any more the Oracle than the fake. I don't even know what the Oracle is meant to do."

Myron shot her a sharp look and a sudden sharp pain swept through her head making her yell.

"I see you are telling the truth. How strange!" he remarked.

Ahlia shouted a string of curses at him, "What did you just do to me?"

"Not just filthy on the outside I see."

Myron made a lowering gesture with his hand and as his hand lowered, Ahlia found herself being forcibly pushed to a kneeling position against her will by an invisible force.

"Did I forget to mention? I control you now. You cannot act against me so do not bother attempting anything foolish."

Ahlia's body was not in pain, but the index finger of her left hand was throbbing violently. She cast her eyes down and found a small incision in the flesh clotted over with dried blood. What had this monster done?

"Perhaps if you told me what the Oracle is supposed to do, it might help," she said through gritted teeth as Myron towered over her.

"Help who?" Myron smirked. "To think, you had it all this time and couldn't use it. You didn't even know what it was capable of. What kind of an apprenticeship did Mora give you?"

"A short and cryptic one, thanks to you," came Ahlia's terse reply.

"Well perhaps I can fill in a few gaps for you. I have no idea why she didn't tell you. Perhaps she didn't trust you enough. Perhaps she thought it might give you ideas above your station, although I don't see why she thought to delay the inevitable. As soon as you did use it you would have realised."

She realised he was taking great pains to display to her that he considered her no threat to him whatsoever. This ritualistic etiquette seemed somehow strangely familiar to her and it took her a while to realise that it was from Sebastian that she recognised it.

"The Oracle is an eye like no other, the eye of the Spirits themselves; 'Wisdom without bound, power without limit'. It sees all things, all things whether hidden or not, magic or not, material or not. All thoughts are exposed too I'm sure. Whoever wields it, speaks with the wisdom and insight of the Spirits."

"And you want it because you want to be named Supreme?"
Myron laughed loudly.

"My dear, I am Supreme with or without the Oracle. Look about you. Compare this palace to that hovel Mora was living in. Do not taint me with the same brush as those pathetic little vermin who have been troubling you trying to get their greedy, dirty little hands on the Oracle, as if they could ever fathom its mysteries even if it should fall into their pathetic clutches."

"But if you are all powerful already, then why do you need the Oracle?"

"Oh novice!" he exclaimed, "One can never have enough power, enough wealth, enough land, enough time. The Oracle is the eye. It points the direction to all other existing power objects, objects that have so far eluded my attempts to locate them. That is why the Oracle is so important. Most Sorcerers have little idea. They chase a thing not knowing what it is. Because the Sorcerers who possessed it through the annals of time were glorious in their power, petty little novices who have barely lived a few years think that by holding the Oracle they too might be great. What they do not realise is that greatness is a thing we are born to."

As he spoke he stood tall and proud and certainly seemed the very figure of greatness and power he described. His face was flushed and the very air about him crackled with the intensity of his energy.

"So how is it that Mora had the Oracle all these years and not you?" asked Ahlia.

She thought with immense satisfaction that she detected him deflate slightly at the question.

"As I said before, Mora was a powerful Sorceress in her day before her conscience weakened her. Her lust for power was stronger even than mine, though it burned out early leaving her without ambition and turning her into the dried old hag you knew. Even then she did not lose her power, merely redirected it into hiding herself and the Oracle for as long as possible so as to keep its power from me. What a waste! I assure you I shall not be so wasteful," he said, his voice full of fervour.

"I just need to learn how to control it and I shall show this world what Sorcery truly is."

His words make Ahlia quake with dread. Myron was clearly mad with power hunger.

"As for you, you can live for now until I am absolutely positive I don't need you any longer. I shall not be rash and make the same error twice. Now if you'll excuse me."

He was about to leave when a thought struck him causing him to hesitate. "Actually, I have thought of a use for you already. A few of the leaders of my outreach dominions have been a little vociferous lately in their complaints. Perhaps showing them that I have captured a powerful Sorceress might be in order to quell their unrest in a more diplomatic manner than the one I had in mind initially."

He smiled to himself as a plan formed in his head. He said something to one of the guards who called out to a servant behind the door. The servant appeared and bowed reverently.

"See that bedraggled heap in there? I want her washed, manicured and dressed. I want her looking like a queen," Myron commanded, "Do you understand? Anything less and I shall have the heads of all concerned. Have her ready by this evening for the banquet."

He clicked his fingers and the door of the cage sprung open.

"There's a rather strong dampening spell on you. Your power is useless here and for miles around."

He waved his hand over the air between them and Ahlia felt the weight that was forcing her to kneel, lift. She jumped to her feet and stepped out of the cage, but had not taken more than two steps towards Myron and the Oracle before he stopped her dead in her tracks with a gesture of his hand. Despite all her efforts, she found she could not move in any direction, but was pinned to the spot she stood in.

She looked again at the cut on her finger. A horrible thought began to form in her mind.

"A little trick my Master taught me. Foolish of him really, he should have anticipated that I would use it on him once I was strong enough. Needless to say there are guards everywhere and they have strict instructions to keep both eyes on you. I fully expect you to be true to your nature and so have anticipated everything you might think of."

"You know nothing of my nature. On that score, you can trust me," she spat out the words venomously.

Myron came closer to her and looked steadily into her dark eyes that burned hotly with indignation. She did not feel him intruding into her mind this time, but she found it hard to look away. Nor did she want to. She was tired of playing the weak victim. She would not be belittled by anyone, not even by her captor. Myron smiled as if pleased at the display.

"Evidently not, though I think I begin to see why Mora chose you. Now you must excuse me, for I have matters to attend to."

He gestured to the servant as he left the room.

"Clean her up."

The servant pulled Ahlia through several heavily guarded corridors where members of Myron's guard stood to attention, each one brandishing sharpened spear. The walls were decorated with tapestries and ornate statues and large porcelain vases lined what space was left vacant. It was clear that Myron had a taste for opulence and excess which spilled out from his energetic Sorcerous desires into material manifestation. He and Mora could not have been further apart in their lifestyles thought Ahlia to herself, though she could not help but wonder why each had gone to such extremes, one living like a pauper, the other like a god.

Finally, they stopped and the servant pushed open a large pair of white doors to reveal a large tiled room with a pool of water in the middle of the floor from which a subtle vapour was rising. As she was ushered in, the scent from the hundreds of flowers that were arranged in crystal vases and strewn about in the water filled her nostrils and permeated the entire room. Four women sat on cushions as if they had been waiting specifically for her. They got up and within seconds were undressing her and pulling her towards the clear waters of pool. She resisted them at first, but as they pushed her down the submerged marble steps into the warm soothing water, her aching muscles got the better of her and dutifully she plunged her dirty weary body in, in complete and utter surrender.

* * *

Myron was sitting in his study with Brade standing beside him. There was an air of displeasure about his countenance.

"You are sure of this Brade. Not that I am bothered about ending his pathetic little life, but if he is loyal, then I do not want to waste a perfectly good pawn."

"I am sure Sire. My sources tell me that Kryfer has been inciting the others to challenge your dominion over their lands. He has been telling them your demands are milking their estates dry. They are becoming increasingly disgruntled."

"And their troops?"

"Enough. The land in question is large enough and lies far out enough to make it a hindrance to maintain martially. A subservient overlord would be infinitely preferable. The nephew of the Chief in question is amenable to the idea of being his uncle's replacement. Of course, it is vital, in order to put an end to the unrest that all be seen to happen according to etiquette... above board so to speak Sire."

"What a pity, Kryfer was so promising. He killed his own father to seize power, you know. I gave him free reign of course to satisfy his bloodlust. It seems however, that lust has overgrown its allotted territory. I agree Brade. It is, as usual, sound advice you give me. In any case, I have something in mind that will take care of the situation as well as send out an appropriate message to the others. You see Brade, the mistake most despots make is that they openly move to control their world. In doing so, they make themselves targets to be toppled. I shall not fall into that category. The lands shall appear to be ruled freely by Chiefs from the Clan blood of the area. The people will happily follow and I shall get my levies and taxes and my dominion and my power. When the people are unhappy, I can place the blame on their Chief and replace him with another of my men. Thus I shall appear ever benevolent, so beautifully simple."

Myron smiled to himself, pleased at his own genius. Brade watched his Master with eyes that blinked unnaturally infrequently. It was a habit that Myron found disturbing in his servant.

"You may go Brade, but be sure to be back before the banquet."

Brade walked towards the door, but hesitated before leaving the room.

"Yes Brade. Ask."

"The woman, Sire."

"You mean the Sorceress I take it?"

Brade nodded. Myron scrutinised his Military Captain for an instant.

"Ah, I see. I'm afraid I have plans for her at present, but when I am done, I will give her to you, though I think she will kill you before you have time to take your fill of her. She is more than she looks I'll warrant."

"I am strong," Brade countered.

"In your way yes you are, but when all is measured, said and done, she is, I'll wager, the stronger. Perhaps you will see that for yourself tonight."

Brade bowed reverently to his Master and left the room, taking great pains not to reveal his displeasure.

*   *   *

Sebastian was complaining at the meagreness of their progress. They had made their way inland, careful to avoid using any magic lest they be sensed, but the pace had been painfully slow compared to what he was used to. Rhianad was about to reprimand him when, suddenly she appeared distracted.

She stopped speaking mid sentence and holding up her finger to silence the others, she cocked her head to one side as if listening intently.

Lex turned his attention to the direction Rhianad was facing and listened, but all he could hear was the sound of wind rushing through the long grass.

"Can you feel it?" she asked softly after some moments.

"Feel it? Feel what?" asked Lex entirely bemused.

"Yes," whispered Sebastian. The hairs on the back of his neck had risen at what he was sensing.

"It's not strong, hardly dangerous."

"Will someone tell me what you are talking about?" demanded Lex impatiently.

"Power," said Sebastian.

"I thought we'd established that already," complained Lex who was eager to continue on.

"No, this is different Lex. The wind carries the signature to us, though it is faint. Rhianad and I sense someone of power close by."

"A Sorcerer?"

"Not exactly, it is difficult to say what it is."

Rhianad's eyes lit up suddenly. "I know what it is," she smiled "and so would you if you had not forgotten what you were once like!"

Sebastian looked at her in confusion.

"Wait here," she ordered and set off on foot through the long grass towards a row of trees that obscured the terrain behind them.

Lex looked questioningly at Sebastian who could only shrug his shoulders in reply.

"I suppose we wait then!"

Rhianad passed through the trees to find that a makeshift settlement lay on the other side, consisting of a series of tents fashioned from animal hide. Doorways were covered with long thin flaps of material that billowed in the rising winds. Domestic animals roamed freely, though they never strayed too far from the area surrounding the tents. Looking more closely, Rhianad could see why. She spied a solitary boy, not more than eleven or twelve years old, sitting amongst the animals. He face was contorted in concentration and he appeared engrossed in whittling a branch with a small blade, though the fervor with which he was attacking the task showed that something else was clearly on his mind. His blond locks hung roughly about his face and shook with the vigor of his movements. The wind whirled and whipped about him as if mirroring his discontent.

As if feeling her gaze upon him, he stopped to look up and gave her a nod of acknowledgement.

"You are not from these parts," he said by way of greeting when she had come within speaking distance.

"That is correct. What gives me away so clearly?" she asked in surprise.

The boy looked her up and down.

"Not sure," he answered finally, "Everything really, your clothes, the way you walk and now I have heard your accent, the way you speak too."

"Very astute," she remarked, "Perhaps you can help me then. I have need of direction. I am looking for the centre of your lands, a city or a citadel."

"The palace, you mean the palace."

"Ah yes. The palace," replied Rhianad.

The boy resumed his task, but with less fervor.

"Has his hand reached across the sea already?" he asked in a sombre tone that was beyond his years.

She looked at him in amazement.

"I don't know what you mean."

"Yes you do. What else would bring the likes of you here?"

"The likes of me?" she asked innocently.

The boy looked up at her and arched his brow.

"I'm young, not stupid."

Rhianad was taken aback.

The boy focused his gaze upon her and as he did so, Rhianad felt wisps of wind gently finger the loose tendrils of her hair in a way that was almost human.

"If you intend to see the Emperor, I hope you have an appointment, but I suspect you don't," he said mischievously. He was toying with her now and his eyes sparkled with enjoyment at the game he was playing.

"You're here because of that woman aren't you?" he said

confident that he was right in his assumption.

Rhianad's eyes lit up.

"You might as well go home. You won't get anywhere near her. Not now that he has her."

"He?"

He huffed impatiently as if annoyed by her lack of understanding.

"The Emperor, Myron. No doubt that's where she is, in his dungeon or something, if she's still alive, that is."

"And how does a young shepherd know so much about such things?" she asked.

This was the question he had been waiting for and building up towards. He had told his uncle the story, but his uncle's eyes had filled with fear. He had been reprimanded for putting himself in danger and ordered not to speak of the matter again. Now, however, he had a chance to tell his tale again. His eyes shone as he spoke.

"It was some weeks ago. We were camped further East then. I was wandering with the goats on the hilltop. They like it up there. Suddenly, though it was just gone midday, the land was covered in shadow as the beast passed over us. It scared the animals into a frenzy, I can tell you. It passed low enough for me to see the scales on its black underbelly, and the beat of its wings raised up all manner of dust and loose grass. Oh, but it was an awesome sight. I had never seen anything like it before. I left my goats and followed it as fast as I could."

He gave Rhianad a conspiratorial look.

"I can run really fast when I want to; really fast."

Rhianad smiled in understanding, but said nothing, not wanting to interrupt the boy's story.

"...and when it landed on the ground I clean lost my balance and fell over so great was the tremor. The beast had landed in a small valley where men on horse back were waiting, the Emperor's guard. I didn't dare get too close, but as I hid in the grass I watched her being carried off by the Emperor's Captain. I knew in my heart the beast had brought her from across the sea and I could feel she was important. I could feel it right here."

He pointed to his solar plexus.

"She was all limp, like she was dead, but I could tell by the way the Captain carried her that she was alive."

She looked at him through the eyes of a Sorceress.

"What is your name boy?"

"Sarl"

"You have the Knowing, Sarl," she told him with a strange formality.

"Is that what it is called?" he asked in wonder, happy that finally someone had put a name to that which so obviously made him different to all those around him.

Rhianad nodded.

"Well I'm not allowed to use it, in case he finds me. Emperor Myron. That's why I'm here with my uncle tending animals instead of with my mother at the palace. She has me hide here so he doesn't bleed me."

Rhiand's brow shot up in shock.

"Bleed you?" she exclaimed in horror. "What do you mean?"

"That's what they say he does; bleeds you of your power and takes it for his own. It is why he is so strong."

Rhianad felt nauseous at the very notion of doing something so repulsive. She had heard legends of such Sorcery, but never imagined that in the present day any Sorcerer would think to use such a barbaric and unethical form of magic. The sooner such a Sorcerer was destroyed, the better, she thought to herself grimly.

"I thank you Sarl."

She turned to walk away, but was stopped by a sudden gust of wind that pushed her to a standstill. The boy's power was active despite his family's well meaning efforts to suppress it. She turned to face him.

"You cannot leave me here!" he said with sudden desperation. "I shall die if you leave me here."

"On the contrary, here you are safe from harm's way. Where I go there will be danger, and your mother will not thank me for taking you into danger when she has worked so hard to keep you safe. Where is your uncle? What would he have to say on the matter?"

"My uncle is inside eating with everyone else."

"And you were not hungry?"

The boy looked at her in disbelief.

"Food? You talk to me of food? What I need to feed me I cannot find in this place! To live without growing is a slow death. I'd rather die quickly and know at least what I am capable of."

Again the boy spoke with wisdom beyond his years. He obviously truly had the makings of a great Sorcerer. Rhianad could see that his power was strong and it was eating him alive as he became less and less able to contain it with age. Soon it would be impossible for him to suppress it any longer. She had been the first to find him. According to etiquette, that gave her a responsibility.

"Take me with you," he said in earnest, "I can help you get into the palace."

"And in return?"

"You help me understand myself. Teach me."

"You wish to become my apprentice?"

The boys blue eyes sparkled like sapphires.

"Yes exactly! Your apprentice."

"Sarl, you must understand that I have a task to accomplish first and our chance of surviving is minimal," she said gravely. "All I can offer you is some learning along the journey, but I fully intend to place you in your mother's care when we reach the palace."

"But if you survive and if you defeat Myron, then you must take me with you. You must promise to take me with you. You must give me your oath."

His eyes locked on her and burned with the ferocious determination of a prisoner who has spied their escape route.

Rhianad adopted a formal stance and bowed to the boy.

"Very well Sarl of the Wylderlands. I accept you as my apprentice. The journey begins here."

The boy looked hesitant for the first time since Rhianad had laid eyes on him. "What about my uncle?"

Rhianad placed a reassuring hand on his shoulder.

"Leave your uncle to me," she said smiling.

* * *

Lex and Sebastian had been waiting impatiently where Rhianad had left them.

"Well?" they asked eagerly when she returned with a boy in tow.

"Ahlia is being held in a palace further inland by the Sorcerer that rules these parts."

"Then we shall go and get her," said Sebastian with simplicity.

"It is not going to be that easy Sebastian. This Sorcerer, Myron, uses... blood magic."

She forced the words out with evident disgust. Sebastian's stomach turned at her words.

"It gets worse. He has command of a dragon which means he has access to dragon's blood. We can only draw upon theoretical knowledge to guess what he is therefore capable of."

"Spirits!" was all Sebastian could say.

"The only thing in our favor is that his power is spread thinly over a wide expanse. He controls these lands by magic first and the sword second it would seem."

"The mark of a man who trusts no one," commented Lex.

"Or the mark of a Sorcerer who is unwilling to share even the smallest morsel of power, and who is this?" asked Sebastian.

"Ah yes, this is Sarl my new apprentice."

Sarl puffed his chest out, much to Sebastian's amusement.

"I see."

"Sarl's mother works in the palace, the palace where Ahlia is being held."

"How convenient that Sarl's desire to become an apprentice should coincide with our need of a way of entering the palace," remarked Sebastian disdainfully.

Sarl shot him a defiant look.

"It was I struck up the bargain," he asserted fiercely.

The wind whipped about him as his cheeks flushed with

indignation at not being taken seriously. Already, despite his youth, the boy's power was strong and radiated far enough into the space about him for it to push against Sebastian's own. Sebastian would have killed another Sorcerer for making such a challenging action. He looked at the boy in surprise.

"Does he remind you of anyone Sebastian?" asked Rhianad, trying to contain her humor.

Sebastian opened his mouth then shut it again as he looked at the determined young boy and realized that he was looking at a mirror of himself as a youth. He bowed his head and conceded defeat.

Lex too had looked from boy to Sorcerer and had seen the resemblance in character far more than in feature. He chuckled gleefully to himself at Sebastian's discomfort.

"Perhaps Sarl would be more suitably placed with Sebastian," he said adding fuel to the already well stoked fire.

Sebastian shot him a look of ire.

"It has crossed my mind," said Rhianad in a serious tone that worried Sebastian greatly. "It has definitely crossed my mind."

"Just throw some of your Witch's veil over him before he alerts all and sundry of any power, of our location," replied Sebastian swiftly changing the subject.

It was a sensible request and Rhianad did as Sebastian recommended. Soon they were on their way once again with Sarl safely seated behind Rhianad on her steed.

Chapter 4

The banquet hall was warmed and floodlit by an array of torches. Table after table was weighted with the cooked and seasoned carcasses of deer and boar. Gold jugs of wine and beakers were scattered about and a myriad of servants stood at the ready. Every seat in the hall was filled. All seemed a picture of reverie, at least from a distance. Chief Kryfer barely touched the feast that lay before him. He smelled the wine before drinking it even after his man had tasted it for him. He thinly disguised his contempt for the man in red and gold who sat at the head of the room as he pretended to be absorbed in the dancing girls who gyrated before him in their bells and sequin covered attire. Kryfer was in fact listening to the man next to him who was whispering loudly enough to be within his earshot, but quietly enough so as not to be heard by any other.

"Uncle it is certain. I have it from a trustworthy source. He'll be bringing her on any minute now."

Kryfer grunted, but said nothing as he listened to his nephew.

"Think. It has to be so. Why would Myron risk unleashing a Sorceress so close to himself? Obviously the minute she felt her power she would attack him. He has to have her magic contained in some way."

Kryfer was thinking intently. He did not entirely trust his nephew, but he did have a point. A cold chill ran down his back which caused him to shiver involuntarily despite the warmth of the hall. He had the feeling that even if he made it out of this Hall alive, he would not make it back to his lands. However, he was not afraid. He was a warrior. This was the way life was. Death was always at his shoulder.

Myron set down his cup and waved his hand to a servant standing in the corner of the room. The servant bowed and lifted the stick his hand high, bringing it down to strike a large gong which hung on a wooden stand. The dancing girls scurried away leaving the centre of the room empty. People hushed each other into silence as Myron stood, commanding their attention by sheer force of presence.

"I thank you all for coming to partake in my humble meal with me. Today, I celebrate yet another victory. After much trial and effort, I have managed to capture the much fabled Oracle of Power, an object coveted and sought after by every Sorcerer in the world."

Gasps rippled through the audience of listeners.

"But this is not all. I have also managed to capture and subdue the great Sorceress and keeper of the mighty Oracle. She has killed many powerful magic workers to keep the Oracle for herself, but now she is my captive. Behold!"

A servant poked Ahlia in the back indicating that this was her cue. She emerged from the shadows into the centre of the room, a guard before her and a guard behind her. Each guard was holding a thick gold chain. One chain was attached to a cuff on her ankle, the other to the gold cuffs that pinned her hands tightly together in front of her. The audience gasped again. She could not understand why. After all, she hadn't actually done anything. She could just be a woman for all they knew. She looked about her as they all stared at her in wonder. She felt ridiculous. The servants had dressed her in the most ridiculous and humiliating garb. They had draped jewels on fine chains around her waist about her belly and round her neck. They had painted her nails and her mouth blood red and she could only imagine what they had done to her eyes and the rest of her face. She had endured hours of waxing and scrubbing and powdering and spraying. Her hair alone had occupied two servants for three hours. They had braided it after much industrious brushing and had woven it into a gold headdress encrusted with rubies. Then they had teased the remaining locks into tight curls. She felt like she was wearing a lion's mane. They had ignored her very vocal protestations regarding the slip of gold material they planned to put her in, but it was to no avail, though thankfully they agreed that it looked better with a train that served also as a skirt. A huge ruby clasp connected the two pieces of material that covered her torso. She dreaded to think what she looked like, but she would not flinch. She was after all a Sorceress, even if no longer a Supreme one.

Myron was almost as awestruck as his audience. He could not take his eyes off her as she stood there defiant even in captivity. The dampening spell he had used to subdue her power had obviously only managed to act like a shield. In his mind's eye he could see it as a grey sphere about her, preventing her power from moving beyond its rim, but Ahlia's power was not like any other he had encountered. The natural direction for a Sorcerer's power was outwards and upwards, but Ahlia's power, angry at being refused freedom, had spiralled and formed dark blue and purple coils about her and through her, that moved ever inward. It was as if being denied access one way, it had defied captivity and taken an alternate route. She exuded power like none other before her. Even the physical shackles that he had demanded be placed on her for effect, in an aim to diminish and degrade her, seemed to serve as ornaments to enhance her beauty and presence. Not even Mora had been this breathtaking. It seemed his Captain had been more astute than he. He should have realised as he remembered the way Ahlia had looked at him as he had stared into those dark captivating eyes. Perhaps he had realised, and had tried to ignore it. Beauty had its own power, and she wielded it without even realising it. She had control of the whole room. She almost had control of him, almost.

Brade saw the look in his Master's eye and instantly knew that Myron would not be granting the concession Brade had hoped for, but would probably take her for himself. Though looking at her now, he was in part afraid of her. There was something so awesome about her, that he could not help but fear her. She was after all a Sorceress. Perhaps Myron was right and he was safer for the not having. However, as he watched her, his fear paled before his desire. He would have her yet he thought to himself. He would have her, and more besides.

Myron finally found his voice and spoke to his guests once

again.

"And now I invite anyone who dares, to execute the prisoner and claim as a reward sovereign ship of the Eastlands from me, a worthy prize for a sizable risk."

There was a long pause as people looked about the room at each other.

"The Eastlands as you well know constitute half of our empire. I would consider any person able to conquer this woman, a worthy co-ruler. I would be glad to finally share the burden of rule. Of course, if none come forward, then I shall execute her myself at a time convenient to me and keep regency of the lands."

He looked round the room in contrived eagerness. Finally, Kryfer could take it no more. Perhaps it was a trap, perhaps it was a test. He could not afford to turn down the opportunity, and he knew no one else would dare to step forward. Maybe if he proved himself, Myron might be impressed enough to accept him. He stood up, knocking his chair backwards. All eyes were on him. He moved to the centre of the room and pulled his sword out as he approached Ahlia.

"Kneel Sorceress," he commanded.

Ahlia took a cautionary step back. "Don't do this," she pleaded.

"I said kneel!" he ordered.

"Please, don't do this."

The man reveled in the moment. She was begging for her life. This was not the action of a powerful Sorceress. She was just a woman of flesh and blood. He could do this. He would rule. He pushed her to the floor and raised his sword aloft.

Ahlia was helpless to defend herself. She had tried to use her power over and over all day but to no avail. Each time she tried to use it, the energy seemed to smash against a solid wall. Unable to overcome Myron's spell, she had subconsciously drawn her power into her, reigning it in as she had done for most of her life. The difference now was that she could sense it clearly seething within her, waiting for a chance to leap outward and express itself. Fear welled inside her as she crouched under the shadow of the sword. As it began to descend she screamed and tried instinctively to shield herself from the blow. A seemingly futile gesture, but she could think of nothing else. In that instant, she felt her power release from inside of her for a second just before the blow reached her. There was an all too familiar loud crack like thunder and a bright effervescent glow. The torches about the room flared up to an impossible height in response to the release of such potent energy. For a split second, she felt free to do as she pleased. Then it was as though a weight had been replaced over her, a magical shackle, suppressing her power once more. It had, however, been enough. The man who had intended to kill her was dead, as were the guards that had stood either side of her. Scorch marks radiated all about from where she was, almost reaching the tables where people sat. The crowd was dumbstruck by what they had just witnessed.

Myron walked into the centre of the room with apparent calmness, though his gaze flickered more than once towards the torches which still burned a little too brightly for his liking.

"You have all witnessed what this woman is able to do. My offer still stands. Who is brave enough to dare?"

No one came forward this time.

"Kryfer was a brave man, braver than any here. He shall be sorely missed. Who can I trust to rule his lands with as much wisdom and magnanimity as he did?"

Narp, Kryfer's nephew stood up. His uncle had been a bloodthirsty power hungry animal. It would not be hard to better him in the eyes of his people, and Narp was after all of Clan blood.

"If my people will have me and Master Myron deems me fit. I should like to offer myself. I shall try to emulate my uncle as best I can Sire."

"If the people are happy, then I am happy. Let it be so," agreed Myron.

Kryfer's nephew bowed humbly. "Now for all to witness I shall execute this Sorceress myself."

There was another gasp from all round the room. Myron bent slightly towards Ahlia to say quietly, "Listen carefully and I shall give you a chance to live. I do not wish to kill you, but if you make me lose even a modicum of face in front of these people, I shall not hesitate. You will be seen to cower and pander to my wishes."

"Never. I'd rather taste your blade," hissed Ahlia.

"I could make life very unpleasant for you, unpleasant enough that you might wish for death. See my Captain there? He has developed quite a penchant for you. They tell me he is a brutal man with a tendency to break the things he touches. Now all I require you to do is agree with whatever I say; a simple thing that will cost you nothing."

"Except my honour," argued Ahlia.

"My dear there are other more painful ways one can lose one's honour," he gestured again to where Brade was standing. Ahlia began to tremble involuntarily from a mixture of terror at what Brade might have planned and frustration that she could not protect herself. When Myron saw this, he addressed his people.

"See how she trembles in my presence. Tell me Sorceress, can you use you power against me? If you can then do so now!"

Ahlia was able to do nothing. Myron had suppressed her power completely.

"Tell me can you use your power against me?"

"I cannot," she said quietly.

"My people cannot hear you." He grabbed her by the hair and forced her to rise to her feet.

"I cannot!" she shrieked in pain. "I cannot!"

"I shall not kill you Sorceress. I am not bloodthirsty though you deserve to die for having killed many of my men. Good men. If Kryfer's nephew allows you to live I shall spare you. What say you Narp, will you be gracious and allow this woman her life though she has wronged you clan?"

Narp had no doubt about how he was supposed to answer.

"I shall Sire."

"Then it is decided. The Sorceress shall be my slave and my slave is the slave of my people. Each of you here will tell your people all that has happened here tonight, so they may know

299

how glorious their kingdom is, but now feast until dawn. My palace is your palace. Dine and be merry. I must leave you to safely secure our prisoner. I dare not let anyone else do it lest she charm them and kill them."

He gestured to the servant by the gong to let it sound and servants scurried to remove the dead bodies and wipe up the blood. The music began to play once again and the dancing girls came to fill in the gap as Myron led his prisoner away.

"Very good!" he remarked as he walked her down a series of winding corridors, "That was very impressive. I only gave you your power back for a millisecond and you radiated enough power to kill Kryfer and the guards as well. I could not have planned so effective a demonstration."

"How did you know I'd kill him in time? I am assuming that you wanted him dead for some reason."

"Oh I had no doubt concerning your ability and you are quite right, Kryfer had become a nuisance."

He declined to tell her that it had taken him some effort to replace the curb on her power, enough effort to make him slightly concerned. Fortunately, the woman seemed to have very little understanding of what she was capable of.

"Mora gave you the Oracle with much forethought. She knew the others would be of minimal threat. It was me she was protecting you from. Even now her power sits about you, but only a powerful Sorceress could wear such a mantle so well. I should have trusted her to be true to her nature and pick an excellent apprentice."

He stopped in front of a pair of double doors and pushed them open.

"Shall we?"

The room inside was unlike any she had ever seen. It was the epitome of decorative decadence. There were furs and silks and large reclining chairs about the place. Long fur rugs lined the already thickly carpeted floors. A large round table was covered with every kind of food and drink imaginable. Ahlia gasped despite herself. Myron seemed pleased by her reaction.

"I like beautiful things," he said and gazed at her intently, but she was so transfixed by the opulence of her surroundings that his meaning was lost on her. He took hold of her cuffed wrists in one hand and passed his other hand over them. There was a click as the lock released. She pulled them off and flung them onto a chair, rubbing her sore wrists as Myron helped himself to a tall glass decanter of dark wine and filled two gold beakers. He handed one to Ahlia, who feigned a smile as she watched him drink first.

"If I wanted to kill you Ahlia, you'd be dead, and if I want to impair your senses, I've no need of drugs," he told her.

She drank from the glass. Myron watched her intently as the colour of the wine added depth and shine to the redness of her painted lips. He moved closer to her.

"Are you hungry?"

"No," she lied. "And this?" she pointed to her ankle shackle, the chain of which was trailing the floor devoid of its keeper.

"Certainly, if you would be so good as to place your foot here," he indicated the padded stool that stood closest to him.

Ahlia was beginning to feel awkward. She realised the customary guards were not present. For some reason, that bothered her.

"No guards?"

"I never have guards inside my private quarters. No guards and no servants, except once a day to clean the room, and make the bed and so forth."

He pointing a finger towards another set of double doors at the far end of the room and they opened inwards on queue to reveal another room, a bedroom. Ahlia's anxiety went up a notch at the sight. She talked to soothe her nerves as he moved closer to her, trying to focus him on the shackle and distract him from anything else that might be in his mind.

"You are a madman. One gem from this shackle could feed a whole town. Iron would have worked just as well you know."

"I told you. I like beautiful things," he said sweeping her skirts away to reveal both the shackle and most of her leg. It was then that he saw her scar. He stopped in surprise.

"Then I suppose my leg's a bit of a disappointment on that

score," she said with satisfied contempt.

Myron ran his finger down the entire length of the scar. "This was done by Sorcery," he commented in fascination.

"Yes it was. You can thank a Sorceress for spoiling your view."

She began to feel horribly self conscious under his gaze. "Um... can you unshackle me now?"

Without removing his hand or his gaze from the scar, the shackle opened seemingly of its own accord and fell to the ground.

"My leg, if you don't mind, and for that matter even if you do!"

As if breaking from a trance, Myron released her leg and stepped back. Ahlia quickly covered her leg.

"That blast should have severed your leg clean off, or killed you. How did you survive it?"

"I don't know. I passed out. Must have been the tonic I suppose. I take it to mend myself."

Myron gave a wry smile.

"Mora's old recipe no doubt. Herbs could not have saved you. The wound was sewn up well, but at a time well after you should have been already dead. It seems the longer I know you the more intriguing you become."

Something was filling the room, creating a prickling energy about the air and Ahlia was beginning to suspect it might be lust. Power always desires more of itself, she thought grimly.

"There's nothing intriguing about a simple wound. I think it's just wider than it is deep is all," she replied.

"Oh I disagree, I happen to be an expert on such wounds," countered Myron. To Ahlia's dismay he began slowly unbuttoning his shirt. As he pulled it open, she realised it was to show her a similar scar to her own running diagonally across his torso.

"Mora gave me this to remind me of my defeat at her hands."

He grabbed Ahlia's right hand and placed it on his chest over the scar. When you run your hand down a scar such as this, and such as yours, you can sense the memory of the event. That is

302

how I know exactly what happened to your leg. Feel!"

He ran Ahlia's forefinger slowly down the scar and instantly she was there.

* * *

It was as if she was in his body. She saw an auburn haired woman aiming both open palms at her and with what seemed all her might thrust them towards her. There was bright light, deafening noise, searing pain. Then all went black. She blinked from the force and vividness of the image half expecting her own stomach to have been ripped open. The room began to spin and she would have toppled over had Myron not caught her.

"You are not used to such things I see. So much power and you have used so little of it."

He laid her on one of the long chairs. Everything was blurred and soft around the edges. She felt as if she were in a dream, there, but not there. Myron loomed over her. He ran his hand over the outline of her features, down her neck and over the curve of her breast before planting a kiss on her bare stomach.

"Please me, and you shall want for nothing. Do not deny me what I might take in any case," he threatened her with a voice soft enough and more suited to utter a lover's sweet nothings.

He sounded far away, more like an echo than a voice. She barely registered that he had taken her wounded forefinger into his mouth and was scraping gently at the scab with his teeth. He had placed his goblet under her finger with the intention of catching the drops of blood as they fell. As somewhere in the back of her mind, she heard him begin to murmur strange unintelligible words, her mind drifted from her control. Then amidst the fog of her consciousness, she felt something erupt to the surface.

"You would destroy all that I am," she heard herself say in a voice that was strangely familiar to her, but not exactly her own. The words came out of her mouth, but she had no idea why she was saying them. The fire in the room crackled loudly at the sound of her voice and the stone of the Oracle that hung about

303

Myron's neck glowed momentarily and burned uncomfortably against his skin. Myron, who had been just about to sink his teeth into her finger in order to open the wound further, flinched at her reply and recoiled instantly. The words had stirred a disturbing memory causing his face to contort. He pulled away from her abruptly and left the room hurriedly. She did not hear him leave. She was already lost in a deep slumber.

As she slept, her head tossed restlessly from side to side against the pillows.

"Ahlia, Ahlia," she could hear Mora's voice calling to her. At least she thought it was Mora's voice. In front of her, stood a slim woman in her mid thirties. Her auburn hair was a mass off wild curls and her eyes were sea green. She was breathtakingly beautiful.

"Ahlia it's me, Mora. I thought I'd shed a few years. You can do that in the Spirit World you know," she smiled warmly and winked at Ahlia, "Not that I give a fig for appearances mind!"

"What vision is this? Am I dreaming or awake?" asked Ahlia confused. Everything seemed real, but how could it be?"

"'Tis a real dream. Let's explain it like that. Your desperation has heightened your ability."

"What am I to do Mora? Tell me please!" begged Ahlia.

"Do not fall for his solicitations Ahlia," advise Mora, "He can afford to be as he is with you because he knows he has possession of the Oracle. Were you to try and take it off him, you would soon see what you are worth to him. He would not hesitate. Remember that. It is his nature to adore power and covet it. He is attracted to your power even more than your beauty. He cannot be changed. Do not repeat my mistake."

Her face became serious.

"Remember all that I taught you and you will be able to use the Oracle. I cannot tell you how to use it, because to use it is a feeling, an indescribable feeling, not a technique. A feeling that is the culmination of, and fusion of all that I have taught you merged with the strength and purity of your own intent. Like all true magic, the Oracle is not controlled nor does it control. It does not bestow power, but it is a powerful object. It does not require power, but only a powerful person can wield it."

"You speak to me in riddles as always!" complained Ahlia.

"In order to help you un-harness your mind and engage it in a different way of thinking. What did you learn from the book I left you?"

"That the Oracle is dangerous, that I am dangerous, that somehow beyond my understanding I am the Oracle."

Mora smiled benevolently. "Daughter in more than blood could ever bestow. You have the answers at your fingertips."

"I have nothing but confusion!" wailed Ahlia. "Your book did not teach me how to use the Oracle at all!"

"The book was not meant to teach you how to use the Oracle, it was meant to teach you how to be the Oracle," replied Mora.

Mora's form was becoming more translucent with every passing moment and her voice fainter and fainter. Ahlia tried to cling onto her image with all her mind's strength, but she could not.

"I understand less and less. The Oracle is an object and Myron has taken it from me. How can I get it back?" Ahlia called in earnest to the disappearing form.

Mora opened her mouth to speak, but her form had all but faded leaving Ahlia alone in the darkness.

*　　*　　*

Myron had retreated to the comfort of his study to consider all that had happened. He had fully intended to draw off some of Ahlia's power in order to weaken her and strengthen himself, but he had left the spell incomplete. Before him, on the table, lay the crystal goblet where a single drop of her blood swirled about invisibly amidst the dark wine. He had taken a sip and it had nauseated him. Just looking at the contents, brought a rush of saliva to his mouth and made his stomach contract. The liquid was entirely unpalatable and he could not understand why. He had worked this kind of spell a thousand times, but he had never encountered this problem before. For a moment he entertained the thought of forcing himself to drink, but his intuition warned him to err on the side of caution. This woman's magic was an unknown quantity and might well poison him for all he knew.

He rolled the Oracle between his fingers as it hung suspended from its chain, frustration eating away at him. He should have mastered it by now. He had tried every technique he could think of and had met with failure every time. He wondered what it was that Mora did to activate it. She had always been so enigmatic about her dealings with the Oracle often, he suspected, feeding him misinformation. Even when they had been at their closest, he realised now that Mora had never fully trusted him. He drew from the recesses of his memory a conversation that had taken place over a hundred years before.

"You are not thinking straight. Ever since you acquired it, you have been different. Its magic is affecting you Mora. You are not strong enough to control it."

"I cannot let you take it from me Myron."

"You would let it stand between us in the way of our love?"

"You think you are proposing sharing power, but Myron I know you too well for that. You do not share anything if you can help it. I have wielded the Oracle I have seen something of its vision and it is not what you think. I cannot allow you to use it the way you would wish to. It is not a tool for conquest. How strong is your love for me Myron? Would you allow me to stand in your way?"

He had deflected the question.

"Why should you wish to stand in my way? You love power as much as I do."

"As much, perhaps, but not in the way you do. I love it as a child loves its mother. From it, I learn. You love it as a man loves his gold. With it you control. It is not the same."

"Give me the Oracle," he had demanded.

"Believe me when I say that I cannot. Even if I wanted to I could not," she had answered cryptically.

"Give me the Oracle. Do not deny me what I might take in any case," he had threatened.

"If I gave you the Oracle, you would destroy all that I am. I cannot let you do that."

306

Those were the words that Mora had uttered over a hundred years earlier, before she had turned against him and disappeared with the Oracle. Ahlia had uttered those same words this very night in a voice that was not her own, but sounded uncannily like that of Mora. Was it a spell or an omen?

As if in answer, the candle that sat on his desk crackled and flickered eerily.

He called to the guard standing outside the door.

"Tell the servants that I want every fire on this floor put out," he ordered.

Chapter 5

Ahlia awoke with a start to the sounds of people around her. It was the servants clearing away the dishes of the night before. Myron was not there. Looking through the open door to the bedroom, she noticed his bed had not been slept in either. She ran a finger down her face and grimaced at the amount of paint that had come off onto it. She grabbed a servant woman.

"Bath. I need a bath and some proper clothes," she said with determination.

"Of course, my Lady. Master Myron has made it clear that you are to have whatever you wish and go wherever you please in the palace."

"He has, has he?" said Ahlia a little surprised. "He's a very trusting fellow."

The servant looked at her in a confused manner. "The Master has eyes everywhere. He has no need for trust."

An involuntary chill ran down Ahlia's spine.

The woman led her to the same chamber Ahlia had been groomed in the day before.

"My thanks, I'll take it from here," she instructed, once the servant had laid some clothes for her on a chair.

"If these garbs do not please my Lady, there are more in the wardrobe there."

"Dress up a lot of women does he your Master?"

"These particular dresses belonged to the Mistress. Her build was not unlike yours, though her hue and complexion different, from what I've been told."

"What happened to her?"

"They say she left after some discord. She was of... violent temperament."

"How long ago was that?"

"Why that was before my time, when this part of the palace was built and when the empire was much smaller. A castle stood here then they say."

"Who says exactly?"

"My family has always served the Master through the generations, just like each of the servant's families. We are his. He owns us." She changed the subject abruptly. There are soaps for my Lady's use. The jug here is filled with fresh juice and if my Lady is hungry, an assortment of cakes and fruit. I will be just outside should my Lady need me. She has only to call."

She gave a little bow and left the room.

Ahlia helped herself to the food. It was good. The juice was sweet and refreshing too. The pool looked serene and inviting. She dipped her toe into the water. It was lovely and warm. The head dress was to her pleasant surprise much easier to remove than she had anticipated and she simply unwound her braids to release it. Undressing was a much more traumatic affair. She struggled a bit with the various clasps that held her garb on, muttering curses under her breath, but was finally free of them and let the cursed garments and trinkets fall to the floor.

"And don't tell me your Mistress ever wore that!" she said to no one in particular. She breathed in deeply her lungs' new found freedom and lowered herself into the pool sighing with delight. As she scrubbed the paint off her face and washed her hair she had to admit there were worse ways of being a captive. She stopped dead in her tracks horrified at her thought.

"Oh, you're good Myron, you're good! Paint the cage gold and the bird will forget it's in one," she said to the empty room. The water gave a sudden odd ripple even though she had stopped moving. She started and despite the warm temperature of the water, she could feel goose bumps forming all over her body. Suddenly, she was not entirely sure that she was as alone as she had thought. She remembered what the servant woman had said about Myron's eyes being everywhere. Suddenly the pool had lost its appeal. She got out and quickly dressed herself. The servant was waiting outside just as she said she would be. She rose to attention at the sight of Ahlia.

"My Lady!"

"Please. I'm not your Lady."

The woman bowed.

"Can you tell me where your Master is at this present moment?"

"Yes my Lady," said the woman oblivious to Ahlia's exasperated sharp intake of breath at being so addressed yet again.

"My Master has business in the Hasgar Province. It is a day or so's ride away. He left this morning at daybreak with his Captain."

"Oh." Ahlia felt relieved.

"It is my Master's wish that my Lady amuse herself in his absence. This floor and the one above are my Master's private quarters. Downstairs are the general halls. Should you lose your way you have only to ask a guard. They are posted... everywhere."

"Yes I had noticed."

"I am to tell you that my Master wishes you to stay and he will take no refusal on this matter."

"I see. That's one way of putting it, though I think the term 'prisoner' would have sufficed."

* * *

They had been following Sarl's directions and had headed East of where they had found him.

"Soon you will be able to see the towers of the palace," he said by way of encouragement.

"Not long now."

Lex looked at the boy suspiciously. He was clearly excited, which might be deemed normal, except that his gaze wandered about the landscape as if he was looking for something far less obvious than a palace. It was not long before the mystery was revealed, when Sarl pointed ahead of him to a large opening in the hillside.

"There! There's the beast's cave!" shouted Sarl squeezing

Rhianad's waist in excitement.

Rhianad let out a short gasp. She had heard of dragons. She had read about them, but she never once in her wildest dreams imagined that she would ever come close to encountering one. Curiosity and fear battled for precedence as she probed the darkness of the cavern with her Sorcerer's sense.

"What are you doing?" asked Sebastian sharply, deliberately breaking her concentration.

"Aren't you in the least bit curious?" she retorted.

"No and let us hope the 'beast' is not at home at present."

As if in response, a low ominous rumbling began to erupt from the cave, shaking the floor beneath them.

Instinctively, the horses all took a step back and neighed nervously.

"Such power! How is it that the Emperor can control such a mighty thing?" asked Sarl in wonder he slipped off of Rhianad's steed and took a few paces in the direction of the cave before abruptly stopping. There was a strange look upon his face.

"The boy has a point. How are we going to defeat someone so powerful?"

For the first time there was doubt in Sebastian's voice. Lex looked at him in dismay.

"Now is not the time to lose your arrogance. Perhaps we should kill the beast so that it does not trouble us later."

"Do you have any idea how hard it is to kill a dragon?" asked Rhianad. Her confidence also seemed to be wavering. The presence of the dragon and the knowledge that the Sorcerer Myron controlled it somehow seemed to be sapping their resolve.

"No I don't. Do you?" replied Lex angrily, knowing full well that she could only answer theoretically.

"The more time I spend with Sorcerers, the more apparent it is to me how different Ahlia is to you all. I wouldn't be having this conversation with her!"

Rhianad stared at him coldly.

"Where is Sarl?" interrupted Sebastian suddenly.

"Spirits, no!" Rhianad exclaimed in horror as she caught sight of him disappearing into the entrance to the dragon's lair at Sorcerer's speed.

"Tell me he's not gone into that cave," pleaded Lex.

She looked at him, her eyes wide and her mouth open.

"I'll go after him," said Lex without hesitation, "You and Sebastian stay out here. If I don't come back out then leave. If that Sorcerer is as powerful as you fear, then it's going to take both of you to help Ahlia defeat him. I on the other hand am expendable, being a mere human."

He trudged with determination towards the cave entrance.

"Lex!' Sebastian called after him, "Do not go to your sword until absolutely necessary. A dragon will not attack without reason, or so I have read."

"Books!" muttered Lex to himself, entirely unimpressed as the darkness swallowed him.

Rhianad looked at Sebastian in disbelief.

"We cannot let him go in there by himself!"

"Do you want your apprentice back or not?" questioned Sebastian.

"Yes, but…"

"Our priority is the Oracle. I am loath to admit it, but Lex is right. It will be up to us to help Ahlia defeat the Sorcerer."

Rhianad looked at him in disgust and turned towards the cave, but Sebastian pulled her back.

"I have him in my mind's sight. At the first sign of trouble, I shall be in there faster than he can imagine."

Reluctantly, she acquiesced. She felt to blame. She knew in her heart that she should have been the one to go into the cave. Sarl was after all her apprentice. What had possessed the boy to do something so foolish?

Lex stumbled down the long dark passageway following the sound of the rumbling until he caught sight of Sarl standing absolutely still as if transfixed at the end of the tunnel. As he came up behind him, Lex was able to witness for himself what had Sarl so entranced.

Before them, the tunnel opened out into a huge cavern. The ceiling was encrusted with yellow and red crystals that seemed to give off a dim eerie light, bright enough to make visible the massive form that sat upon the floor of the cave; the form of a great black dragon. The beast seemed to be at rest, its great head lay upon its forearms and its membranous wings were folded down and resting upon its back. It had curled its heavy scaled tail around itself as a cat might. However, this was no cat. It had been watching Sarl intently, but on seeing Lex it broke off its stare to take in the new visitor.

"I did not call for you," boomed the dragon, flaring its large nostrils to release wisps of grey smoke.

As if released from a trance, Sarl came to his senses and placed a hand on Lex's arm.

"It's alright. He doesn't want to hurt me. We were talking."

"Talking!" Lex looked at the child sceptically.

Sarl tapped his forehead. "In here. We were talking in here. He's young like me and he wants to become great and powerful like me too, but he cannot because he's stuck here. He called me to tell me."

Lex looked about the dragon. "I don't see any manacles," though he noticed there was a silver chain about the dragon's neck. Nevertheless, it was not attached to anything and the dragon appeared free.

The dragon arched its long neck with the elegance of a swan. Its curved talons tapped and scraped against the bare rock of the cavern floor as it shifted its position. Lex watched its every move warily, but he heeded Sebastian's warning and did not allow his hand to move anywhere near his sword handle, though the temptation was strong.

"You work for the Sorcerer who rules these parts," Lex called out, his voice echoing about the cavern walls.

"He has control of me under duress. I was taken as an infant barely out of my shell and blood stolen from me so that I might be controlled," replied the dragon in a voice so resonant that it that almost burst Lex's ears.

"I cannot help you because it is not in my power to do so, but I shall grant you this boon. I shall not hinder you either," it thundered.

The dragon fixed a yellow eye on Sarl.

"What is it about the boy that fascinates you so much?" shouted Lex suspiciously.

The dragon ignored him, unbeknown to Lex, it was in the middle of saying something to the child, communicating mind to mind, Dragon to Sorcerer.

"In the Palace is a box. In the box is a vial on a chain. In the vial is my blood. Smash the vial and you free me. Only you can smash the vial to break the spell that binds me. Free me, and I shall be in your debt. I shall show you secrets that other Sorcerers can only dream of."

"I shall try Dragon, I shall try," promised Sarl silently as Lex pulled him away and ushered him back down the tunnel and into the daylight where the others stood waiting anxiously.

* * *

Ahlia was exploring her prison. After what seemed like an age of wandering from room to room and often having her entrance barred by guards, Ahlia came to a room that did not have guards posted outside it. Intrigued, she gave the door a tentative push to see if it was locked. It wasn't. The room inside was a library. Dark wooden bookcases lined the wall from floor to ceiling. Ahlia gasped in delight. It had been an age since she had indulged her passion for reading. She began to browse through the titles. Every book was on Sorcery of every kind. Some looked very old, even older than Myron might be. Perhaps she would find something about the Oracle here or better still, something about her captor. She began to scour the shelves and soon lost track of time as she delved into book after book.

Suddenly she became distracted. Something felt strange. She looked about her, but the room appeared to be entirely empty. Shrugging her shoulders, she buried her nose once more in the book she was reading. It was a chronicle of ancient history and started from five thousand years ago. It documented disputes and battles, risings and fallings from power, and philosophies old and older that the Sorcerers of those times had advocated. She was absorbed in a chapter relating to the old lineages of Sorcery, when father passed his knowledge down to son. There was little mention of women at all. Her eye focused on one family tree that bore the crest of the Black Dragon. The names and dates stopped at almost a thousand years ago, but the line had been continued on in different ink on a loose piece of parchment that had been inserted into the book. She did not recognise any of the names except one. Myron's was the last on the list. What was obvious throughout, by the scarcity of names, was that these men had lived incredibly long lives.

Her eyes began to ache from the strain of reading the small print in the fading daylight. Longingly, she looked at the cold empty hearth and shivered. It had not escaped her notice that all the fires were out and even the torches were being kept to a minimum. In a palace where everything else was available in abundance, this seemed more than strange. What did Myron have against fire? She closed the book and leaned forward to rest her head on the book case as she stood. She closed her eyes and tried to relax. In the back of her mind, she vaguely registered a strange draft about her neck, but there had been lots of odd drafts blowing through the room while she had been there. Then, something brushed by her in a way that was tangible enough to make her start. For a split second it was as if there was a person standing close behind her. She opened her eyes with a start and looked around the room again. It seemed as empty as ever. She tried to reach for her inner senses, but she was met with a fog of confusion. Myron's mental shackle was addling her abilities. The thought of it made her boil with indignation. He might as well be suffocating her she thought angrily. The angrier she felt, the harder it became for her to breath. The musty smell of the old books and parchments that surrounded her became increasingly imposing and she began to feel dizzy, as unbeknown to her conscious mind, her power seethed within her and filled the space about her, crashing furiously against the force that held it at bay.

The book still in her hand, she went over to the open window to breath in some fresh air. On looking out, she could see that below her there were ornate gardens filled with flowers of every colour and description. When she turned around again she gave a startled jump. Myron was sitting in one of the chairs by the door. She had not heard him come in. How had he returned so quickly? Perhaps he had never left.

"I see you have found my library."

"Yes."

"The chronicles are enthralling are they not?"

She nodded reluctantly.

He walked up to her and gestured for her to hand him the book.

"Ah the lineage, but you disappoint me. I had thought you would for sure be researching the power objects."

"I have, but there is precious little on them except that there are seven of them and that they are not of this world. I had thought that there were only four."

"Only four of them can be physically manifested in the material world; the sword, the chalice, the staff and, of course, the stone."

"But what about the other three?"

"The remaining three must be of purely astral existence."

"Astral?"

"Yes, or of ether, of spirit, intangible. I will be honest with you in saying that I do not know for sure. Only one Sorcerer, it is said knew of them and he left no description that I know of."

"Oh yes, Mazon. I read about Mazon the Great scattering power objects."

"Seven objects, one for each centre of power. Six scattered, but one kept back. Mazon could not quite bring himself to let go. Can we blame him?"

His creamy voice softly lulled her into an almost hypnotic state.

"I imagine he must have been a rare man indeed to have all the objects of power in his possession and succumb to keeping only one. Did you see Mazon's lineage?"

Ahlia had been far too busy looking at the Black Dragon line to even register the others.

Without waiting for her reply, Myron flicked through the pages.

"Ah here it is. It ought to be of some interest to you. You will note, it is not a blood line. Mazon had no children. This line traces the holders of the Oracle."

He partially handed the book over to Ahlia so that she might see more easily. She followed the line down. It was a very different picture to Myron's line. For one Ahlia noted the name of at least one woman and for another, not all these Sorcerers had been graced with longevity. Quite the opposite it seemed. Towards the bottom of the list she saw Mora's name and to her surprise, there was her own name in fairly fresh ink. She was so engrossed that she did not notice that Myron's attention had drifted from the contents of the book to her.

"Her dress suits you. It was one of her favourites as I recall. You chose well."

"I didn't choose it. Your servant laid it out for me," she answered curtly.

"Then my servant chose well," he said unperturbed, "the result is the same. Her dress fits you as though it were made for you."

He did not take her eyes off her and she was beginning to feel uncomfortable under so intense a stare. "I thought that seeing as she had given you her power, she would not object to me giving you her attire."

"You've said that before about me having Mora's power, but I don't understand what you're talking about."

"You didn't know." he said as if the realisation were just dawning on him. "Ah, but which part did you not know? That Mora was once my partner or that she sacrificed the last few hours of her life to give you her power, her power for your protection."

He watched to see what her reaction would be. She tried to hide her shock from him in vain.

"I see. She told you nothing, absolutely nothing. How convenient for her purpose. She created a cloak, a powerful cloak. She cloaked you to hide you from me. It still left you open

317

to the others, but she was not concerned about them. She knew you would take care of them. It was me she was worried about. It took me quite a while to unravel the nature of the spell, and I still as yet haven't figured out how to reverse it entirely. You appeared and disappeared like an intermittent beacon. It became easier when you started killing Sorcerers, but you cleverly kept mobile, never staying in one place long enough for anyone to get a strong fix on your whereabouts. It was all Brade could do to keep up with you."

"And why did you not come yourself?" asked Ahlia.

He waved his hand about him. "You see my responsibilities."

"And you weren't sure about my abilities, so you sent expendables," she accused.

Myron shrugged. "It was the intelligent thing to do. Of course, when you finally disappeared into the forests, it was as if the trees themselves banded against me to protect you. I lost sight of you completely for a while."

"How did you find me then?" she asked.

"You have no idea how much power I had to pour into that little venture. I had to awaken Valamar and send him to find you. Do you have any idea how difficult it is to control a dragon? Had I lost control for an instant, you would have perished and the Oracle with you, and Valamar would have come for me next, but you left me with no choice."

"Why would the dragon harm me?" she asked in confusion. "It has no reason to."

"Ah my dear Ahlia. Do you know nothing of magical beasts? They do not operate with reason. We are but flies to them, irrelevant pests at best. It takes a huge amount of power to maintain control over such creatures."

"I do not believe that, though I must confess, I would not know," admitted Ahlia, "There are no creatures of magic over the seas that I know of."

Myron nodded knowingly.

"No. The Wylderlands have always been the breeding grounds for such creatures and even here they are fewer than ever before. Times have changed."

He moved closer to her breathing in the air about her as though it were scented.

"Mora was one such creature of power. She was born here in these lands and she loved them. Her power clings to you still, you wear it like a mantle, and now you also wear her dress. Both seem to fit as though they were made for you. Already they are changed. You have made them your own."

Ahlia wondered to herself, what manner of force would cause the magical beasts to disappear. She wondered too exactly what had occurred to force Mora to leave the land she was born in and, according to Myron, loved so much.

Myron smiled at her. "Tell me. Don't you find it strange that Mora told you so little? Have you considered also that the little you do know might be inaccurate or dare I say it, deliberately misleading? Can you be sure that Mora was in the right? Maybe her motives were less than noble regarding the Oracle. Maybe she simply did not want to share its power."

"Mora wasn't like that."

"Mora was exactly like that. I should know her better than any. One does not become as great as she was without coveting power. She had thirst for power, stronger than mine perhaps."

"If that is so, how is it that she lived in a run down cottage and dressed in old smocks and you live in a palace and call yourself King?"

"Superficial differences, outward manifestations are nothing but shadows cast by the true possession of power. She had the power of the Oracle. The flavour of that power coursed through her veins like a drug mingling with her lifeblood, her essence. She became the addict who lets their outer world fall to ruin because they have become so absorbed with the inner riches they have found."

"Mora cared about things. The Oracle changed her. Whatever she was before doesn't matter. She changed."

"Did she change so much? If the Oracle changed her for the better, which according to you it did, why did she not trust it to change me for the better? Perhaps if I could see for myself, I would understand and change also."

"You don't know how to make it work though do you," said Ahlia.

Myron pursed his lips.

"Not yet, no."

"Well even if you win me over it won't help. I don't know how to make it work either. Besides, you've curbed my power."

He grabbed her around the waist and drew her close. She turned her face away from him.

"Not all of it, it seems. A part of you eludes me," he whispered into her ear. He released her gently.

"Am I such a monster?" he asked in a tone that indicated he was amused rather than hurt by the notion. He lifted her chin compelling her to look into his eyes.

"Why you have had all the fires put out?" she demanded.

"To protect myself from you," he said softly, "You say Mora cared. Would you kill the man you loved to keep the Oracle from him?"

Ahlia cast her mind back to what she had seen and the pain she had felt when she had traced her fingers along Myron's long scar. She thought of Sebastian. She tried desperately to avoid his searching eyes, but it was to no avail. He found the answer he was looking for.

"No. I didn't think so. Only a monster would do that," he said gravely.

She did not know what to say. About her the room had grown gradually darker as the sun had journeyed down and the moon had risen. Myron gently took her hand in his and raised it to his lips and planted a gentle kiss there.

"I must leave you for the present, but feel free to stay here for as long as you wish."

The irony of his statement was not lost on Ahlia.

"I am not free though am I Myron, and my wishes have little to do with the matter," she said tersely.

Myron sighed heavily.

"Perhaps in time, you will decide to stay of your own accord, and there will be no need for restriction."

"I doubt it," she called after him as he left the room.

After the episode in the cave, Lex had insisted that Sarl ride with him on his horse so he could keep an eye on him. Sorcerers might be powerful, but they had a tendency to overlook the obvious, he had argued. Rhianad had not felt able to argue back, though she felt guilty that Lex was taking responsibility for her charge.

Sarl, oblivious to the trouble he had caused, was chattering endlessly about the dragon, to the point where the others were becoming heartily sick of it.

"Another word from you and we shall return you to your uncle," warned Rhianad finally.

"I am deeply disappointed in you Sarl. You put others in danger without a moment's thought. You may well have been as safe as you believe, but what if the dragon had turned on Lex?"

Sarl looked downcast. He was truly sorry for putting Lex in danger, though he sincerely did not believe the dragon ever had any intention of harming either Lex or himself. Moreover, he was quite annoyed that the others did not share his amazement concerning the fact that the dragon had chosen to communicate with him. Of course, he had been selective in what he had told them. He wanted to be the one to free the dragon and learn its secrets as the dragon had promised. If he told the others about the vial, he was sure either Sebastian or Rhianad would take charge of the task. He could not let that happen. The dragon had chosen him and it had made him feel special and important. He liked that feeling.

Sarl was so wrapped in his thoughts, he failed to notice the worried looks that Sebastian and Rhianad were exchanging. Had the boy really communicated with the dragon? If he had, then there was more to the boy than met the eye, and if he hadn't then his insistence was worrying in that it bordered on delusion. It was not uncommon for young Sorcerers to go mad if their power was suppressed for too long.

"Childish musings," Sebastian had said at last.

"What would you know about children?" asked Rhianad scornfully.

"I was one once, remember? I believed I could communicate with birds when I was a child."

"Sebastian, you can communicate with birds."

"No, I can be a bird. It is not the same thing."

"So what, are you saying that Sarl can 'be' a dragon?"

"Perhaps," said Sebastian, but then immediately realised had tied himself in a knot of reasoning, for only a powerful Sorcerer could accomplish such a shape shifting feat.

"There is another possibility of course," he said.

"Oh?"

"The dragon could be using him. I for one have no idea what dragons are and are not capable of. They are creatures of magic, with their own agenda."

"Then we must be vigilant Sebastian. We must be very vigilant indeed," stressed Rhianad casting a wary eye over her young apprentice.

* * *

Myron's study was as beautifully decorated as every other room in the palace, except that here he had favoured darker more subdued colours. His desk upon which an array of parchments were scattered was of a dark mahogany, and the floor was covered in thick black carpet. Ahlia ran her fingers across the parchments scanning them. There were maps and decrees and letters, but all pertained to affairs of state rather than magic. Disappointed, she turned her attention to an ornate box that sat at one corner of the desk.

A glimmer of hope seized her as she sensed with what little ability Myron had left her access to that there was something of power in the box. Surely he could not have let the Oracle here unguarded? The closer she got to the box, however, the more certain she became that whatever the box contained, it was not the Oracle. This energy felt different, somehow more organic. Tentatively, she tried to open the clasp, but it was, of course, sealed. She quietly cursed in frustration.

"It is locked."

Ahlia spun round to find Brade standing at the doorway. How had she not felt his presence? She silently cursed in fury at Myron and his magical shackle.

"You cannot blame me for being curious," she said simply, "If Myron wants an explanation, you can tell him that I was bored. I am stuck between these walls all day every day. I was running out of rooms to explore."

Brade came a few steps closer.

"It is a beautiful box is it not?" he said in a strangely conspiratorial manner, "but what is in the box is perhaps more interesting."

Was he taunting her? He seemed to be deliberately arousing her curiosity further.

"And what is in the box?" she asked, fully expecting to be rebuffed. To her surprise he answered her eagerly.

"Blood. Dragon's blood."

He held his hand out to receive the box from her. She knew she had no choice but to give it to him. As she went to place the box in his open palm, her eye caught sight of the small red scar on his forefinger. The cogs of Ahlia's mind began to click into place.

"Ah!" she exclaimed, "Blood!"

Brade smiled as if he had won some small victory. Then his attention seemed to be caught by something. He cocked his head slightly as he replaced the box upon the table.

"He will be approaching soon. You should leave."

It was too late. Myron appeared at the doorway. He raised an eyebrow at his Captain. "I hope, Brade, that you are not bothering our guest."

Brade bowed his head and was about to speak when Ahlia interrupted.

"Actually he caught me rummaging through your papers and was just insisting that I return to my quarters."

Myron looked at her in surprise. "I see. He cast an eye down to see what manner of documents he had left exposed. As he

323

noticed the map, it occurred to him that Ahlia had been searching for an escape route. He frowned slightly. No, he was not about to part with her just yet. Perhaps he had been too liberal in allowing her to wander so freely through the palace.

"I think it would indeed be best if you returned to your quarters for the present. If you would escort our guest, Brade, to ensure there are no more 'detours'."

The captain nodded and gestured for Ahlia to go before him. Ahlia watched Brade intently as he led her back to her room on the other side of the palace. Once they were safely far enough out of earshot she stopped and turned to him pointing her scabbed forefinger in his face.

"He controls you too doesn't he, like he controls me. Like this!" she told him shaking her wounded finger at him. "How?"

A strange pained expression appeared on Brade's normally severe face.

"It is...complicated," he said stiffly.

He turned his head as if expecting someone to be behind him.

"No more talk of this nature," he said sternly and gestured for them to continue on.

Once back in her own quarters, Ahlia sat and contemplated what she had learned. Was dragon's blood the key to Myron's power?

Chapter 6

"Stop," Sarl called out suddenly. Lex reigned his horse in to a standstill accordingly. "What now?"

Sarl pointed to a spear that had been stuck firmly in the ground next to a monolith. Beside the monolith someone had constructed a small shrine from loose stones.

"This is Clan country. We cannot pass without permission."

"Permission from whom?" asked Sebastian.

"Kryfer the Chief."

The others looked at each other.

"Of course, he'll go directly to Myron's guard to notify them as soon as he realises why you are here."

"Then why did you bring us along this route?" asked Lex irritably.

"Because it's the most direct and you said you were in a rush," answered Sarl sulkily.

He got off his horse and knelt before the shrine while the others looked on. The boy was murmuring quietly to himself and touching his lips to the earth at the foot of the shrine at intervals.

"What in Spirits name is he doing?" asked Sebastian in horror.

"Isn't that obvious?" answered Rhianad, "He is praying. They must still revere the old Deities in these parts," she mused with wonder, "I had thought the practice all but dead! Would that Samia were here to see."

Sebastian pulled a wry face. "Barbaric superstitions," he commented in disgust.

Rhianad shot him a scathing look. Sometimes Sebastian's narrow mindedness was almost too much to bear.

"What difference between your Spirits and his Earth Mother, Sebastian?"

325

Sarl had concluded his prayers and turned to them with a smile upon his face.

"I know what we must do. We must pay Kryfer for passage across his land."

"Your Gods tell you that?" asked Sebastian with sarcasm.

Sarl's face screwed up in indignation.

"Don't your Gods speak to you?" he asked, his face flushing with ire.

Sebastian opened his mouth to answer, then realised he did not know what to say.

Rhianad laughed. "It seems Sarl, that Sebastian has not ever bothered to listen."

It was Sebastian's turn to look indignant.

"Can we leave the theological debate for another time?" asked Lex impatiently, "The boy's plan is sound, however he may have come by it. The only problem is we don't have enough money to wet the appetite of a Clan Chief."

"I could spell cast for gold I suppose, though we would risk detection."

Rhianad mulled something over in her mind.

"Not necessarily. Myron will look for the magic of Sorcery, but there are other forms of magic that may well evade his attention. I wonder," she looked at the shrine, "Sarl that shrine was blessed and consecrated was it not?"

"Of course, are not all shrines in your land?"

"And Myron tolerates such worship?"

Sarl thought for a moment. "Why yes, I suppose he sees no harm in it."

Rhianad smiled. "One thing that can always be counted upon is the arrogance of a Sorcerer. The most powerful magic of all right under his nose and he overlooks it."

She turned to Sebastian.

"Those stones are sacred and blessed with Natural magic. People have come here to meet with the Gods."

"And?" asked Sebastian completely bemused.

"That means this place lies between the worlds. It exists in this place, and also in the other realm. It is protected and we can enhance that protection further. We can use the stones from the shrine for the spell."

"This smells of witchery to me," remarked Sebastian unhappy at being made to dabble in a magic he had little knowledge of, but dismounted and walked to the shrine. He was about to pick up the first stone when he was stopped by Sarl.

"No! If it has to be done, then I shall do it myself."

With great reverence, Sarl slowly and carefully dismantled part of the shrine to create a small pile of stones. When the task was done, he sat back upon his heels, his face full of concern.

"I hope the Gods will forgive us," he said anxiously.

Rhianad smiled. "Do not worry Sarl. We do not do this for personal gain. We do this for Ahlia and she is well loved by the Old Ones. I would not dare disturb such a sacred place otherwise."

Sarl seemed reassured by her words.

Rhianad pulled a small bone knife out from a small scabbard that was attached to her belt. She thrust it into the ground as if to mark a starting point. From her bag, she pulled out the small pouch of pungent smelling powder that they had come to know as witches veil. Motioning for Sebastian to move close to the stones and for Lex and Sarl to stand back, she began to trace a circle about them, dowsing the ground with the powder and murmuring strange unintelligible words as she walked. When she had returned to the place where her knife was, she nodded to Sebastian.

Sebastian bent over the stones and began to murmur softly, sweeping his hands over the stones again and again. Sarl and Lex watched in amazement as the stones began to glow with ethereal brightness changing in colour from grey to gold. In moments, a pile of gold ingots stood where the stones had been. All the while Rhianad cocked her ear to the wind as if listening for something. Finally she smiled as if pleased.

"I think that went well," she said finally.

"I like that spell!" commented Lex. "I shall be getting you to do that again at a later date, as my bill has yet to be settled."

They had not ridden long into clan territory when two scouts on horse back approached them. Lex greeted them with the respect of one warrior to another.

"We seek passage across your land," he explained.

"We have orders to let none pass that is not known to us."

The scout looked at Lex, then at the others behind him. You are not from these parts."

Both scouts were watching the travellers intently, alert to every movement, and were clearly poised to retaliate if a weapon was drawn. Lex raised his hands, palms open in a gesture of acquiescence.

"That is true, we have business with the mother of this boy," he pointed to Sarl, "We are returning him to her."

"That is of no concern to us. You must find an alternate route."

"We can pay handsomely," said Lex coaxingly, "We can pay very handsomely."

The two scouts looked at each other as if communicating telepathically. Finally, one spoke. "Bribery, you propose bribery?"

"We prefer to call it tribute."

"Ah tribute, an admirable notion. What is it that we must do to earn this tribute?"

"Allow us passage, so that we can get the boy home."

Carefully, he gestured to Sarl to open the back he was clutching to him, to reveal the shining contents within.

The scout's eyes lit up with greed at the sight.

"It's gold!" he called to his comrade.

"All we ask is free and discreet passage across you land," said Lex, "It could not be simpler or less bothersome."

The scout turned to his comrade who gave him a nod. As if by way of justification he said,

"Kryfer was a formidable Chief. I would have died rather than cross him, but he is dead and Narp our new Chief is a man of politics, not a warrior," he said as he spat on the ground.

He held his hand out for the bag and Sarl thrust it at him.

"We are collecting another such bag from my mother," Sarl told the scout as he had been instructed to do, "You would be welcome to half that bag too on our return, if our journey is unhindered and undisturbed."

The scout nodded in understanding.

"None shall know of you passing from us, though not all is in our control. We shall do what we can."

He tied the bag safely to his saddle, and pulled on the reigns to turn his horse.

"May the Gods be with you!" he called as he and his comrade rode away.

"A blessing from their Gods!" remarked Sebastian with amusement, "They'll be cursing us by those same Gods when my spell wears off and all they own is a pile of rubble."

He shook his head. "It would have been simpler and quicker to kill them," he said with idle casualness.

Rhianad sighed heavily. "There will be death soon enough, Sebastian," she said gravely.

*   *   *

Ahlia mentally braced herself before entering Myron's study. She walked in to find him busy with some parchments, a quill in his hand. He did not look up as she entered.

"You asked to see me?"

"Yes. I will keep you prisoner no longer. You are free to go."

"I am?"

"Yes. You may leave now if you wish. The servants will see to your travel needs."

He put his quill down and let out a long drawn out sigh. He appeared morose. Ahlia knew this had to be some kind of trick.

"And my power?"

"It was a shield I placed over you, for my protection. I cannot release it until you are off my lands. I cannot risk it. You are Mora's disciple after all. How can I be sure that you will not attack me?"

"What reason would I have?" she asked then realisation hit her. "You are keeping the Oracle."

"Of course I am."

"But you don't even know how to use it."

"I will with time find a way. You do not want to be a part of this. You are free to leave." Myron turned his back to her and pretended to be absorbed in the view from the window.

Something stirred in her. Until now, it had not mattered too much to her that Myron had possession of the Oracle. She thought this was because she knew he was unable to use it, but now she knew it was more than that. The Oracle at least had been close. She was indirectly still connected to it both in proximity and through Myron. Though her own power was suppressed, it was in a sense still active through its contact with the magic shackle Myron placed upon her. She was connected to him and he was connected to the Oracle. The idea of being entirely disconnected from the Oracle filled her with a huge sense of foreboding and dread. It was as if someone was asking her to hack off one of her own limbs. She stood rooted to the spot, unable to take even one step towards the door. Myron waited for her to leave. When she did not move, his lips curled into a sly smile.

"You can't can you!" His eyes gleamed with satisfaction at being proved right.

"You see, you are helpless. Mora infected you with the Oracle without even warning you. She prepared you carefully for the taste and she knew once you had tasted you could never let go. Ask her about that next time you dream journey!"

Ahlia gasped.

"It is not my restrictions that create your prison. Your whole life has become one long obsession to which you are enslaved. You will never be free of it until perhaps you finally see what it truly holds. Maybe then it will release you from its grip.

Ahlia remembered Mora's words to her in her dream,

'Once you have used the Oracle you will have no need for magic. You will be at peace.'

She held her head in confusion. Perhaps he was right, her whole life had been turned upside down and her inability to use the Oracle had secretly tormented her. She had struggled to keep hold of the Oracle. She had killed. She wanted to taste the fruit of her labour. She needed to know it had been worth the cost, worth the sacrifice.

"I don't see how this can be resolved Myron. I need my power and the Oracle to try to make it work and you are not prepared to give me either," she argued.

"It is myself I am protecting. Mora nearly killed me. It took me decades to recover. What if you were to do the same to me or worse?"

"Myron you may find this hard to believe, but I have never attacked anyone in my entire life. I have only ever acted out of self defence."

"To kill is to kill Ahlia. The dead are not concerned with how they were made dead, only that they are dead. How many have you killed already?"

Tears sprang into Ahlia's eyes as she remembered. Myron walked up to her and kissed her on the forehead. He stroked her hair tenderly.

"Who else but I can understand your burden, your torment. Who else but I can see that though you are beautiful of form, your mind is more delicious still. Where else but here can you find the answers that you seek? I will risk my safety. I will trust you. I will lift the shackle in return for your promise that you will not try to kill me. That is all I ask of you, your word."

Ahlia felt wretched. "You have it," she answered wearily.

"Then I shall give you the Oracle and you shall work it."

"But how? I have tried Myron. I have looked into it, I have worn it round my neck, I have held it in my hand, I have poured my intent into it, but nothing works."

Myron looked at her in utter disbelief.

"How would you speak if you could not see? The Oracle is an eye and as such it is worn over the eye when in use. You cannot tell me that you did not know that, surely!"

"Which one?" asked Ahlia. "Left or right?"

Myron was astonished at her ignorance. To think that this girl had held onto such an object of power for so long and had not the presence of mind to know where to place it in order to activate it. He had always assumed that her problem had been her inability to amass enough power. Could it have been the oversight of a simple technicality that had kept her at apart from the Oracle's power?

"I mean *the* eye." He pointed to the space between his brows. "The eye that looks inward. I am sure that is where Mora must have worn it to activate it. I have tried to do the same, but nothing happens, absolutely nothing. I have tried over and over again, until I have become almost mad with frustration. I cannot understand what I am doing wrong. I can only surmise that the Oracle chooses who it will yield its power to. I am assuming that you are that person."

He handed her the talisman, carefully laying it in her open palms. She looked down at it for a moment before curling her fingers around it. Myron was watching her like a hawk. She could feel his eyes boring into her, scrutinising her every move. She fastened the chain around her head so that the talisman rested over the space between her brows. She reached out mentally to the Oracle until she detected its power, like a personality. She thought of the fire, of the water of the earth and air. She spoke to the Oracle in the language of natural things, not imposing her will upon it, nor allowing it to control her, but endeavouring to reach an understanding. She remembered the words that Mora had written in her book, '*the world is the Oracle, not the talisman.*' Ahlia pushed her focus through the Oracle and out into the universe about her, and in doing so she suddenly realised that the Oracle was merely a door, a gateway into another world. For a few seconds nothing much happened. She was beginning to think she had got it all wrong, when she felt the stone beginning to heat up. It no longer rested against over her brow, but was stuck fast to her skin. It began to press hard into her flesh all the while increasing in heat until Ahlia was sure it was burning her. She gritted her teeth to endure the pain as it soldered her flesh, imbedding itself there. It became too much to bear and she tried to pull it away, but it would not come off. Myron gasped as the stone began to glow with supernatural luminosity. Ahlia was clutching at the arm rests of the chair, trying desperately not to buckle, her face contorted in pain.

Suddenly the pain instantly vanished and she could see it. She could see it all. The Great Map, the very fabric of the universe, the thread and the seams that held the world together. She saw her part, her place. It filled her with incredible joy to understand her place in existence and know that she was in every way a deliberate and essential part of the Great Map. Everything was an interconnected interplay between essences. All the knowing of the universe was here, the past, the present and the future. She knew she could search the vastness for the answer to any question she might have. She looked out across the worlds and there she saw them, the power objects, each one in its own specifically chosen hiding and resting place. She could see why they were there, she could see the many potentials they guarded against and she understood.

A scene materialised before her. She saw Myron's face. He was standing amidst the flames and sounds of battle. In his hand there was a golden sword. The Oracle hung from his neck, bright against his black chain-mail. Behind him a banner flapped in the wind, the crest of the Black Dragon on a blood red background. He stood amidst the carnage, indifferent to the suffering around him, revelling in his victory and in his power.

'More!' his mind cried out in demand, 'More!'

The scene changed and Ahlia realised that the vision she had witnessed was part of another. Someone else had seen the same thing and Ahlia was looking through their mind's eye. As Ahlia pulled herself out of the scene she saw Mora as she had looked in her youth, dressed in the dress that Ahlia had been wearing, her auburn hair hanging about her shoulders. She saw Myron leap forward to attack her. His eyes were full of fury. Mora thrust out a hand and all became a blaze of fire.

Now Ahlia understood, and the horror of what might come to be filled her with dread. She felt she had seen enough, but the Oracle seemed to have an intent of its own. It burned on, and like a beetle tried to burrow deeper into her forehead. In a voice that was not a voice, it told her how much more it could show her. It could show her everything about everything. A huge picture was trying to form in her head of all existence, of past, present and future, but the sheer vastness was too overwhelming. No, I cannot grasp it all, she reasoned with the stone, I cannot!

As if heeding her plea the images faded as Ahlia negotiated with the Oracle to break the connection. Gradually, the stone began to lose its glow and the talisman began to cool a little. There was a soft hissing sound as the metal seemed to release its grip on her flesh, and return once more to her skin's surface. She reached to unclasp the chain and took the Oracle off, rubbing her forehead to see if there was a burn mark there. There was none. She clutched the Oracle tightly in her hand and looked at Myron with contempt.

"She was defending herself wasn't she? She was defending herself from you. It was you who was attacking her."

"I would not have killed her. I simply wanted the Oracle and she refused to yield. I would not have killed her. Her blow on the other hand was intended to be fatal. You have felt the scar, you know that."

"Because she saw! The Oracle showed her. She saw what would happen. She knew you wanted the other power objects and she saw what you would become if you had that power. It wasn't that you were a threat then or even now. She tried to kill you to prevent you from becoming a monster in the future. You cannot change a person's nature. Power enhances what is already there. It amplifies our qualities both good and bad. She saw that the bad in you was stronger than the good."

"That's rubbish. Tell me what you saw. Where are the power objects?"

"What happened to Mora's first apprentice Myron?" asked Ahlia. It was more of an accusation than a question.

"Where are the power objects?" he asked more impatiently.

"They are... scattered. I cannot explain," she said cryptically.

"Tell me what you saw!" he shouted, snatching the talisman back from her. She felt the weight of the mental shackle return, dampening her power once again. She had hoped that the Oracle would have given her some protection against him, but it clearly had not.

"I swear to you, I cannot. There are no words, it was more a feeling," she screamed back.

"Do not make me search your mind. Do not make me hurt you," he warned.

"I cannot..." she tried to reason, but Myron was not listening.

He reached his hands out towards her as if gripping her very brain between them, and sent searching tendrils through her mind. She screamed from the searing pain that erupted in her mind as he tore her thoughts apart as if ransacking a room. Then without warning, he released his mental hold and she fell to the floor in a crumpled heap. In fury, he swept his hand across the nearby tables sending everything flying across the room. He smashed his fists in rage on the now cleared table, pounding it over and over.

"Why can I not see? Why?"

As suddenly as his anger had erupted, it subsided. He became uncannily subdued. Ahlia was not sure which was the more frightening. He focused on her once again and reached a hand out towards her. She felt herself lift from the floor as he moved her up and across onto a soft chair. Without saying another word, he turned and left the room.

* * *

Ahlia wept, but not from physical pain. Where the Oracle had sat there was a sensation of loss so acute that she could hardly bear it. It felt to as though a part of her mind was missing. As she lay semi-conscious upon the chair, flashes of the images she had seen flitted across her mind intermingled with her own memories. She saw herself as a child, and relived the estrangement she had felt in the knowledge that she was different from those around her. She saw herself as a young woman, struggling to find her place in the world, and she saw herself as a Sorceress capable of destroying anything which stood in her path. As she was flung from painful impression to painful impression she called desperately and silently into the root of her soul for relief, searching for something that might make existing seem possible. An image of a form floated into her tortured mind, and flooded her with such intense hope that it made even the loss of the Oracle pale by comparison. Even in her state of delirium, Ahlia was taken by surprise as the form became increasingly focused. Was she falling into madness she wondered or had she been mad until this moment and was finally falling into sanity. She let out a silent cry in her mind, of such intensity she though her head might shatter.

Miles away, Lex suddenly grabbed his head in his hands and cried out in excruciating pain. He fumbled to dismount, but his foot became displaced from his stirrup and he fell to the ground writhing in agony.

Sebastian jumped off his horse, but could not imagine what was causing Lex's distress. He turned frantically to Rhianad for help, but she was equally dumfounded.

"Is he having a fit?" asked Sarl.

No one answered him.

Sarl dismounted and walked cautiously towards Lex. He tentatively put his hand out to touch the writhing man.

"No," called out Rhianad in fear, but it was too late. Sarl had just for a few moments placed his hand upon Lex, and in those moments transferred some of his power into Lex's tortured body. The gesture created a connection, the force of which was enough to send Sarl hurtling back amidst an array of blue sparks. Rhianad rushed to the boy's aid.

"I'm fine, I'm fine," he said weakly, "But I feel suddenly tired in a strange way. I cannot explain."

"You have drained yourself. Stay still. You will replenish in time."

Sarl smiled to himself. So this was what power was. Despite his fatigue, he felt incredibly good. He had never seen his own power before so clearly.

"Did you see?" he asked.

Rhianad nodded. "I did."

The boost of energy that Lex had received, succeeded in bringing his convulsions to an end though this seemed to be much to everyone's relief except his own.

He remained upon the ground curled in a ball like a child and did not move, his face buried in his great hands.

The others looked at each other questioningly. A strange muffled sobbing sound fought its way out, but still Lex kept his face covered.

Sebastian found this even more alarming than the convulsions. Finally, Lex raised himself from the ground. His face was ashen and his eyes had the look of one half mad with emotion. As he looked at them, he winced as though their eyes upon him somehow hurt. Silently, and with some difficulty, he got back on his horse. When Sebastian started to speak, Lex turned his head away and raised his hand, spurring his horse on to indicate that this was not the time for explanation.

*   *   *

Lex remained intensely sullen as they journeyed towards the palace. His countenance did not lift for one moment and a tension hung in the air like the crackling of a Sorcerer's emotion. Fearful that he had erred in some way Sarl approached him with the single minded determination of a child who wants the truth at any cost.

"You were having a fit," he said to Lex. It was more of a question than a statement.

"No I wasn't," replied Lex with such anger that Rhianad's ears pricked up in concern.

"I did I help you though didn't I?" asked Sarl.

"No you didn't. Typical of your kind, you chose to interfere in something that did not concern you."

Sarl's lip trembled slightly. "I thought you were dying."

"I was, in a way. You should have left me be, boy. You should have left me be."

"Sarl!" Rhianad called to the boy who was clearly upset, and motioned for Sebastian to pursue the conversation with Lex.

Sarl's face was a picture of distress. By helping Lex he had hoped to atone for his previous escapade in the dragon's lair, but he seemed instead to have made things worse.

"Rhianad I was only trying to help. I thought he was dying. I didn't think he could survive her touch."

"Her touch?" asked Rhianad in bewilderment, "What do you mean?"

"Of course now I see I was wrong. I didn't know that he was like us. I thought he was…"

"What are you talking about Sarl?"

Sarl looked from Rhianad to Lex's sombre figure and mulled something over in his mind.

"Nothing," he said finally, "I'm just all confused is all."

Sebastian was fighting to drag information out of Lex who was being less than forth coming. Finally he lost his patience.

"If you do not tell me what happened, then I shall place my hands on you like the boy did and take the information I want," he threatened.

Lex shot him a look of pure fury.

"I'll kill you first!" he said with such venom that even Sebastian was taken aback.

Lex's knuckles were white over his reins and his jaw clenched with such tension that Sebastian could not fail to realise that though the physical pain had gone, Lex was in some form of pain still.

"Have you considered that what you conceal from us might put us all in danger?" he asked in a tone of concern.

Lex relented. "It's not like that," he paused, "it was Ahlia. Somehow she managed to reach into my head and…" words seemed to fail him.

"And? What did she say?" asked Sebastian.

Lex looked at him with wild eyes full of indefinable emotion.

"No words, but she made me see…I can't explain. It was like she and I were one person. I felt what she felt, saw the world how she saw it. I thought my mind would burst, if my heart didn't first."

Unable to speak anymore, his last words were hardly a whisper.

Sebastian was astonished by what he heard. Looking at his

338

friend he came to a realisation.

"She soul-merged with you. It is unheard of!"

"What do you mean?"

"We just don't do it. For one, it involves relinquishing anything one might wish to keep private and for another, it involves a huge amount of power. I have tasted some of her power in a superficial merge and I could barely tolerate its intensity. You should be dead. How could she be so reckless to attempt to soul merge with a human? Sarl probably saved your life, by interfering with the connection."

Lex seemed to retreat into himself brooding over what he had heard.

"Is there something you are not telling me Lex?"

But Lex would say no more.

Chapter 7

"Sit, please."

Ahlia sat and watched as servants filled her plate with food for her. When they were done, Myron waved them away. She started to eat slowly and quietly. She had no idea what to expect. As far as she was concerned, Myron was utterly insane. She just couldn't figure out whether he had always been like that or whether it was a turn of events over the years that had sent him over the edge. Looking at him now, he appeared completely calm, but his eyes betrayed an inner turbulence. He got up and moved into the seat next to her. He went to take her hand in his and she flinched involuntarily. He seemed genuinely distressed by her action.

"You despise me. You think me mad. You think me the monster that Mora thought me."

She said nothing. The images that she had seen flickered through her head. He took a deep breath.

"Would it make any difference to know that to search a person's mind is equally painful for the Sorcerer as well as the subject? I felt it too."

He brought her hand to his cheek. "You and I are battling with forces that no one else could ever understand. I have been battling longer than you. It is harder for me. You have youth, freshness, vigour on your side. Wait until you have lived with power as long as I before you judge me and deem me insane."

"You manipulate me," she said quietly, "You manipulate me at every turn."

"And Mora did not? Tell me Mora never interfered with your life, with your destiny. Tell me she led you here with your eyes fully open. Can you say she was not manipulative, erratic, frightening?"

He watched her for a response, but she gave none.

"Did you ever dare cross her? Did you ever stop to think what might have happened if you had? Of course you did not know her for very long and all that time she had control of the Oracle. You were no match for her. She knew that and so she had no need to show you the other side of her nature, the side I knew only too well. Ask yourself what if? Then you might have seen the Mora that was my Mora, the Mora that shared my hunger for power, that shared my riches and my castle, that shared my heart, and that despite it all tried to kill me."

Ahlia's head was spinning. She was no longer sure which thoughts were hers and which thoughts Myron had planted in her mind and to add to her confusion, the visions of the Oracle came and went, floating through her memory. Everything was the same and nothing was the same. She knew things that she did not want to know and she knew also that she did not know enough.

"I know what you suspect me of. You think I killed Mora's first apprentice."

Ahlia shifted uncomfortably in her seat.

"Did the Oracle tell you so?"

Ahlia shook her head. "No it did not."

"Because I did not kill her."

"Then what happened to her?"

"I do not know for sure Ahlia and that is the truth. Dead she is, that much I know, but not by my hand. For all we know it could have been by Mora's. It would not be the first time a Sorcerer has killed their apprentice."

"Mora would never do such a thing!" insisted Ahlia fervently.

"No? why did Mora never tell you about the Oracle? Even when she knew she was going to die, she could not bear to give up her secret. Did she stop to consider the danger she was leaving you in? No, she left you to flounder about. In truth, it was Mora that placed you in my hands. No one else could have helped you to use the Oracle, but me, No one."

All the phrases from Mora's book floated through her mind. She recited them quietly as if to herself.

'The stone is bathed in blood. The stone bears the weight of the world. It is the eye that cannot be shielded from the pain of infinite joy and infinite pain.'

She was a speck in the universe, vital, and at the same time insignificant. She would live and she would die and shed her body to take another. She would have a new place and purpose, for the Great Map would always continue. She would be rock, she would be breeze, she would be dew, she would be dust and ash and so too one day would Myron, for all his power.

"Myron what is it you want of me?" she asked wearily.

"Show me how to use the Oracle."

"The Oracle cannot be 'controlled' in the normal sense of the word. It requires the perfectly balanced blend of its own power in conjunction with someone else to work. If you try to draw power from it, it doesn't work. If you try to pour power into it, it doesn't work. You can't tell it what to do nor can you ask it what you should do. It's more like a discussion, a partnership, a relationship. Sometimes it agrees, sometimes it doesn't. If you can convince it of your cause, it will work with you. That is all I can tell you Myron."

He mulled over what she had said and murmured something about Natural power to himself. He thought for a moment then reached a decision.

"Take me to the other power objects. They can't all be ruled by Natural power. The chronicles say there is a sword. A sword cannot be ruled by the same inclination as the Oracle. A sword is made for battle. It desires battle. Once I have the sword, I will give you the Oracle."

Ahlia felt sick to her stomach.

"I don't want it," she said.

"You may think that, but you could no more reject it than you could will yourself to stop breathing. It has of its own inclination bound itself to you. There is no say on the matter. I was a stupid arrogant fool to doubt it, but if I might have the sword!"

His eyes were wild with excitement at the thought.

She looked at him and said clearly to him in her mind defying him to hear, but willing him not to, 'By all the Spirits and all that is good, there is no way I am taking you to the sword'. Out aloud she said to him, "Myron I have to sleep. I am so weary. Can we talk tomorrow? There is no urgent rush is there?"

He smiled and kissed her forehead.

"Of course, of course, tomorrow we shall start afresh."

She breathed a sigh of relief as she withdrew back to the room that served as her sleeping chamber.

* * *

Narp was in discussion with his second in command, when four clansmen entered his quarters with the two scouts whose hands were bound with thick rope.

The clansmen pushed down hard on the scouts shoulders, forcing them to their knees.

"They tried to deter us from making our rounds and when we questioned them, they tried to bribe us with some of this."

The clansmen threw a bag onto the ground.

Narp's eyes gleamed with greed as to his surprise and delight, gold ingots tumbled out of the bag onto the floor.

"Where did you get it?" he demanded of the scouts, "Do not lie if you value your lives."

"Travellers. They said they were returning a boy to his mother and asked for passage through our lands."

"Our lands? Our lands?" cried Narp with rage, his eyes flashing dangerously, "My lands. You gave them passage through my lands without my consent! Did you not stop to wonder who this boy was that they should pay you a king's ransom so easily? Or that they may have had a completely different reason for seeking easy passage? No! All you saw was the gold and you thought no further."

He gestured to his clansmen. "Take these traitors away, out of my sight."

Narp was stroking his bare chin thoughtfully as he looked at the gold. His mind flitted back to Myron's banquet hall and a Sorceress from foreign parts who was being kept prisoner.

"Shall we send a messenger to the palace?" asked the clansman who was his second in command, interrupting his thoughts.

"No," replied Narp, "There is not ample time, the damage is done. How would it look? We let these strangers have passage across our lands. Myron does not take kindly to mistakes."

He looked out into the distance.

"Besides, I think it best to act cautiously. Change is afoot and we must make sure that we are on the right side of it."

"The scouts?"

Narp's eyes narrowed with displeasure.

"Kill them," he said.

*　*　*

It had taken no small effort to reach the palace walls, but they had somehow managed to do it without being undetected. Rhianad's witch dust had helped, but it was now running dangerously low. They hid behind the cover of a bush that had managed to plant its roots firmly in the foundations of the wall and had refused to be uprooted. Lex looked up at the great building in dismay.

"There must be a thousand rooms in there. How are we ever to find her or even be sure that she is in there?" asked Lex.

"I could try scanning for her," suggested Sebastian.

"Don't you dare!" warned Rhianad, "At this proximity, we'll be noticed in an instant. Besides I have a better idea."

She pulled a small box from the pocket of her tunic and carefully opened it. Whispering strange soft words, she gently coaxed the creature that dwelled inside to come out. Two insect like legs tentatively poked out from the rim as if savoring the evening air.

"We have need of you Badaria," Rhianad crooned as if to a child, "Only you can do this task for us. Only you can find the lady for us."

"What in Spirits name is that? A spider? How can a spider help us?" asked Lex in disbelief.

"No ordinary spider are you Badaria. You are old as the hill and wise as the trees. A witch's familiar you are and you shall find the lady for us," Rhianad whispered on.

Badaria responded by jumping out of the box and resting for a moment upon the rim. She leapt into open space, seemingly to her doom, but an almost transparent silken thread served to stop her falling to the ground below. Downward the spider spun until her skeletal toes touched the hard ground. Breaking her thread, she scuttled towards the brick and mortar of the palace wall and began to climb feeling with her sensitive legs for a crack in which to fit. Sure enough, she found one and disappeared from sight.

"Her eyes shall be my eyes," chanted Rhianad "and I shall see what she sees." She seemed to enter an almost trance like state and swayed gently where she stood. Sebastian took her by the shoulders and lowered her to the ground, behind the cover of the bush while Lex and Sarl kept vigilant watch.

Badaria scuttled through the bricks and all was darkness until a chink of light appeared in the distance. She moved towards it and carefully poked two legs through the hole. Yes, it was big enough. She found herself high above the main hall. People moved down below, but they would not notice her. She crept across the wall with surprising speed and across the open door. She would find this woman for her Mistress, but it could take some time.

Back outside Lex was growing impatient.

"It will take your spider an eternity to search through that place. This is a foolish plan!"

Sebastian hushed him silent before turning to Rhianad and softly asking.

"What do you see?"

As if dreaming, Rhianad answered.

"I am sitting on a guard's head. He cannot feel me. He is walking to the upper floors. Time. Give me time."

Sebastian nodded in agreement.

An hour or more passed and Badaria scuttled from place to place, hitching rides upon the heads or shoes of guards until Rhianad let out an involuntary shudder.

"I see him!" she gasped.

"Who?"

"The drinker of the blood!"

Badaria had shrunk behind the lapel of the guard to shield herself from view. The guard she was riding on was in fact Brade who had come to report to Myron.

"All is well, Master."

Myron was distracted by his own thoughts and barely registered his guard's presence.

"Yes, yes." He waved Brade away.

Brade did not wait for Myron to change his mind. He withdrew quietly and ascended a flight of stair by his Master's study. He just wanted to check on her, he told himself, after all, it was his job to ensure that the prisoner was not up to mischief. He nodded to the two guards who stood by her door before knocking upon it. There was no answer. He was about to push the door open when the door opened a crack and Ahlia's face appeared.

"What do you want?" she asked coldly.

The iciness of her voice hurt him, but no matter. To her he was the enemy. How could she know of his true plans.

"Do you want for anything my Lady?" he asked softly.

"No. Thank you," she replied curtly, but less coldly.

"Are you sure?" he stepped forward then cursed himself inwardly for his earnest as she closed the door a little in response.

"Quite sure. I was asleep."

Brade nodded and retreated, but not before he had unwittingly left behind his eight legged passenger.

"I see her, I see her!" gasped Rhianad. "She is alive and well!"

Sebastian and Lex both breathed a sigh of relief.

"Badaria shall stay with her until we come."

"Well tell her to be careful and stay out of sight," warned Lex in a troubled voice, "Ahlia is not overly keen on spiders."

Rhianad chuckled as she withdrew the link between her and her familiar to see with her own eyes once more.

She turned to Sarl. "Now let us see about getting you to your mother and getting us into the palace."

                                * * *

The two sentries at the palace gate did not feel threatened at the
sight of a boy and a young woman approaching, however, they
had a job to do and so barred the entrance without hesitation, by
crossing their spears.

Sarl dutifully took this as his cue to speak.

"I am Sarl son of Laida. She works in the kitchens. I have
come to see my mother."

The guard looked first at Sarl and then his gaze lingered on
Rhianad.

"This is my cousin. She walked me here."

"Lucky you to have so tasty an escort," leered the guard.

Rhianad smiled sweetly at the man who hesitated for a
moment before pulling back his spear and scrutinizing the boy's
features.

"I know you. Been a while hasn't it? Laida's son. Yes. Of
course I know your father too," commented the guard turning
to the other and laughing.

Sarl looked at him in astonishment. He had never heard
anyone mention his father before, but before he could say
anything, Rianad had ushered him through the gates.

"Where will your mother be?" she asked.

He remembered as if it were yesterday, though it was six
years or more since he had set foot in the palace. The last time he
had walked through this courtyard it was under cover of night.
His mother had wrapped him in a warm blanket and handed him
over to his uncle. She had wept tears over him and begged her
brother to keep the child safe. Sarl had not been able to
understand why he was being sent away. It had something to do
with a monster who wanted his blood. He had had nightmares
about the monster for months after leaving the palace, but
eventually, these had been replaced with dreams of fields and
games. Now he had returned to face the monster that wanted his
blood, not as a child, but as a Sorcerer's apprentice, he thought
proudly to himself.

The heat emanating from the open doorway of the great

kitchens hit them as they entered. Before them lay a large room lined with a dozen clay oven fires. Some were open as kitchen staff shoveled bread dough and carcasses into them to cook. It took a few moments for Sarl to spy his mother, though she had changed little over the years. She was kneading bread dough, her forehead covered in a film of perspiration and her concentration fully absorbed in her task. He walked to stand opposite her and waited silently for her to notice him. Would she recognize him? He did not have to wait long to find out. The woman looked up from her work to see who it was demanded her attention. On seeing Sarl, she let out a whimper before rushing round the large wooden table to clasp him to her breast, covering him in flour as she did so. Sarl didn't mind. He had dreamed of this moment.

"You should not be here!" his mother exclaimed. "It is not safe!"

"I am not alone mother. Things have changed. I'm an apprentice now, an apprentice Sorcerer."

The woman looked horrified. "No! It cannot be! Your uncle was supposed to keep you from such things. I made him promise."

Rhianad stepped forward. "I am to blame. I found your son and I saw in him the Knowing. It is his destiny. It was only a matter of time."

The woman renewed her grasp upon her son. "My son is not for that life of slavery. Myron will use him and discard the husk without thought."

"Rest assured Lady, that your son will be a free Sorcerer in his own right and a powerful one moreover if I and my comrades succeed in our task."

"They've come to defeat him," said Sarl excitedly. "Imagine! Everything will change."

The woman huffed in disbelief. She pointed her finger at Rhianad. "Myron has ruled these lands for hundreds of years. Do you hear what I am telling you? Hundreds. He cannot be defeated. You have brought my son into danger and you have signed your own death warrant by coming here."

Rhianad would not be deterred.

"The woman they keep prisoner in this place has immeasurable power. With our help, I believe she can defeat Myron. We have to reach her. Your son will be safe with you. All I need is for you to help me get to her."

The woman shook her head.

"Myron does not allow us to roam above the kitchen level." She tapped her head. "We are village people see? Brought here as children, but free thinkers yet. All the servants above this floor are different. Controls them him he does. They do not speak to us. I do not even know where they are keeping the woman you speak of."

"I know where she is. Is there no way you can think of to get me to her undetected?"

"There are guards everywhere. You'll be spotted instantly if not by them, then by the other servants. It is a stroke of luck you were able to get this far."

Rhianad bit her lip in frustration. Lex and Sebastian were still outside the palace walls waiting. She had hoped to avoid bloodshed, but there seemed no other way. They would have to fight their way through.

She made her way back to the gates and was stopped by the guard once more.

"I've left the boy for a short visit with his mother. I'll be back to collect him in a while," she said smiling sweetly. The guards nodded and allowed her to pass.

Back in the kitchen, Sarl seized the opportunity to ask his mother the question that had been burning in his mind since speaking to the guards at the gate.

"The guards outside said they know my father. You have never spoken to me of my father. Why?"

The woman looked deep into her son's eyes and sighed heavily. "Because child your father is Brade, Captain of Myron's guard. It was he helped me to conceal you from Myron when we discovered that you had the gift. You would have been found long ago if it were not for his help. However, he made me promise never to tell you who your father was, a promise I have now broken."

She looked at her son in earnest.

"You must tell no one Sarl. You will not be accepted anywhere if people know. They will treat you with fear, or worse, hand you over to Myron."

"Why would they do that?" asked Sarl.

"Because of the blood child, because of the blood," was all she would say.

*   *   *

Rhianad rushed to where Lex and Sebastian were waiting.

"Sarl's mother cannot help us."

Lex's face dropped in disappointment.

"Magic it is then," replied Sebastian. "Magic and the sword."

Rhianad was not listening. She was rummaging through her bag. She pulled out a small tub of ointment and a packet of crushed herb.

"Why did I not think of this before?" she chided herself. As she scooped up some of the ointment and mixed it into the powder, she explained to the others.

"Los Root."

"Poison!" interpreted Sebastian for Lex.

"I would normally use it for darts, but the guards here wear thick armor and visors. So means must find a way. A deadly kiss I shall create. I can protect my own lips with bland wax ointment then smear the poisoned wax over the top. Then all I have to do is get the guards at the gate to kiss me!"

Sebastian grabbed her arm.

"This is not the time to get possessive Sebastian," she commented.

"It is dangerous. What if you absorb some of the poison?"

"I am far too professional for that," she replied archly. "I'd put them to sleep, but I have nothing that works fast enough and we cannot wait."

Moments later she had returned to the palace gate. She presented herself before the guards and smiled coquettishly.

"I have come to collect the boy,"

"So you have returned my pretty," leered one of the guards, "Perhaps you should leave him a while longer with his mother and stop with us a while."

The other guard sniggered.

"Oh? And might you hope to gain from that?" she asked enticingly.

"What might you give?" replied the guard suggestively. His comrade sniggered again.

Rhianad bright eyes flickered provocatively. "Ah what must I do to pass? A kiss then, but only one though, my kisses are deadly," she warned as she closed the gap between her and the first guard, enticingly.

"Is that so, then I should like to partake of such a kiss," he chuckled. He pulled off his visor and with his free hand grabbed her about the waist and kissed her. She kept her lips pressed to his despite her feelings of revulsion. After a few moments the second guard pulled her away and grabbed her to him.

"Now, now, there'll be none left for me!"

How right he was, thought Rhianad to herself as she pressed her poisoned lips to his exposed mouth.

Soon Sebastian and Lex were gingerly stepping over the two dead bodies and padding across the courtyard, trying to make as much headway as possible before they were inevitably spotted.

Chapter 8

Ahlia lay in bed deep in thought. Since her merging with the Oracle, and Myron searching her mind, her memory was a maze of broken images. She knew she had seen things of importance and she was certain that she had done something incredibly significant, but she could not piece together the torn fragments. Still, she took comfort in one thing:

Myron had not been able to see her thoughts. She was sure of it. Nor could he see what the Oracle had showed her. She could hide things from him. Was his power diminishing or had hers grown? It did not matter either way. The small victory filled her with hope. She could get away!

She wondered if she could lift the shackle he had placed on her. What did she have to lose? She concentrated all her effort on lifting the block. She could feel its edge pressing down on her like a solid cage. She felt about for any sign of a chink. For a split second she thought she found one and pushed against. It yielded momentarily before slamming shut. She cursed in the dark to herself. She sat up and pointed a finger at the candle next to her bed and asked it to light. Nothing happened. She tried again. This time it lit. A shiver went through her. How had she done it? It didn't feel like she'd done anything. She got up and walked over to a table over by the window where she knew there were three or four candles. Each of them lit instantly, but she was not happy. Something was wrong. A sneaking suspicion crossed her mind. She picked up one of the candles to see more clearly. In the dim light, she looked about the room to see the silhouette of a figure in the shadows by the door. Suddenly, the dying fire burst into flame of its own accord. Myron stepped out of the shadows.

"You cannot break the dampening shield, although I adore the sensation it gives me when you try. It is truly exquisite."

"Not for me it isn't," Ahlia retorted.

He moved towards her. Even by the soft light of the fire, there was no mistaking the deadly look in his eye. She stepped backwards, instinctively trying to maintain the space between them though she knew there was no where to go. He was moving in mentally as well as physically. He may not be able to read all her thoughts, but he was quite able to impose his on her.

"Wait... Myron... you said..."

"I lied," he said simply. "So did you. Why else would you be trying to break the shield?"

He quickened his pace like a hunter who knows his quarry is trapped. She was forced to retreat back, falling backwards over a chair. He leapt towards her, and as he roughly hauled her upright by her night dress she could hear the sound of linen ripping.

"Do not deny me or I shall break you."

Panic welled up inside her. "Myron, please listen..."

He grabbed her by the throat to keep her head still, as he violently bored into the recesses of her mind. The more she struggled, the more intent he became, and the tighter his grip, until she could barely breathe. She tried to scream out for help, but the only sound that escaped her crippled voice box was a desperate gasp. She did not have the heart to try again. She knew there was no one who would come to her rescue.

Yet as if in answer, there was an abrupt loud knock at the door. Myron ignored it. It came again, this time more insistent.

"Not now!" Myron snarled at the door.

Then a voice called, "I am sorry Sire, but this cannot wait."

Myron cursed venomously and rose from the bed. He opened the door to find Brade standing there.

"What!" he snapped.

"We have intruders in the Palace Sire."

"Impossible. I would have detected them myself."

Brade leaned slightly to one side to look past his Master into the room. "It appears you were otherwise engaged and perhaps therefore distracted Sire. It seems they too have magic. They have slain a number of the guard already."

Myron let out a violent curse.

"Whoever they are, they must be after the Oracle. I shall deal with this myself."

Closing the door behind him, he ordered,

"Guard this door. No one enters no one leaves. I shall be very displeased if she is not here when I return."

Brade bowed reverently. When his Master was out of sight, he smiled to himself and opened the door to Ahlia's room.

Ahlia shrieked at the sight of him. She had just been thanking the Spirits from releasing her from Myron's clutches.

"What are you doing in here?"

Brade sat down on one of the chairs.

"I am guarding you for my Master."

"Why? What is happening?"

"We have intruders."

"Well doesn't he need you? Why don't you go help him or something?"

Brade looked at her. He took in the dishevelled hair, the torn nightgown, the fear in her eyes.

"He thinks they are after that power talisman," he said.

Ahlia's heart jumped. She had expected the intruder to be a disgruntled warlord. Only another Sorcerer would be after the Oracle.

"I think he is wrong," Brade continued. "I think, it is you they are after."

"Me?"

A faint hope sparked to life in her.

"One of them is definitely looking for you. He is carving through my guards at an impressive rate, cursing all the while."

She did not dare to hope. Could it be?

"How do you know it's me they're looking for?"

Brade tapped his head.

"I can feel it, in here. He thinks loudly," he said, causing Ahlia to start. Brade, a Sorcerer?

"But I shall be waiting," he said smugly, "I shall be waiting."

Ahlia shrieked as he leapt out of the chair towards her and grabbed her by the hair.

*   *   *

The stream of guards was endless, but Ahlia's rescuers fought for all they were worth. Lex had thrust himself into battle without a care for his life and seemed tireless as he took on opponent after opponent. Not for the first time, Sebastian wondered where he got his strength from as he watched him tear through the guards with incredible determination. It seemed the closer they got to Ahlia, the stronger Lex became. More than once, blows that should have hit him and at least wounded him, seemed to miss their mark for no apparent reason. At times, he thought he could see a suspicious thin blue haze about Lex's form as he moved. Had Sebastian not been so distracted with his own opponents, he might have paid his suspicions more thought. As it was, at present, his only concern was to survive. He returned his full attention to bringing his sword down upon the guard before him and advancing to the clash swords with the next guard that stood in his way.

There was a momentary lull, but it would be moments before more guards rushed towards them. They ducked into the nearest room, and dragged heavy chairs to block the door. All three of them were panting heavily from their exertions.

"She's on this floor," said Rhianad in between deep breaths and pointed further down the corridor.

"But he isn't anymore," said Sebastian as he sensed Myron's presence, "He's waiting for us downstairs."

"Good," said Lex. "That means I can get to Ahlia.

Guards had arrived at the other side of the door and were hammering against it.

"We can't fight our way through all of them. We'll have to use magic," said Sebastian looking grave. He had hoped to save all their power for the Sorcerer, but there were too many guards.

"As little as possible," he advised. Rhianad nodded, "Just enough to clear a path."

He turned around to find Lex looking out of the large window. "No need. There's a balcony on the floor directly below. You can get down that way."

355

Rhianad went over to the window. She looked down. It was too far for a human to jump but an easy distance for a Sorcerer.

"Go!" urged Lex.

Rhianad jumped and landed deftly on the balcony below to wait for Sebastian.

"You too!" insisted Lex. "I'll get Ahlia."

The guards were smashing through the door and it would be minutes before they were upon them. Pulling Lex as far away from the door as possible, Sebastian let out just enough power to do what was required. A surge of white mage-fire smashed through the door and scattered the guards over the floor of the corridor. Lex took full advantage of the lull in the attack and headed out into the corridor. Sebastian meanwhile, jumped from the window and landed beside Rhianad on the balcony below.

"I can feel him from here. He is powerful Sebastian, very powerful."

"I know, but we can beat him, if we work together."

Rhianad smiled. "How you have changed," she remarked with satisfaction.

They made their way with remarkable ease to where Myron was waiting for them. It seemed as though he had deliberately left a path clear for them, so great was his belief in his own power. Of course he had probably not been challenged in decades, Sebastian thought to himself grimly. Perhaps he was looking forward to a little exercise.

* * *

Myron stood deathly still as his opponents paced the marble floor of the great hall, a few metres before him. Only his sharp eyes followed their every move.

"You have come for the Oracle I presume," he said calmly.

Sebastian shook his head. "We have come for Ahlia," he replied.

"Ahlia is the Oracle you fool. The power of the stone has chosen her. It will not cease pulling towards her, it yearns to merge with her and it will have no other. She has wielded it."

Sebastian's eyes opened wider, and his brow rose slightly at the news.

"Then I am surprised that you are still standing."

"I said she has wielded it, but she has yet to merge completely with it. For some unimaginable reason, she chose not to. Like her Mistress before her, she hesitates. I still hold the Oracle, and more besides. I advise you to turn around and leave."

"We will not leave without Ahlia."

"As I have explained, I cannot give her up."

Myron turned to face Rhianad and gave her a fixed stare, his eyes boring deep into her. She clutched her head in her hands as a sudden strong energetic force swept through her. He smirked coldly.

"The two of you put together do not have enough power to overcome me. You are committing suicide."

Sebastian and Rhianad both stood firm, their resolve unshaken. They locked eyes with each other as if making an unspoken agreement. Then each of them raised their arms and thrust all their power towards Myron with all their might.

* * *

Lex had slashed his way through guard after guard, carving a path towards the room where Ahlia was being kept. Rhianad had given him directions, but he found he did not need them, he could feel her and he could feel that she was terrified. He burst into the room to find Brade using Ahlia as a human shield. He was holding a knife to her throat.

"I have been expecting you."

"Let her go!" Lex growled.

Brade remained calm. He raised his head for a moment as if sniffing at the air.

"I can feel my Master is otherwise engaged with your colleagues. I wonder if they are strong enough to contain him."

Lex paced warily, circling about them throwing his sword from hand to hand.

"Lex, he has power," Ahlia warned, keeping her head still so as not to disturb the blade. "She is right you know. I have power. My Master never allows me the use of it, but even he cannot stop the natural course of things."

Lex bided his time, looking all the while for an opening.

"He probably fathered me specifically to drain me. He taps into me like a parasitic leech sometimes, but it has made me strong and able to replenish quickly."

"Let her go," commanded Lex.

"Oh. I can't do that. I know you want her. So does my Master. I tried to hide her from him. I rolled her in dirt and smothered grass in her hair so that she would not please him. Normally he is a shallow man, but she would not be hidden, her light could not be hidden."

Lex took a small step forward, but quickly stopped when Brade tightened his grip on Ahlia.

"If you cared for her you wouldn't hurt her," reasoned Lex.

"If you cared for her, you would give her up," countered Brade.

"She wants none of you or your Master. I will not let you keep her against her will," said Lex his voice bristling with fury.

Brade pushed Ahlia onto the floor behind him. She tried to get up, but her hands and feet were too tightly bound.

"I can see you're not going to go away until I kill you."

He pulled his sword out of its sheath and walked towards Lex. Lex let out a piercing war cry and blade aloft, rushed to meet Brade.

* * *

Myron was a touch disconcerted. He had expected to be rid of these would be Sorcerers by now, but they were stronger than he had anticipated. They moved with one will against him. It was almost as if they were nurturing each other's power as opposed to feeding off it. This had to be some kind of Natural magic. He thrust an arm towards the column that supported the ceiling just behind them, cleaving it in two in the hope that it would smash down upon his foes, but as it fell, Rhianad with a wave of her fingers caused the column to burst open scattering thousands of tiny marble dust particles through the air. Sebastian aimed at the floor on which Myron was standing, renting deep cracks in it. Myron simply levitated and moved to another part of the room, thrusting ball after ball of mage-fire at them as he travelled. From the corner of his eye, Sebastian could see that blood was beginning to ooze from Rhianad's nose, but she fought on, not giving an inch of ground. He strained himself internally to try and take on more of the burden and ease hers, digging deep into the recesses of his power. This was a worthy battle. This was the battle that should have been. If only Myron had always been the holder of the Oracle, Sebastian could have proven himself without complication. His very clothes crackled with static electricity, his feet barely touched the ground as his heart sang its battle song. He could do this! He would be victorious!

Myron however, had other plans. His lips began to form strange shapes as he began to mouth an incantation. His stream of power grew stronger in fits and bursts as he recited his spell, pushing back Sebastian, and causing Rhianad to buckle and fall to her knees though she refused to withdraw her attack. It was all Sebastian could do to remain standing. His entire body was shaking from the strain of the renewed onslaught, beads of sweat running from his temples. Where was Myron's power coming from? How could he not be tiring? Sebastian could sense a wetness on his lip that felt too warm and thick to be sweat. Was this the beginning of the end?

* * *

Brade was strong and fierce and Lex was astonished that Myron's Captain had not already beaten him by now. There seemed to be a strange inconsistency in the way he fought. Some of his blows reigned down heavily upon Lex and other times, Brade seemed to falter and lose his strength. There was no pattern or obvious reason and it was definitely not through fatigue because he always managed to somehow return strong once more after a weak series of blows.

Ahlia too was watching the fight, her heart gripped by terror. She too saw the strange ebb and flow in Brade's fighting, but she also saw the reason. It was Myron. It had to be. Somewhere in the palace, Myron too was engaged in a battle and he was drawing on Brade's power to fend off his attackers. Brade seemed to be fighting off his Master's demands as much as possible and the result was this strange push and pull in energy. She could feel the shield that enclosed her falter at times too. She pushed against it over and over, desperately hoping that it would eventually give way. If it did not, she could only hope that Myron would drain Brade dry, and weaken him enough for Lex to be victorious. Her face screwed up in frustration as she realised if that were to happen, then Myron would have enough power to defeat his attacker, and she knew that attacker was probably Sebastian.

*   *   *

Sebastian was fighting hard against an overwhelming desire to fall to his knees. Blood was pouring from his nose and his body was so hot, he felt his organs might be roasting inside him. He dared not look over to see what state Rhianad was in. His eyes were so swollen and dry that he could not blink. Myron's onslaught remained constant and focused, and then without warning, he pulled back for a few seconds. Sebastian basked in the respite, before Myron's attack continued with renewed vigour only to suddenly pull back again in a way that could only be described as jerky. What was he doing? Was he playing with them? It happened again and this time Sebastian was sure that Myron was trying not to look perturbed. Something was wrong. His power was beginning to fail at last. Sebastian tried desperately to maintain his stream of power. Perhaps if he held on for just a little longer.

*   *   *

Brade's sword crashed against Lex's sending him hurtling, but instead of closing in for a death blow, Brade let out a mighty bloodcurdling yell.

"My power! Not yours, mine. To me! Come to me!"

Ahlia could feel the air crackle as Brade drew in all his power, withdrawing it from Myron with all his ability. She felt the shield about her begin to crumble until she was able to push through it and release her power. Like a caged animal set free, it surged into the space about her, sending sparks into the air. A sense of immense wellbeing and omnipotence filled her. She had access to her power once again.

Before Brade had a chance to lock his newfound power on Lex, Ahlia attacked him with all her might. Brade met her with his own blast and they were locked in stalemate.

"I have more to lose Brade. I have more to lose," she screamed above the roar of energy.

"You shall not take him from me!"

Beads of sweat were forming on Brade's forehead. He knew he was powerful, but he was unschooled and while Myron had had his own power in conjunction with Brade's, Brade had only his own and he was beginning to feel unsure that he could sustain this intensity for much longer. Somehow, he managed to raise his sword to plunge it down on the heavily wounded Lex.

"No!" Ahlia screamed and diverted some of her power to create a shield over Lex's body, stepping forward as she did so, though she need not have bothered for somehow, a shield had appeared about Lex's body before she could muster one up.

Brade seized his chance. He still did not have enough power to defeat her, but when she had moved, Ahlia had exposed the large arched window behind her. He sped past her and flung himself out of the window without a moment's hesitation.

Ahlia ran to the window just in time to see a smoky blue film form around Brade's body as it hung suspended for a moment in mid air. Then Brade disappeared completely and all was left was the fast fading blue film.

"Please tell me he's dead," murmured Lex weakly.

"I can't I'm afraid. But he is gone for now," she rushed to help him.

"I'm alright, I'm alright." He reached into his jacket and pulled out a bottle. He pulled off the cork with his teeth.

"Lex!" said Ahlia in dismay.

"It's tonic woman!"

"Oh. How did you manage to create that shield over yourself?"

"I thought you did that."

"No. I didn't get a chance…"

"Talk later. Find Sebastian." he urged.

Coming to her senses, Ahlia ran to the door, disappearing as she crossed through the doorway into thin air.

"Guess she's learned a trick or two since I saw her last." Lex mused to himself as he nursed his wound.

*　*　*

Myron was furious. He had been feeding primarily off of Brade's rather vast resource of power for the battle, but Brade had somehow denied him access and he could no longer tap in. Brade was obviously much more resourceful than he had imagined. He would have to deal with him later. No matter, he still had plenty of power to finish off the remnants of the two pathetic figures before him. They were already on their knees.

Suddenly, a small orb of light appeared in the far corner of the room. It grew in size until it resembled a doorway. There was a bright flash as a figure appeared from within the light and rushed towards him. It couldn't be! Ahlia! She hurtled towards him thrusting out the power and the fury that had been boiling in her, suppressed for so long. He threw bolt after bolt of power at her but to no avail, her pace quickened as she gained momentum. She was heading straight for him. He pushed out shield over shield, but she tore through them, her mouth contorted as she let out a bloodcurdlingly piercing scream. None of his blows seemed to touch her. As her power surged through her, memories of the visions of the Oracle flashed into focus. She could see him now not as flesh and bone, but as pure energy. He was a dark murky writhing patch that sat like a parasite in the fabric before her, throwing its tendrils out destroying all that it touched. Her hands opened, fingers outstretched as if to form claws, her rage forming hazes of red and orange in the air about her. Soon she was just a few metres away and still, she showed no signs of slowing down. Myron opened his mouth, but before any sound could come out she had reached him, hitting him at an impossible speed and smashing right through his body like a boulder through glass. His body was torn limb from limb at the impact, his head rolling across the marble floor until a column stopped it from going any further. Two lifeless eyes stared out from it, locked in an expression of sheer panic.

Ahlia unable to stop, was screaming now for an altogether different reason as she found herself hurtling towards a solid wall. A blue haze formed about her as she reached the wall, and a second before impact she disappeared, only to reappear at the point in the corner of the room where she had first materialised. This time she had enough space to slow herself down and came to an abrupt halt which caused her to lose her balance and fall backwards to sit like a child's doll, on the floor, her legs out in front of her, her arms limp by her sides. Even in his weakened state, Sebastian had to laugh weakly, wincing as he did so from his wounds.

"Well hello!" he called out. It took a few seconds before Ahlia could focus on him.

"Hello," she said as if in a daze. She looked down at her bloodied clothes and hands and grimaced.

"I'm covered in Myron! Covered!" was all she could say before she fainted, her head hitting the ground rather loudly. From the human debris of Myron's remains, the stone of the Oracle glowed warmly. As if sensing Ahlia's proximity, the talisman twitched of its own accord. In fits and starts, it began to slide across the floor, dragging itself some way across the floor towards her. Then it jumped into the air and hung as if suspended by some invisible thread. As it hung, it began to rotate, slowly at first, but gradually speeding up. The blood that had stained it was flung from it by the centrifugal force of its motion until it was utterly clean. It sped through the air and flung itself into Ahlia's open hand, still glowing brightly. The action seemed to rouse her slightly and closing her hand over the talisman, she moaned as the energy of the Oracle began to course through her.

"What a bloody mess!" said a voice from across the room that Sebastian recognised only too well.

"Trust you to show up when we've done all the work," he said to Lex smiling with as much mischief as he could muster in his present weakened state.

"Are you alright?"

Sebastian nodded. "We're all alive."

"I see Ahlia's been here then. Blood splattered everywhere, hewn limbs scattered about the floor. Yes, it's her trademark alright. I wish she'd learn to kill a bit more tidily, you know, with a bit more finesse. Judging by the state of that Sorcerer, I take it she's alright?" he asked.

Sebastian grinned and nodded, gesturing towards the blood soaked heap that lay sleeping on the floor. "She's activated the Oracle. I think its healing her. She's grown in power quite substantially since we last saw her."

"Yes, I was pretty sure she wouldn't be beaten this time, even by the likes of him. She had that look in her eye. You know the one."

He tossed a bottle towards Sebastian.

"Tonic. Drink it. All of it. It'll help."

Sebastian picked up the bottle from where it had fallen and crawled over to Rhianad. She was barely conscious and very weak. He pried open her mouth and coaxed her to drink some of the tonic little by little. With each sip, she seemed to gain a little more colour in her pale haggard face.

Lex looked on with approval.

"Has to be love," he said to himself softly.

He walked over to Ahlia who had curled herself into the foetal position and was snoring very softly, oblivious to how she looked. He stroked his stubble thoughtfully.

*   *   *

364

Brade re-appeared in the moonlight by a field, miles away from the palace. He walked with purpose towards an opening in the side of a nearby hill. The dark tunnel wound downwards until it finally came to a huge cavern where curled about a rock, lay the black dragon that had captured Ahlia. Smelling his presence, it reared its head up from its resting place and focused a yellow eye on him.

"What do you want?"

Its voice boomed in his head.

Brade with a gesture of his hand yanked at the chain around the dragon's neck. In his free hand, he held up a small dark vial on a silver chain.

"I had hoped to be finally free. How is it that you can command me still?" asked the dragon with more than a hint of displeasure.

"He used my power to subdue you. He was nothing more than a pathetic leech who drank your blood to maintain his youth and mine to steal my power. I have reclaimed my power, and I shall rise and claim my destiny. You serve me now."

The dragon was disappointed. The boy had failed to free him, but if the boy still lived, perhaps there would be other opportunities in the future. It could only hope.

"Until the spell is lifted." warned the dragon, "only until then."

Reluctantly, it lowered its head to the ground and allowed Brade to climb on.

"For now I must be far from this place," ordered Brade.

"So be it," replied the dragon. It raised itself onto its hefty legs and crawled out of the cave. It unfurled its colossal wings and lifted itself into the sky with Brade holding on for all he was worth. Soon the dragon was but a mere dot in the moonlit night sky.

* * *

Sarl had waited impatiently downstairs with his mother. She had refused to let him out of her sight, and the very air crackled around him as he paced the floor of the kitchens in frustration. The large kitchens were near sound proof, and almost separate from the rest of the palace. Everyone was going about their work entirely oblivious to the what was happening above stairs, but Sarl could feel the surges of power in the rooms above his head and it was all he could do keep silent.

Suddenly after what seemed like hours, they heard a commotion at the top of the stairway that connected the kitchens to the banquet hall. A wounded guard partly staggered, partly fell down the stairs. Some of the kitchen women rushed towards him in horror.

"We have been attacked. Myron is dead. Myron is dead!" he cried.

The kitchen women looked at each other in disbelief.

"He is dead I tell you. Sorcerers have killed him."

Sarl's heart leapt at the news, but there was something else he wanted to know.

"And what of Brade?" he asked as the woman began tending to the guard's wounds.

"What of Brade?" he repeated the question despite hearing his mother's sharp intake of breath.

"He abandoned us. He has fled. We do not know where."

Sarl swallowed the news like a bitter pill. His father was a coward. He turned to his mother.

"Why did he not come for us? Why did he not come for you at least?" he demanded angrily.

"My child it was not like that between us. I am a servant. I was never dear to him, and he does not even know that you are here. You cannot judge him so harshly."

Sarl was unconvinced, but let the matter go for the present. What did it matter that he had been abandoned for a second time by a father that he never knew. He would travel across the seas and become a mighty Sorcerer like Sebastian. As if reading his mind, his mother tried to hold onto his arm, but he pulled away and ran up the stairs to find his future.

* * *

Upstairs Lex was in the room that once served as Myron's study flicking through the parchments on the desk. A middle aged manservant appeared at the door and waited to be noticed. During the fighting, all Myron's personal servants had kept themselves safely hidden, and it was only now that the fighting had stopped that they had reappeared to survey the damage.

"Who will rule this place now?" asked Lex more to himself than to the servant.

'The Clan Chiefs will continue to rule their stretches of land, only now they will no longer have to answer to Myron," replied the man.

"And this palace?"

"Ah, this palace was built and sustained by Myron's magic. I suspect it shall begin to crumble now that he is dead. Or perhaps Brade will return in due course and claim his birth right."

Lex's stomach turned involuntarily at the thought as he contemplated what the future might hold. A shiver ran through him as he looked about the room.

"I've had enough of this place," he said to himself and nodding to the manservant, left to find the others. He was so absorbed in his concerns for the future that he barely registered Sarl running past him at an unbelievable speed towards Myron's study. The boy burst into the room, his eyes wild and glistening. He ran to the table and grabbed the ornate box that sat to one side. The box opened easily in his small hands. It was unlocked and empty.

"Gone!" wailed Sarl, "It's gone!"

The manservant, who was still in the room scrutinised the child for a moment.

"Brade is also gone," he said in a subtle, but pointed manner. It was enough for Sarl to make the connection. He threw the box upon the floor in fury and stormed out of the room.

Chapter 9

Ahlia stood on the deck of the ship, staring out to sea as the journeyed homeward. Her eyes skimmed the surface of the dark waters as the moonlight flickered and reflected off the waves. Deeper and deeper she sank in her mind.

"There are questions I would ask," she sang softly to the sea as she abandoned herself to the act of scrying. Her brief merging with the Oracle had left her with enhanced abilities. She could feel the difference within her. Where there had once been fog and confusion, there was now clarity and ease. She could feel the power of the waves and she knew that they would answer her. Deeper and deeper she sank, deeper and deeper.

She saw a girl lying in a bed. Her face was deathly pale and body obviously wracked with fever. Beside her sat Mora as Ahlia had seen her before, younger, though by now, her hair was greying. Mora's face was grave and full of concern.

"I did not call for you," said the girl.

"How could I not come, Nila?"

Mora leaned across the sweat soaked sheets and gently cradled the hand of her apprentice.

"I do not want you to interfere. I want this," the girl insisted adamantly.

"But you are dying child. I can help you."

The girl shook her head, tears began to fall over the rims of her lids and spill onto the pillow.

"Nila it is not too late. Let me help you."

"No," the girl answered firmly. "I want no help."

She took a sharp breath as a wave of pain washed through her body.

"You did not help him, when his horse threw him, you did not help him," she said accusingly.

"His back was broken beyond repair, his head badly wounded. It was his time. There was nothing I could do."

"Why could you not save him?" asked Nila, fresh tears springing from her eyes.

"My child, it was his destiny. There was nothing to be done," Mora replied.

"You could have foreseen it! You could have stopped it from ever happening!"

Mora shook her head regretfully as she wiped the sweat away from Nila's feverish brow with a rag.

"It was his time, if not by that way on that day, then by another on another day soon to follow."

"What use is the Oracle if it cannot help us in such situations?" cried the girl wretchedly.

Mora could say nothing that would be of any use on that point. The Oracle was not designed to help change destiny, but to help accept it.

"Did you know Mora? Did you know?"

"I did not my child, for I was not looking in his direction. I cannot hold the entire universe in my mind all the time, I would surely go mad if I tried. My attention was directed elsewhere. I am sorry, though even if I had known, what benefit would it have been to you to know that the man you loved was to die?"

The girl whimpered. Mora held her hand and continued,

"I accept that you have turned your back on the magic of the Oracle and want no part of it. I accept that because it is your free choice, but I have seen that this does not have to be your time. Let me heal you. It is only your wish die that stands in my way."

The girl pulled her hand away and turned her face away.

"Then honour that wish Mora. It is my free choice. Can you not see? It is the only way I can see him again. You have taught me that there is life after death. I am not afraid to die. All that matters is that I will see him again."

Nila's life was draining fast, her breath was becoming increasingly laboured. Mora knew that the window of opportunity was fading fast. The porthole to the otherworld was already open and waiting.

Nila turned to Mora in as fear as doubt suddenly gripped her.

"I will see him again won't I? He will be there waiting for me?"

Mora looked deeply into the eyes of the dying girl. She could not have loved her more if she had been her own daughter. The knowledge that she was losing her when she could have saved her was excruciating. Mora thought bitterly that once upon a time, she would have not hesitated to over-ride Nila's wishes and do what had to be done, but the Oracle had shown her too much of the Great Map and she had changed as a result. Already through the Oracle she could see Nila's life force disbanding and merging into the Map, to become streams and trees and stones, just as her lover had done before her. One day she would live again in human form, and so would he. One day.

"Yes, child," she answered softly, her voice full of emotion as she held back her tears, "He will be there as he has always been, for he never left you."

The girl's pained expression eased as she took her last breaths. Finally, her hand went limp and she breathed no more. The candle flame beside her bed flared for a moment before dying out completely. Mora thanked Fire for the appropriateness of the gesture.

Ahlia pulled back from the vision. The feel of Mora's grief was too intense for her. She blinked several times until the water was water once again. Turning to her right, she was startled to find Lex standing there.

"How long have you been there?" she asked in surprise.

"A while," he gazed at her intently examining her features. "You're upset," he said finally as if disclosing some great revelation.

Ahlia smiled weakly despite herself. "It is nothing."

Lex looked entirely unconvinced, but did not press the matter.

"You should get some rest Ahlia."

She nodded in agreement and made her way to her cabin. Lex watched her leave, then turned his face to the sea, succumbing to the soothing, hypnotic call of the waves.

*   *   *

They touched land early the next morning and Lex for one was mightily relieved to have his feet on solid earth once more. The ride homeward was wonderfully uneventful by comparison to all that had gone before. There were no attacks from Sorcerers, no creatures to fend off and no sense of urgency or danger. Everything had changed however, and Ahlia knew she would never be able to return to her old life in Avor. She could not, for the woman that had lived there was long gone and a Sorceress stood in her place. With one hand she held tight the reigns of her horse and with the other, she clasped the Oracle, stroking the stone with her thumb thoughtfully as it now hung in around her neck once more.

"It speaks to me," she said in wonder, "It speaks to me all the time now."

"What does it say?" asked Lex who was riding beside her.

"It wants to merge. It wants to share its knowledge. It has seen so much."

"Do you know why it has taken so long to activate? It would have been nice to put this all to an end much sooner."

Ahlia smiled and nodded. "I wasn't strong enough. It didn't want to hurt me. Moreover, I had to learn its language and that took time. I had to change the way I think. I see things differently now."

She seemed distant for a moment.

"And will you merge with it? What will happen if you do?" questioned Lex in a concerned voice.

"I have opened a door I cannot close. I can't go back now, but it is not as I thought."

She was talking in riddles. Lex was beginning to feel that he had found her only to lose her again.

"There is always choice Ahlia."

"I have seen the Great Map and my place in it."

She was going to disappear back into the woods and he would never see her again. He knew it in his heart and he was not sure that he could bear it.

371

"You are wrong. People can choose and they can make their destinies. I don't care about that Great Map you keep talking about. I don't care what happens eons away. I care about here and now."

"Lex," she said gently. I am a Sorceress. It is my nature. I cannot change my nature."

"You are wrong you know. A person can change. They can change for love."

She shook her head. "No they can't Lex."

"Yes they can. A man can change for love if the love be true."

"No he cannot. He will be what he will be."

"I say he can," he insisted defiantly, "I say he has."

Ahlia looked at him inquisitively as she realised that they were not speaking hypothetically as she had thought.

"Who has?"

"I have."

Her jaw dropped open in astonishment.

"You are in love? With who?"

She wondered what manner of barmaid had finally snagged him. An emotion erupted within her that she did not recognise. She knew she ought to feel happy for him and she wanted with all her heart to feel happy for him, but something seemed to be in the way, something that hurt.

He looked her straight in the eye, holding her gaze for a long time before answering.

"I cannot believe that you who have the 'oh so great' Oracle in your grasp, have to ask me such a question. You have looked at the fabric of entire universe and yet you can't see what is under your own nose."

He paused to quell the emotion that was beginning to surface before uttering the words he had until now not even dared to think.

"You. I am in love with you and when you soul-merged with me, half killing me might I add, I thought you might be trying to tell me that you loved me too, but I see I was wrong. All you wanted to do was share your despair."

Kicking his horse in the flanks, he cantered off, leaving Ahlia with much to think about, the Oracle still glowing brightly in her palm.

Lex remained sullen and ill tempered for the rest of the day and all cautiously gave him a wide berth for fear of having their heads bitten off. Ahlia watched him with a heavy heart. She felt the weight of the Oracle far more at that moment that she had ever done before: more than when her life and been in danger, more that when Sebastian had rejected her and more than when she had endured the loneliness of her solitude. This was, however, her destiny and she could not walk away from it.

At nightfall, the travellers put into an inn, finally thankful that they did not need to look over their shoulders anymore. Ahlia was seated by a warm fire and deep in thought when there was a knock on her door. It was Sebastian.

"I am sending up for some food. Are you hungry?"

Ahlia shook her head.

"You will be merging with the Oracle soon?"

She nodded, unable to find her voice at that moment.

"I know that it is over Ahlia, and I want you to know that I am glad. Thanks to you I have been saved from the baser part of my nature and no doubt countless others have been saved too. There is no doubt in my mind that you are the chosen because you are the best."

"The most appropriate," she corrected. "It has nothing to do with best."

"Can you at least tell me what you have seen?" he asked eagerly.

She gave him a weary look.

"Sebastian you know what I have seen. You know the Oracle shows the whereabouts of the objects of power. You even sang me the spell-song once, remember?"

"And will you pursue the other objects?" he asked.

"Mora did not. What reason would there be for me to?"

"Is that not the whole purpose of the Oracle?" he asked confused.

"No it is not, far from it. The true purpose of the Oracle is much, much more than that. It has nothing to do with power.

Not in the way that we understand it, nothing at all. Its eye is not directed at the physical or the material world, but the otherworld. The Oracle is a gateway to the Otherworld."

"And why should we concern ourselves with the Otherworld?"

"To help us preserve the equilibrium of this one Sebastian."

"I see that I have much to learn still," remarked Sebastian.

"As have I," replied Ahlia wondering how she would cope with life once she had merged with the Oracle. At least she knew that Mora had found a way. That at least gave her great comfort, but Lex's words had disturbed her greatly too. For was she not, when all was said and done, a human and a woman? A rift was forming inside of her. She had nearly killed Lex with the intensity of her desire to reach him. How could she have been so selfish? What puzzled her even more, was how was it that he had not died?

Sebastian mistook her silence for preparation.

"I shall leave you to it," and because he had no idea of what might happen, he added gravely, "Journey well Ahlia."

She looked up with eyes that hardly saw him before resuming her ruminations.

When Sebastian returned to his room, Rhianad, Sarl, and Lex were already eating.

"Will she not even come out for some food?" asked Lex crossly.

"She is preparing to merge. It will be soon," said Sebastian gravely.

"And then what?"

"I do not know. We have only Mora's example to go by," replied Sebastian.

Lex threw down his plate of half eaten food and stamped angrily out of the room.

Fearful that Lex might disturb Ahlia, Sebastian went to follow him, but Rhianad held him back.

"Leave him be. He will come to terms with things in his own way."

They heard the door to Lex's room slam shut. Sarl quietly put down his food and taking advantage of the fact that Rhianad's attention was entirely on Sebastian, discreetly slipped out of the room too.

Rhianad was scrutinising Sebastian.

"And how do you fare?"

Sebastian sighed.

"What can I say? It is over. The Oracle has chosen. Ahlia will not pursue the other power objects. It is not her ...way. So life will resume as before, except that I must choose a new path. I suppose eventually, I will take an apprentice and the wheel will turn again."

Rhianad's eyes narrowed.

"That is not what I meant."

Sebastian caught her sharp gaze.

"I am not in love with her if that is what you mean. Not in the way that he is. I look at her, and I see a powerful Sorceress. He looks at her and he sees a woman. I think first of her ability. He thinks first of her heart. There is no comparison."

"And what do you see when you look at me?" asked Rhianad. It was a loaded question. He knew his answer would matter more than he probably could appreciate.

"I think I see a powerful Sorceress."

She looked away and tried to fix her features in a steady expression, to hide her disappointment.

"But," continued Sebastian. "I would beg for a chance to learn about the woman who is that Sorceress. I have much to learn I think."

Rhianad's face lit up with an inward smile. The corners of her lips rose.

"Well," she answered a little coyly. "I am looking for an apprentice," as she drew him towards her.

* * *

Sarl knocked on Lex's door, but there was no answer. Carefully, he opened the door and poked his head round.

"What!" snapped Lex on seeing the boy.

"If you care for her that much, then why don't you stop her?" asked Sarl.

Lex sighed.

"It's complicated. You're a child. You don't understand," he said in a softer tone.

Sarl's features sharpened in indignation. He came into the room and shut the door carefully behind him.

"I understand very well. I understand about you. I see what they do not. I felt it when I touched you. I can't understand how the others haven't noticed. It's obvious when you think about it."

Lex looked at the boy in surprise.

"How old are you again?"

"Eleven, I think."

Lex smirked in wonder at the wisdom of babes. He tapped the side of his nose.

"I'm very good at hiding it, our secret."

The boy shook his head.

"Not for much longer Lex. She will find out."

On seeing Lex's countenance turn to one of concern, he said quickly, "but it will not be as bad as you think."

He paused. Then in a way that seemed far too cynical and grave for his age he added as if speaking from experience, "Secrets are bad things Lex. They stand between us and the people we love."

Then all of a sudden, he was an ordinary child again announcing he was off to his room to bed because he felt sleepy.

Lex shook his head.

"Sorcerers!" was all he could bring himself to say.

*   *   *

Ahlia's brow was knotted with determination. She had made her decision. There was no point in delaying any further. Tentatively, she placed the talisman to her forehead as she had done once before, only this time she had removed the chain. For the second time, she opened her mind to embrace the magic of the stone. In response, it stuck fast to her skin and she was able to take her hand away. As the stone heated the metal encasing it, the Oracle began to burn with Otherwordly heat into her flesh. This time there was no pain because she was no longer afraid, nor was she fighting against its desire to merge. The Oracle burrowed deeper through the flesh, hitting the bone of her skull and penetrating it, sending a myriad of fast flashing images through her mind. It moved in deeper still until it was entirely imbedded in her skull with flesh and skin forming over the wound to hide it completely from view. She put her hand to see if she could still feel it, but the skin was smooth without trace of burn or scar. This was how Mora had concealed the Oracle from Brade that fateful day. This was why Ahlia had never seen the Oracle in Mora's possession, and this was why Mora had told Myron that she could not give him the Oracle, nor could he take it without destroying her.

As the power of the Oracle fused with the energy of her inner eye, Ahlia, was bombarded with image after image. Vertigo caused her to drop backwards onto the bed. Her entire body trembled as her metabolism adjusted to the surges of power that were beginning to course through her. She could no longer see the room about her. She was floating in an entirely different existence. For what seemed like an eternity, she lay there, in absolute awe and wonder of what she was seeing and how she was seeing it. Then very gradually, her heartbeat began to slow once again, and she ceased to tremble. She realised that she was able with some effort and concentration, to change her focus in a strangely similar way to how she focused her physical eyes from distant objects to closer ones and back out into the distance again. She drew the focus of her inner eye closer pulling herself away from the outer reaches of the universe, through the stars, back to her world. She tried to keep her focus as steady as she could as each wobble sent her off at vast tangents of time and space. She drew in ever closer, pulling with all her ability to bring her awareness to her surroundings and to the room she was in. The Oracle naturally wanted to thrust her awareness back out again, but she worked with it until her physical vision returned to her enabling her to see her surroundings once again. She stretched her hand out in front of her and scrutinised it, experimenting with her new gift. Playing at altering her focus, she could see her physical hand, then look right through it into the flesh and bone, then look in further still to see it as pure energy. It was fascinating. She cast her vision out further to the surrounding rooms, sweeping through person after person, object after object. She realised that though for her, eons seemed to have passed, not much had changed about her at all. She could feel the energies of all the people downstairs and she could clearly see the brighter, less dense energies that she realised were the mark of the Sorcerers upstairs. She started in surprise as she counted them. She lingered over one mass of energy that was a few rooms away. She lingered there for some time.

Finally, she rose and padded barefoot down the corridor until she came to the last door. She knocked softly on the door and waited. Lex opened it and she stepped inside.

"What is it? Are you alright?"

She nodded. "Did I wake you?"

"No, I wasn't asleep."

He was still dressed, though his creased shirt hung open and he had loosed his belt buckle in the name of comfort. His boots stood by the bed, his sheathed sword propped up next to them.

"I was just lying down and resting my eyes."

The fire was dying. Ahlia mentally lifted a log from the pile next to the fireplace and lowered it onto the fire. She teased the flames with her finger and they sprang into a new lease of life.

"Is it done?" he asked.

"It is." She gently tapped her forehead. "It is lodged in here."

"Does it... hurt?" he asked awkwardly.

She smiled. "No, not at all, I think in time I will forget what it was like to be without it. I feel like centuries have passed already."

"Well you seem... not very different," he said as if surprised. In truth he was relieved. He had not known what to expect. He had not even known if he would see her again. He had expected her to slink away into the night. Then it dawned on him.

"You have come to say goodbye," he said grimly. His brow creased, but his expression remained steady.

Ahlia looked at him though the Oracle's eye, through her own eyes, through love's eyes.

She took a step closer to him and slowly raised her hand towards him letting it hover for a moment over his bare chest. She paused there gathering the courage to make the connection with his flesh. Finally, she placed her hand over his heart.

"Essence does not change Lex. Things act to enhance or detract from what we are, but our essence remains the same. A man cannot really change for love. If love seems to make him greater, it is because his essence was already great. He just may not have realised it."

"You speak in riddles more and more. Perhaps you are right. Perhaps it is impossible even for what I feel for you to cross the boundary between us. You belong to the world of Sorcery."

"As do you," she said gently.

"What are you talking about?" he asked in seeming ignorance.

"Well, consider the facts. You have slain Sorcerers, you have spent much time speaking with and in a sense, learning from Sorcerers. You have been in close proximity of the Oracle for much time."

"So?"

"You survived my outburst of mage-flame, Lex. I thought that Sebastian had shielded you, but I realise now he did not. He had barely enough time to shield himself. Moreover, you shielded yourself from Brade. You shielded yourself with your own power. You talk to me about the Oracle sometimes almost as though you had yourself looked through it. Even Sebastian has trouble seeing the Oracle as anything other than a way of finding the other Objects of Power. You intuitively understood its design and purpose."

She paused for a moment.

"Of course, as you quite rightly said, I could not see what was under my nose, and it was not until I merged with the Oracle and learned how to focus it that I realised what was blindingly obvious. I have seen you Lex, and I have seen through you."

He remained silent.

"I must have realised, the very first time when I partly merged with the Oracle at Myron's palace. My mind was in such disarray, I could not piece together the parts of my memory until you reminded me earlier today. I would never have merged with you had I not known at that point. I would never have put you in danger. Now I remember what the Oracle revealed to me."

She tried to look into his eyes, but he averted her gaze.

"Have you always known Lex? Or did the awareness creep up on you slowly," she asked softly.

"I wasn't sure. I could feel that I was changing, but I wasn't sure what was going on. You must believe me on that score. I was never interested in the Oracle, and I had nothing to do with Sorcery until I met you."

"But Sorcery has had everything to do with you it seems. It is and has always been in your soul. I have been such a fool not to see."

"And does this make it easier or harder for you to leave me?" he asked in earnest.

She laughed softly. "You have cursed at the Great Map because you thought the Oracle would create a rift between us. Yet it has done the very opposite. You are a remarkable man, and you also belong to the world of Sorcery, even if you never cast a single spell."

She moved in a little closer to him, but he held himself back and did not respond. A flicker of hurt ran through her at his seeming rejection and he felt it as if it were his own emotion. Unable to bear it, he met her gaze.

She looked deep into his eyes until he could not help but yield. He sighed deeply as he placed his hand over hers and enfolding her with his free arm, drew her in tightly and kissed her tenderly.

*   *   *

She awoke in the early hours of the next morning to find Lex's arm wrapped tightly around her. He was holding her so close that she could barely move. Trying not to wake him, she tried to gently move his arm. It proved impossible.

"Lex," she whispered.

"Yes," he replied. He was wide awake and had been for some time.

"If you hold me any tighter, you'll suffocate me!"

"Sorry," he released his hold a little, but just a little so that she could turn round to face him. He was looking a little apprehensive.

"What's wrong?" she asked.

"I was afraid I'd wake up and you wouldn't be here, like when I used to dream of you. Sometimes things seem different in the cold light of day. I thought you might have regrets and I wanted to be sure you didn't disappear on me before I had a chance to quell them."

She kissed him. "I've no regrets."

He seemed unconvinced. "You left before."

"I didn't leave because I didn't care for you. I left because I did. The world of Sorcery is harsh and dangerous and at times unfair. I thought it was not your world and I feared you would not survive in it. When you got hurt, I became afraid you'd end up dead because of me. I couldn't do that to you. It is only now I see that in trying to keep you from harm, I harmed you myself. I am deeply sorry. The last thing I wanted to do was harm the one I love."

He stroked her face tenderly.

"There is nothing to be sorry about. I was a mess then anyway. Couldn't tell my feelings from my…" he decided not to finish the phrase. "Anyhow, I should have told you how I felt. I should never have let you go."

"The Great Map will have its way. It exists to evolve each and every one of us. Consider yourself evolved." She giggled as he pulled a face, and she kissed him passionately.

"I take it you're not going to turn me into a toad then," he teased back, playing with her hair.

She grinned mischievously and made as if to spell-cast, but

Lex grabbed her hand and kissed it.

"I love you," he said to her, his voice filled with his heart's emotion.

"I don't think I can ever tire of hearing that," she said smiling radiantly. They lay in each others arm for hours, loathe to quit the warmth and sanctuary of their bed. Ahlia could think of nowhere else she would rather be. Right now everything seemed perfect. She had never known such bliss or such peace. She hoped he felt the same way. As she looked into his eyes, she knew that he did, but there also seemed to be a faint shadow lurking there in the background, a cloud.

"What is it?" she asked.

"I was thinking about Brade," said Lex grimly.

Ahlia sighed heavily. She knew Brade would surely return once he had mastered his newfound powers and then their lives would surely be in danger once again.

"It will probably take him years to develop. He has no teacher."

"Except his own ambition, and ambition is a motivating task master."

"When he comes we will be ready," said Ahlia firmly.

"We will have to be," replied Lex holding her close.

Outside their window, a cock crowed to herald the slow rising of the morning sun and the coming of the new day.